ONE YEAR ON MEADE STREET

A Novel

by

Patrick Sean Lee

Patrick Sean Lee

For information about permission to reproduce
sections from this book, contact Patrick Sean Lee at
patrickseanleeauthor@gmail.com

Book cover design by Laszlo Kugler,
sitkajoe@msn.com

Printed in the United States of America

ACKNOWLEDGMENTS

There are too many people who contributed to the conception, actual writing, and the editing of this book to name individually, but I must thank Jim Warren for his teaching and unflagging devotion during the first drafts.

Trish Munroe, who read those drafts and told me, "Write like *you*, Patrick. Find your voice. That unique, charming one I know you possess." It took me a while, but I finally understood. Thanks, dearest friend.

Cherilyn DeAguerro who read every word in every draft; who suggested many things, making such a difference. You have always been right here beside me.

All my wild and crazy friends at Bookrix who first met Skip and Jimmy inside a flip-book cover. Who support and believe in me. You're the best. A special thanks to Chris Clarke, Judy Colella, and Valerie Fee.

To Allen Ginsberg and his phenomenal poem, *Howl*. My deepest respect, admiration, and thanks.

Joss at Canstock for Jimmy's face on the cover. Kozzi for the back cover image.

Lastly, to my dear wife, Pam, who more so than any and all of the above, read, believed, and encouraged me over those long years of writing. I love you.

Contents

One Year On Meade Street

1980

*I*t *is near dawn, March 21ˢᵗ, and I haven't slept. I've been staring at a spot on the wall half the night—a particular spot, that when the moonlight is just so, lights up the picture I hung there many years ago. A small photograph in a simple wooden frame. I turn my head slightly to see if I can find it and make it come alive by the strength of my will alone, by changing my perspective, but it is hopelessly lost in the dimness of the room.*

Outside, the gray dawn slowly climbs the arc of nighttime sky, pushing the moon gently along before it. Soft shadows awakened force their way through the frosted glaze of glass, across the bedroom walls in search of the picture. I turn and follow the weak light back out the window for a moment. I can see the dusty fingers of smoke from a fireplace chimney somewhere nearby curling without effort, skyward, waiting patiently to be absorbed high above me, out of reach. It reminds me of what happens to love, really, in the end. Absorbed into other worlds...taken far away from us because of laws that now I know we simply cannot comprehend.

The photograph of Jimmy and Carol is with me here in my old room, but they are gone.

They are only part of the shadows, now, kneeling in a brown and ochre field of leaves, caught forever, captured, with their arms thrust upward. The leaves they'd just thrown are still in jumbled, carefree movement, ever frozen in that moment. They were laughing.

ONE

The Claw and Dennis the Menace

Denver, 1957

There we were again.

We were standing between the old rock and a hard place. Up a creek without a paddle—not even a boat. Jimmy had started another fire, which wasn't so bad, except it was in some girl's hair at the old Comet Theater in our neighborhood. He'd done this before—not torched a girl's head, just started a fire that got out of control. It wasn't so much that he was criminal with matches, only that something deep down inside him was thrilled in a way I couldn't understand with anything burning. I guess that's pretty much a sign of a pyromaniac? It isn't like he did screwy things like that everyday though. Only at the worst times, and with the most predictable and damaging results. So far we—yes, I was always there with him—hadn't gotten busted.

I wasn't so sure this time. At some point I knew our luck just had to run out. It finally did, though not for reasons you might think. The real bolt of lightning would strike a little later.

It was a gorgeous April afternoon. Sunny and shirtsleeve-warm. No soot-covered snow lingering on the north sides of the buildings in my hometown of Denver. Neighborhood dogs cavorting with their tongues hanging out. Kids on bicycles everywhere. Shoppers without overcoats out visiting the local stores.

Jimmy, Mickey, and I gone to the theater that day to see a new movie called, "The Claw". It was so stupid it was brilliant. An

7

atomic chicken monster had come to Earth somehow from deep outer space. When it got here it was hungry from the long trip, and was expecting a baby, because before it went off to eat, it laid a huge egg in a cave. I won't go into the details. The point is, every kid in the neighborhood had packed into the movie house that afternoon to see the movie. That was the beginning of the problem, because among them was Inky Minkle and his gang, and they took their seats in the balcony not fifteen feet away from us. They didn't see us, and they didn't see Jimmy shoot the stick match over the railing, but I know they saw us hightail it out of Dodge after the thing landed in the girl's hair.

After that, things got more complicated. It went something like this.

"Jesus Christ, Jimmy!"

That was Mickey Fumo yelling after we raced past the theater manager who was on his way in to find out what the hell all the screaming was about, and *we* were running lickety-spit toward the glass doors, because we knew. I was dead certain he'd seen us.

Dear Mother Mary...

Me praying in situations like this. I knew moms always listened and helped out whenever they could, and Mary was a very important mom in my young life.

"Shut the fuck up and run."

Jimmy cussing. He was older than me by a year, and nearly two years older than the third part of us, Mickey. Jimmy's voice hadn't changed yet. It was kind of on the high side, and when he gave that command it sounded like a 45 record playing at 78 speed. He was tall and lanky still at thirteen, and in no time flat was ahead of us by miles. Well, when you think about it, it was his ass more than mine or Mickey's that would pay the biggest price for what he'd done. Me and Mickey had just been "accessories after the fact". That afternoon Jimmy was super-fast. Dumb jerk.

Honestly though, I loved the guy, devoted to trouble though he was.

We got away. We stopped three blocks down to take a breather in the local library parking lot, and after we'd slunk back against the brick wall we relaxed. Mickey changed his tune suddenly.

"That was cool!" He was referring to the little clothespin matchgun Jimmy had made, but which neither Mickey nor me knew anything about before Jimmy pulled it out of his pocket in the balcony at the Comet. "You're a genius, McGuire."

In a way Mickey was right. Jimmy was a miserable failure in school when it came to English and History, but brilliant with starting fires and things like that. Science things. Those kinds of things he understood, like he was Albert Einstein. *Applied* science, that is—which I'll tell you a lot about as we go.

So he'd made this gun out of a wood clothespin, the ones with the springs that open and close when you pinch the ends. I don't know how he did it, but it worked great. All you had to do was pull back the wire spring that he'd somehow flipped over, until it caught in a slot in the wood. Then you would shove a stick match in headfirst, aim it, and then release the spring. Instant fire missile. Mickey was right. It was cool. I know for a fact that that girl didn't think so though.

We sat there admiring it, shooting some matches into the weeds beneath this big billboard across the alley in a vacant lot—solid wood and dry as a dead tree, just begging to go up in flames—when we were interrupted by this little craphead of a kid.

He'd been watching us the whole time from his yard on the far side of the parking lot we were in, and he commented to us that he thought it'd be neat to take the thing to school. To the gym or the auditorium. "Ta' scare girls with," he said.

Jimmy gave him a dirty look, and told him that if he *ever* mentioned seeing the three of us and our matchgun to anyone we'd come back and string him up by his little balls. The kid looked to be about eight or nine, and he had this intense look on his face that said to me he might be able to describe the three of us pretty damn well, and that for the time being he could care less about *his* balls or anybody else's. By then I was beginning to feel a little like a genuine criminal, a little paranoid. But the kid offered a solution.

"I won't breathe a word of what I just seen to nobody. Promise...if you let me have that thing."

We all knew what the word for that was, but what we didn't realize was that that's when we lost our paddles. The boat, too, if we'd had one to begin with. If we didn't give the evidence away the little blabbermouth would for sure run through the neighborhood telling everyone who'd listen all about us. If we did give it to him, he'd most likely burn down Barnum Public School—and then tell the cops and everyone who'd listen all about the three older kids who gave him the gun, and even showed him how to use it. We were screwed.

Jimmy walked over to him.

"Lemme say it again. You say anythin' about what you just saw here and I swear I'll personally come back and bust your ass good. You got that?"

"Yep," the kid said as he stuck his hand over the fence, palm up. Jimmy stood very still for a second or two sizing up the situation. Finally he took the matchgun and slapped it into the kid's waiting hand.

"Remember what I just told ya', ya' little snot. You tell anyone...and DON'T go pointin' that thing at me! Make a target or somethin' out of an old box. Don't shoot no one. Got it? Crap...are you fuckin' dumb or what?"

I had a feeling that Jimmy's instructions were falling on deaf ears. The kid took his other hand and shoved it over the fence.

"I'll need some of them matches."

"Goddam'!..." Jimmy started to cuss.

"Let's get out of here," I said. "Don't give him shit."

"I'll go right in and ask my mom to give me some, then. Bet she'll wanna' know what for. I'll have to tell her they're for this thing you gave me."

Jimmy reached over the fence to grab hold of the little brat's throat, but the kid was as slick as snot. He shot back a few feet into his yard, stopped, and then demanded matches again. What could Jimmy do short of hopping the fence and beating the daylights out of him? If he could even catch him. He shoved his hand into his pocket and pulled out a handful.

"Here, ya' little asshole." He threw them at the kid. "You get into any trouble with these and I'll personally come back down here and whup your ass good. You got that, you little..."

The boy jumped forward, bent down, and snatched up a few of the sticks. He paid no attention to Jimmy at first as he tried to figure out how to make his new toy work. Jimmy cussed at him some more, and then turned back to Mickey and me. He shook his head sideways, and shrugged his shoulders. Beat by a lousy eight year-old. "Let's get outta' here."

We started to ease away from this little rat, who now had the lantern in Mrs. O'Leary's barn, Lex Luther's smarts, and, I somehow knew, an aching desire to burn down the entire city of Denver.

The kid yelled at us. "Hey! How do you cock the trigger? Come back here and show me!"

Jimmy raised his middle finger over his head and we took off, back out onto First Avenue.

"Hey! Come back here! Hey, Mom, look what three guys gave me! Hey..."

So we were running again. We hadn't heard or seen the last of that snotty little rat.

TWO

The Dancer

We got to Meade Street, which was about half a mile west of the Comet. Jimmy and Mickey must have forgotten about everything that had happened because they were carrying on about what a freaky movie The Claw was. Jimmy was doing his imitation of the pissed off bird, flying around like it did, eating battleships and airplanes. Jesus, I could have found something better to eat than steel boats and aluminum airplanes. So did it, finally, when it discovered people. Between eating people and the fact that it ate military equipment, the Army got involved. Well, so did the Air Force and the Navy. But that didn't do much good. This bird just got madder when they shot machine guns and missiles at it. It took some smart scientist to figure out you've got to fight fire with fire—I shouldn't bring fire back up. But anyway, he and this woman invented an anti-matter gun. Thing. None of us understood the science part of it, except maybe Jimmy, but finally they killed it. I guess. We were long gone by then, like I said.

So Jimmy is jumping up and down, and Mickey is laughing and pulling these invisible puppet strings like he's directing Jimmy's moves, because that's what the people who made the movie did with the bird. Only in the movie we actually saw the strings.

I'm a little ways behind them, worrying about the burned up girl and that kid we gave the matchgun to. At school, Sister Mary Dolorine told us back in fifth grade the story about Nero. How he loved playing his violin and burning stuff up, and that he went so far as to torch Rome, which of course you know he was the emperor of. He blamed it on the Christians, and then started feeding my ancestors to the lions in the Coliseum. It went okay until Constantine told everybody who wasn't Christian the real story of what happened. The Senators stuck Nero in jail, and then later fed *him* to the lions. That's when Rome became Catholic and elected Peter as the first Pope. I think that's how she told the story.

That's what was going to happen to us I was certain. Except they don't feed pyromaniacs to lions anymore. Maybe just hang them.

I'm thinking about all this, when out of the corner of my eye I see this girl standing on her front porch, about halfway up the street. She's got this ballet tutu thing on, and she's dancing away. She was really pretty and looked to be about my age, and I could kind of hear some symphonic song playing in the background, inside her house. Of course I stopped, and I forgot all about going to jail or getting hanged on the county courthouse steps.

I think she saw me too, because she stopped dancing and looked over at me. All I could do was smile, and wish I had the guts to march across the sidewalk and her front lawn and tell her my name, and that I thought she danced really well—and that I thought she was the prettiest girl I'd ever seen.

I instantly memorized the lines of her face without thinking, smiled at her again as my cheeks flushed, then I turned and caught back up with my friends. I looked back every now and then to see if she would continue on with whatever she'd been practicing when I interrupted her, but each time I did I caught her just staring back at me. Or maybe it was at the back of Mickey's head.

We approached Ellsworth Avenue, the street running east and west intersecting Meade Street. Mickey's house was a big two story brick home sitting on the corner at the top of the hill. It made the hair on the back of my Irish mother's neck bristle whenever she saw it. Mick's mother never drew the drapes open for reasons all her own, and that made Mom very suspicious. What, she always asked if the subject of the Fumo family came up, was the woman hiding?

"She has to have the lights on inside that place all the time, for God's sake. How else can a person see with drapes that thick covering all those windows?"

13

Good question maybe, but not one I ever asked Mick about. I'd never been inside his house, elegant palace that it looked to be, but that was most likely because he was always inside mine or Jimmy's. Why his mother kept the curtains drawn tight was her business though. Mom thought it was snobbery, the sin of the rich looking down their noses at us poor folks. I wasn't so sure of that, and I really didn't care anyway.

Mickey turned at the corner and left us. "Well, I'll see you guys later," he said as he smacked Jimmy one last time and headed up the grade.

"Where you goin'?" Jimmy asked him. "It's only three-thirty. There's plenty of daylight left."

"I have to mow the lawn. Promised Dad I'd do it after I got out of the movie. I'll come down later."

"Mow the lawn? It's still all brown, for cryin' out loud! It ain't even growin' yet. Why's your dad makin' you mow dead grass?" Jimmy went on and on as Mickey climbed the hill. I saw Mickey shake his head, and he finally turned when he'd gotten about half way up the street.

"You blind? Dad took this huge torch last Fall and burned all the dead grass away—doesn't hurt the roots, he said. And then he threw fertilizer on it in January. It's growing like gangbusters already. I'll come down when I'm done. Later."

"Burned it up?" Jimmy said to me.

"Hey Mick! What kinda torch?" he yelled, but Mick was too far away to hear, and he didn't answer.

Jimmy was already thinking. I was seeing the hedge in front of his house, the tall Elm tree—all of it going up in smoke.

"I think Mick was pulling your leg, but I don't think you have to worry about cutting your grass anyway," I answered. "You've got a couple of months yet before...what the heck?"

I saw them first—the woman running in our direction on the sidewalk halfway up the block, and then turning up the driveway into Jimmy's yard. My mom was right behind her, headed in from the opposite direction. I looked over at Jimmy. He lit out again, this time faster than he had thirty minutes ago back at the theater. Not half a minute later we reached his house and saw the reason for the commotion in his yard. Mrs. McGuire lay sprawled out on her front lawn behind the low hedge, a bottle of whiskey still clutched in her right hand.

Jimmy rushed up to her and knelt down. He was cussing softly, shaking his head. I suffered some of the embarrassment right along with him, but thank God it was only Mrs. Baumgartner from two doors up and my mom who must have seen Mrs. McGuire fall down drunk. It wasn't the first time she'd made a fool of herself in public, and God knows it wouldn't be the last.

"Help me get her inside, Skip. Goddam' her."

I rushed to the other side of his mother and took half of her deadweight into both hands. Mom and Mrs. Baumgartner skirted around Jimmy and me like two old hens, advising us how to get Mrs. McGuire out of there without hurting her. Like she was a newborn baby and not just a hunk of pickled meat. Mrs. Baumgartner reached down and picked up the bottle that Mrs. McGuire had finally let go of, and looked around to see if anyone else was looking. She brushed the speckles of earth and dead grass clippings off its mouth very carefully, then tucked it close under her arm beside her huge right breast.

"Hurry up, boys, before the bus comes by," Mom whispered. "We don't want no one to see her like this. Hurry up now."

I groaned under that half of the weight I carried and looked over at Jimmy whose face was fixed tight and emotionless. A tear had already begun to run down his cheek.

THREE

Welcome, Lawrence

Much later that afternoon I entered the dining room of our house on Meade Street, the image of Mrs. McGuire lying on her front lawn clutching the half-empty bottle in a death grip still spinning in and out of my head. I don't recall if I felt sorry for her as much as simply feeling ashamed for Jimmy's sake. Pop was seated with is back to me at the old parlor piano at the far end of the room that shared the wall dividing the kitchen from the more or less formal eating area. He hadn't heard me enter.

I stopped under the archway near the front door and watched him bring his long, thick fingers up to the keyboard, then place them gently down. He spread them out. His gaze was fixed straight ahead at the music sheet stand, but of course there was nothing on it. A cigarette dangled out of the corner of his mouth, hidden to me; a blue-gray stream of smoke drifting toward the ceiling. My dad was thinking of notes, or tempo, or something I didn't have the power to imagine myself. He was composing.

Suddenly, as though God had whispered "Go!", his shoulders shot forward. His head lifted slightly, and then what looked like twenty-five fingers began striking the keys all at once. The sudden flurry of hurricane-speed notes made me jump. His playing always did that to me, even when I knew what was coming on the heels of his stone-like hesitation. Pop's arms and hands were a blur, racing up and down the keyboard.

Pop was self-taught, he always admitted modestly whenever someone asked how he was able to play like a concert pianist, unable to read a note—and the music he made was marvelous, even if it wasn't what I liked. I don't think Mom ever told me that much about his early life, how he had come to be so accomplished at the keyboard, or why he'd chosen to upholster furniture and stay poor instead of trying to make it as a classical composer or concert pianist. I do know he was born the same year Mark Twain died, and that he grew up in a flea-sized town north of Denver called Longmont. The same town that Mom was born in, except she arrived on the planet the year the first shots of World War I were fired, instead of on the tail of a comet. That might explain the sometimes-polar difference in their dispositions, and, maybe, the stellar power of his imagination.

I listened for a while until the furious pace slowed. His head dropped then, as though his eyes were searching through the keys themselves to the very soul of the instrument for something more. I knew without seeing his face that his eyes were closed, that he was somewhere far away, and that he was happy.

"LaVerne, it's time for dinner."

Mom's voice brought the curtain down, so to speak— ushered Pop back to earth filled with its grinding sameness. His fingers curled closed a little, he leaned back, and then he stared straight ahead again. Mom poked her head through the doorway opening, a large steaming bowl in her pot-holdered hands next to her stomach.

"Skip, wake your father up. Let's eat, dear." She abruptly left the opening after saying that and carried the bowl away into the small eating area off the kitchen. Pop turned when he heard my name. He grabbed onto the curved, corbelled end of the keyboard with his right hand, surprised, I think, that he had had an audience. He re-entered our house with the blink of his eyes, then smiled.

"Hello, Skip."

"Pop." I nodded.

"Did you like it? It's brand new, you know. I think I *can* write an entire concerto. Working on it, anyway."

"Yeah, Pop. Really good. It sounded great." I wondered what the word concerto meant. I'd heard it many times over the years, standing there at the end of the piano, watching him in his world so distant and huge. So far away from our small house.

"A concerto is pretty long, isn't it?"

"Sometimes." He pushed the piano bench back, stood up, then looked back down at the keys for a minute. I don't know what he was thinking, but he was that statue again.

"C'mon' you two. It's stew," Mom called out.

I left the dining room first, and made my way without another word into the eating nook to the left of the kitchen. It took several more minutes before Pop finally arrived and took his place across from me.

Saturday evening was Mulligan stew night—and Lawrence Welk night. Mom and Pop loved the man, maybe because they loved to dance, and related on some weird level to the spectacle of ever-smiling men and women dressed in lederhosen whirling around the stage in a blizzard of bubbles. In those days I neither danced (although I had nothing against it), nor could I see anything particularly interesting in a TV program that in my mind mimicked a washing machine gone crazy, with insanely happy Germans frolicking around it. Also, I failed to see any connection between Mr. Welk's music and the music my father wrote and played. So, after filling up on the stew and whistling through the dishes as fast as I possibly could, I figured I'd rush next door to have my friend entertain me. If he wasn't in a deep pit of anger and disgust over his mom.

Jimmy had no interest in Lawrence Welk either, but for very different reasons than mine. He'd explained that the host was either a communist spy—he didn't explain why or how that would be, or a space alien who'd come to earth and taken over the guy's body. The Body Snatchers had invaded our planet, Jimmy said. Not giant anti-matter chickens, but real, nasty creatures who needed *host* bodies.

Lawrence Welk wore his pants up to his chest, but people loved him anyway. And so, being a trustworthy American, one that everyone over forty seemed to go ga-ga over, the creatures must have found him irresistible. I questioned whether or not an intelligent species, no matter how nasty, would choose someone so out of it as a host.

I'd usually find Jimmy in his bedroom reading Mad magazines, or throwing darts at a picture of Alfred E. Neuman pasted on the wall, maybe drawing pictures of some crazy new invention he'd dreamt up. I wasn't sure about that night after the mess of his mother in the front yard though. I thought twice about going over the back fence to his house.

The Morley clan now seated, we bowed our heads, said Grace, and then began to eat. Of course the main topic of discussion fell immediately to the sad condition of Ruth McGuire.

"Poor old gal. She's a mess...pass the salt and pepper, Skippy," Pop said. I did.

"Yessiree to that. She ain't been worth a good goddam' since that no-good Fred lit out on her and Jimmy if you ask me," Mom said, motioning for Pop to hand her the salt. She waved off the pepper.

Pop seemed to agree. He shook his head and added, "You're right, Rosie. The woman's traded one louse for another one. I don't know which of the two is worse, either. That whiskey's gonna' kill her if she doesn't quit throwin' it down the way she does. She oughta' stick to beer." He emphasized that opinion by shifting his fork from his right hand to the left, then picking up his bottle of beer.

"If she drank beer instead of whiskey the result'd still be the same. She'd just pee a lot more, that's all," Mom corrected him. She continued to eat, then shot a quick glance at Pop. "How many is that for you tonight?"

"Oh, I don't know. A couple. Maybe three," he answered, as if the question hadn't been all that important. Maybe it wasn't.

"Hmmph."

Then again, maybe it was.

I didn't say a lot. Just sat there across from Pop sliding the wormy-looking slices of onion out of the way with my fork while they talked about my best friend's mom. I felt so bad for Jimmy. No father, and a mother who couldn't say 'shit' without slurring it. He lived alone in his house these days, pretty much fending for himself, the victim of some *thing* that had snatched his mother's good sense. And yet I knew way down inside he loved Mrs. McGuire deeply in spite of what she'd become. He didn't, I didn't, even Mom and Pop didn't realize the tenacity of the demon that had taken hold of her; that would keep clawing at her until her brain finally turned to the consistency of Jello.

"I'll give her five years, best," Mom said. "Unless someone talks her into goin' to one of those sanitoriums for the drunken disabled."

Pop couldn't see the sense in that statement. "Now how the hell would she do a thing like that, Rosie? What would happen with her job? There isn't an employer on the face of the earth that'd put up with letting her be off the line for more than a week, especially for something like that."

"Maybe not, but she can't go on fallin' down flat on her face, drunker than a skunk. And what if me and Gracie hadn't a seen her an drug her inside before the neighbors caught sight of her layin' there with that bottle in her hand? Good God Almighty."

"Ah, to hell with the neighbors. Skippy, hand me over the bread, would you?"

I passed the plate of bread to him. "Me and Jimmy got her out of sight, Mom."

"Well, you know what I mean."

"Jimmy was pretty...messed up. He didn't say anything, but I sure could see it in his face," I said to her.

Mom lifted her eyes and I could see the sadness in them. She shook her head and laid her fork down.

"Skip, I know honey. I know it. Just thank God you got parents that take care not to make fools o' themselves in front of everyone. I know he was hurt. Clean up that stew, now."

But when it came down to it, it wasn't really a question of her making a fool of herself. Not in my mind, or in Jimmy's.

The colors of the sky outside were weakening in the twilight, bleeding through the bank of windows behind Pop's head. Ghostly pink-orange stirred into the purple of the clouds hanging over the snow-covered Rockies to the west. It was close to seven, and Lawrence Welk would be on soon. I wasn't hungry anymore, but looking back and forth between my parents an idea hit me.

"Why don't we move Jimmy over here and talk Mrs. McGuire into going to one of those sanitoriums? She'd listen to you, Mom. I don't want to see her die. Do you think the whiskey will really kill her?"

"Fat chance of that—her listenin' to me, anyway. She don't think she'll die, and even if she did, she loves that whiskey more than anything in this world—more even than death," Mom said.

"Even her own son?" I couldn't quite understand that. How could a mother love something that made her sick, that made her turn her back on her child? And force her to become such a terrible spectacle on top of everything else.

"It isn't a question of her loving the booze *more* than Jimmy," Pop explained. "She loves Jimmy. But the whiskey...well, she loves it, but she hates it at the same time."

"I see," I said. But I didn't. How could you love something and hate it at the same time?

Why, I thought, couldn't we bring Jimmy over here for a while? Just for a while? At least he'd have decent meals and someone to talk to while he ate. Okay, he'd have to put up with Mom's sometimes fanatical, often nutty ramblings about the Republicans, the non-Catholics, the anyones who weren't sitting in the same leaky boat that we were in, but even so, *that* wasn't insanity. Yet, I didn't think Mrs. McGuire was possessed by demons. I was beginning to see her as nuts. Just plain nuts, and a moral weakling, because everyone else knew drunks were just moral weaklings.

"Can he come live with us?" I looked across the table at Pop, his hair graying at the temples, his fork in hand, and his eyes lowered toward his plate. His thoughts must have been mixed. I think he wanted to say yes, but he knew he would have to say no. Mrs. McGuire would get sober by tomorrow, as usual. She wasn't about to leave her home or her job, and especially not her lover in the dark amber bottle. No way.

Mom rose abruptly, gathered her plate and silverware, and carried them to the sink in the other room without answering.

So, Jimmy was stuck. For all I knew he wouldn't accept an invitation to live with us anyway. He had his own room. His picture of Alfred E. Neuman with a hundred holes in it. His bed with dirty sheets. His freedom to come and go, to create anarchy whenever he saw fit. He had his own demons, and maybe he was happy in a terribly tragic way.

It was a bad idea. I let it pass and stayed away from Jimmy that night. The Lawrence Welk Show was terrible as usual, but I looked the man over closely to see if his eyes, maybe, betrayed a hint of alien madness.

FOUR

Inky and Butch

We got up as usual at five o'clock the next morning, Sunday. Father Stone, the younger of the two priests at Presentation of Our Lady Catholic Church, would say the six o'clock Mass, and us Morleys would be in faithful attendance. Mom and Pop adored the chubby little man, in part because he had gotten so good at getting the Service down to twenty-five or thirty minutes—and that included communion and a short, to the point, no bullshit sermon. Further, he was neither stuffy nor old like our pastor, Father Blinker. He was able to out-cuss my mom if he thought us kids weren't close by, and if he wasn't inside the church, of course. And he was a two-fisted drinker at church functions, which made him A-okay in all the men's eyes.

Naturally, Ruth McGuire wouldn't be joining us at Mass because of another raging hangover. Not that she often did come along. She wasn't a strict adherent to the letter of the Church law that said "Thou shalt attend Mass every Sunday. Drunk or sober." Mom's version.

When I hopped the back fence in the darkness and tapped on Jimmy's window at quarter after five I got no response. Neither of them would be visiting God that day, at least with us. Just so they made their Easter Duty. It was a sin to miss Mass on Sunday, but going an entire year without attending one was grounds, Mom pointed out, for excommunication, the very worst word in the Catholic/Irish dictionary. Next month, or surely by May, Mom would go next door and drag Mrs. McGuire out of bed by her ankles if she had to so that the sodden woman could get past that book outside the gates of Heaven. In five years, I supposed.

We arrived and took our usual seats at church, and true to our expectations Father Stone ripped through the Latin prayers, hardly letting the two altar boys have time enough to stumble through their Latin responses. Extine Noye, the Negro kid from our school with jet-black skin and the constant smile of a fat little cherub, had to nearly run with his paten to keep up with Father as the priest put the hosts on everyone's tongue at the communion rail.

People coughed. Frankie McGregor, the other server, dropped something up on the altar steps that clattered and echoed against the brick walls and the ceiling. That made Father Stone hesitate and look. Four seconds lost. Then came the sermon, a five minute commercial on "the misplaced devotion we Catholics have for brand new automobiles." I thought, as I sat there looking around me at the parishioners dressed like pretty common poor people, that maybe his comments were a little ridiculous. Then again, maybe it was just a general observation on his part—not applicable to those of us who lived in *his* parish. Anyway, Mom shook her head and said "Yes." over and over, and then the sermon ended almost as quickly as it had begun.

Father whipped around after it was all done with, blessed the dozen or so in the congregation with a quicksilver-fast sign of the cross, then raced down the marble steps and back into the sacristy, followed by two tired out boys. Mass was officially over in record time.

We left the church. It took Mom the whole of fifteen minutes to say hello to every one of the brave souls outside who'd gotten up at the crack of dawn like we had to hit the six o'clock. Three times longer than Father Stone's short, strange sermon a few minutes earlier.

Pop drove us home. Mom thanked God on the way in her follow up to Father Stone's sermon, saying that *us* Morleys put no particular importance on shiny new automobiles. Our 1949 Ford Station Wagon with a few scratches on the driver side door where Jimmy and I had gotten too close with our bikes' handlebars, was plenty good enough for us. She said.

She cooked the usual Sunday fare of bacon, eggs, and French toast. She also sliced an apple into eighths and placed it on a chipped saucer onto the table, of course knowing neither Pop nor I would be interested in it that early in the day. By afternoon the cream-colored fruit would be sitting exactly where she had put it hours earlier, dark tan by then, and all but the pieces she'd eaten would wind up mixed into whatever she cooked for dinner that evening.

"See you guys later," I said after finishing my breakfast. "I'm going next door to see what Jimmy's up to."

Pop was reading the entertainment section of the paper and didn't hear a word I'd said. Mom sat to my right. She looked at me and just *had* to say something. It wouldn't do to simply say, "Okay, sweetheart. Have a wonderful time over there." No. Mom could be so complex and baffling sometimes.

"When you get in their house, see how many whiskey bottles are layin' around. See if she's up. Poor goddam' woman."

"What?" I said.

She went back to her garden section of the paper without answering. Maybe she'd already forgotten she'd even made the comment. I got up and left through the back door shaking my head, wondering if she really gave a hoot whether or not the entire house was carpeted in empties. As I pulled the door closed behind me I heard her say something to Pop about needing to get bulbs ready for planting. He didn't respond, or maybe I just couldn't hear it against the squeaking of the door hinges.

I drifted across the yard and hopped the fence into Jimmy's yard. It was half past eight, and I spotted him rummaging through his trashcan out in the alley, making a terrible racket, cussing. It was warm that morning, the kind of beautiful early spring day when Chinook winds came floating into the city and sent the thermometer skyrocketing. A perfect day to tramp the gravel alleys looking for interesting things people had thrown into their trash cans, poke sticks through the fences at snarling dogs. Whatever struck our fancy.

"Whatcha' doing?" I asked him.

He had his head stuck deep into the fifty-five gallon drum so that when he answered me it had a kind of rumbling quality to it.

"Lookin' for empty bottles." He pulled his head out of the trashcan and looked over at me standing inside his yard. "Pop bottles. I told her not to throw 'em away with all her goddam' empty whiskey bottles, but she don't hear shit I say anymore."

"Why don't you empty the trash, then? Beat her to the punch?"

He shrugged. "I dunno'. Just don't."

Beside him on the ground lay a pile of Coke bottles in good shape, and one with the neck broken in a nasty, jagged line. I don't know why he'd bothered hauling that one out of the barrel; it wasn't good for anything, except maybe to use in a fight.

"We going up to Rashure's for candy?"

"Maybe. I wanna' get a Coke later. Eight bottles'll do." He glanced down at the pile beside him, counting them quickly. "Six. We need a couple more. Go check out Baumgartner's trash," he said pointing to the cans across the alley.

I left through the gate attached to his garage, crossed the alley to the trash cans over there, and dove into the drums filled with all kinds of smelly crap. After holding my nose and pushing garbage-stained bags and other stuff around, I found the two that we needed, as well as two more. Sort of a reward I thought, for having gone to Mass and not causing any trouble there. I figured Jesus was still happy with me, still close by—well, still hanging around in my stomach because I'd gone to communion.

"Here you go.

"How's your mom?" I inquired.

Jimmy crossed the alley to take the bottles from my hands. "Dunno'. Still sleeping it off I guess."

"Oh. Did you eat yet?"

"Yeah, I ate. Let's get these bottles into the yard, then we can work on somethin' for a while until Mrs. Rashure opens her store."

And so we carried the ten empty bottles into his yard and laid them next to the red brick barbecue that his grandpa had made when he built the house for his only daughter—next to the patio, midway between the rear of the red brick house and the back fence. The barbecue had been well-constructed by mason grandpa. Would withstand horribly cold winters and a lot of other normal abuse. But it would never be the same, to Mrs. McGuire's horror (in one of her sober spells), after Jimmy loaded it up with M-80s to test the integrity of its several hundred, tightly mortared bricks. A portion of the stack was missing since last year—since the summer afternoon when Jimmy satisfied himself that the firebox was as solid as the Rock of Gibraltar, having loaded it up with the explosives. The stack hadn't been so lucky when he decided to test its soundness.

"Let's go in and watch TV," he said after laying the bottles down.

Here was my chance to answer Mom's instructions to check out the number of bottles lying around—as though Mrs. McGuire actually guzzled the stuff like pop, and then pitched the empties wherever she wanted. I followed him across the patio to the rear door. We went in. I counted about six empty bottles of Old Crow stacked like soldiers on the kitchen counter, but the linoleum floor was free of trash, except for a few candy bar wrappers, which I figured had held Jimmy's breakfast.

He led the way through the opening into the living room and went directly to the TV that sat against the wall next to his mother's bedroom. In a few minutes the picture began to appear, along with the sound of preacher Oral Roberts' voice whining for something, a call for faith and healing, I guess—and his pleas for money. Jimmy turned the volume up full. It didn't take long for Mrs. McGuire's whinier voice to break in.

"Jimmy! Godammit, turn that thing down. I'm sick!"

Jimmy turned to me and snickered, but left the volume where it was.

"She needs some o' this.

"Heal!" he yelled.

Mrs. McGuire was in no shape to come out of her room—probably in no shape to even get out of her bed—and so she went on for a few more minutes in a voice that sounded like that of a witch being burned at the stake with a gag stuffed in her mouth, and then Mrs. McGuire went silent. This seemed to satisfy Jimmy, kind of like the dynamite test on the barbecue had, and so he turned down the volume. He grinned at me, and then turned the channel to something worth watching. Bugs Bunny cartoons, I think it was.

We watched Bugs and Elmer for a little while, then wandered back outside to his garage, leaving the TV on. Jimmy wanted to experiment with a pipe rocket he was thinking about making. One that would shoot a broomstick missile into the stratosphere if he could figure out exactly how much gunpowder to pack into the pipe without blowing us to kingdom come. The big question mark in the design still on the drawing board.

"If I don't get enough powder into the bottom of the tube, the rocket'll peter out at forty or fifty feet up. If I get too much, it'll blow the fuckin' pipe into a million pieces, like a hand grenade," he said.

I would watch, that's all. When it came time to test his launcher though, I promised myself I'd be long gone, and I'd be saying a prayer to whoever was the patron saint of...what? Coal miners?

We farted around the rest of the morning, chopping up Lady Fingers and Inch and a Halfers, separating the powder into little piles, checking out different sized pipes to make a good guess as to which would work best without disintegrating into deadly shrapnel after HE lit the fuse.

"How will you know how much powder to stuff into the pipe?" I asked him.

"Trial an' error. We'll make an educated guess or two," he answered seriously.

I couldn't see that. No way.

I stepped outside the overhead door of the garage and looked over at the chimney stack of the barbecue. I wondered if the destruction there had followed one of his educated guesses?

"Let's leave this till later. I'm getting thirsty. Rashure's should be open by now," I said to him.

"Yeah, okay. We can finish up after we get a cold pop. Goddam' it's hot, ain't it"

"Sort of."

Mrs. Rashure was most likely some kind of Protestant—one of those who saw no wrong in opening her business doors on Sunday if she wanted. I suppose we shouldn't have gone there on that first, holy day of the week, but I shrugged off that unwritten commandment, and off we went, bottles in hand, down the long driveway onto the sidewalk leading south to the corner where the old lady's store stood.

We made the short trek without a care in the world, still talking about the hilarious shock of weedy hair on the chicken monster from outer space, wondering if by our experiments we could invent a super-weapon more powerful than plain old gunpowder that would blast through its force field. When we crossed the street, I saw them standing outside the store on the porch, leaning against the white painted columns holding up the small gabled roof.

The Minkle brothers—Inky and Butch.

Butch was the shorter of the two. Stocky, and ugly as a basket of rotten apples. But Inky—he was tall, athletically built, and good-looking. He must have spent hours each morning in front of the bathroom mirror with a jar of Brylcreem and a comb getting every strand of hair in that jet-black pompadour just perfect. I admired him for that, but trembled at the thought of stumbling into his path without Jimmy, Mickey, and every other kid I knew beside me. The hairdo alone would have made me sink to my knees and pray for mercy.

Inky stood on one side, at the top of the wooden steps, Butch across from him with his thumbs inside the waistband of his jeans. Both of them had a lit cigarette dangling out of their mouths, and a pack rolled up in their white tee-shirts at the shoulder, common for hoods and delinquents. Butch looked stupidly at us, mostly because, I figured, he *was* stupid...but Inky sneered with his head-devil smarts as we stepped between them, single file. We didn't want any trouble, just a cold bottle of pop. I even tried not to think back on the teepees we'd built in the vacant lot across the street from our houses last summer, and which I knew positively they'd smashed to the ground on one of their midnight raids down onto our block. Now, here they were, ready to smash us to the ground.

"Where you buttholes goin'?" Butch greeted us when we passed by, mangling the words out of the side of his mouth opposite the cigarette.

Inky didn't say a word. Neither did Jimmy or me. We continued on into the store, with its glass-faced display cases standing on either side of the main aisle, without a peep. The Coke box stood at the far end near the doorway entrance to Mrs. Rashure's living area at the rear. We were in, but we were trapped. I knew we weren't going to get back out of that place without a fight, unless we ran like scared chickens. Thinking about the alternative to having our faces used as punching bags, I was all for the chicken idea. Worse, I'd heard about Butch's devotion to switchblades. I sure didn't want a knife stuck into my belly on that or any other morning.

Mrs. Rashure shuffled out of her apartment when she heard the little bell above the screen door ding, and I saw the look on her face when she saw the load of bottles we'd lugged in. She was a widow, stooped over, wearing an ankle length, dark blue polka dot dress, and she was for sure a hundred fifty years old if she was a day. Her thin face looked like a potato left out in the sun for a month. Her scraggily arms and hands could have been the shoots that'd withered and died after having sprouted from it, screaming for water that wasn't there.

"I don't want no more bottles, boys. I got too many already. They're all over the place back there," she said in her faltering voice, pointing back at her living quarters.

"But you get money for 'em," Jimmy complained. "We just want a cold Coke. We even got an extra couple we'll let you have. That's four cents profit."

That seemed to move her. Four cents wasn't much, but it was better than nothing, I guess she thought. She turned up her nose, but she opened the cash register drawer and slipped a dime and a nickel out for us.

"Actually, that's five cents profit," Jimmy told her as he took the two coins. "It's all yours, and we thank you, don't we Skip?"

"Yep. Thanks."

I looked behind me as Jimmy went to the machine and lifted the top. Inky hadn't moved a muscle, but Butch had slithered across the porch, and was standing just outside the dusty screen looking in at us. Mrs. Rashure noticed him, too, and she went for him like a shot.

"You hoodlums take those cigarettes and get on outta' here before I call the police. G'won," she said wagging a finger at them, "you ain't hangin' around my store like two banty roosters. Get on up the street!"

Butch turned up his boxer's flat nose and sneered out of the free side of his mouth. He turned slowly, and with an air of arrogance retook his position at the column a few feet back, staring in at me, blowing out a slow puff of smoke. Inky didn't budge.

I turned my head to Mrs. Rashure, and without daring to ask her, used my eyes to inquire whether Butch's retreat might not have been far enough—which I was sure it wasn't. She must have thought otherwise because she turned and shuffled back toward her living quarters.

"Don't bring no more of them bottles in here, boys. I got too many of 'em already. They're all over the place back here." She disappeared without another word through the doorway, leaving Jimmy and me to face certain annihilation in another couple of seconds—and without the benefit of a cop, or even an old lady, to referee the slaughter.

I looked to Jimmy, who didn't seem to be all that frightened, and mouthed the question, "Now what?" He gave me a little smile, snapped the cap off of the Coke at the opener attached to the side of the bright red case, then led the way back out. We had our ratty old Keds sneakers on—Inky and Butch were sporting their engineer boots with rock-hard toes. I could feel the pain in my shin bones already. Why did we have to go and get thirsty when we did? Well, the remorse was useless, so I said a little prayer for help under breath.

Dearest Virgin Mary, I know you don't want to see us get our rear-ends kicked. I just know it. Can you maybe give us a hand here? Ah, please! We don't have much time, so you're gonna' have to be quick! Sorry.

I followed Jimmy outside to the firing line, not having a great deal of faith in that too-short prayer. A current of warm air hit us as we stepped onto the porch. Jimmy stopped directly in front of Inky, who wasn't much taller than my best friend, even

31

though he was three years older than Jimmy, and held out the bottle to him.

"You an yer goofy lookin' brother want a sip?" he asked Inky.

He could have said anything, *anything* but that. I watched with terror as Butch quickly pushed himself away from the column with the foot he'd planted against it. I instinctively clenched my fists. Inky stayed locked against his column and didn't offer any response, or even twitch a muscle for a few seconds. Finally he lifted one hand and extended it toward Jimmy.

"Yeah, I'll take a swig. Butch don't like Coke much, though, do you Butch?"

Butch stopped dead. He must have been trying to think about his brother's question—maybe that he *did* like Coke? I watched his eyes crashing against the corners of their sockets, and his mouth open and close rapidly. Yep, he was trying to come up with the correct wrong answer. And then he replied to his older brother's question like the obedient little dog he was. "Nah. I hate the stuff. I think I'd like to kick this sissy's ass, though."

That sissy would be me, and that would be the correct wrong answer. Inky grinned.

This was not good. Jimmy was making friends with Inky while I was preparing to get knifed. Where the hell was my miracle, I wondered? I kept glancing at Butch, waiting for him to pull the switchblade, and then over at Inky, hoping he'd say "Heel" to his brother.

Inky grabbed hold of the Coke Jimmy offered him, brought it to his lips without shifting his dark eyes off Jimmy, and then slowly emptied it. That kind of made me nervous. After *that,* he burped very loud...and very long. When he'd finished with the entire insult he handed the bottle back to Jimmy, who took it without a complaint. Butch let out a roar of approval. For sure he would never have been able to think of something as clever as that himself. I waited with growing apprehension.

Jimmy lifted the empty bottle and looked it over, and then tossed it past Butch's nose into the small, weed-infested garden beyond the porch. Butch stood totally upright at that, pulled his shoulders back, and raised his clenched fists. I moved a step closer to Jimmy waiting for the shit to hit the fan. Strangely, Inky didn't flinch. Neither did Jimmy.

As Butch began to strut around like a boxer waiting for the bell sounding the beginning of Round One to clang, Jimmy calmly walked off the porch. I wasted no time following him.

"You owe me one, Inky," he said without looking back.

Inky responded, deadpan, "Yeah, I'll bring it by as soon as you kiss my ass." He burped again, and Butch began to howl louder.

Jimmy and I walked across the gravel toward the sidewalk at the corner. We were forced to stop when the number 75 bus rumbled up and the doors opened with a loud hiss. Half of the people in the neighborhood must have been on that bus and decided to jump off at the very same stop. Providence? An answer to my prayer, at least, because Butch had decided to follow me off Mrs. Rashure's porch. The appearance of the people getting off stopped him cold.

Clifford Childers, a dumpy little ten year-old who lived three doors down from me, tumbled out of the bus first with his mother and another woman, both of them with feathered hats on their heads and shopping bags dangling from their arms. They were followed by an old woman and someone I took to be her husband of more than just a few years. She stepped down, firmly planting both feet on each step before going on to the next, and then when she'd reached the sidewalk, she turned and fussed over her husband as though he was helpless in the face of the two steps he must get down. He managed pretty well—that is to say he didn't fall. A bunch of other passengers patiently waited their turn to get off the bus. When they were all safely out and standing on the sidewalk, the driver closed the doors and prepared to pull away. Suddenly, as if on some unspoken cue, the entire group in front of us seemed to sense a coming battle. They stopped dead and stared at Jimmy, the Minkle brothers, and me. I heard the soles of Butch's boots scuffle to a stop behind me in the gravel. The bus pulled away with a roar.

How could I not help but see the next vision? In the frozen second when everyone waited for the boots to fall, I beheld her radiant face in the rear window of the bus. The girl. The dancer. Beside her sat the drip of the neighborhood, Allen Jung, his mouth screwed up in some word he must have been trying to get out, and that would make sense. The sun twinkled for an instant off the thick lenses of his Buddy Holly glasses. She seemed almost like she didn't give a hoot, as though whatever he was blabbing about actually irritated her—and she looked straight out at me.

I bit my lip, hoping she wouldn't see what was going to happen in the coming seconds. Hoping the driver of the bus could whisk her and Allen far enough away so that my beating wouldn't be observed. Then I turned my head quickly to find out where Butch was. He'd backtracked a few steps, hands shoved into his rear pockets again, waiting, I think, for the crowd to break up and go away. Or maybe reaching for his knife.

Jimmy had already sidestepped the crowd and had hustled into the street. He turned about halfway across and did what I should have expected, and what made me cringe with terror. What sent the ladies in the nervous crowd straight into cardiac arrest—and what forever made the two of us state enemies of Inky. Jimmy bent over in the middle of the empty street, dropped his jeans, and told Inky and his idiot brother exactly what he thought of them with his bare ass.

"Kiss this!" he said pointing at his lily-white cheeks with both hands.

When I saw that, I excused myself immediately and made a beeline for the safety of my house. Jimmy was right behind me, laughing like he'd just K.O.'d every one of the world heavyweight champs from John L. Sullivan on.

Really, I don't know if the Minkle brothers bothered to follow us—I didn't hear their footsteps over the shouts of disgust from the rest of the crowd—but I suspected our days of semi-peaceful co-existence with them were now numbered. Numbered zero, to be exact. All the way home Jimmy laughed like he had no sense at all. He might think it was funny, but I knew differently. They'd be down to pay us a real glad-to-have-met-you visit, and to thank Jimmy for his parting thoughts very soon.

At the far end of the block the bus had stopped again. The dancer hopped off, followed by Allen right on her heels. He waved his arms and spoke as though she really *might* be interested in whatever it was he'd been blabbering to her about. I just knew she wasn't. She walked away from him, but before she got too far, she turned and glanced back at Jimmy and me just as we hit the front fence of my yard. I wondered as I crossed the top bar what her name might be. Sandra Dee or Elizabeth Taylor, maybe. I found the image of her exciting, even knowing I would sure enough die within seconds if Inky and Butch caught up to us.

FIVE

World War Two and a Half

I could never figure this one out.

Pop didn't have a sister that I'd ever heard of. Mom had three or four. So I had three or four aunts. Only that wasn't true. I had five or six. The extra two came from Pop's side of the family, but like I said, he didn't have any sisters. I wondered about that sometimes, but never enough to ask him to explain the existence of the extra aunts.

They came down to drink a beer and visit one afternoon a couple of weeks after Jimmy committed the mortal sin against Inky and Butch up at Rashure's store. I'd kind of put worrying about the two of them on the back burner—not too far back, though. They'd come visiting, too, eventually.

I wasn't thinking about them that day—wasn't even thinking about my "aunts". Oh, Aunt Corey was the older of the two. Aunt Sylvie was her daughter. That should have made Aunt Sylvie my cousin, except that Aunt Corey wasn't Pop's sister. I think someone screwed up somewhere, or else someone was lying to me.

Well, anyway. Like as happened to Ruth McGuire, Aunt Sylvie's husband had flown the coup for reasons that were never explained to me, and so she lived with her mom, my aunt, four or five blocks away from us.

Their big thing in life was collecting salt and pepper shakers, and every time they got their hands on a new pair of them, they'd come visiting, or else I'd be dragged along up to their house and be forced to have a look at them there. And Mom and Pop, and Aunt Corey and Aunt Sylvie would always have a beer or two or three as they talked about the dumb salt and pepper shakers. Honestly, I think sitting around drinking beer was their real big thing in life. It would have been the same, probably, had my two aunts collected rocks or bugs.

We all went to the same church, though my aunts had brains enough to go to a later Mass than we did each Sunday. Aunt Corey was a sweet old lady. Aunt Sylvie was nice, but she had some nervous tick that made her jumpier than a bug on a hot rock. She shook constantly, and her eyes were always like a pair of bullets banging around in a tub after they'd been fired from a gun.

Me and Jimmy and Mick were in the basement when they came that day—Ruth McGuire not far behind them with her bottle. Through the floorboards we could hear their voices rising, the more beer they opened and drank. Downstairs the three of us had dragged out all my little plastic soldiers at Jimmy's suggestion—because he wanted to stage a "real war." I wasn't keen on playing with kid's stuff anymore, and at first I didn't understand what he was talking about, but I said okay anyway. And so down they went onto the concrete, divided into three armies. The Nazis, the Americans, and the Commies. I had to be the Commies, even though all the soldiers were mine. But I said okay again.

I wasn't too excited about any of this toy soldiers stuff, and at first neither was Mick, but Jimmy was all beside himself, which should have been a tip-off.

"The Americans invented flame throwers," he said smiling at me. "The Nazis were pretty smart too, and they stole our idea. But the Commies were dumb as rocks." He pulled out a brand new matchgun and tossed it over to Mick, and then pulled out another for his guys to use.

"War is hell," he said, and then loaded up and started shooting at my guys. Once in a while, just to keep Mick interested, I think, he'd shoot one at the Nazis. It wasn't long, though, before the Americans and the Nazis ganged up on the Commies, and the basement started to smell like sulfur. As much as they shot at my guys, though, their matches didn't do a lick of good. They'd either hit me, or else land beside one of my Commie guys and burn out.

This went on for a little while. Every now and again someone upstairs would bust out laughing, or cussing, or both. Finally Jimmy threw the matchgun down and stood up.

"I'm gonna' go get some napalm."

"What's napalm?" I asked.

"Gas. These fuckin' matches ain't doin' their job. You guys wait here."

"Oh no you're not, Jimmy," I said. "No gas down here. Are you nuts?"

Mickey wasn't often the one who came up with a good alternative solution to Jimmy's screwball plans, but that day he had a good one. A safe one, I thought.

"Why not we go up and get some charcoal lighter fluid? It ain't as explosive as gas."

I didn't mind that so much, and so I agreed. Again.

Ten minutes later we were back with two cans of charcoal lighter fluid, and one squeeze bottle filled with gas that Jimmy snuck in. Me and Mick got the charcoal lighter. We made our armies back up a ways, because battles are sometimes fought at long distance, and can get real messy. Jimmy fired the first shot. He loaded up his matchgun, stuck the tip of the squeeze bottle right in front of it, and then depressed the triggers of both at the same time.

It was really cool.

Two of my soldiers caught on fire right away. Just to make sure they got burned properly, Jimmy squirted some more gas on them. Mick was pretty awestruck at all this, and he laid into Jimmy's Americans, yelling, "Tora, tora, tora!" And then he went for the Commies.

Real battles in real wars happen fast sometimes, I'd heard, and the outcomes are never predictable—unless the Americans are fighting. But Jimmy's guys were burning up almost as fast as mine and Mickey's, that is to say they were melting as fast. So as not to lose the fight, Jimmy started running around, stomping and squirting on our soldiers that were looking a lot like two armies of The Wicked Witches of the West.

38

It stunk pretty bad, and my aunts and folks and Ruth must have noticed, because pretty soon Pop started stomping on the floor and cussing. "What the hell is going on down there?"

Jimmy looked up while he was busy stomping and squirting napalm. A stream of it hit me, but I got out of the way of the main part of it, which landed on my bed. Which started to burn. Which sent all of us into a panic.

"Now you've done it, McGuire! Grab that blanket!" I screamed that, and like all things screamed at the wrong instant, everyone upstairs had gone quiet at the very same instant.

I heard Pop's footsteps on the floorboards. Jimmy tried to yank the cover off the bed, but it was burning like gangbusters already, so he nixed that idea. Besides, he could hardly move for all the gooey plastic on his shoes. Mick dropped his can of lighter fluid and headed for the door. My left pant leg had gas all over it, and so I wasn't stupid enough to try and put the burning bed out. I backed up next to the furnace, which, thank God wasn't on, and went through the list of saints I hadn't asked for help from lately. Was there a Saint Nero? No. For sure. And I thought Mary was probably getting tired of bailing me out, so I just closed my eyes and waited for God to come roaring down the stairs in the form of Pop, and slap the generals silly. After he put the fire out.

He got there, almost busting the door off its hinges when he came in.

"Jesus-H-Christ!" were his first words. They were okay, and not a mortal sin because of the gravity of the moment. Pop came stumbling in, waving his arms, trying to make the smoke go away.

"Who the hell is down here? Skip! You here? Jimmy McGuire, I know you are! The two of you get yourselves out of here. Now!"

Mick somehow slipped underneath him and shot up the back stairs, but he was collared at the door leading to safety by Aunt Corey. As he was making his getaway, and me and Jimmy were coughing our guts out, trying to get out, too, the window above my bed busted open, and a hose came flying in, open full blast.

"Laverne? You down there?" That was Aunt Sylvie, and it took her a couple of tries before she got those two questions out. She must have been holding the hose—God knows where Mrs. McGuire and Mom were—and I'll bet poor old Pop...well, that's why when he finally got upstairs again he was soaked.

But the fire got put out.

The peace treaty was not very good for any of the three armies. Mom told the Nazis to "Get on up to your goddam' high-fallutin' house, and don't come back!" The Americans were banned forever from ever stepping foot into the Morley residence. The Commies were grounded "...until you're goddam' twenty-one. You got that?"

"Yes, sir."

"Ah, Mister Morley, that ain't fai..."

"Shut up, Jimmy."

Jimmy was allowed to stay in our house for a little while longer though, because Aunt Corey and Sylvie hadn't finished showing Mom and Pop and Ruth their salt and pepper shakers. That and there were still a couple of six packs that hadn't even been touched in the fridge.

"Let's go outside, LaVerne," Aunt Sylvie said after everything settled down. "It stinks to high heavens in here. G-goddamn kids."

Jimmy and me were stuck on the couch in the living room. That day he couldn't be trusted to be home alone, though in Ruth's condition it wouldn't have mattered much anyway.

"You two stay put.

"Godammit anyway."

When they'd all gone away, between coughs, Jimmy tried to cheer me up.

"Don't worry a bit, Skip. By the end of the week none of 'em will remember a thing, and we'll be about our business as usual. Trust me."

"Shut up, Jimmy. Where am I gonna' sleep tonight on account of you?"

He was quiet for a minute. I was busy testing the springs of the couch we sat on. At last he said, "My house?"

"Oh right! You heard my dad. I'm grounded till I'm twenty-one."

"Crap! You put way too much stock in their threats. Your dad was half-shit faced when he said that, an' he was just mad cuz your blanket was on fire..."

"My *bed,* you idiot! And you started it—everything. And like always I'm gonna' have to pay the price for something that was all your fault! Why don't you just get out of here and leave me alone—for the NEXT EIGHT YEARS!"

He sat there in shock for a second or two, and then Jimmy got up and walked out the front door. No one, for sure not his mom, would care that he'd disappeared. I felt a little bad for having said what I did, but like you sometimes do when you've smacked your best friend, I hit him again, harder, when he was halfway out the door.

"My dad ain't no drunk like your fuckin' mom, either!"

He stopped, but didn't turn back. I saw his hand clench the edge of the door, and then he pushed it all the way open so hard it banged into the plaster wall. Then Jimmy was gone, and I figured I'd never ever see my best friend again.

SIX

Lockdown-It Ain't Necessarily So

I was busted again the following afternoon for violating the terms of my being "grounded for the duration," whatever that phrase was supposed to have meant to begin with. This time around Mom, after catching me sneaking out the front gate, ushered me immediately back into the house and told me I would be looking at those walls until I graduated from *college*.

"We was gonna' send you to Notre Dame, Skippy. Notre Dame! *Now* you're gonna' have to go to Regis—and you'll be stayin' here at home where I can keep an eye on you. Goddamit'."

Regis was a good Jesuit college in the north part of the city, not exactly on an academic par with the home of the Fighting Irish, maybe, but since it was taught by that vaunted order of intellectual priests, The Society of Jesus, she decided Regis would have to do, even if it wasn't technically Irish. Where she and Pop thought they would get the money to send me back to that other Catholic college in Indiana was beyond me. He probably had no idea about what school she intended for me anyway; I was definitely not scholarship material. Perhaps someone upstairs had given her the what-it-is concerning board, books, and tuition? Perhaps the dimes under the statues were working? I cannot deny, even now, the power of dimes placed reverently beneath statues of saints.

Anyway, it was Regis College someday, she said, and I was going to have to stay, not just in the house, but in my room until then.

Unless God Himself intervened.

Which He did.

A spring snowstorm swept into Colorado. A vast, black cloud climbed quietly over the mountains and then stalled directly over the city a few days after my second sentencing. Every ounce of moisture in the Pacific Ocean had been gobbled up and sent specifically to unload itself on Denver in my behalf, I believed, and so I fell to my knees beside my bed in fervent prayers of thanksgiving.

*Our Father, who art in Heaven, hallowed be...*but somehow that didn't seem quite good enough, so I began again on a more personal level.

Lord, I'm grounded, as You probably know, but I'm still so grateful. Regis will be a good school, I think, and I thank You for helping Mom pick it for me. I began to lose direction, become tongue-tied. Us Catholics weren't practiced, like the Protestants, with extemporaneous praying, but I pressed on.

Lord, I'm pretty certain You don't want to see me tied down in my room until I'm...gosh, twenty-two or twenty-three? So...Well, thanks ever so much for sending this snow. It gives me a great idea. I mean...well, You already know what I'm thinkingI suppose. I mean seeing as how You know everything...ah, what I'm trying to say is, I sure need Your help! I gotta' get out of here! But I'll stick close to home. If You'll help me. Promise. One thing, though—and I don't want to push my luck with You—I'm for sure gonna' need Jimmy on this one. I'll leave the details to You. Thanks so much again.

Amen.

Oh, P.S. This is the last thing I'll ever ask You for. Promise.

The emptying of the Pacific lasted for three long days. When it ended in those early morning hours of Saturday, March 30th, I got up, went upstairs, and peered out of our kitchen window at the rear of the house into a wonderland of deep, wet whiteness. Standing at the end of the property ten feet inside the battered chainlink fence, our old elm tree had weeks ago begun to bud its leaves, but the weight of the wet snow had crushed its branches so effectively that—well, it was as if God had sent cement trucks inside the clouds to unload on the city.

Now I needed the second part of God's mysterious but marvelous plan for me; how to get Mom to let me open the back door and go outside.

Standing there looking at the ravaged limbs of the tree, the grace of the Lord shown down upon me. That was when it hit me. Many of the cracked branches would need to be cut off, lugged through the yard, and then tossed onto the front parking for the city clean-up crews to cart away. I could see that. Someone in our family had to do it, and I was the logical choice. Another of those little details had miraculously been taken care of. If I worked diligently, I was certain (at least hopeful) Mom would forgive me and let me have my freedom. She loved the idea of a man sweating to earn his keep. It was what we Irish were good at historically. Working and sweating. Drinking too, of course. Once I got outside the entire yard would be my domain. If I happened to stray near to the fence...but I wouldn't hop over it. I'd let Jimmy do that. She hadn't mentioned a word about his coming into my yard as being part of the conditions of my lockdown.

It all sounded sensible enough, so I ran to hers and Pop's bedroom, the only room in the house without a door.

"Hey you guys, wake up!"

"Wha...?" Mom groaned. I couldn't see under their pile of blankets where she ended and Pop began. The early morning light barely broke the dimness of the small bedroom, thank goodness, but I turned my head slightly away from them anyway.

"Mom, Pop! Get up. Come see what the snow did!"

"What is it Skip? Whatd'ya want?" Pop asked.

"The old tree in the backyard...gosh, half the branches are broken."

Part two of The Plan...

"We gotta' get out there and clean up the mess. It's terrible. And the other trees...they're pretty wrecked too! Hurry, we gotta' get started!"

Silence fell on them for a moment. Pop turned over onto his side and squinted in the dim light at the clock on his nightstand. "What time is it?" he grunted.

44

"A little after six," I said.

"Six? Good God Almighty." He rolled onto his back again and laid an arm across the top of Mom's pillow against the headboard, cleared his throat a little. "Go on out and start cleaning it up. I'll be out a little later," he said.

Mom sighed, rolled over in disinterest—at least in me—closer to Pop, and threw her arm almost casually across his chest.

"Go do what your father says, Skip."

I think they were happy in a way that I'd woke them, and that I had a chore outside that would occupy my time for a while.

I was free.

SEVEN

The Fortress In The Sky

S tanding on the covered patio gazing out at that tree, the image of something beautiful, straight out of House and Garden, formed in my head. A treehouse. Not a wimpy platform up in the clouds to sit on and watch the birds fly by, but a real house, with walls and a roof—maybe even a fireplace for Jimmy.

I'd clean up the busted branches and then construct a mansion in the sky. From our perch a mile above the earth we'd be able to scan the city from horizon to horizon. Inky's approach unseen would be relegated to a mere nightmare from the past because the minute he and his idiot brother opened their front door two blocks away we'd spot them. They'd have to come down the street in tanks if their attack was to succeed. We'd be waiting for them up there in our castle with our rocks and slingshots—maybe even pots of boiling oil, if we could build a stove to boil the oil that wouldn't set the place ablaze. Better still, when they tromped down the alley with their knives and clubs and zip guns, Jimmy could stick his bare butt out the south window and greet them with near-impunity. That's what I thought.

The storm had been a sign from God—a blessing bestowed on me and my friends at no small cost to the city. The tree had been readied by Providence; an answer to my prayer for freedom. What other explanation could there possibly be?

I took it upon myself to slog through the snow in the back yard, out to the garage to grab a snow shovel, and then begin the task of plowing a path to the tree. I needed to work up a good sweat, even in the arctic air of the morning.

Pop had built the garage by himself fifteen years ago, soon after he'd purchased the house. He possessed a laundry list of character strengths and oddball mechanical abilities, but carpentry wasn't among them. The walls he erected were as thin as butterfly wings and covered over with corrugated sheet metal. The metal alone, I think, carried the weight of the roof. As for the roof, it had a pronounced sag midway along the ridgeline for as far back as I could remember, but that morning under the burden of a three foot high load of snow I could almost hear the splintering of the fibers. If it survived the day I figured he'd be lucky.

I pushed open the door he'd hung with straps of heavy leather instead of hinges, and grabbed the old coal shovel leaning against the matchstick walls. Half an hour later I'd managed to carve a ragged "V" through the snow from the corner of the garage, to the base of the tree, and then back to the rear door of the kitchen. Sadly, even though I had overworked myself, there was no sweat, except that frozen just below my nostrils.

"Hey Skip, how's it goin'," I heard just as I was about to pull the door open and go inside for a little breakfast and some welcome heat. It was Jimmy, with his head stuck out through a hole in the screen of his bedroom window. I guessed he'd forgiven me, just like Mom and Pop would do pretty soon when they saw how industrious I'd gotten.

"Thought you were grounded."

"Shh! Not so loud," I said, pointing to my folk's bedroom window. "I got a reprieve for a while."

"Uh...okay. Hey, that was one big-ass storm, wasn't it? Whatd'ya say we build a snow fort today?"

"Nah, I don't think so...waste of time. We got a bigger project to do," I answered. My toes were numb and my stomach was growling.

"What kind of bigger project?" he asked.

"Look at the old tree back there," I said pointing to the rear of the yard.

"Yeah...so what about it? We gonna' cut it down?"

"Nope. We're gonna' clean it up and build a Hilton Hotel up there at the top. Soon as I warm up and eat. Get dressed and meet me over here. And be quiet about it!"

"Hilton Who...? What are you talkin' about?"

"The best damned treehouse in all of Denver. The best! I gotta' go eat. Just come over."

He pulled his head back into his room, and I went inside where I stripped my boots and socks off, then sat in front of a register vent for a couple of minutes to thaw out my toes, one ear cocked in the direction of the door-less bedroom. When I could stand without grimacing, I tiptoed into the kitchen to eat. Before I'd even gotten the milk poured into a bowl of Rice Krispies, the back door opened and in Jimmy waltzed, covered to his knees in white.

"Treehouse?" he asked.

"Yep. Big one, too. One we can use as a lookout. They're coming for us, you know."

"They? Who's they?"

"Inky and Butch."

He stared at me for a minute and then laughed. "Baloney. They ain't comin' after us. An 'sides, I ain't scared of either one of 'em."

"Yeah, sure. You'll be shaking in your boots when they come down here with guns and knives and baseball bats. We've gotta' prepare. Make a fort they can't get into even if they had a thousand guys behind them. A fort at the top of the tree!"

That blank look came over his face again, and I knew he was visualizing the treehouse—but not the one I had in my head.

"Wow. At the top...in *that* tree? But how we gonna' get the wood up...where are we even gonna' find any wood?"

I shoveled a spoonful of cereal into my mouth, chewed it up, and then beamed at him. "Lemme' eat, then we'll go out and I'll tell you all about it."

By mid-morning the hundreds of severed limbs lay in a dense, tall pile not more than ten feet from the thick trunk of the tree. Jimmy figured it would be a waste of precious time to shovel the walk to the front yard and lug the limbs there, and besides, he said, maybe we could use some of the heavier ones to build parts of the castle.

"Not a chance," I said to him. "We're gonna' find the best wood there is. Straight ones. Nuthin' but the best."

"Where we gonna' find good wood?" Jimmy asked again as he hatcheted off the last of the broken limbs.

"They're building a new house up on Perry Street. I saw it a couple of weeks ago. There's tons of two-by-fours and plywood, and lots of other stuff. Won't nobody be around there in this mess. We'll just go borrow what we need," I answered.

Jimmy dropped the hatchet as I laid out the inspired plan of larceny, and it bounced face-first off of a thick branch at the base of the tree with a thunk, three inches from my right foot.

"Damn, Jim! Watch what your doin'!" I screamed.

"Sorry, Skip."

"Let's get movin'. I'll get the sled and we'll go up there and load it with wood," I said.

Jimmy shinnied back down the tree while I went to dig out the sled where it lay buried by the side of the groaning wall of the garage.

The late March sun had risen high enough to break up the remnants of the clouds, and the temperature was beginning to climb steadily higher by the minute. It was going to be a warm, early-spring day. By tomorrow the lion's share of the snow would be melted, but for now we had to Lewis and Clark it out the gate, down the alley, then onto Bayaud Street which would carry us up the long hill to Perry Avenue...and our lumber yard.

Arriving at the scene of the crime, we casually dragged the sled over more drifts of dirt mounds covered knee-deep in melting snow. The new home stood half framed, with walls shored up, and roof rafter lumber stacked, waiting to be cut— conveniently close to the street.

"They knew we'd be coming," I quipped. "Damn nice of 'em to put this stuff where we could get at it easy!"

"Yeah," Jimmy said. "How much you think we'll need? Those boards are really long."

That they were. Longer than our tiny Flexible Flyer by a mile. The question arose concerning just how the two of us could get ten or twenty of them cut and loaded onto the sled without a saw and then drag the whole mess back home. And without being too obvious.

"Well...let's see." I thought long and hard, but it was Jimmy who broke the back of the problem with a simple solution.

"I got it. Let's get 'em loaded up. Most of the length we'll let stick off the sled, behind it in the snow. We'll get some rope or wire or somethin' layin' around here and tie it all up onto the sled. Then we can drag it like a twenty-foot toboggan back down to the alley. Simple."

He was sort of right. The journey back was all downhill, and deep ruts had been carved and packed in the snow by passing cars. Someone seemed to be smiling down on us at first.

It took us until almost mid-day to get the shipment home though, because the toboggan refused to slide as effortlessly as expected with all the wood dragging behind it. Worse, negotiating the two required turns along the route lay outside the parameters of Jimmy's simple solution. The ends of the wood leading the way acted like the prow of a ship. At each turn they sliced into the higher bank beside the rut, and we were forced to either dig a new channel through the slush or else abandon the effort. We pushed on.

When we finally dropped anchor in the alley outside the rear gate, Jimmy and I collapsed. It required three peanut butter and jelly sandwiches and two glasses of milk apiece in order for us to regain our strength and focus. We ate, we rested, and then I laid out a very rough verbal draft of the logistics of our attack on the stack of wood we'd stolen. Of course the plan was all in my head, clear as water in a mountain stream, but the material translation was clearly in danger, as neither of us had ever even sawn a toothpick in half. Still, rested and jazzed, we gathered up some of Pop's rusted tools, a rickety ladder, an assortment of nails, and then we began.

We violated every common sense rule of carpentry, but soon enough we'd hacked a couple of the boards in two despite the fact that Jimmy had to use a hammer to complete the dissections.

"Now what?" he asked me.

There was no hesitation in my answer. "Let's build!"

By late afternoon when Pop poked his head out the kitchen door, we had something of a not-quite-level, but reasonably secure underpinning erected.

"What the devil is going on out here?" he asked with a big, broad smile. Behind him stood Mom, her arms wrapped around his midsection. Aside from the little swearing we'd done when boards fell, or my thumb found itself between the hammerhead and the nail, we'd been exceptionally quiet. Jimmy stepped to the fore with a timely answer.

"Hiya', Mr. Morley, an' whoever that is huggin' your belly! We're tired of trompin' around the neighborhood gettin' ourselves in trouble, so we decided to build a little treehouse out here. Could ya' get dressed and help, maybe?"

That did the trick.

I noticed all ten of Mom's fingers dancing around on his stomach as though she were trying to play one of his compositions, her head and the rest of her body invisible behind his broad chest. He laughed. "No, I don't think so...maybe later."

I gave them ten seconds at most before they disappeared again far into the interior of the love cave.

Pop hadn't even noticed the clean, stolen boards, which were now ready to become some sort of floor, four walls, a roof—and afterward, the home for a tin can fireplace. His love-induced blindness to our stack of wood had to have been another divine intervention. Who says God was the author of that commandment about stealing? *Someone* was blessing our construction project. We even miraculously figured out that if we nailed some boards at a downward angle from the perimeter of the floor framing back to the tree trunk, the whole thing would remain remarkably stable. We became instant master craftsmen and monkeys.

***

"You are a little jewel in my crown," Mom said.

Not only had I cleaned up all the broken branches and shoveled all the walks, I'd quietly scrubbed the kitchen counters and taped a red plastic rose in the outstretched hands of the Blessed Lady, whose statue stood on a dark wooden, polished dais in the living room next to the TV. All of this before she and Pop tumbled in exhaustion out of bed for the second time that day.

I leaned forward and kissed her whisker-burned cheek softly. "And you're the Queen of all Mothers," I said. "Did you sleep well?"

She simply took hold of my face with her warm hands and smiled.

"Yes."

EIGHT

Veni, Vidi, Vicious

Monday, April 8th, was a religious holiday, and so the students of our school were given a reprieve from our studies to commemorate the miraculous events surrounding the Virgin Mary's wondrous appearance in a European village high in the Alps somewhere, with a name that couldn't be pronounced, except by language scholars.

The Fumo gardens were clean beyond all mortal comprehension, and so Mickey was released from his bondage, having overturned every clod of dirt on his property in search of anything even remotely resembling a weed. Jimmy, Mickey and I made the most of the holiday and our new freedom.

It turned out to be one of those brilliantly blue, shirtsleeve-warm days that made Mom and Pop curse my Uncle Wayne for having "gotten snippy" and moving off to California; out west at the edge of the ocean where rumor had it every day was sunny and hot, and everyone who lived there was rich. I didn't know anything about why he actually went, what fortunes the state actually possessed, or what the weather was really like in California, but I did thank the Blessed Virgin for favoring us with another excellent day for building. The thought of how Jimmy and I swiped the material had begun to eat away at my conscience though. I figured—or hoped at least—that there existed a prayer or an indulgence or a candle that could be lit to cover the sin. Anyway, I'd decided to deal with it later. That morning the warm sun and the tree beckoned more than the price we'd have to pay when we died someday and went before St. Peter to explain how we'd come by the wood.

Jimmy arrived first, of course, with a brand new saw. God knows where he'd gotten it—or how. His mom sure had no use for one. Hail Mary time again. Anyway, between the two of us the rest of the two-by-fours got cut into reasonably equal lengths—eight/five-foot pieces for the roof rafters. We continued to work harmoniously and pretty effectively.

53

Mickey blew in at a little after ten, both hands waving above his head, screaming at the top of his lungs. "They're comin'! They're comin'!"

That could mean only one thing to me, but Jimmy who was on his hands and knees, straddling the studs of the one wall still lying on the floor, studying the five huge nails that he'd bent, looked down in some confusion as Mickey hit the tree like a cat escaping a pack of dogs.

"What are you babblin' about? Who's comin'?" Jimmy asked.

"Inky and Butch and three other guys I never seen before. They got pipes and bats!"

Jimmy dropped his hammer and jumped to his feet, nearly knocking me over the edge of the deck. We both peered south over the roof of the garage, over the line of backyards buffering us from the Skulls, and our mouths dropped the same distance in horror. How had we so foolishly neglected the inevitable? Why hadn't we worked faster? There they were, as plain as day, marching like Huns in our direction. Inky led them single file, and in no more than five seconds they'd be turning down our alley, ready to stop at my house and beat the living daylights out of us. Mickey must have thought twice about offering his body to the slaughter by climbing up beside us, and so he beat a quick retreat toward the front yard.

"What are we gonna' do?" I asked Jimmy.

"Dunno yet. I'm thinkin' though."

"Well think fast. There's five of them and only two of us," I replied.

"Yeah. Yeah..." He paused and turned in a circle, looking, I figured, for something we could use as a weapon. The crummy old hammer with one claw broken off lay where he'd dropped it, but I don't think he wanted to kill any of them, so he left it where it lay and twisted his mouth all out of shape. "I dunno'. I dunno'. Let's make a run for it!"

"There isn't time."

"Well then start prayin'. I guess we're gonna' get our butts kicked good."

NINE

Duh, My Name Are Butch

Jimmy and I ducked down low, backs against the wall, quieter than two nuns in a church. For sure we were listening to the terrible cursing they did, but the chances of The Skulls seeing us were next to nothing if we kept our cool—and kept our mouths shut.

They stopped beside the trash barrels just beyond the fence, and I turned my face to see the scourge of Meade Street and his brother through a small hole in the plywood siding. The three other hoods standing beside them were every bit as nasty looking as Butch, and it was my guess they'd just been released from juvenile hall, or maybe even prison. They were big. No, not just big—they were professional football-sized monsters. Three linemen from the Chicago Bears, looking dumber than blocks of stone, but probably meaner than a nest of hornets. And all of that wrath apparent in the faces of those five thugs was directed at us three chickens hiding somewhere in my yard.

From my vantage point high above them I saw Inky surveying the property as he tapped the sawed-off bat he carried onto his thigh.

"Maybe they ain't here," Butch growled. He squinted his weasely eyes, shading his face from the sun with an open hand. I knew he must be terribly nearsighted, as every time he looked in another direction he squeezed his eyelids even harder. Little help that would be to us if any of the others spotted us, though. Butch was a close-in fighter, an arms length puncher, I'd heard. I could be a blur to him and he'd still knock my head off.

"Nah, I think they're in there...somewhere," Inky replied, scanning the yard.

"Maybe in that shed, or the garage," Butch followed, "or up in that...what the hell is that 'spose to be?" he said pointing up at us.

"It's a treehouse, dimwit. Put on your glasses." Inky paused. "Hey, wait a minute...that's where I'd be if I was them. That's *exactly* where I'd hide!" said Inky. "Hey, you up there! Get your asses down here and face us like men. We just want to talk to you, that's all."

"Yeah. We ain't come to beat up on ya'. We just wanna' talk," Butch laughed.

Fat chance of that being true, I knew. They were armed to the teeth. Talking was probably pretty low on their list of priorities. I turned to Jimmy who already had an index finger touching his lips. He mouthed the exact words I'd just been thinking, "Don't say a word!"

One of the thugs in the alley picked up a rock—Mickey's preferred weapon—and slung it up at us. It hit the side of the treehouse with a bang, and before I could peer back out through the hole, another one hit...and then another. Had two cowards other than us been sitting up there in the clouds, trapped and paralyzed with fear, the barrage of stones would have driven them screaming for mercy, out, and down to the ground. But Jimmy and I weren't your ordinary cowards. We figured we'd call their bluff and sit tight. Eventually they'd tire of demolishing the treehouse and wander back up the alley. They knew, I'm sure, that time was on their side. They could always catch us later.

"Gimme' that gun," I heard Butch say.

"What gun?" Inky answered in a low voice.

"Yers. The one ya' brang."

"You stupid shit. I didn't bring the gun. What's the matter with you?"

I heard a thwack!, followed by the shocked voice of Butch. "Ouch! Godammit, somethin' hit me!"

I peered through the hole again and saw him holding the side of his throat, squinting every which way. Inky and the other guys immediately went into a defensive posture, lowering their bodies, snapping their heads right and left to see if they could find the location of whomever was attacking them.

Thwack!

"Jesus Christ!"

This time it was Inky's turn. He grabbed hold of that perfect pompadour, digging into it at his skull, and I thought I saw smoke spewing out of his nostrils. "Somebody's shootin at us. BB gun or somethin'."

One of the dumb guys pointed toward Pop's garage. "They's over there somewheres. I saw somethin' move on top o' the roof."

Good old Mickey! He hadn't run out on us after all. I slid across the floor and peeked through the window opening of the south wall. Running along the alley on the property line stood our old abandoned chicken coop, and separating it from the garage was a weed infested driveway that Pop had intended to pour concrete in many years ago but had never gotten around to doing for one reason or another. The five invaders swarmed to that side of the yard yapping and cursing and looking for Mick. I saw him scoot down the front gable end off the roof into Mrs. McGuire's yard, and then in a flash he reappeared, darting behind the lilac bush in my yard. He carried his Wham-O slingshot by the surgical rubber tubes draped across his wrist, and sported a bulging pocketful of pebbles. The weapon was silent, highly accurate in the right hands, and deadly. Had Mickey loaded it up and fired at Butch with a quarter inch steel pellet instead of the pebble he'd used, Butch would have found himself lying on an operating table later that morning, looking up at the masked face of a surgeon holding a scalpel.

I glanced at Jimmy who was kneeling next to me looking down at the chase. "Did you bring your slingshot? Please say you did!" I whispered.

"No. It's in my room, dammit'!"

"Did you hear what Butch asked Inky?" I asked in a panic.

"Yeah. Shit."

We stuck our heads over the windowsill up to our noses and looked out again. Mickey was standing in the open next to the bush now, taking aim at the narrow space between the coop and the garage, waiting for a body to appear. Sure enough, dumb-shit number three wandered into his line of sight, and Mickey let another rock fly. In less than a heartbeat the ragged bullet hit the guy, catching him in the muscle of his shoulder. He let out a scream as he turned to see the sniper darting across the lawn to reposition himself behind the other elm tree near the patio.

"There he is! We got 'im!"

I thought the five of them would kill one another trying to knock down the two-foot section of rotting fence between the coop and the garage in their effort to get at Mickey. He realized the jig was up, abandoned his tree, and took off like a jet toward the front yard and the street beyond. From our conning tower Jimmy and I watched the foot race, an intermittent play broken by the obstacles of the Linden's two-story roof, towering elms farther down the street, and a board dangling over our own treehouse's roof that blocked part of the view. Mickey was a world-class sprinter, and he was running for his life. Those two factors saved him, I'm sure, and put an ever-increasing distance between the howling mob and himself. Inky was no slouch runner himself, and though he didn't gain on Mickey, he quickly outdistanced his thug friends and Butch. I saw him stop in front of the Jung's house three doors down and motion for the slower Skulls to return to my house. I couldn't hear what he was saying to them, but something told me Jimmy and I weren't out of the woods yet.

"We'd better get the hell out of here, Jimmy. They're coming back."

"Don't have to tell me twice!" he answered.

We shot down the ladder rungs nailed onto the tree trunk and made a bee-line for the house. Mom was busy in the front room with the vacuum when we darted in, nearly knocking her over to get to the window overlooking the street. Butch and company came marching into view about the same time, and so we jumped to either side of the drawn curtains, backs against the wall again.

"What the heck is goin' on, you two?" Mom asked after she'd flipped off the cleaner. She stood dead center of the window opening questioning Jimmy and me. I imagined the gorillas passing by outside, not daring to enter the yard, staring in at Mom yakking away at the pane of glass like an imbecile.

I explained to her what was happening, without moving, praying that stupid Butch and his stupider buddies wouldn't catch on that we were hiding just out of their sight. Mom's eyes narrowed at the conclusion of my short explanation. She glanced back out through the glass, and then she rolled up her sleeves and went for the front door, banging it against the wall when she left.

I looked over at Jimmy. He smiled weakly and then shrugged. Without a word we left the room and followed Mom. We stopped together on the front porch at the top of the steps, but Mom had already reached the gate. The Skulls, minus Inky, had halted and stood on the sidewalk like four roosters ready and egging for a good fight. Mom slung open the gate and advanced toward them with the cockiness of Babe Ruth. Of course she didn't have a bat, but that was okay. Her fists would do just as well. They were closed tight, and I knew she meant to kick a lung out of one or two of them at least. I'm absolutely certain she could have.

Fortunately for them, Pop pulled up at the curb in our station wagon just in time to save them from the beating of their lives. I don't know where he'd been—probably at the bar— but when Butch and his friends noticed the car they scurried on up the street. Mom was hustling after them, but she stopped when Pop stepped out of the car and called to her, "What in blazes is going on here, Rosie?"

I learned from Mickey's own mouth on the telephone later that evening after dinner how Inky had chased him all the way to his house.

"He's a fast sonofabitch. Nearly caught me! I got to my house though, and ran up to the front door. This is the best part!" He laughed. "I had one more rock left, and so I loaded up, turned, and warned him not to come any closer. He stopped for a sec and then took another step, sneering at me. Daring me to shoot him. So, I did. Hit him right in the belly! Man, was he mad!

Mother opened the door at the same time, just as Inky was doubling over. She was pretty pissed when she saw me with the slingshot, I gotta' tell you.

"She ran down the walkway and tried to help that no-good s.o.b. but he pushed her away and took off down the hill. He didn't look back, but I heard him cussing at me. Mother came back up and grabbed my slingshot, and then she beat me good for a while. I'm grounded again. She said she didn't care if he was going to beat you guys up, using a "deadly weapon" was the wrong thing to do. Deadly weapon. Crap! I knew what I was aiming at. If I'd wanted to kill them I'd have got 'em right between the eyes!"

I didn't bother to tell Mom that Mickey had used his Wham-O on the Skulls—she probably wouldn't have known what it was anyway. I just said that he had his beanie-snapper, which has about as much power as a good fart, and was trying to protect me and Jimmy, who'd done nothing to provoke the gang. Kind of true, and it did the trick. She was so angry that she threatened to march up to the Minkles' house and lay into their mom each time I added another detail to the account. Pop calmed her down, though, and refused to let her go, saying it'd do no good to have her wind up in jail for beating up some poor woman just because the other lady's kids were so reprehensible. The image, too, of my mom thrashing another woman—indeed, another anybody— makes me chuckle. Like I said, I had no doubts she could do it, but she stood only four foot-eight.

The Skulls' attack had failed. Jimmy and I had come out smelling like roses. Mickey hadn't fared quite as well. Still, we'd all escaped alive, thanks to him. The matter wasn't finished though. Not by a long shot. Jimmy might think so, he was an eternal optimist and sometimes idiot. I knew better. They'd be back for round two and the knock-out punch. It was just a matter of time. I knew Inky had a gun.

TEN

HEADLINE

Rocky Mountain News. Page 2. April 10th, 1957.

Blaze Erupts In Westside Elementary School

I said a hundred more prayers of supplication after reading that, but Jimmy and I decided against finding Dennis and stringing him up by the thumbs...or the balls. Local investigators somehow failed to add up two and two, to our greatest relief, and so the mysterious fire in Mr. Kimple's lot across the street, the girl with the incinerated scalp at the Comet, and the roaring blaze in the auditorium at Barnum Public School remained isolated incidents.

We thought.

We decided to forevermore curb our fascination with Fire...well, kind of. Jimmy boasted that he'd nearly solved the problem of the amount of gunpowder needed to propel his broom handle rocket into orbit.

ELEVEN

Five, Four, Three, Two...

I headed over to Jimmy's house Friday afternoon after getting my chores finished to see what was going on. We still had lots of work to do on our treehouse stretching into in the clouds. Maybe the two of us could scrounge up some shingles to cover the hundred cracks in the roof. With Inky Minkle out of the way for the time being, Jimmy and I were free to head back to the house being built up on Perry without fear of being ambushed, I hoped. Mickey was busy picking more weeds in his mother's garden, so Jimmy and I were on our own.

I found him in his mother's garage working on a piece of pipe about a foot in length. He'd capped one end of it and was busy drilling a small hole close to the bottom near the cap where the threads ended.

"What's up, doc?" I asked him as I walked through the wide opening.

He stopped drilling for a second and smiled, the way he always did when trouble lay waiting for us just around the corner on account of one of his projects. Reaching down, he grabbed an old spark plug and handed it to me.

"Feel that thing. It's just the right weight," he said.

"Right weight for what?" I asked him.

"Here, drop it into the end of this pipe."

I did. The plug slipped down to the cap with only a slight rattle, and then seated itself with a thunk. Jimmy closed his eyes tight and smiled again. A slight refinement of his rocket. Trouble for sure.

"Oh, shit..."

"I think I solved the problem."

Now everything was beginning to fit together; everything except how much gunpowder he figured was needed. I knew it had to have something to do with the hole he'd been drilling in the end of the pipe.

"What's the hole for?" I asked.

"The fuse. And we don't need to pack the pipe with gunpowder."

He bent down again and fished through a shoebox loaded with sparklers, Roman Candles, and more firecrackers. Five or six fresh packs of Lady Fingers, a dozen or two Inch-and-a-Halfers, and more M-80's and Cherry Bombs than I could count.

"Cool, huh? One of these Cherry Bomb kickin' it in the ass should do the trick?"

"Jeez Louise. It's great! For sure it'll go out of sight! Are we gonna' rig it up with a parachute?"

He stared down the muzzle of the pipe as he answered, "Yeee-aah, I think we should. That'll make it easier to see when it's comin' back down, too. Goddam', it'll go half a mile up with a quarter stick of dynamite pushin' it! Why didn't I just think of that before? There's no need to pack the powder down the stupid pipe. It's already packed!"

"We'll need to make some kind of base to hold it straight up," I said.

Last Fourth of July Jimmy had thrilled Clifford Childers, Mickey, Allen Jung, and me, by stuffing a lit Inch-and-a-Halfer into the back pocket of his jeans and then strutting around in a circle like the leader of a marching band. After it exploded and we all roared, he did it again, and then again until the pocket of his pants shredded. I knew his butt was throbbing, but it didn't seem to have fazed him a bit. Jimmy was crazy sometimes. Today I knew he'd want to hold the pipe and aim it, but that was nuts. An Inch-and-a-Halfer would burn his ass, but an out-of-control Cherry Bomb would blow his arm off.

"Hell no. I'll hold it like a Roman Candle," he answered.

"No you won't. Damn, Jimmy, you're gonna' kill yourself one of these days."

"Yeah. Yeah. Okay." He looked around, and sure enough spotted a pipe strap in the pile of junk littering the floor of the garage. He grabbed it and very quickly bent it around the perimeter of the pipe until its sides met, then splayed the ends back out to form a very questionable two-pronged base. It wasn't perfect, but it beat the hell out of holding the launcher steady with his hands. We shook each other's hand and then took the apparatus, the box of firecrackers, and our Sputnik outside to the wooden picnic table.

"This is our best idea yet," Jimmy said proudly.

I naturally agreed. Well, it might not have been the *best* idea we'd ever come up with, but it was the best so far that year. Jimmy had me hold the pipe upright on the warped boards of the wooden picnic table, and he grabbed the first of the Cherry Bombs and then dropped it down the open mouth of the tube, fuse first. A weapons engineer couldn't have predicted a more unfavorable result. The tip of the fuse was lost somewhere down there at the bottom of the pipe, and no matter how much he shook the damned thing he couldn't coax the fuse out through the hole.

"Shit! Now what?" I asked in frustration.

Jimmy remained silent, analyzing the problem. The tide of his genius swelled, finally, and with a smile he snapped his fingers.

"We're idiots. Here, gimme' that pipe wrench layin' over there."

I fetched the wrench, handed it to him, waiting anxiously for his solution. He turned the missile launcher upside down and dumped the Cherry Bomb out the way it had come in. He carefully loosened cap of the base that I had no faith in and then unscrewed the cap from the bottom.

"Simple enough. Gimme' the bomb."

I gathered it up off the ground and handed it to him. I would never have thought to remove the stupid cap, but it had come to him so easily. That was only one of many instances when I was certain Jimmy was blessed outside the parameters of human understanding. He pushed the fuse through the opening, grabbed hold of it, and then screwed the cap back on. After re-attaching the base we set it onto the tabletop and dropped the spark plug in.

"Ready?" he asked me.

No, I wasn't. I nodded anyway, and then took a quick look around for a place to duck when the bomb exploded. Visions of shrapnel ripping through his backyard leapt into my head, yet…yet. I had faith in his calculations and the thickness of that pipe.

"Hey! We forgot the parachute!" I shouted just before he struck the match.

"Screw the 'chute. We'll put it on the next one." And then he lit the fuse and flew under the table. I stupidly stood my ground ten feet away and watched in amazement as the powder ignited. There was a horrific bang, and a ferocious cloud of gray smoke rushed out of the open end of the tube, which toppled onto its side immediately afterward. I never saw the spark plug leave the barrel, but my eyes shot upward anyway, expecting to see it sailing into the clouds hanging high above us. I saw nothing. Jimmy screamed in delight at the sound and crawled out from his bunker to join me in my search for the rocket.

"Goddam'! Maybe we sent it into orbit!" he said. As if in answer, we heard a distinct THUD on the roof of Pop's garage a couple of seconds later. I looked toward the garage abutting his mom's property and then, with eyes the size of a Cadillac, back at Jimmy.

"Wow! That sonofagun was in the air for a solid minute! How high you think it went?" he asked jumping up and down.

Math was one of my weak subjects and I really had no idea, but my guess was that it came very close to the stratosphere we'd been aiming for before it plummeted back to smash into Pop's roof. Without another word we ran to the fence, and from there hopped up onto the snow-ruined roof. There it rested, heavy threaded end first, in the red rolled-roof covering. Remarkable.

We retrieved it and conducted several more launches, pleased with each small improvement we made in the projectile. Chief among them was to wrap duct tape, that miracle material Jimmy had long ago discovered, around the base of the sparkplug to fill up the space between it and the wall of the pipe so that all of the explosive energy was confined behind the missile instead of escaping in blow-by. No matter how hard we tried, though, we couldn't get the parachute to stay in one piece, or in place, after the plug left the barrel. It either shredded, or if it did not, failed to open at all. No great loss. Through some twist of luck or blessing by the Blessed Virgin Mary, the sparkplug continued to land on the roof each time it descended, adding another hole to the roof of the garage. Really, except for the excitement of actually seeing it float earthward, there was no need for a parachute. We knew precisely where to recover our rocket.

The loud noise of each blast drew a crowd in no time. We were sorry that Mickey couldn't be with us to revel in this new endeavor, but Clifford Childers and Allen Jung wandered up the alley and quickly began to applaud each launch.

Clifford, who was dumpy and attended Barnum School, clapped his hands, making these weird, indecipherable comments that reminded me of the noises made by the chicken monster from Planet X. I guessed they were meant for Jimmy and me and not so much the rocket. Anyway, I took them as such. Allen wore his thick glasses with the black frames and had brought his brand new pair of binoculars with him. Just before each explosion he ducked, then reappeared without the glasses, binoculars in place of them. If he was as blind as I thought he was, I wondered if the binoculars were doing him any good. Apparently they were, because he was all beside himself and pointing skyward after each blast.

On the south side of Jimmy's property a man and his wife had moved in three or four months earlier. My mother was suspicious of them. She counseled me, though, to be respectful of them. They were "Injuns", she'd said. Good people, probably. Probably not Catholic, as Injuns prayed to trees and deer and such. But, treat them well, Mom reiterated. They were people too, just like us, and at least they weren't Protestants.

The family, whose last name I never heard, had three small children. I don't know—three, five and seven years-old, I supposed. Something like that. At any rate, they played peacefully enough in their back yard; kept their distance from Jimmy and me, more because of the age difference, I suspected, than because of the fear of a thrashing at our hands. No doubt they'd heard about our routing of the thugs from two blocks up and feared us terribly.

All three of them had gathered like little lambs on the other side of the chainlink fence separating their property from Mrs. McGuire's. They silently watched us send the rocket into the sky, just like Allen and Clifford out in the alley. The older boy was so wowed by the noise and the excitement that he hung on the top bar of the fence, nose pressed into the wire just below it. The two younger kids kept their distance, though, unsure of what was going on next door.

After ten or twelve launches Jimmy and I found ourselves standing within two feet of the table, proud of our handiwork, and confident of the integrity of the steel pipe (which fell over immediately following every explosion). Clifford was leaning over the alley fence with his index finger planted inside one of his huge, flaring nostrils. Allen had abandoned his glasses entirely and stood beside Clifford with the binoculars glued to his face. Everything was perfect.

"How many Cherry Bombs we got left?" I asked after launch twelve.

"Enough. Four or five more, I think," Jimmy replied. He busied himself reloading the pipe. Because of the frequency of ignitions, the cap had gotten very hot, and Jimmy had grabbed a pair of leather gloves from the garage so that his hands wouldn't get blistered from the heat each time he unscrewed the cap, shoved the bomb quickly in, then screwed it all back together.

Launch Thirteen. I should have known something would go wrong. Though I wasn't particularly superstitious, the number hit me as I watched Jimmy's gloved hands struggle with the blackened, expanded threads of the cap and pipe. He finally got it just the way he wanted it, though, and set the space weapon onto the table again. Then he lit the fuse.

Clifford whooped it up, as did Allen, and the little Indian kid tightened his grip on the fence. To my horror I saw in slow motion the failure of our tube stabilizer. It fell with a light thud onto its side and couldn't have aimed itself better had the devil himself been there to help it along. Jimmy froze when he realized what was about to happen. The muzzle-end was pointing dead on south, three feet off the ground. The little Indian kid stood looking down the barrel, dead on north, three feet off the ground. We were going to become murderers.

"Jesus Christ! Move!" I screamed. But the kid probably didn't understand. Or something. Maybe it just didn't occur to him that the spark plug would come ripping out of the pipe at nearly the speed of sound. I don't know. He remained welded to the fence in any case.

Jimmy jumped up and down, and for the first time in his life was lost for words—clever or otherwise—and he was freaking. There was no time to return to the launcher and shove it in some other direction, so I did the only thing I could think of. I closed my eyes and prayed to Our Lady of I Didn't Care Who to give us a miracle.

The Cherry Bomb exploding sounded louder than an entire case of dynamite going up all at once. For some reason I opened my eyes at the same instant and watched the remainder of the scene in true awe. The plug rocketed out of the tube. The little Indian kid strangely drew his nose off the wire about two inches at the same instant. When the plug hit the wire and I was certain he could count the threads on the frayed duct tape, the miracle materialized. It ricocheted off the wire and whistled past his left ear, which made him jump—finally. The fence rattled but Jimmy and I were saved from murder.

"Are you fuckin' crazy?" Jimmy yelled.

I fell to my rear and thanked God, and Mary, and every saint in Heaven, and asked them, also, to ignore Jimmy's mouth.

The three kids next door took his comment badly, and ran crying into their house.

We packed the fireworks and our launcher up after that, at least for the time being, and went shaking into his house, leaving the rest of the audience to hang around or go home, whichever suited them.

But, the next day...

Patrick Sean Lee

TWELVE

SEARCHING FOR THE KING OF SNAKES

The three of us ran into Allen and Clifford the next morning. That was a stroke of bad luck for them. Both were still in a state of awe over what Jimmy and I had done in his backyard the day before, and now they wanted to kneel down and worship us. Neither of us wanted their homage.

Clifford's family had bought the home three doors down from us several years ago; a modern split-level with perfectly manicured grass, and a real cement driveway leading to a two-car garage that I swore was bigger than our entire house. It had been built right after the war, so it boasted a raft of wonderful, modern features that the Morley residence lacked; things like doors that didn't need to be jerked in order to get them open, closing off *all* the bedrooms. A big kitchen, too, with glistening white, metal cabinets, an electric range, and something else I drooled over—a dishwashing machine. I knew because of that machine he and his little sister, Annie, were spared the horrible job assigned to every other kid our age; washing and drying the dinnerware every night. That stuck in my craw, and I believe was a major part of the reason I looked down on him. That dishwasher somehow made him better than me. He paid for it time and again, though, when I lost sight of my Christian upbringing and lorded it over him. Clifford was chubby, too. God knows why that should have bothered me, but it did. I suppose I subconsciously saw him overindulging in eating—the sin of gluttony—and lying around while the rest of us were working— the sin of sloth. The fact that I suffered from a serious case of envy completely slipped my mind, though.

Now Allen, on the other hand, was of average height, neither skinny nor fat, and as far as I knew, helped his mother with the dinner dishes. He wore those damned, black-rimmed glasses, though. He claimed to be a scholar, and thus his eyes had gone bad on account they were always stuck inside a book. He boasted about being an A student, though in attending a public school I figured that didn't mean too much. He was an only child, a Protestant of some denomination or other, and the apple of his mother's eye. He was never up to a dare, had absolutely no imagination, and always wore perfectly pressed clothing, whether it was to go out to play or parade off to Sunday School.

This session of trouble began innocently enough after a gulley-washer of a rainstorm in the early afternoon. Jimmy, Mickey, and I found ourselves bored stiff. The treehouse we'd suddenly found uninteresting, and as far as sending Cherrybomb rockets into space—well, we'd decided to hold off on an encore on that one for a while.

A creek ran through the neighborhood several blocks northwest of our street. The three of us had been sitting on the steps of my front porch picking at the splintered boards, cussing, and trying to think up a new idea for having fun when the vision of that stream popped into my head.

"Damn! Let's go down to the creek and hunt for Garter snakes," I said. "There oughta' be lots of them by now. It's warm enough."

"Hey, yeah! Great idea. I'll go get the jars," Jimmy said, giving me the look of a man saved from drowning.

He dashed over to his house and returned a minute later with three mason jars. Jimmy handed one of them to me, one to Mickey, and we headed down the street. Low and behold that's when we spotted Clifford and Allen sitting together on the lawn in front of Clifford's house.

"Crap. They'll probably want to tag along," I said.

"Nah. Allen'd never risk gettin' his shoes muddy. He's prob'ly scared to death of snakes, too," Jimmy answered.

As it happened, Jimmy was wrong. When we passed by them, Allen greeted us.

"Hi, Skip. Hi, Jimmy. Hi, Mickey. Your cannon was really keen! Where are you fellas going?"

71

"To the creek to catch slimy snakes and get our shoes filthy muddy." I figured that the words snakes and mud would make him cringe, but they only fired his dull imagination and kindled his desire to join us. Allen had been studying reptiles over the course of the weeks Jimmy and I had been designing the finest treehouse and the most powerful rocket in the city, and he jumped to his feet in joy.

"Wowee-zowee! Can we go? I've been researching the vast variety of..."

"Jesus...Yeah, okay. But keep your mouth shut!" Jimmy broke in before bothering to consult me or Mickey concerning our feelings about the matter. He glanced at us and smiled. I understood without his having to say another word that before the afternoon ended poor Allen and Clifford would be returning to their homes in tears.

Weir Gulch was the name of the small creek that meandered in from the far western part of town before dumping itself into an algae-infested mudhole called Barnum Lake. We loved the lake and the gazillions of crawdads it was home to, but the creek was far more interesting because of the tangle of weeds, never-been-pruned trees that overhung it, and the hundreds of sharp rocks that lined its banks. Here was a wonderland of disorder that appealed to our gang's natural propensity for exploration and trouble.

All along the banks of the gulch in the late Spring the harmless little Garter snakes cracked out of their eggs and went slithering everywhere, practically inviting us to capture them and haul them home to become pets until, for whatever reason we never could figure out, they simply died. We always did our best to toss plenty of crickets and spiders and grasshoppers into their sealed jars so they'd have tons of food, but the little buggers never failed to croak after a few days of captivity. That was okay, though, because there were always plenty more waiting for new homes after the funerals of their relatives had been attended to.

Clifford was a kid of few words, but Allen always seemed to want to pontificate on every subject under the sun. Clifford fell in behind us, but Allen danced around Jimmy, Mickey, and me like an excited puppy, yapping about Corals and Pythons and the dreaded King Cobra. Within a couple of steps he'd already gotten on my nerves and I began to wonder. What could I do? How could I best make him cry?

Jimmy began the assault. "Shut up, Allen. There ain't no King Cobras or any of those others you said in Colorado. You dip."

"Yes, I know that. I know it. But there *are* rattlesnakes and other vipers here. I was reading about them and I know how to suck the venom out if one of them bites you."

I stopped immediately at that. Clifford ran into my back, which earned the pudgy little guy his first rough shove of the day. "Watch where you're going. Dummy." I turned to Allen. "Hey, butthead. If I get bit by the biggest rattler in the whole world...you touch me with those pukey lips of yours and you're dead. I'd rather die first. You got that?"

Allen quit dancing, and the look on his face told me he was definitely getting what I'd just said. I was hoping he'd feel sufficiently threatened to backtrack for home, but either he was as thick as mud in the Mississippi, or else begging for a miserable day at the creek.

"Oh, I didn't say I would actually remove the poison from you, Skip, just that I knew how to..."

"Shut up," Jimmy said. Which Allen did for the remainder of the six-block trek. He moved to the rear alongside Clifford, and whistled some song over and over that I knew I'd heard on Lawrence Welk. It was terrible when it'd come out of Myron Florin's accordion, but ten times worse in Allen's rendition.

The five of us arrived at the portal to the paradise of mud and weeds and slithery little snakes just in time. Allen's whistling had begun to make Mickey and Jimmy grit their teeth and narrow their eyes.

The street along which we'd walked passed almost inconspicuously over the swollen creek. A four-foot diameter cement pipe carried the water and trash under the street, and on either side of the road the abutment ended abruptly, the barricade picked up by a bent and twisted, terrible excuse for a fence. Jimmy was first to go in. He stepped easily between the fence post and the cracked concrete, and then skiied down the steep, muddy slope to the edge of the water. I followed him, and then came Mickey. We stood shoulder to shoulder at the bottom waiting for Clifford to squeeze through the opening, and when he'd managed to get himself down to us on his rear-end, Allen eased through the opening. He stood pensively, with one hand on the fence post and the other on the concrete. He'd worn a pair of neatly pressed white cotton trousers, and a black and chartreuse polo shirt tucked in at the waist, gig line perfect. His horn-rimmed glasses hung down on his pointy nose, and he remained motionless for a second or two surveying the steep grade below him.

Watching him standing there, I was imagining trousers soaked, muddied glasses lost, and a shirt one uniformly gucky color. But then in that vision the characters changed slightly. I saw Inky Minkle looking up at me. For a brief instant I felt a pang of shame, but then the vision died a shameful death. Just like that. No remorse for what was certainly about to happen.

"C'mon, Allen. Are you chicken or what?" I asked.

The dare hit a nerve. He pushed the glasses back up onto his nose with his index finger, bent down with one leg extended straight out like a figure skater, and then let loose of his moorings. I do believe he meant to use the extended leg like a brake, but having the coordination of a rock, he immediately toppled onto his right side and skidded sideways down at us through the mud.

Directly behind Jimmy, Mickey, Clifford, and me, the water gurgled along, waiting for Allen's arrival. The question in my mind—and it was a quick one—was whether to sacrifice myself and stop him before he plummeted over the edge, or do the obvious: step aside and let him take the dive. Instinctively, Jimmy and Mickey, who were standing on either side of me, stepped sideways and watched Allen's slide into home with the most bemused and casual of looks painted on their faces. Clifford moved sideways, covered his eyes with his hands and cried, "Ooh!"

Without blinking an eye I joined Jimmy to my left and watched Allen bounce over the bank and into the brown, murky water. As he hit I thought about the hundreds of inane, pseudo-intellectual, verbal pontifications he'd pestered us with, and chiefly, his desire to suck poison from my body with his lips.

He disappeared for a moment, then bolted headfirst out of the cauldron of crud-infested water as though he'd been submerged for five minutes.

"*That* was cool!" Mickey remarked. "I'd have to give him a solid ten for form."

"Well done. Well done," Jimmy added.

Allen glubbed and thrashed about as though he was destined to go clear to the bottom for good next time, even though the depth of the creek near the culvert couldn't have been much more than two feet. His eyes were locked shut, but thankfully for him the glasses hadn't been lost in the churning fathoms. If he opened his eyes, the vista might be murky, but at least it would kind of be in focus. When he realized that he wasn't going to drown or be swept away, he stabilized his stance, opened his eyes, and stared blankly at his four friends on the top of the bank for about five confused seconds. Then he let loose.

"I'm dead! Oh, God help me, I'm dead!"

"No you're not. There isn't enough water in this whole creek to drown you," I reassured him with a laugh. "Come on, get out. You'll be dry before we get home."

"You don't understand! My mother is going to tan my rear when she sees me. Why didn't one of you stop me?"

"We tried to back in front of Clifford's house," Jimmy said, holding his hand out to him. "Just ditch the clothes as soon as you get home. Your mom'll never be the wiser. Next time, maybe you'd better stay home. The woods can be real dangerous."

We all helped tote him out of the water, and once ashore, we even tried to dry him off with some old newspaper and dead leaves we found lying around nearby. He would have nothing of it, though, and left in a huff—back up the slippery slope, which would have defeated him except for the rat-like clawing he did, and his determination to be away from us.

75

Clifford was beside himself, though I don't think he entirely blamed Jimmy or Mickey or me for Allen's clumsiness. After all, he could have thrown himself in front of the speeding train just as easily as anybody else. Be that as it may, he waited until his friend had nearly gotten to the safety of the street above us, then left himself to escort the drowned rat home. As the two of them disappeared down the avenue, Jimmy called after them. "We'll bring you guys back a King Cobra!"

With that we left with our jars and grins, and began the season's first snake finding expedition. An hour later we took the easy way out of the gulch through the fenced backyard of a family living just beyond the wilds, jars seething with green and yellow-bodied snakes.

THIRTEEN

Frank

By midweek all but one of the snakes had died, due, I had a pretty good hunch at the time, to a lack of breathable air and the unsanitary living conditions inside the jars left inside the heat of the garage behind Jimmy's house. It seemed obvious to us that we couldn't trust them to stay inside their quarters if we took the lids off, so we punched half a dozen holes in each lid for fresh air. It did no good. We pulled their smelly, lifeless bodies out one by one, held quick services for them, and then buried them behind the trashcans in the alley. The last fellow, the one who'd struggled valiantly for his life in Mickey's jar, looked as though he might pull through given a little individual love and care, and so we placed a fan beside the jar, wished him well and left him for the night.

Saturday morning came along. Mickey was absent, confined somewhere to a dentist's chair. Jimmy and I pulled the overhead door to the garage up and walked to our captive's jar expecting to see him peering out at us through the glass. The poor thing must have taken a turn for the worse overnight though, because he lay all curled up on the glass bottom, and refused to move even after we'd shaken the container over and over trying to wake him up.

"Well, looks like another funeral," I said.

I believe that shook the critter out of his lethargy. His tail moved first, and then his head—just slightly, but enough so that we knew for a fact there was still a breath or two left in him.

"Hey! He's gonna' make it," Jimmy said, lifting the jar close to his face. "He's a tough little bastard. Let's dump him out on the grass and let 'im get some sun. I don't think he'll run away."

That was a pretty safe bet. Frank, as we'd christened him, lay comatose in the deep, cool grass after Jimmy let him drop from three feet in the air. The snake slowly curled its tail once, and then went totally motionless. We watched. We watched, and watched some more until something told us Frank was nearing his end.

"Wha...what the hell! We can't just let him die on us!" Jimmy said.

"Maybe not, but whatdya' suggest we do? Take him to a vet? I don't have any money. 'Sides, he looks too far gone, and I don't think vets work on snakes anyway."

"I dunno. Shit. I guess let's just leave him here until he either gets some life back into himself of else kicks the bucket like his friends. I'm gonna' go watch cartoons," he said rising up from his hands and knees.

We walked off into the house, and Jimmy turned on the TV in the tiny living room adjacent to the kitchen. In a few moments the screen flickered to life. Jimmy clicked off Howdy Doody on Channel Two as soon as Buffalo Bob took a squirt from Clarabelle's seltzer bottle. Channel Four was pretty much the same—a local kid's show called Fred and Faye—pretty lousy stuff for thirteen year-olds. Channel Nine was our last hope, and as luck would have it, the people running the station had put on an old horror movie for us, the original Karlof classic, "Frankenstein".

"Ah, that's better," Jimmy said. He turned the volume up so that we could hear every one of the mad scientist's words, which brought cursing from his mother in her bedroom immediately beyond the wall behind the TV.

"Jimmy! For Chrissakes, turn that goddam' TV down. I'm tryin'..." the rest of the words got lost in her pillow.

"Okay, mother." He didn't bother to do as she'd asked, and we sat down on the carpet very close to the screen, watching Dr. Frankenstein power up the dazzling array of life-giving machines in his laboratory. The inside of the medieval castle was lit up like the Fourth of July. Outside the lightning was ferocious, unending, powerful. With a crazed look on his face, the doctor cranked the torturous looking wheel that slowly began to raise the sewn-together body of his insane creation upward toward the open roof. One look at its hideous face with the bolt spikes jutting out from either side of the monster's neck was enough to make the heavens explode in anger.

We knew what was going to happen, of course. Every kid in the world with a TV set had watched it at least a dozen times. The dead thing would come to life with a massive jolt of lightning, and then it would kill the doctor, terrorize the village, and die in a fiery conflagration inside a windmill at midnight. Poor Mary Shelley.

We looked at one another without uttering a word, rose in unison from the carpet and rushed out to gather up Frank. How appropriate that we'd named him that. It was Providence working in our lives, and his, once again.

He was still lying right where we'd left him a few moments ago, more or less in the same pitiable condition, pleading silently for help. I looked up dolefully into a clear blue sky. Who was the patron saint of storms, I wondered?

"What's the weather forecast?" I asked Jimmy, who stood poking at Frank with his index finger.

"Don't know. Maybe we won't need to worry about a storm. I have an idea that just might work. Let's get him out of the sun and then we'll start to build!"

I kind of knew where we'd be going with this one.

Mrs. McGuire woke up again several hours later when we dragged the pyre-ish looking contraption over the linoleum in her kitchen, through the living room, and then into Jimmy's bedroom directly across from hers.

"What is THAT?" she asked holding the palm of one hand over her forehead when she came out to see what the terrible noise was all about. She looked like she might be a candidate for our electrical arc super-zapper resurrection platform. Frank looked more alive than she did.

"Relax, Mother. It's a science project for school. Go back to bed. Once we get it bolted down you won't hear a sound—it's as quiet as a baby."

"Bolted down? You're not puttin' any bolts in the floor..."

"Just kiddin'," Jimmy said. "Go back to sleep."

And so Mrs. McGuire trusted us once again, closing the door to her bedroom, hung over and mumbling, happy, I'm sure, that we weren't going to launch a full-sized rocket from inside her son's room.

We bolted the platform down to the floor just as a precaution. It looked much like a rabbit hutch in miniature, complete with a netting of wire looped around its open sides, three tiers of tin with an array of holes crudely knocked through each that allowed superior ventilation. The very bottom floor we'd connected two wires to—positive and negative, north and south, the right end of the floor and the left. This was the initial power transfer floor where Frank would receive a mild buzz from a nine-volt battery when we touched the leads to its connectors. We had no faith that the anemic shock would cure him, but we were certain it would awaken him from his coma. Whence he would be transferred to the second floor.

The second floor was something like the ICU at a hospital in that we'd hooked up a strand of Christmas lights to mimic the blinking machines. We'd step the voltage up a notch or two here, but as the current would be shared with the lights, we figured its lethality would be diminished dramatically. Frank would be roused to definite movement and, hopefully, cognizance of his surroundings. After he'd rested for a spell, we planned to move him up toward the open ceiling and the storm. The top floor. 120 volts of pure life-giving electricity—not nearly what the monster received, but more than adequate, we were confident, to do the job. Frank would be back among the living. As a final gift to our stalwart friend, we vowed to return him to his rightful home at the creek after his recuperative rest ended.

"Are you ready, Doctor Morley?"

"I am indeed," I answered.

"Then bring in the patient."

Frank was lifted ceremoniously out of the shoebox we'd laid him in, positioned onto the first floor, and then the bare ends of the light-gauge wire were connected to the battery. Jimmy and I waited for a moment. Two moments. Frank didn't move.

"Put your tongue on the floor," Jimmy said. "I don't think he's gettin' any juice."

"You put your tongue on it!" I answered with a laugh. "What do I look like? An idiot?"

"It won't hurt you for cryin' out loud. It's only nine lousy volts."

"Yeah, then if it won't hurt me it won't hurt you either. Go ahead, you do it."

Jimmy bent over and stuck the tip of his tongue onto the greasy tin floor. He waited for a second or two, then spread as much of its surface onto the tin as possible. After a few more seconds he pulled his tongue back in, turned to me, and said, "No juice. Nuthin'. Not a tingle. Let's move him up to ICU."

Poor Frank was hoisted up one floor to the Christmas wing where a maze of wires looped from the leads, into the lights, and then into their connections at each end of the tin. The leads on this floor ended at a plug we'd stolen off Mrs. McGuire's iron, and after a short, hopeful look, Jimmy plugged it into the wall outlet beside the Resurrection Platform leg. The ceiling light in the room flickered instantaneously, and then went out. We looked down at Frank, who still refused to move, and then at each other.

"You sure you got it hooked up right?" I asked.

"Yeah, I'm sure. I think we blew a fuse. Damn."

"Now what?" I asked.

"Unplug the cord. Let's go put a new fuse into the box and then move him up to the top floor. We're not lettin' him die!"

"Won't the new fuse just blow too?"

"Not if I put a penny behind it."

I wasn't sure what putting a penny behind the fuse was all about, but the way Jimmy said it, I believed he knew exactly what he was talking about. We bypassed the fuse (I learned later), and then returned to his room. The ceiling light was on again. Frank was moved up to surgery.

81

"I think we need to connect the leads to his head and his tail—so that he gets a continual flow of electrons, one end to the other," the head surgeon said intently.

"Whatever you say. Connecting them to the floor sure hasn't done the trick so far."

Frank was hot-wired, we said a quick prayer for his speedy recovery, and then Jimmy turned to me.

"Ready?"

FOURTEEN

Hell's Doors Open Wide

The detective arrived at my front door about the same moment that Frank left this world.

Jimmy and I were still bemoaning the failure of the resurrection platform, staring at the curls of smoke that rose from that courageous little snake's body, when Mom shouted at me from the side yard.

"Francis Patrick Morley! Get over here right this minute!"

The only times I heard my full Christian name come out of her mouth was when she gushed with pride over some rare scholastic accomplishment, or when I was being called onto the carpet to answer for one of my crimes. I hadn't done anything noteworthy at school lately that I could remember, and so that left only one other possibility.

Hail Mary, full of grace...Mom's tone of voice led me to believe that I was going to need a great deal of heavenly help. I glanced down at Frank—lifeless, having suffered the ultimate capital punishment for crimes he'd never even thought of committing. A real victim. Was there such a thing as snakeslaughter? Or involuntary snakeslaughter?

Could Mom *even* have somehow known what Jimmy and I had just done? Impossible. And besides, she was no lover of snakes, so probably could have cared less about Frank's electrocution. Maybe she'd discovered something else. The picture I'd carefully hidden among my school papers; the one that Johnny Marley had given to me at school at recess a few days ago. The one of the naked woman with very large bosoms that made my eyes pop completely out of their sockets when I saw it.

Hail Mary, full of grace! I really didn't like that picture all that much. I swear it. Please forgive me. I promise that if Mom didn't find it I'll rip it up...

I wracked my brain, looked at Jimmy, who was staring back at me with a large question mark on his face.

"Francis Patrick Morley! GET OVER HERE, RIGHT THIS MINUTE!"

"Oh shit," I muttered to Jimmy. He tightened his lips and raised his eyebrows.

I left him, Frank, and the smell of burnt snake flesh and ran through his house, out the front door, and back to the lightning storm brewing at my place.

There was a moment of total confusion when I spotted the guy in his dark blue suit, hat pulled down nearly to his eyebrows, standing with a notepad in his hands on the front porch.

Cop? I thought. Mom, in a headdress of curlers, had gone to the fence by then and was glaring at Jimmy's bedroom window, her hands on her hips. I opened the front gate, which made a low clanking sound, and that brought hers and the cop's eyes to bear on me. She marched down the yard with a look on her face that made me shudder. Whatever it was that I'd done had nothing to do with pictures of naked women, unless there was some law I knew nothing about saying it was a serious crime for kids to have them. Even if they didn't intend to look at them.

It was pointless to wonder any further. I was going to find out within the next few minutes why the man had come, and why it appeared as though Mom was going to strangle me as soon as he left.

Mom reached the gate about the same instant that I turned and quietly closed it, hoping in vain that the action would have some calming effect on the two people about to charge me with an offense I prayed wasn't too serious. I was still half-facing the street when I felt her fingers clamp down on my right ear, and then she yanked. The separation of my outer ear from the inner made we wince. I caught a glimpse that rivaled in horror whatever trouble I was headed for. Across the street under a sullen sky, a crooked smile smeared on his evil face, stood Inky

84

Minkle. Mom either didn't see him, didn't care if he was hanging around waiting for his turn at me, or thought right then that he was less a hoodlum than her only begotten son. She dragged me to the foot of the ragged wooden steps leading up to the wooden porch.

Before the man—who suddenly appeared to be at the very least eight foot-tall—had an opportunity to begin addressing me, Inky's voice rang out.

"Better get the other guy over there. He's in on it, too." And then Inky laughed.

I turned my head, one ear gone stone deaf thanks to Mom, and watched him shuffle on up the street in the direction of Rashure's little general store, shaking his head, laughing, glancing back at me every other step. Mom grabbed hold of my other ear in order to get my attention fixed back on the officer. He stepped down two creaking steps, and then stopped on the last one, spreading his legs wide.

You are innocent until proven guilty...except in the Morley household.

The cop began the investigation.

"Francis Morley?"

That wasn't really a question. I'd seen Broderick Crawford start his questionings of rapists and thieves a hundred times on Highway Patrol in just the same way.

Who wants to know? I'd seen the criminals answer that way, but I figured I'd better not try it today. "Yes, sir?"

"You know anything about a clothespin that shoots matches?"

Oh shit! So that was it.

I'd been looking up at him kind of sheepishly when he asked the question, but after hearing it my eyes fell, as if someone had stuffed lead in them.

Busted.

"Well, sir...I've heard of them..."

"I see. You have one by any chance?"

"Oh, no sir! I mean, I threw it away. I, uh..."

I learned this in the next couple of minutes:

Dennis the Menace, who was clever, but not clever enough to escape the trail of witnesses who'd seen him plucking his Nero harp all over Barnum Public School, was dragged into the principal's office where the local Fire chief and Detective Ryan— this guy—stood on either side of Principal Sweetman in the stench of water and burnt bleachers, waiting with their hands clasped behind their backs. Dennis spilled his guts in tears of great remorse, pointing the finger of guilt, though, at three "older boys" living somewhere in the neighborhood. It wasn't really his fault that he'd done what he'd done, he said. Those boys, he cried, had laughed when the tallest one offered him the matchgun and told him it would be very cool to take the toy to school and scare all the girls with it.

"No officer, sir, that isn't what happened at all."

"Well then suppose you tell me what exactly did happen."

And so I told a slightly different version of the story.

"Jimmy hopes to be an inventor someday when he graduates from Harvard..."

Mom laughed at that pipe dream.

"Who's Jimmy?" Ryan asked.

Mom was more than willing to explain who Jimmy really was in order to save my butt, but the detective held a hand up, motioning her to be quiet.

"Let the boy speak, ma'am."

"Jimmy's my next door neighbor, and a real genius, sir. He's very inventive."

I forced myself to stop and take a deep breath; to think fast.

"We were sitting around one afternoon talking about how dangerous it was to start up barbecues and stuff like that with a match—especially those kinds that come in books. It wasn't me that figured out you didn't even have to reach in with a match...it was Jimmy."

I thought I did pretty well considering all of it was a fat-ass lie (I had the fingers of both hands crossed behind my back), but there seemed to be glaring holes in a few of the important details, mostly those concerning another incident in a certain theater about a month ago.

"Theater?" I asked. I began to sweat. The jig was up. I did the only thing I could think of in that critical moment, and which I regretted almost immediately; I compounded one lie with another that was even worse.

"Well, we were walking out of the theater because the movie was so bad. We'd, um, gotten to the corner when we heard the doors bang open behind us. Me and Jimmy and another friend. These two guys came running past us. They live up the street, I think. And one of them threw the clothespin at us. So we watched them for a second, then Jimmy...I mean me...I picked it up, but it was Jimmy who figured out right away what it was."

"I thought you said you and your friend had...how did you put it? invented something to start fires in the barbecue with? Like a matchgun, maybe?"

"Well, yeah. We did. I guess we weren't the first to come up with the idea though."

"I see." He scratched a few words in the notebook he had in his hand, and then glanced down at Mom, who was frowning, her bottom lip caught between her teeth.

"Go on."

"Well, me and my friends started walking home. It was hot that day, and so we stopped behind the library to rest for a minute. Jimmy was checking out the clothespin gun, saying how whoever made it had carved a notch in the wood for the spring to catch tight in. Which the one he invented wouldn't do...so it didn't work...so we never bothered to use it. Pretty soon I picked up a twig layin' on the ground about the same size as a match and started shooting it. Just to see how the thing worked, you know?"

It was a great story I was making up. I could actually see us in my mind, innocently shooting the twig around. "And that's when that little snot across the fence asked my friend Jimmy to let him see it for a minute. So Jimmy walked over to the kid and handed him the clothespin-match-shooter-thing. I remember the kid gave Jimmy this creepy look. Sort of evil...well, not exactly evil. Sort of...what's the word, Mom?"

Her eyes were piercing.

"Piercing. Piercing look. And then he took off running into his house. We couldn't believe he'd swiped it! See, we go to a Catholic school, officer, and we're taught..." I glanced once more at Mom. Her eyes were slits. Her lips were drawn tight. If the detective was buying my story, I knew she definitely wasn't.

"That's it, then?" the detective said.

"Uhh, yes sir. We went on home. What happened anyway?" I asked innocently.

The detective closed the cover of his notepad, clicked the pen he'd been taking notes with closed, and slowly placed both in his suit coat pocket.

"That'll be all for now," he said, tipping his hat to my mortified mother. He stepped down onto the sidewalk, brushing gently by me, and began to leave. When he reached the gate, which seemed to have a voice that was shrieking, "LIAR! HE'S ON HIS WAY TO HELL. HE'S LYING!" he turned suddenly.

"What did you say that boy's name was that threw the matchgun at you outside the theater?"

"I don't know his name for sure..."

"It's Minkle, officer. He lives up at the top of the hill. 295 South Meade Street. Minkle. He was just walking by," Mom cut in.

The detective tipped his hat at Mom again, shot a suspicious look at me that I'd seen on Crawford's face on TV, and then he left.

"Get into the house, Skip," I heard Mom croak in a whisper.

FIFTEEN

MISS MARILOU JENKINS

Detective Ryan visited the home of the Minkle family. Yes he did. I learned much later that Butch Minkle had answered the door with the ever-present cigarette dangling out of his mouth that day. Unlike me, he didn't make a good impression on Detective Ryan. But he did make a lasting one. Being stupid, Butch's vocabulary was limited to sentences which made little sense, were contradictory, or else splattered with four letter words—and that didn't set well with the detective. All told, his explanation of the events that terrible day at the Comet Theater sounded very much like a lie to Ryan. Suspicion concerning who committed the crime fell immediately onto his and Inky's shoulders.

Still, the matter was easily settled now that a battery of suspects had been tracked down. Ryan requested that my parents bring me, and that Mrs. McGuire bring Jimmy, down to the home of Dennis to star in a line up. All hope in my heart vanished when Mom informed Pop at the dinner table in tears that her son would likely be going to juvenile hall soon—if not the state penitentiary. Afterward she left the tear-stained room and marched next door to awaken Mrs. McGuire, if such a thing was possible, and inform her that Jimmy must accompany us on the death march. Mickey's name was never brought up.

"Did you do it?" Pop inquired calmly after Mom had disappeared in her breast-beating state.

I did not lie. "No, sir. I had nothing to do with it."

We walked; Mom two steps in front of Mrs. McGuire, Pop bringing up the rear, Jimmy and I sandwiched in between. Down past Clifford's big house, past Allen's tiny one, then across Ellsworth Avenue we walked. Midway down the street we passed the dancer's front door, and a sort of hellish feeling welled up in my stomach. She sat on the porch swing with a friend—or maybe the other girl was her sister. I tried not to glance over at them, or at her I should say, but a morbid impulse latched onto me and I turned my head. She'd noticed the parade, and she must have known it was more a procession of calves to the slaughterhouse, or murderers to the gallows. I dropped my eyes and cursed the moment.

When we reached our destination I saw detective Ryan standing on the doorstep of Dennis' house, the door ajar, the boy's mother halfway in and halfway out, holding a handkerchief over her mouth and nose. At her side peeking out at us stood the bane of creation himself. I shot a look at Jimmy. He was sweating bullets this time around, and he whispered to me, "By his little balls." Dennis eased farther behind his weeping mother's skirt.

"Ah. Here they are, Mrs. Humboldt," Ryan said when we came to a halt at the foot of her porch. "Terrence, can you step out here and take a look at these two boys? Do you recognize them as the ones who gave you the matchgun?"

Dennis, or little Terrence as it turned out, poked his head out from behind his mother's broad posterior. He wasn't looking at me, I'm certain. His eyes locked on Jimmy's immediately, and the necessary words were quickly communicated. Even little Terrence valued the jewels he had not yet had the opportunity to use. He crumbled in the face of Jimmy.

"No."

"No?" repeated Detective Ryan.

"No. I never seen these guys 'afore. They ain't the ones. There was three of 'em."

Detective Ryan's brow fell at that lie. He addressed Pop matter-of-factly. "Wait by my car."

And so the five of us turned and marched back out to the street. Ryan, Terrence, and his mother had disappeared by the time I took a seat on the curb and looked back at the house. A few moments passed in that state of Limbo out in the silence of the street. Then Ryan exited the house alone and strode down the steps, down the sidewalk, and came directly to me.

"You told me yesterday that you'd given the boy a matchgun, Francis. Now he tells me he's never seen you before. What's up here? Did you or did you not give that boy the weapon that enabled him to start a fire at school?"

I stood alone in the universe after that question. A concept I'd never truthfully encountered on a real level surfaced in my head. A moral dilemma. I had two options, and neither of them was particularly palatable. Deny my involvement, or tell the truth. I answered Detective Ryan.

"No sir. I didn't. Jimmy did...but I was there. And it was us who shot the match inside the Comet..."

Mom let out a sound that was not a wail, nor a screech. I had kicked her in the stomach, and her response was a muted bellow, a groan, a whimper.

Pop remained quiet.

Mrs. McGuire merely seemed confused.

I thought better of speaking at the dinner table that evening; of even being there in fact. But, my presence was requested, and my replies to the questions pitched at me were duly noted, as if Detective Ryan had seated himself with his notebook and pen at the ready directly across from me. A rancorous veil was thrown across me, this time not only by Mom, but also by Pop.

"Even if it's true you didn't actually shoot that match in the theater, or have anything to do with handing the gun to that boy," Pop lectured me waving a finger in my face, "you're still guilty by association."

"Yes, and I'll tell you another thing, and it ain't two..." Mom began.

"Be quiet, Rosie, I'll handle this," Pop said. The color in his face deepened to incendiary red as he continued, at long last not the least lost for words. Mom sat back in her chair, defeated, or content with his command, or waiting—but in silence.

"So here's the deal. I'll drive you to school for the remainder of the year, and pick you up at 3:30 every afternoon. I can't stop you from talking to Jimmy or that Fumo boy while you're out of my sight, but by God if I hear even a whisper that the three of you have done anything—*anything*—that would make me raise an eyebrow...do I make myself crystal clear?"

Like looking through a window in God's home on high. "Yes, Pop."

"Good. You've shamed your family and yourself. Don't ever let it happen again. Understand?"

"Yes sir."

"Alright, then. You'll stay in this house until I say you can leave. Now, finish eating, get the dishes done, and then go to your room."

I looked up. Mom had placed her hand on Pop's forearm, and though I'd pierced her side with a spear a few hours ago down at little Terrence's house, I saw her mouth curl upward into a tiny smile. She remained silent as I rose and took my plate to the sink in the kitchen.

"And one last thing," Pop added. "You'll go along with me to that girl's house and you'll tell her you're sorry. God help you if her folks decide to press charges."

"What about Barnum School?" I asked in dread.

"We'll wait and see there."

At last Mom decided it was probably safe to interject her feelings on the matter.

"Skippy. That was a courageous thing you did...telling the truth. I'm proud of you."

***

The smoke cleared two weeks later, and I heaved a sigh of relief. The girl at the Comet had a name, I discovered. Marilou Jenkins. She was very pretty, an honor student at a private school for girls on the eastside of town. As promised, or as threatened, we visited her.

Jimmy, Pop, and I drove to her home one morning when the sky had abandoned itself to a somber rug of gray. We pulled up to the curb, and at first I was shocked and disheartened when Pop checked the address he'd written on the back of an envelope, and then announced, "This is it." He cut the engine of our dusty old station wagon, emitting a cloud of smoke out through the tailpipe thicker than the dreary sky above us. We had driven to another planet.

"Je-sus H. Kee-rist," Jimmy remarked, and I had to second the invocation.

The home, sitting in Versailles elegance on the corner lot looked more like a grand museum or an important public monument, except for the park-like expanse of golf course lawn and the English gardens meandering through the acreage spanning the distance to the mansion that would have made Mom explode with envy. Bordering the broad parkway towering elms stood, perfectly aligned and spaced. They were trimmed as if a small army of tree barbers spent innumerable hours each day manicuring them, until even the squirrels and birds donned tuxedos before entering the branches.

The three of us exited the truck in a state of awe—Jimmy and I, anyway—and hiked up the meandering flagstone walkway to an entry as imposing as that of Monticello. I glanced nervously at my ragged sneakers as Pop pushed the doorbell button.

We waited.

The door was opened halfway by a predatory-faced woman dressed in the attire of a maid instead of what in my mind should have been spots, or stripes. She smelled strongly of lemon oil mixed with mothballs, and she showed us into a foyer the size of our entire house where we were politely instructed to wait. She then padded silently across the black and white checked marble floor into an adjoining gallery lined with ten foot-tall paintings and milk-white statuary. Standing in the foyer peering in, it seemed to me none of it had any practical use beyond its grandiose statement of sinful wealth and extreme snobbery. Undoubtedly Mom would have agreed. And, the statues were naked.

But such was not the case with the occupants themselves.

A middle-aged gentleman dressed in a Lord and Taylor black suit strode across the floor several minutes later as I stood gawking at the smooth, sculpted, firm breasts on one of those statues. He was followed by a much younger woman, fashionably attired, who at first I mistook for Sophia Loren. Miss Marilou Jenkins, sporting a blonde, pixie-cut hairdo, followed her beautiful black haired mother. My eyes fixed on the young woman immediately, trying to imagine if she could have looked any more angelic with locks like waterfalls of silk drifting all the way to her shoulders, and snow white wings that had not been savaged by the fire. I shuddered and drew in a breath as inconspicuously as my instantly smitten condition would allow. I glanced again quickly at the undressed statue directly over her shoulder—and then as quickly made an abbreviated act of contrition.

Miss Marilou Jenkins surveyed the three visitors from the west side; Pop and Jimmy, impassively, briefly, and then she let her gaze fall on me where it rested as she followed her parents into the foyer where we stood waiting. Whether she was counting the droplets of sweat that had begun to form on my forehead after seeing this creature Jimmy had lit on fire, mentally sneering at the apparent rags I'd thrown on not two hours ago in ignorance of the impending audience, or simply wondering what alien universe I'd escaped from, I could not tell.

"Mr. Morley. Thank you for coming across town with the boys," Mr. Jenkins spoke in a clear, mellifluous voice as he walked toward my father, his hand extended in greeting.

Pop seemed very comfortable, or at least not particularly ill-at-ease. He shook the gentleman's hand.

"I'm very sorry, Dr. Jenkins, that this visit became necessary. This is my son, Francis, and his friend Jimmy." He motioned with a nod of his head for me to say something. But what was I to say in that ambassadorial place, standing before these people who likely had just removed wreaths of laurel from their heads before entering the cavernous room?

It's so lovely to meet you, sir. May I kiss your daughter?

And so I merely said, "Hello, sir." To my undying horror, my voice cracked mid-sentence. The velvety mid-range C of 'hello' suddenly kicked up three octaves at the next short word, 'sir'. I cursed my vocal cords and would have bolted for the door right then except that Miss Marilou Jenkins' aquamarine eyes had brightened like twin novas, and she smiled across the room at me. I cleared my throat. My cheeks and forehead bled heat.

"Please," Dr. Jenkins gestured to us, "Come into the library. Right this way." He waited until Pop drew alongside him, and then walked with him, trading small asides, grinning at my father's pithy replies.

The amiable doctor's wife lingered a step behind the two of them. She smiled at Jimmy and me and then inquired. "Your mother could not make it, Francis?"

"No, ma'am. Saturday is laundry day."

"I see. That is a shame. And your mother, James?" she said turning to Jimmy, who turned up his nose at the appellation.

"Umm...she's emptyin' bottles."

I cringed, certain that...

"I see. Baby bottles? You have a younger brother or sister?"

Jimmy nodded, as if he had rehearsed his answer. "Yeah, one of each."

"Ah. How lovely." We crossed the expanse of the gallery of naked statues, Miss Marilou Jenkins gliding between her mother and myself as though one of those marble images had come to life and stepped down from its pedestal. I thought I caught the faint scent of lilacs drifting from her. "The younger ones must keep her very busy, indeed."

"You can't imagine," Jimmy laughed. "Bottles everywhere. And crappy diapers."

Mrs. Jenkins' pencil-thin, dark eyebrows soared upward at the remark, and she shot a mildly disdainful look at my best friend. Miss Marilou Jenkins put a hand to her mouth, stifling a giggle. We moved on, me wishing I had at least worn my old suit.

At the end of the gallery of statues and paintings, an ornate archway of stone led into a wide hallway lined with several imposing carved wood doors, their polished brass handlesets set midway up on one edge in the European style. Dr. Jenkins stopped at the second room on the right, opened the door inward, and indicated with a gracious wave of his hand for us to enter. Again, and not for the last time that day, my jaw dropped. This was the library.

Four wingback chairs—that Pop took only casual notice of, but probably would be able to describe down to the last luxurious thread later—were set in a semi-circle in front of a kingly desk of mirror-polished wood. Floor to ceiling bookcases stood, packed with volume after volume, and except for the doorway in, and a single, tall window behind the desk, the books dominated; a dense wallcovering of thousands of lofty, written thoughts.

We took a seat. Pop, Jimmy, me, and to my right, Miss Marilou Jenkins with her faint scent of summer flowers. Dr. Jenkins sat imperiously in his leather chair opposite us behind the desk. A gray-mist shaft of light shined through the window making him appear otherworldly, lit from a passageway leading back out into a place that was not the city I inhabited. He leaned back and surveyed the two arsonists, the fingertips of his right hand tapping his chin, and then he let his gaze fall on his daughter.

"That was a very serious and foolish thing you boys did in that theater. You understand that, don't you," he said, as though the statement was being directed at her.

"Yes sir," I concurred holding onto my vocal chords with all that I possessed.

"Yeah, I guess so," Jimmy followed.

I didn't wait for anything further to erupt out of Jimmy's mouth. I turned to Miss Marilou Jenkins and melted into an apology worthy of my finest moment inside a confessional.

"Please accept my sincerest forgiveness, miss. If I had it all to do over again I wouldn't of...well, that is...I would have..."

Miss Marilou Jenkins' smile broadened in amusement at my comments. She turned full-face to me and said, "I accept your 'forgiveness'. I was planning to have it cut anyway."

I heard Jimmy exhale in relief. If we were to be chastised and made to kneel in sackcloth outside their door for one or two weeks, made to survive on moldy black bread, and water from the gutter, it appeared it would not be at the hands of the girl sitting beside me. Jimmy and I both looked imploringly over at Dr. Jenkins, as if to say, "See, sir. No harm done. None at all."

"What were ya' doin' at a theater clear across town?" Jimmy asked Miss Marilou Jenkins in the momentary lull in the conversation. Pop looked over at Jimmy in astonishment. I dropped my gaze and squinted with pain. Still, it was a good question, but I would never have had the courage to ask it. I waited for her answer.

"Our daughter wished to visit her cousins who live near a park on your side of town," Dr. Jenkins emphasized the phrase, 'near a park'. Barnum, I guessed, as there was nothing as grand as City Park where we lived; just the small, hilly half mile square home of smaller trees, smaller trails, a smaller playground, and the smaller lake. "Her mother and I were going out of town. Perhaps we should have taken her with us?" he asked in a serious tone, but with a glint in his eye.

Probably so.

In the moments ahead we learned these things:

Dr. Jenkins had been in Minneapolis with his lovely wife that weekend attending a convention of Proctologists. The eminent rectal repair specialist did not tell us exactly what one hears at such a convention—perhaps long hissing sounds punctuated by laughter and the pinching of noses?—but he lectured us, punctuated, definitely, with extremely long words neither of us had ever heard before. We sat before him nervously, and I'm certain shook our heads yes once or twice, when in fact we should have shaken them no.

The inferno in Miss Marilou Jenkin's hair turned out to be not an inferno at all. In fact it was only a minor brush fire of really little consequence. The cousin sitting at her side had had the foresight and prize-fighter reactions to smother it long before it did more than eliminate most of the split ends caused by teasing and hairspray.

"Young gentlemen such as yourselves from good Christian families..." Dr. Jenkins turned his head slightly toward Pop and nodded. Pop nodded obligingly back at him. "...must consider their actions very soberly, weighing the consequences..." And we listened to it all again.

An hour later as we left his mansion I couldn't help but overhear Pop inquiring of Dr. Jenkins whether he knew the little known fact that Wolfgang Amadeus Mozart suffered from Tenesmus, brought on by an unwillingness, or forgetfulness, to run to the chamber pot due to his complete immersion in composing. Of course, Pop continued, the physicians of the day diagnosed the discomfort as nothing more than gas.

"Not precisely true," corrected Dr. Jenkins (who certainly would have known). "Herr Mozart consumed entirely too much beef, and drank cheaper wines far in excess of what would even then have been considered moderate to heavy alcoholic consumption. While he imagined his bowels..."

At the end of which Pop quipped that never in his life had beef, or beer, at least, "...caused any discernible deviation from other than a normal bowel movement in my life. At any rate, I bow to your probable expertise concerning Mr. Mozart's unfortunate condition. It certainly didn't affect his fingers."

With a hearty laugh, the doctor agreed wholeheartedly. I moved down the corridor toward the entry at the side of Miss Marilou Jenkins, lost in a cloud of medical shadows cast by the doctor and the upholsterer. My father, I suddenly realized, inhabited a world far below the one he should have lived in.

"He loves to speak to his guests about stuff like that. My father is so weird," Miss Marilou Jenkins whispered to me.

"So is mine," I whispered back, my lips touching the strands of sweet-smelling hair covering her ears.

At the entry, Dr. Jenkins grabbed hold of Pop's hand once more, clasping over the top of it with the other. For the short moments of our visit they had looked in each other's eyes on an equal plane, but I knew the moment we left that the invisible barrier separating their worlds would have to be erected again.

We returned to Barnum along the same streets that had taken us to that place of refinement and beauty, relieved, silent.

SIXTEEN

Mom and Pop

Time passed, quickly spinning the threads of hours into fabrics of weeks. No longer threatened by arctic fronts pushed far to the north, now, by the slow, tilting dance of the planet, the early-June sky turned a deeper azure. The days grew longer and warmer. Mom's gardens burst into forests of flowers and greenery, as if possessed by unlikely enchantments unleashed by heavenly visitors.

The crocuses along the fence dividing our yard from the McGuire's had long ago broken through the surface of the ground, but had by then begun to fade, replaced by clustered stands of red and yellow snapdragons, the beginnings of four o'clocks and violet hyacinths. Mom bloomed right alongside them. The unpleasant months behind us, her raw nerves began to melt under the warmth of the sun, the soft texture of the soil, and my recent saintly behavior.

I looked for Jimmy through the interlaced triangle wires of that fence, but he'd begun to fear Mom I think, and so he stayed away. I think he believed as well that I'd stabbed him in the back with my confession, and perhaps I had. But the unintentioned treachery aside, I'd walked away from the adventures he had created able to say I'd grown, nurtured by a different sun and a brand new, hope-filled season.

Detective Ryan paid one final visit to our door the last week of May, informing us that in view of the fact Terrence Humboldt had not fingered us in the lineup, the case was officially closed. As far as he was concerned, the weapon had been given to Terrence by "persons unknown."

"Personally," he suggested with a wink as he prepared to leave the yard and our lives that day, "I'd stick to inventing things like two-way wrist radios, or telephones that don't need wires—that can be carried anywhere."

Such a stupid idea, I remember thinking at the time. But I was finished with fire, and rockets propelled by explosives; finished buying into Jimmy's quest for self-destruction. Flower gardens could not possibly present any dangers to me or anyone else on the planet. And so I thrust my fingers into the earth.

I helped Mom each day after school to cultivate the rich, black soil, and strike down the armies of clover and grass that constantly attempted to jump the low brick edging like steeple chase mounts. We labored together and spoke to one another—tentatively at first, but then as if we really had become mother and son. She sat sideways, on one of those ebbing May days, along the border of the garden in her faded black pedal-pushers, the ankle of one leg folded under the thigh of her other extended leg. Very high above us, to the west, a cloud crawled lazily over the edge of the late afternoon sun. A broken, silver-blue shaft of light fell across the black curls of her hair creating waves of shadows, illuminating emerging strands of silver, uncovering the effects of passing years. The foot of her extended leg rested against my calf. She glanced over at me as I sat plucking the invading greenery, and instructed me in the proper maintenance of the garden and its residents.

"No, not them, sweetheart. Those ain't weeds. They're flowers. Leave 'em be."

"They all look the same to me, Mom."

"No, they're not, just the thin-leafed ones that grow in clumps. See?" She raised a hand clothed with spots of earth and greenery, and pointed. "Those are weeds. And the jagged-leafed ones. And the dandelions, of course."

I blinked. The sheer variety and number of weeds got quickly out of hand, out of my grasp. To my untrained eye the weed-green looked exactly like the flower-green, and the flower blooms began to resemble the weed blooms. Dandelions became just yellow violets in my bored eye, and so I allowed them all to stay.

I laid the three-clawed hand tiller onto the grass, a little bored, leaned back on an elbow, and asked her a question.

"When did you meet Pop?"

She'd returned her attention to the strands of grass in the garden. "I grew up with him, Skip," she replied.

"You grew...you mean you lived in the same house together?"

She laughed. "No, honey. He lived across the way, on Grant Street...our street...in a big two-story house with a long front porch, with columns all along it that held up the roof. And green trim boards on the tall windows...and it had a wooden swing way down on one end...hanging. And..." Mom's eyes left the garden as she stood in front of her old house looking over at his, far away in Longmont. Her fingers rested for a moment in the dirt.

"That's where we grew up together." She sat frozen then in time, and drifted into silence. I waited. Perhaps her eyelids might descend to her cheeks. Maybe she would melt like a shadow in the waning sunlight and float away to a younger him, so far away and long ago when they were nearly still children, and she'd just begun to fall in love with my father.

I watched, and wondered, sitting close to her side, what memories played inside her head and deep in her heart.

"What was it like, back then," I asked in a hushed voice, as though we were kneeling side by side inside a crowded church.

She continued to stare for a moment, straight into the tangle of stems in the garden before us, but she'd heard my question. She answered, at length.

"We were young." Mom hesitated and seemed to look straight through the fingers of my hand that she had interlaced in hers. "Just a lot younger is all."

A tiny white butterfly fluttered casually from one bloom to another, folding back its wings each time it came to rest. I glanced at it as I sat waiting for Mom to continue. The delicate creature rose after a moment's pause on a daisy, then flittered away.

"Everything was much quieter, I guess. Mostly. Longmont was a small town with only six or seven blocks of houses, surrounded by beet farms in those days." She closed her eyes and tilted her head upward in search of the images. "Our street, Grant. And Hoover, and Lincoln...goodness, what were the others? A hardware store downtown, two taverns, of course. A general store owned by the Meinkes. There was even a blacksmith, but old man Gray who owned it and shoed the horses for all the folks who still had horses eventually put in a big red pump out front, with a glass top—where the gasoline went up into before..." Mom hesitated and glanced over at me. A wistful smile formed on her lips. "Before it went down the hose into the new cars that started showing up. More and more each year. But it was quiet. That's what I remember most. Except for your father."

I looked at her questioningly. Pop was in my mind the most reserved soul on the planet. Contemplative.

"His mother, your Grandma Morley, bought a piano one summer when we was about twelve or thirteen...yes, it was thirteen 'cuz both of us was just startin' high school in a month up at Saint John's. But if he didn't talk and yell as much like all the rest of the kids who lived there, he made up for it at that piano..."

Grandma Morley, who died long before I was born, wanted a piano because she loved the sound of the notes she heard coming through the open doors of the beer halls on Main Street, and from the tinny mouth of her parlor Victrola. But more so because in her mind it would somehow elevate her in stature in the small community of hayseed farmers, shopkeepers, Mrs. Pendragon, whose husband owned the local mercantile bank downtown, and the mill owners. And so, with money she had hidden from Grandpa, who was loathe to work, but not to disappear at the drop of a hat, she boarded the southbound train early that summer with Pop and Aunt Corey sitting on either side of her in the sparkling coach in their Sunday clothes. The three of them traveled down to Denver and bought a fine new upright piano—with no cigarette burns or coffee cup rings on the music sheet stand. A few days later the instrument arrived in the back of an open bed truck. Two husky Swedes carefully lugged it up the front walk in full view of the Cowdens, the Sturges, the Petersens, and every other neighbor up and down the street, Grandma beaming with pride and a pose of subdued arrogance. Grandpa, of course, was nowhere to be found, beaming with visions of a carefree life among the few remaining tribes of Indians who still camped and roamed along the banks of the upper Platte River.

"I always thought your father was the most handsome guy I'd ever laid eyes on. It was his eyes, Skip. Oh my gosh, them eyes!" Mom opened hers and glanced over at mine. "Like yours. You got them pretty blue eyes, just like his, though the rest of you is me. We played all the time, me and him and your Aunt Corey...up in the branches of one of the Cottonwoods that was out front of his house. I was a tomboy, and was always the first up into that tree, though your father was strong, and athletic and coulda' beat me anytime if he'd really wanted. Just look at his shoulders and his thin waist. You can still see it. But when that piano came..."

Much to Grandma's everlasting delight, Pop took to it like Patton to his pearl handled revolver. She purchased music scores and scads of little books and pamphlets to help him learn to read notes, even sent him to the home of Mrs. Agnes Purdy, the wife of Reverend Purdy who ministered at the Methodist church three blocks north, and who taught piano. But perhaps because of some crosswire in his brain, or maybe simply a disdain for fundamental music structure, he grasped only the very basics of the instrument's possibilities at first. Even so, he loved the sound of the notes vibrating off the harp of strings, and spent hours sitting in another world, pounding on the keys, mastering tempo and chords, falling prey to its charms.

"I used to stand beside him. Me and Corey sometimes. There in the parlor off the entry. That's one of them things I remember so well, like it was yesterday. He didn't even know we was there half the time. He loved that piano more than your grandma ever coulda', and for the right reasons." Mom's gaze drifted away once again.

"I was in love with him even then, as kids. God almighty. There weren't no one else like him. When we got into high school, that's when I knew it for sure. He had the softest voice, and by then he could play just about anything he heard just by listenin' to it once or twice. I wanted him to go to school somewhere and really learn...but he never did. He never did anything with it."

Mom snapped her head, uncurled the leg beneath her that had begun falling asleep. She winsomely picked a few brown-edged blossoms from one of the flowers, tossed them onto the grass beside her, and then continued.

"We was always together there at Saint John's. At the bonfire before Homecoming, sittin' in the bleachers when the basketball team played. Him and me and Corey, who was two years younger than your father. Your Aunt Betty was still in grade school, raisin' Cain...she was wild as a March hair, that girl, even then. And May was still a baby. We used to sneak off, me and your father, after a dance, or a game, leavin' Corey behind." She pursed her lips and then winked at me. A very impish wink, and said nothing further about that.

"Old Doc Ryan adored your father. Knew he was smart as a whip—and he was. Doc even offered to give your grandma the money to send him off to college to get his education, to give him the money to get him through medical school afterward."

"Honest?"

"Oh yes! He was smart as a whip, and he shoulda' done it. He coulda' been a doctor. He coulda' been a concert pianist. He coulda' done anything he wanted, but somethin' held him back, like whatever it was, it had reins on him."

Pop turned his back on college, on a conservatory, on the world exploding with opportunity for a young man with far ranging vision—or even modest vision. For some reason I don't know it frightened him, as though all of it was a war and he'd been thrown at the very gates of it, scared witless by the terrible noise and ugliness beyond. But Roseanna Cowden did not frighten his gentle soul. The beautiful raven-haired young woman captured his heart and soul early on in his life back in Longmont. Sympathized, even identified, with the unspoken, foolish fears deep inside him as though she'd read them clearly, which, of course, she had not.

To Grandma Cowden's eternal delight, and Grandma Morley's never-ending horror, they were married the day after graduation from Saint John's High in 1929, the year Wall Street went down in flames. Grandma Cowden rejoiced at the marriage because there was one less mouth to feed in a family of eight; Grandma Morley raged because she'd lost another man, and with him the possibility of weeding her way into high society in Longmont on the coat tails of a doctor or concert pianist.

As the story of my father unfolded that afternoon in the weakening sunlight, I thought of Miss Marilou Jenkins' home far away, across the railroad tracks, the downtown district like a dividing line in the city, just beyond the sprawling city park. I thought about her father who had somehow had the courage to become a doctor. Is that what it all boiled down to in life, I wondered? Having courage? I saw her grand home set on a corner lot, with flower gardens tended, not by her mother in her silk dresses and chic hairdo, but by hordes of servants. I wondered. I wondered about what my place in the world would someday be; if I would summon the courage when the time came to pursue dreams that I hadn't yet dreamed?

"Well. It's time I went on in and started dinner."

She rose abruptly, awakened back to the reality of life in Barnum in the year 1957. Without another word she walked across the lawn and into the house, leaving me with the flowers, the corpses of weeds, and the dying sun.

When she pulled the rear door open I heard the sound of Pop's piano in the background; a soft, haunting, melancholy tune. How sad, I thought as the door closed behind her and the notes died, that no one other than us would probably ever hear his song.

SEVENTEEN

Floating Down The Mississippi Drain

Had I grown up in a cave, I think I would probably have loved my bedroom in the basement just as much as any one of the many, and probably luxurious, bedrooms in the home of Dr. Jenkins across town. Home is, after all, where the heart is, or at least where you hang your baseball cap.

In my unassuming room I had a bed, a nightstand of sorts thrown together by Pop in one of his final building furies, some very poorly done pictures photo-printed on cardboard hanging haphazardly on the walls, and an old, used clock radio I was given on one of my birthdays; I think my tenth. Really, what more could I ask for?

Relief from the monotony of incarceration came to mind after about the fourteenth day, so I gathered up some books to ease the boredom. One of the ones I found was Huckleberry Finn. Huck reminded me of Jimmy. I laughed. I guess I was Tom. As I sailed through the pages near the end of week two, the thought welled up inside me that one day, after escaping the prison of the basement, I'd get Jimmy and Skip together, if either of them would talk to me after what I'd done in my moment of contrition at Terrence's house, and the three of us would build the most incredible raft. Though I knew the Mississippi was a much larger river than the Platte, I was still certain we could navigate the body of water God had seen fit to give our state. Out of Colorado, through Kansas, or Nebraska, or wherever the Platte flowed. We'd eventually wind up on Mr. Twain's beloved Mississippi, I was certain, and there experience...most likely some destructive experience, like somehow setting New Orleans ablaze.

Scratch the raft.

106

I listened to the radio more than ever during those dark days, too. Singers like Fats Domino, The Coasters, Jerry Lee Lewis, and Buddy Holly filled me with brand new passions. The strangest desire to be with the opposite sex—Carol, maybe. She lived much closer than Miss Marilou Jenkins after all. I'd learn how to do dances like the bop, and the chicken, and feel the...her body. I began to dwell on what it all might be like. Down there in my bedroom. Down there. All alone. *Something* deep inside me was stirring. Outside my little window I imagined her waiting on hands and knees, smiling. She was tapping. Tapping. Tapping ever so softly on the glass...

"Hey, Skip. Skip!" What an ugly voice, I thought. *She* turned out to be Jimmy.

Behind him, with his hands on Jimmy's shoulders and a grin as big as could be, was good old faithful Mickey, lately sprung from his house arrest and no doubt come to rescue me from mine. I left my wistful daydream of floating down the mighty Mississippi, head in the lap of my Nubian princess.

A visit by Mickey—or Jimmy, especially—was strictly forbidden. Lock-up meant lock-up. Period. Had the Pope himself come to visit me he would most likely have been denied access to my quarters. That was the depths to which my mother's ire had sunk, even in the face of our heart-to-heart talks at the edge of the flower gardens. Should she have caught my two best friends trying to woo me out of the dungeon, God only knows what fury would have been unleashed. They'd have been railroaded out of the yard with a rake or a broom, and as for me. Well.

"You aren't mad at me anymore?" I whispered.

Jimmy answered as though the question was ludicrous. "Nah. Everything turned out okay. I ain't mad. Get up! Open the window."

"No! I can't. You'd better just go," I said, motioning for them to be quiet. Mom was somewhere in the house upstairs, maybe heading for the broom closet as we spoke.

The small awning window set high up in the wall of block immediately below the floor joists was locked shut, and so I hopped from my bed and darted over to it. Jimmy motioned for me to open it, but I shook my head.

"Get out of here, you idiots! You want me to stay locked up forever?"

"Just open the window."

"No! I already told you I can't."

"We have to tell you something," Mickey tried to whisper.

"No. I want to get out of here someday, and if Mom catches you..." The vision of a beautiful raft popped back into my head suddenly, and I wavered. Could it be they'd been thinking about it, too? "Well...what's so important?"

They both looked at one another, grinning, knowing they'd won the first part of the battle. Jimmy indicated once again that the window needed to be opened. I knew very well that I shouldn't, that giving in to my curiosity would be my downfall, but I did it anyway. The open space between the dusty window glass and its casement was just big enough for a pint-sized burglar to enter, and so Jimmy slid through, followed quickly by Mickey.

The radio on my nightstand sang out a current hit by a very hip new group. Danny and the Juniors. I tuned the volume up a little, and then returned my attention back to my friends, confident that the noise of *At The Hop* would mask the chatter of the upcoming conversation.

"What is it?" I asked.

"We gotta' get you outta' here," Jimmy told me. "Mickey and me was just over at Mrs. Rashure's store an we saw this paper taped on the front window. There's gonna' be a soap box derby race next Saturday! We just gotta' build one an get in on the action, but there ain't much time left."

"Yeah," added Mickey, "and you're going to be the driver! We pulled straws. You won!"

"We did?" I asked.

"Well, since you're stuck down here all by yourself, we put one in for you. You drew the longest," Mickey said.

"What are we going to build this racer out of...and when?" I asked.

Jimmy plopped down onto the bed excitedly, and then answered. "Clifford has a pretty cool wagon with a perfect set of wheels for what we need. Real new. Slick as snot! You could give that wagon a shove, and it'd keep rollin' forever! No sense askin' him to donate it after the creek deal, so we'll just borrow it for a coupla' weeks when he ain't lookin'. We don't need the wagon part of it, just the wheels and axles. 'Course we'll give it back after we're done with it. Not sure where we'll get the stuff to make the chassis, but we figured you'd have an idea there—bein' good with wood an all."

The "borrowing" thing again. We were skating on thin ice already, but I let Jimmy continue.

"We need your mechanical help, ya' know. You gotta' sneak outta' here, somehow. You just gotta'! Come with us tonight, ok? We'll get Clifford's wagon, take it over to my garage, then go find some stuff to build the rest of the chug with tomorrow."

"Nope. Not on your life. I'm not stealing any more stuff, and I'm not sneaking out. No way."

Sure, there was a way. For the next fifteen minutes while the radio blared and every angel in Heaven kept tapping me on the shoulder telling me to continue shaking my head no, I listened to the plan. The vision of a glorious first-place winning chug grew stronger with each of Jimmy's colorful words, and, eventually, my better judgment perished.

"Well, maybe..."

"We'll come by at seven," Mickey said beaming. "Be ready!"

Jimmy shook his head, emphasizing his agreement, and then the two of them crawled back out the way they'd come in. I stood looking up at the window as *Come Go With Me* wafted from the speaker of the radio. The background vocal, deep and rich, played against the lead singer's tenor voice and the piano, "...never, never, never, never..." The drumbeat on my shoulder grew stronger.

***

"You've been a regular little angel," my mother announced out of the blue when she'd set the platter of hamburgers down and taken her seat at the dinner table. "I think you've learned your lesson, right LaVerne?" She had a bad habit of addressing my dad while looking at me, or vice-versa, and I often couldn't be sure just who the comments were supposed to be directed at. This particular time, though, I was certain my father was not the one who'd learned a lesson. I sat silently while she waited for Pop to fill up his plate and answer her.

"I hope so," he said.

"Yes, I think you have. And Jimmy and that Mickey haven't come around, neither. I don't want you playing with either of 'em for awhile. But they're steering clear of this house." She rambled on for a few more minutes in short, disjointed sentences concerning bad influences, trouble, and more bad influences.

"So I think we've decided, haven't we, La Verne, to let you off the hook tomorrow. You can leave your room. You've had enough punishment...but if you ever pull off another stunt like you did last month, goddamit', well...what did we say we'd do to him, LaVerne?"

Pop shook his head. He had no idea, I'm sure. This was one of Mom's extemporaneous soliloquies, loaded with assumptions that anyone else might be involved, or that any prior discussion had even taken place.

"Well, you won't like it, will he LaVerne?"

"No, he won't."

I ate quietly after Mom had abruptly dropped the remainder of the charges against me and then moved on to other topics, none of which had a blessed thing to do with me or my friends, thank goodness. I was a free man as of tomorrow at sunrise. Unless something bad happened in the meantime—and it looked like something might.

Excusing myself from the dinner table, which made both of my parents blink with surprise, I left the kitchen dinette and headed out the back door and onto the enclosed back porch with the steep basement stairs leading down to the basement. What, I asked myself, was I to do? It was 6:45. In fifteen minutes Jimmy and Mickey would arrive, expecting me to join them in the merry hunt for unsuspecting Clifford's wagon. Of course I couldn't go.

Not now. But that is not to say that I wouldn't. Jimmy was a master of persuasion when he needed to be; when there was something stuck in his mind like a heated metal splinter screaming to be yanked out. If I said no, he'd list a hundred reasons why I should recant and say yes. And all of them were bound to make perfect sense in that moment.

The idea occurred to me to retrace my steps. Go back upstairs and leave my bedroom as dark as an abandoned mine shaft. I could do the unreasonable; begin to fill the sink basin with soap and water and start the dishes without a fight. Jimmy and Mickey wouldn't dare try to approach me up there. Something deep inside told me, begged me not to take the coward's way out, though. Face them—face Jimmy. Simply tell him my time of confinement wasn't quite finished. Tell him that borrowing Clifford's wagon was really just stealing Clifford's wagon. He'd understand, he'd...no, he wouldn't. For the second time in my life a cloud of real anxiety descended over me. It wasn't so much that I didn't possess the courage to make the right decision—I knew I did not under Jimmy's pressure. It wasn't even that stealing the wagon was the worst caper we'd ever planned. It was the realization, as clear as crystal and hard as a diamond, that this time around giving in would be unforgivable. I knew the stakes, knew that the voice in my head and the ever-increasing tapping on my shoulder really meant something which I'd only once before been called on to acknowledge. I was about to make the second meaningful moral choice of my young life.

I continued on to the basement and the waiting dilemma. In my room I turned on the radio and sat in the darkness, waiting apprehensively. Upstairs, the muffled voice of Mom drifted through the floorboards, breaking every now and then for a brief instant when she allowed Pop to offer his one or two word response. Through the folds of the curtain the shadows outside moved furtively; elm leaf lines of fingers fidgeting like those of a nervous felon tapping on the table in an eerie courtroom, awaiting his sentencing. The minutes ticked on. The jury arrived.

"He ain't down there," I heard Jimmy say in a dejected whisper to Mickey. "Damn it. Now what?"

"Maybe he's doing the dishes. Let's go around to the kitchen window," Mickey answered.

"Yeah, okay."

I summoned the dot of courage hiding inside me and jumped across the room to the window. "Wait!"

The shuffle of their feet stopped and they returned. Jimmy spoke first. "What the hell are ya doin' down there in the dark? Open the window!"

"No. I'm not going. You guys go on without me."

"What? Whatd'ya mean you ain't goin'? I thought we decided it was time..."

"I can't. I can't help you steal Clifford's wagon...I can't. You'll just have to do it and build the chug yourselves." There, I'd said it. My heart beat madly as the words left my lips. I felt a cold blanket of fear; of another betrayal of Jimmy. As far as opening the window, I knew that if I did I'd be outside with them before I took another breath, and then be on my way to deeper pits of trouble. The dusty glass separating us was my only protection, a shield against their beckoning. Jimmy pressed his face against the glass and I could see his cat-eyes searching the room. He said nothing for a minute as he looked about, then spoke again as he pushed against the window with his fingertips.

"Open up."

"No."

"What's got into you? We ain't stealin' the wagon...just borrowin' it for a while."

"No, we're...you're stealing it, and count me out. I'm in enough trouble. I don't want any more."

Behind Jimmy I could see Mickey begin to pace, the moonlight making his movements all the more muted and apparent in their frustration. I'd crossed the first bridge, but I knew the fight was anything but over. Mickey might walk away, but Jimmy, I knew, was loading his cannons in the silence. Soon enough he opened fire.

112

"It ain't stealin'! We're givin' it all back. There won't be no trouble, for God's sake. He won't even know it's gone. We'll even let him hold the trophy."

"No."

"C'mon. What's come over you? Just come help us. Your ma'll never know you was gone! Think about flyin' down the street in the best racer in the city. Why, even that stupid Clifford'll have to cheer when you cross the finish line! Think about the fun. The glory. Open up!"

"Uh-uh. You guys go on without me. I'm not leaving. Sorry," I answered with as much courage as I could muster. A heretofore unknown strength began to creep over me in the darkness, in the silence that followed. Maybe Jimmy *would* lose this time around.

"C'mon, Jimmy. Leave him be. We'll do it ourselves...we don't need him. Let's get outta' here," Mickey finally said. Then he directed the next words to me. "Eat your heart out when you see Jim flying under the checkered flag. We don't need you. Chicken."

And so they crept away, over the cracked and narrow concrete walk, in the direction of the alley behind the house. Clifford would lose his wagon—for a week, or a month, or maybe forever. Maybe they'd get away with it, maybe not. Maybe they'd even win the race. But it was all going to happen without me this time. It looked as though I'd lost my two best friends.

I returned to my bed and sat down with a mixed feeling of duplicity and relief, wondering if tomorrow's news on our TV would show the two of them being led away in handcuffs by a stony-faced cop. Probably not. Jimmy was blessed by the devil when it came to dodging bullets. I turned the volume of the radio up, crawled under the covers without undressing, and stared out at the moonlit shadows dancing across the yard until I fell asleep with the best feeling in my heart that I'd ever had. For once I hadn't caved in.

***

As promised, I was allowed to step outside the following morning into a bright and beautiful day, free and forgiven.

"Now don't you go and get into more trouble with Jimmy and that Mickey. Stay away from 'em," Mom cautioned me as I pulled the front door open. "Your father will skin you alive."

"Nah, I won't. I mean I will. Promise."

When she'd turned her back and gone about her business, I hopped down the front steps and ran to the side fence separating our yard from the McGuire's. The garage door behind Jimmy's house was open wide, and inside I could see him and Mickey working furiously to remove the sleek wheels from Clifford's wagon. My first impulse was to call out to them and ask them what was up. To make amends; defy my parents' warnings. Both of them took notice of me standing there, but continued with their task without saying a word to me. I watched for a moment and then turned and walked away.

EIGHTEEN

Mr. Peepers And The Denver 500

I didn't leave the yard the entire week. Where was I to go all by myself? To Clifford's or Allen's house? I really had no desire to stir up any more trouble with either of them for the time being, and besides, word had spread up and down the block that Mrs. Childers and Mrs. Jung were gunning for me and Jimmy and Mickey after the incident at the creek. An alliance had been struck between the two women, even though Allen's muddy clothes, lack of dexterity, and injured pride were entirely of his own making. I hadn't thrown him in the creek, for Pete's sake—none of us had. And as far as Clifford was concerned, I couldn't for the life of me understand why he would have chosen that dorky neighbor of his over me and Jimmy and Mick. But, he had. I guess his wagon getting Shanghaied served him right in a way.

I was over my mea culpa state of mind, and itching to dismount the spiritual horse I'd uncharacteristically hopped on while in prison. Jimmy and Mickey had worked like two tigers tearing up a gazelle on that chug, had hidden the body of the stolen wagon high in the rafters of the garage after they had dismembered it, as I stood beyond the fence watching. They glanced over at me every now and again, but neither of them bothered to acknowledge my presence.

"Tough luck, chicken," I knew they were saying to one another, and to me. "Tough luck. You ain't gonna' share in any of the glory." That would be Jimmy speaking, of course. Without me being around him, his grammar would be hopelessly spinning ever farther down the whirlpool of the toilet bowl.

I spied on them each afternoon the week following my release from bondage; looked on with certain pangs of envy as they sawed and hammered and cussed the chug together. Now I was no connoisseur of motor cars, or un-motor cars for that matter, but I must say that the thing they'd pieced and patched together was unlike anything I'd ever seen in my twelve and a half years on this planet. It was just plain ugly. Still, beauty was no requisite for speed, I knew, and the litmus test would be their first test run down Mrs. McGuire's long driveway. If it stayed together I figured they might have a fighting chance of at least getting into the derby. Winning the whole bag of potatoes would be something else again.

The chug was a little noisy during that first run, so they dragged it back into the garage for some minor adjustments, then shot it out again. It didn't sound as if whatever they'd done to it had corrected the problem, but after the second run they patted one another on the back, shook hands, and likely would have danced together except they knew I was looking. They were all smiles, and confident their larcenous labors were going to pay handsome dividends the next morning at the race. I wasn't so sure. The thing had been born on the outskirts of Hell, as far as I was concerned, kind of like a Dr. Frankenstein's monster on wheels. No good could come of its birth.

***

I wandered along at a discreet distance to the site of the competition, curious to see if Jimmy's and Mickey's labors would ripen into a good showing. From all across the city dozens of toe-haired kids had gathered, led by a retinue of beaming fathers and the machines they'd built. Looking over the field of entries it seemed obvious to me that none of the kids could possibly have fashioned those marvelous, perfectly painted, sleek-bodied racers without the help of Ford Motor Company designers. They were beautiful. Somehow the title "Soapbox Derby" applied only to the Jimmy-chug. Indeed, he and Mickey had scrounged up a ratty looking crate and mounted it onto the front of the rickety chassis, while everyone else must have scoured the pages of "Car and Driver" to come up with the jet-like fuselages their dads had put together for them.

On the side of the crate, either Jimmy or Mickey—I figured Mickey, because it was spelled correctly—had painted the name

"Rocket Flyer" in black letters, and like the first launches down at Cape Canaveral, the Flyer was unfortunately doomed to die.

The sponsor of the race, Peepers' Hardware Store, located over on the eastside where tons of those rich families lived, had erected a grandstand and stuck up a banner on the temporary fence strung out along the street. Mr. Leo Peepers was a well-known personality in the city. Having made some kind of fortune selling rakes and shovels and lawnmowers, he must have tired of that small accomplishment because he'd talked his way into the TV business. This guy named Dick Clark was having a phenomenal success with his program out of Philadelphia called American Bandstand, and ever the one to seize on an opportunity when it presented itself, Mr. Peepers started up his own version of the program on a local TV station soon after American Bandstand hit. The Denver Bandstand became the ugly little sister of her counterpart back east, but for a couple of laughable years it captured the eyes and ears and questionable dancing abilities of many local teens. After each song ended on his program, the dark-haired, black-suited, balding man with horn-rimmed glasses never failed to grab his mike, dance into the crowd of nervous-looking kids on the set, and say, "That was a real humdinger, wasn't it?" No, I had always thought after hearing him say it, it was not a "humdinger", real or otherwise. I think his absolute lack of coolness and that idiotic phrase were the two reasons his dream child got buried after two incredibly rotten seasons. Anyway, he still had the hardware store and tons of money, so he sponsored events like the derby to do his part to help keep us kids out of trouble—and of course to acquire more fame and fortune in the process.

Mr. Leo Peepers himself was the official who pompously raised the white flag and slung it downward to send each pair of racers off, down the long incline toward the finish line. The blazing morning sunlight hitting the back of his bald head sent showers of multicolored beams ricocheting in all directions. Were it not for the cat's-eye sunglasses worn by almost every high-fallutin' woman standing in the bleachers, dressed to the *nineteens,* cheering on their sons and booing the rest, they each and every one would have suffered corneal damage for sure.

Jimmy was entry number sixteen. Four feet away sat number seventeen; some kid in a coupe de-ville looking machine, smirking and mouthing something at my friend. Jimmy's hand left the wheel for an instant when he flipped the other kid off. Twenty or thirty outraged mothers saw it and let out a chorus of their own mild cuss words, demanding that the shithead from the west side be thrown out of the race. The kid's father, a swarthy, arrogant-looking man wearing a white suit, Panama hat, and expensive shoes, lit out of the bleachers like the shell from a Howitzer, fuming and blustering till Hell wouldn't have it. He bounded over the fence, program waving in front of his head as if he were swatting a swarm of flies. Mr. Peepers had been entertaining the rest of the officials on the opposite side of the street when Jimmy flipped the kid off, and he hadn't seen a thing. I guess none of them had.

"Did you see what that little s.o.b. did! Did any of you see that?" And so on, and so on.

When he turned around, Mr. Peepers' beady little pupils dilated—I could see them burst forward against the coke bottle lenses of his horn rim glasses like exploding black bubbles. The kid's father continued on, demanding something or other. Well, something. He definitely wanted Jimmy and his "blankedy-blank, whatever you call it..." to be "blankety-blankety blankety out!" And I thought my mom knew how to cuss. She would have blushed in the face of that man's language. He must have been a drill sergeant once. That or else a Catholic.

Mr. Peepers got all flustered by the time the tirade ended, and he strode over to Jimmy, past the still smirking little asshole in his formula racer. He said some things to Jimmy, who shook his head yes, and no, and no intermittently during the course of it, and then Peepers turned and questioned the now angelic-faced kid next door. Whatever answers the other boy gave seemed to stymie Peepers to no end, because he threw up his hands and walked away, leaving Rocket Flyer poised and at the ready behind the wheel chocks.

I just knew our chug was going to more than do justice to its name. I just knew it. To be safe I searched the lengthy list of patron saints in my head to say a quick prayer to, but the nearest I could come to anyone worth a damned was Saint Christopher. He'd have to work.

"Dear Saint Christopher, patron of all those..." Mr. Peepers' flag went down. "Help him! Amen!" I don't think Saint Christopher appreciated the necessary brevity of my prayer, or maybe he just didn't quite understand it.

Number seventeen took off slowly at first. That seemed good. But then it gained speed, as though...as though that damned Saint Christopher had gotten behind it and pushed it himself. He got the wrong chug! I scratched him off my list.

Rocket Flyer sat like a rock on a flat plain. My heart fell to my feet. Several seats away I saw Mickey raise his hands and cover his eyes. Finally, when number seventeen was half a dozen yards away from the finish line, one of the officials loped up to the rear of Jimmy's chug and gave it a good push. The run went well after that for thirty feet or so, until the rear wheels began to shudder. I knew what was coming next. They folded outward like a pair of dancers in a supremely polished ballet movement, then left the axle altogether. The aft end of the craft hit the pavement and stopped on a dime, and I gawked in horror as the now-free wheels went sailing past a stricken Jimmy. The wheels crossed the finish line not very far behind the coupe de ville, then roared on down the street all alone. Everyone roared except Mickey and me, and of course Jimmy.

Mr. Peepers took his cue and grabbed hold of the pineapple-sized microphone from the officials' table. Parading around like a carnival barker, he announced over and over again to the delight of the crowd, "That was a real humdinger, wasn't it?"

A few of the men in the bleachers, those who rightly suspected Jimmy's vulgar middle finger statement might have been an answer to something said by his opponent, and not simply a hoodlum's goading, exited their seats with the intention to help him remove the chug from the racetrack. Mickey joined them, but I, being persona non-grata, stayed where I was for the time being. The removal of the downed Rocket Flyer reminded me of Grandma Cowden's funeral procession a few years back—four men in the lead, with a hand on each corner of the casket-chug, solemnly carting it away. Mickey escorting a downcast Jimmy a couple of steps behind. Despite the fact Jimmy had constructed the thing with stolen wheels, and probably stolen everything else, I felt immense pain for him. It's one thing to be beaten in a fair competition, and I'm not saying the race was particularly unfair, even though most of the boys had very little to do with the engineering and building of their entries. It's something else again, though, to be utterly humiliated and then looked down on like an abandoned dog on the streets. That's how my best friend looked in that moment. I swallowed my pride and ran down to offer my support in that, his ignominious hour of need.

The four men laid Rocket Flyer down at the far end of the bleachers, well out of earshot of the crowd who were by that time unconcerned with the spectacle that had occurred only moments earlier. Three of the men left immediately after patting Jimmy on the back. I stood at a distance and observed the remaining adult, a kindly-looking guy with graying hair, dressed impeccably in a dark suit. He lingered momentarily, as Mickey consoled Jimmy, and then approached them, placing a hand gently on Jimmy's shoulder.

"Bad luck, young man. Bad luck. But don't be too disheartened. Things like that happen to the best men in the world. You'll survive. We all do. Do better next time. Try again."

Jimmy glanced up at him with tears in his eyes, his unkempt shag of hair poking out in all directions. I thought I saw him force a tiny smile, a flicker of thanks, before dropping his head down again. That was probably the first time a grown male, someone responsible and even remotely sympathetic, had ever offered Jimmy a word of encouragement after a defeat. The man turned, walked with an unpretentious air of civility past me, and returned to the races. I cautiously joined Mickey at Jimmy's side, half expecting to be told to shove off.

"You just get here?" Mickey asked. His tone of voice held no sign of rancor, and that eased my mind. Jimmy sat on the rear end of the Flyer and didn't look up.

"Nah, I saw the whole thing. I'm sorry. Don't know if it would have made any difference had I helped you guys build the chug, though. I mean...I probably would have made it even worse. I'm sorry," I answered.

Jimmy finally looked up, his eyes a little red and swollen. "What coulda' been worse? That kid told me before the race that I was a fuckin' loser, an' my racer was uglier than me. He told me I'd get my ass kicked by him an' his fancy racer, an' he was right."

"Nah, he wasn't. You heard that guy who just left. You lost, but you're not a loser. Next year we'll build another one and come back. Maybe you'll get to have a shot at him again. It'll be different then. We'll make it better; better than any chug in the universe. I'll help."

Another tear began to form in his eye, but he quickly wiped it away. He stood up and hit me on the shoulder with his fist, and the old smile grew slowly back onto his face. The time had come to shake the dust of defeat off, gather up the remains of Rocket Flyer, and head back across town to our lowly homes. Next year would be different.

NINETEEN

Martian Girls

With great trepidation I related the story of Jimmy's unfortunate shellacking at the Denver 500 to Mom and Pop that evening at the dinner table. Of course I left out the part about where he and Mickey had gotten the wheels for Rocket Flyer, one of which we were unable to find after it finally came to its rest. Wherever it wound up on its merry trip down the street, our best efforts to locate it proved fruitless. If we returned Clifford's wagon to him, it would have to be done very quietly, late at night, and minus one leg. But she didn't need to know anything about that.

Surprisingly, Mom was very sympathetic, especially when I told her that most of the spoiled kids in the race were from wealthy families. Perched near the top of her list of character defects was a deep, vocal dislike of anyone who resided higher on the economic ladder than the Morley family. I think that deficiency had something to do with the fact that many years ago our ancestors had moved to America from Ireland, penniless; suffered the same social ostracization that the majority of shanty Irish had suffered while they were rewriting New York history, and (not the least) her twisted interpretation of the gospel according to Mahoney, which stated something to the effect that, "Blessed are the poor, for they shall get even with all the rich people someday in Heaven."

"That's just like those goddam' Protestant buggers, ain't it LaVerne?" She didn't wait for Pop's one-word reply. "Using their filthy money to lord it over us working class people. It's a shame Jimmy didn't win. He's a good boy—better than the whole lot of them hoighty-toighty little snots from the east side. You want some more spuds?" she asked me without a pause in her speech.

"No thanks, I'm full," I replied.

"I tell you, if it wasn't for President Roosie-veld, this whole blessed country'd still be in the poorhouse..." and she went on for five more minutes about how the "goddam' rich Republicans" back east had screwed up the country in the stock market, precipitating the 1929 Crash, sending every noble, hardworking laborer—mainly the Irish—into the bread lines. She was wound up like a spring, and on top of her soapbox now. Mom loved to explain why things were what they were, at least her interpretation of the reasons, but she never could quite explain how us "poor folk" could escape the grinding doldrums of poverty. Work harder, I supposed. Manually harder.

Pop sat quietly in his chair beneath the bank of windows overlooking the back yard, filling up his plate again and again until all the meat and potatoes had disappeared from the table. I'm sure he agreed in principle with some of the things Mom was pontificating about, but I do believe his reasoning dictated that non-stop eating at dinnertime meant not having to answer some of her sillier questions.

"You know, Mom," I jumped in during an unusual pause in her dissertation. Her dark, un-Irish looking eyes had gone vacant for a moment, following a thought, maybe, that was wheeling around in her head. God knows, if Pop or I wanted to say something, that was the time. She was never quiet for long, but when she was, look out—she'd be brooding about something, and hell would follow her silence. "You know, Jimmy told me today that he felt real bad about what we did down at the Comet. He was very sorry. Maybe it had something to do with him getting trounced today. I'm not sure. But he isn't such a bad guy, is he?"

She woke up. "Why, no. I told you that. If your dad up and left me the way Fred left Ruth, you'd be just as lost. Just as lost. He ain't so bad, though. He's a lost soul wanderin' around lookin' for...well, for someone like your dad and *me*. That's all."

"Do you think I could go over and see him after dinner then? I mean, I could kind of keep him on the straight and narrow. You know, when he wants to go and get in trouble. I sure learned my lesson."

Mom smiled at me. I think she knew I was incapable of saving him; knew, too, how he could persuade an Arab to buy sand for a dollar a pound if he set his mind to it, but the compassionate side of her nature was beginning to awaken. When it came right down to it she'd take Jimmy into our family in a heartbeat if Ruth ever croaked from all her drinking. And that was a high-odds probability. Mom exhibited the wackiest judgment of her peers, had a fiery temper, it's true, but she also possessed a strange quality that always softened that hard-edged side of her—a love for the down and out, especially if they were kids. As bad off as she often claimed our family was—no matter that she darned my socks and bought my clothes second hand—I had a dad, she never failed to remind me when the subject of Jimmy or some other down and out kid came up. Pop might straggle in from The Aeroplane Club on occasion with a stupid, sheepish grin on his face, loaded to the gills, risking a frying pan to the head if her mood was sour. Still, the sun would always rise on schedule the next morning, finding three Morleys in the house, even if one of them was snoring off a drunk on the living room couch with a black eye or a lump on his head.

"Yes, I suppose you can. You behave yourself, though, and make sure Jimmy don't go talkin' you into any more trouble."

I rose from my chair and headed for the door. Pop, who had been scraping up the last of the gravy on his plate with a piece of bread, stopped me just before my hand hit the knob.

"Before you get out of here, get me a beer from the ice box, would you, Skippy?"

"Sure, Pop." I backtracked to the refrigerator, grabbed a can of Coors, and then handed it to him. He stuffed the piece of bread into his mouth as he took hold of the beer. "Thunk ya. Nah, gut outta' huh. Un duh like yer mutha says an stuh outta' trouble."
I *think* I understood what he was saying.

I ran outside, across the grass, and hopped the fence into Jimmy's yard. All sins had been forgiven, and now the official quarantine from Jimmy's sphere of bad influence had been lifted. I found him in his bedroom lying atop the covers staring up at the ceiling, and I followed his eyes to the swirls of textured plaster without saying a word. He'd glued a hundred or so black cutout stars up there, and I immediately recognized the rough shapes of constellations—The Big Dipper, Orion, with its three-starred belt, and Gemini, the dancing stick figured twins. In his lap in the twilight of the room I noticed a large book, open, a picture of the night sky in the Northern Hemisphere.

"Hey," he finally said without looking away from the ceiling.

"Hiya. What's all this?" I replied.

He pointed up at the paper stars. "Those are some of the constellations we're gonna' look at tonight."

"We are?"

"Yep. Allen left his binoculars on his front lawn. I saw 'em when I was walkin' up the street this afternoon an took 'em. I think they'll help us see the stars really good."

Jimmy never learned. Well, not moral or ethical things anyway. He was still a genius of sorts, though. Buried in that larcenous mind was a miraculously natural affinity for the sciences. And math. He was a wizard at calculating. I didn't understand much of that stuff, but he fell into it all as if his father had been Einstein instead of ne'r-do-well Fred. True, he spoke like a barbarian, but he was in no way ignorant. Tonight it seemed we would be investigating the universe, which until recently I had thought was contained in a tangible, understandable bowl extending around the planet we lived on. The zillion dots of light up there were simply pin holes poked by God into the balloon covering. What was outside it on the other side I had no idea, nor interest in. A gigantic room with tons of light bulbs, maybe. Jimmy knew better. I do think he dreamed of somehow getting out there someday; getting away from the world he found himself trapped in, traveling a hundred million light years away in some incredible rocket ship he'd build.

"I put them stars up there. Cool, huh?" He continued to marvel at his creation on the ceiling, not looking over at me.

"Yeah, I suppose so," I said.

"Go get your sleeping bag. Mickey's on his way...what time is it?"

I glanced at the alarm clock on his nightstand. "Seven-O-Five."

"Good. 'Nuther hour and it'll be dark enough. You see the Big Dipper?" he asked.

"Yeah. Everyone knows that one."

"Well, it's not really a constellation, and I couldn't put up all the millions of littler stars around it, but we can see 'em tonight." He hopped up onto his hands and knees and pulled the curtains aside. "Sky's clear. We'll see 'em all." He looked back at me. "Go get your bag. Meet me out in the back yard!"

"Yeah, okay. Sure." I took another look at his star ceiling with constellations that weren't really constellations, shrugged, and wondered what so possessed him about it? Then I left to dig Pop's old down-filled, arctic weather mummybag out of the garage.

As part of the unspoken terms of my probation I checked into the house to let the folks know about the sleepover after unburying the sleeping bag from its resting place under a mountain of junk Pop had collected. He and Mom were still seated at the table in the kitchen, talking and laughing like old, young lovers. Pop had one hand on his can of beer, and the other extended across the small table where it rested in a fidgety sort of way on Mom's hand. She had that goofy grin on her face, and jumped with surprise when I bolted in the door.

"Godammit', Skip! Knock before you come breakin' in here next time," she exclaimed.

"Huh?"

"We was talk...what is it you want?" she asked, pulling her hand free of Pop's stymied fingers. I could see she was flustered, as she turned a couple of shades of red, and I wondered what the topic they'd been discussing might have been? I don't think it was finances, Republicans, or the condition of the roses in the garden outside. I put on my best innocent smile and answered.

"Can I sleep outside in Jimmy's backyard with him? We're going to look at constellations with his new binoculars."

Pop took a quick swig of beer as he turned his head toward me, and he beat Mom to the punch with the answer I was hoping for. "Yeah, go ahead. Now, get outta' here. Don't forget to grab your transistor, some blankets and toothbrush, and anything else you can think of before you go, though."

He didn't come right out and say it, but I knew he didn't want to be interrupted again, so I played dumb, figuring he and Mom just wanted to play kissy-face, huggy-bod as soon as I left. I know I was right because Mom got the dumbest look on her red face after she smiled like the cat in the canary cage and winked at him.

"Good idea. I'll just go get the radio—don't need a toothbrush or blanket..." I said, voice trailing off as I hightailed it out the door to the basement stairs. I gathered up the radio and left the house through the porch door. Crossing the patio behind the kitchen I said, "Bye," without glancing in at them through the windows. For all I knew they were long gone anyway.

Tonight Jimmy, Mickey, and I would dance across another undiscovered field, mostly one filled with conjecture, along with our journey through the universe. I suddenly began to wonder if on Mars or Venus there were girls, and if there were, were they pretty like some of the ones on our planet, or were they like the ones in the horror movies, with long spaghetti arms and legs, and one ugly eye in the center of their green faces? Jimmy would probably know. He knew a lot of stuff about sex, and I guessed he knew even more about what kind of creatures inhabited the worlds out there in the night sky, and how they looked without clothes on. More importantly, though, I wanted to know what the girls here looked like without any clothes. I was pretty sure he could answer that question, too.

So began the night. Mickey had already arrived with his flannel-patterned sleeping bag, a pillow, and something else I would never have imagined he'd bring—a pack of cigarettes and matches he'd rifled from his father's stuff. He was displaying them proudly, sitting cross-legged across from Jimmy on the lawn when I walked up. Sex and cigarettes. Forget the stars.

"Want one?" he asked before I'd even unloaded my bundle. Both of them had already lit up and were cupping the glowing weeds with their palms. It was an exciting prospect. I'd never tried that forbidden pleasure before. Tonight was going to be some kind of thrilling adventure. I looked furtively across the fence to our house, which was dark as the inside of a sealed box, and then joined them on the lawn. Five minutes later after several bouts of severe coughing, I found myself lying on my back, nauseous as I'd ever felt, looking up at the Milky Way. The mass of lights was spinning crazily, and each time I blinked it was like someone had jerked the twinkling vista backward to its starting point. Jimmy and Mickey sat upright, laughing and puffing away like old veterans. When my head stopped spinning and my stomach quit wanting to escape through my raw throat, I swore off that vice forever.

"Do they always make you sick?" I asked them.

"Nope. Only till ya' get use to 'em. Otherwise nobody'd bother," Jimmy replied, holding the pack in front of my face. "Have another. You'll feel better after about the third or fourth one." He laughed as I started to turn green and clap my hands over my mouth.

"No. I'm gonna' puke. Get those things away from me."

He left me alone to suffer through the effects of the chemicals I'd ingested and returned his attentions to Mickey, who graciously accepted another smoke from the pack he'd so kindly brought.

The evening wore on and the sky high above us slowly carried the incredible blanket of stars east to west as precisely as the movements of a Swiss watch. I was forced to lie on my back atop the mummybag so that I wouldn't throw up from the cloud of smoke drifting lazily skyward from the cigarettes my buddies lit up, one after another. As I lay there I peered at the sky, trying to find a point of reference to gauge the stars' movements by, but that was useless. They were crawling along the arc of blackness, I knew, but they made snails look like sprinters by comparison. Still, the sheer numbers of lights filled me with something of the awe that I'd seen in Jimmy's eyes earlier in his bedroom. I grabbed Allen's binoculars and trained them on a dusty sheet of whiteness directly above me. The cloud evaporated after I'd focused the lenses, and in its place were countless more points of light.

"Wow!" As I marveled at the clarity, a moment ago just a foggy mass, a gigantic eyeball burst onto the scene, like a flying purple people eater come to scope me out.

"Whatcha' lookin' at down there?" Jimmy's tobacco drenched voice chimed.

"Man! That cloud above us isn't a cloud at all. It's a bunch of stars!" I exclaimed.

Jimmy grabbed the binoculars and looked up. "Yep. That's the Milky Way. That's our galaxy. Must be billions of stars in it, too, along with our sun."

I thought about that statement for a second. "Wait a minute. If our sun is in that cloud, how can we see it? We'd be in there, too. That doesn't make sense."

"Because we're on the outside edge of all of them stars. We're lookin' across the galaxy at them." Any fool could see that, but I certainly couldn't.

"If we're on the edge, well...why is there all that empty space in between us and the cloud?"

Jimmy laid the binoculars down and motioned for me to follow him to the driveway. He knelt down and drew an imaginary circle with his finger on the concrete, then pointed to its imaginary edge. "See, were out here lookin' sideways across it. The Milky Way is like a plate. The stars in it are thousands and thousands of light years apart though. That's why it seems like there's nuthin' between us and the nearest one."

"But if they're so far apart, why do they looked so bunched up, like they're right on top of one another?"

"BECAUSE! Most of the ones you see are so far away they get lost in perspective! Get it? It's like lookin' at a bunch of leaves in a tree from a block away. Just a load of green until you get right up on 'em. Think how big our galaxy is. Try to imagine it!" he answered.

I couldn't for the life of me. "Where's Mars?" I asked.

"It's over there somewhere, near the horizon. Hard to see, even with binoculars. Just a red dot."

"Do you think there are girls on Mars?"

Jimmy craned his head backward and closed one eye as he thought about the question. "How should I know? What makes ya' ask somethin' like that? Who cares?"

Mickey joined us and slapped Jimmy on the back. "He wants to kiss one of them, dummy!"

Jimmy roared. "Oh, I get it. Yer horny..."

"No I'm not! I just want to know if people live on Mars, that's all."

That answer didn't satisfy Mickey. "Yeah, right. Then why'd you ask if there were girls on it?"

"Yeah, there are as a matter of fact," Jimmy said. "The Air Force shot a spaceship down a couple of years ago out over the desert. They say that they found some bodies inside it. One was a girl."

"How do you know?" Mickey asked.

"'Cuz the guy had a foot-long moustache, but the other one didn't have any hair...none! She was naked as a Jay-bird."

"You're kidding!" Mickey began laughing, and like myself, was no doubt trying to conjure up a vision of the fully undressed Martian lady.

"I swear it's true. I saw a pitchur of it in Sci-Fi Gazette. She was bald as an egg everywhere, 'an she didn't have a doink," said Jimmy.

"Wow..." chirped Mickey.

"Well, okay. Say it was a girl Martian, then. How do they do it if she doesn't have a doink," I began.

"No, no, no. SHE can't..."

Sitting there on the driveway, Jimmy explained in fantastic detail over the next half hour how creatures from outer space had sex. Something told me he was making most of it up, but I drank in every lurid word of it just the same. He was right, though. Part of that new sensation I'd felt down in the basement had quite a lot to do with a strange, pleasant rustling down below. I was beginning to see the opposite sex in an entirely new way.

After we'd returned to the comfort of our sleeping bags, and he and Mick had fired up another smoke, he expounded further on the topic of "doing it"—this time, earth-style. I didn't say a word as I listened intently, gazing up with a profound thrill at the sky, brilliantly alive, dancing with undressed earthling girls. I began to perspire at the thought of them, and imagined the most sinful but rapturous of conjugal pleasures.

TWENTY

Peg Leg's Return

Mom and Pop encouraged me in the days following my sleepover at Jimmy's house to continue with that enjoyable educational experience, saying something to the effect that stargazing could only improve my "universal view". Whatever that was supposed to mean. Little did they know that my universal view had expanded rather earthward to terrestrial bodies. There were no questions concerning what I'd learned about the heavens above, and no reports from neighbors that we'd been prowling the alley or streets, therefore any anxieties they might have had about my conduct were put to rest. I was pretty sure that the real reason they wanted me to sleep out of doors was because of the amount of stargazing fun they'd probably been having over there in their sleeping bag.

Both of them absolutely glowed that next morning. If kissing and hugging—and the other activities Jimmy informed me of in explicit detail—went on in all grown-ups' bedrooms, and had the power to transform the often dour complexion of Mom's disposition in the manner it had, I could only imagine how heavenly sweet my own outlook on life might become. That is, if I was somehow able to partake of that forbidden fruit. Which I was not. The rules seemed unfair, but I supposed God in His wisdom had good reason for setting them up the way He had. Of course, for every law there is a loophole I'd heard my father once say. Now, if I could only find it. My new quest for the summer would be to become a canonical expert. Since school was out and access to the expansive spiritual library there was now barred, I'd have to make use of our small, local library three blocks away. With any luck I'd manage to get my hands on a copy of some arcane volume—"How To Hoodwink God", or

"Acceptable Sex For Catholic Minors", or better yet, "Loopholes In The Laws of The Church". I intended to ask Jimmy if he thought any books might have been written with titles like that. Of course he wasn't an avid reader, especially in the field of Ecclesiastical Law, but he was my only hope. I certainly didn't dare ask the frumpy old librarian. After not a great deal of consideration it dawned on me that books of that sort had probably never been written, and if they had been, they'd most likely been burned centuries ago, or else wound up in a secret collection in a witches' coven somewhere. That scholarly dream died before it even had a chance to be born. So, I tried to put the entire problem of sex out of my mind until I reached the ripe old age of twenty-one or twenty-two when I graduated from Regis College, at which time I could marry and safely investigate the landscape of love. Another possibility occurred to me before I exited that door however—how to make time leapfrog forward. Maybe there was a way to sleep for ten years or so, like Rip Van Winkle had. I'd ask around.

In the meantime life went on about its business as usual. I slept out of doors most every night, sometimes in the company of Mickey, sometimes not, but always lying in my bag beside Jimmy, listening to his tales of outrageous scope and dimension.

One evening Jimmy and Mickey decided that the wagon should be repaired and returned to Clifford. Though I hadn't had a thing to do with stealing it, I became party to that act of amends as, in principle, it seemed to mesh with every good instinct in my soul. We waited patiently that evening until the last of the lights in the neighbors' houses had been extinguished, Jimmy and Mick smoking cigarette after cigarette and laughing about how seamlessly the original plot had finally worked out. True, they'd lost the race, lost a wheel, and suffered great humiliation, but the surprised look on Clifford's face when he discovered his wagon the next morning would make up for some of the pain. "Besides," Jimmy said, "it's the right thing to do." That was a first for him.

Jimmy had found a replacement wheel for the one that had frolicked into hiding so effectively weeks ago. He said he'd stumbled across it down by the creek, but I knew better. It was a tricycle wheel, with no mud or weeds on it, barely even a pebble in its treads. Some kid somewhere was probably crying her eyes out. I tried not to think about that, though, and silently watched as he and Mickey slid it onto the axle under the light of a full moon, a foot or so outside the open garage door.

"You think he'll notice the difference?" Mickey asked as he looked down on the wheel, scratching his head.

"Yeeeahhh...prob'ly." Jimmy chuckled. "It's a tad smaller than the others, but it's the thought behind it that counts. I think he'll 'preciate the gesture."

Looking down on the crippled toy, I had to join in their laughter. We dubbed the revitalized wagon, "Peg Leg", and set off under the cover of absolutely nothing to carry it down the alley to Clifford's yard. Before we'd gotten very far an idea popped up in my head; a good one I thought. I posed a question to my two friends in a whisper. "Don't you guys think it would be nice to leave a note on it? You know, something thanking Clifford for the use of his wagon?"

Jimmy was aghast. "Are you nuts? Why don't we just wait until morning an' knock on his front door with it?"

Mickey agreed. "You wanna' be grounded for another month, don't you Skip? God, sometimes I wonder about you."

"No, no. We don't have to sign it, and we could cut out letters from a magazine and paste them onto the paper so him or his parents couldn't trace the writing, like that gangster did last week on Dragnet. I think that'd be keen!"

Jimmy stopped dead in his tracks and dropped the front end of the maimed wagon onto the gravel. "Yer abs'lutely right, Skip! That's exactly what we'll do. *I'll* write the letter. Let's get this thing back to my house."

And so we backtracked up the alley, stashed the wagon back inside his mom's garage, then went into the house to find some magazines, scissors, and paper.

Mrs. McGuire had left for work two hours earlier in a cloud of exhaust and a warning to Jimmy to stay out of trouble. That meant we were free to scavenge the few magazines needed from her nightstand and make use of the house in any way we saw fit. Jimmy gathered a few of them up and dumped them onto the coffee table in the living room, and then went to fetch the scissors and a piece of paper. He returned from the kitchen a moment later with the paper and scissors, three glasses, and an opened bottle of Old Crow.

"Let's have a shot of this stuff while we work. It does wonders for Mother when she's writin' letters."

Someone began tapping on my shoulder, and it wasn't Mickey, who immediately agreed with his friend, the Frank Lloyd Wright of trouble. I stood up and began to voice my opinion.

"Whoa! We're not supposed to..."

"Oh pipe down," Jimmy interrupted me. "We ain't gonna' get drunk. Just have a drink or two to celebrate our genius. Don't go chickenin' out on us again, Skip."

"I dunno, you guys."

"C'mon. It ain't like cigarettes," Mickey urged me. "Won't hurt a bit. You'll like it!"

"Well...all right. Just a swig though. I've never tasted whiskey before, just Pop's beer."

"Yeah, beer's good—but whiskey is...let's see...thirteen times better!" Jimmy said after quickly doing the proof math. "Mick, run out to the ice box an' get some ice an' pop."

"What kind of pop?"

"I don't care. Coke, Mountain Dew, Orange...whatever's in there."

Mickey darted into the kitchen and then returned with a bowl of ice and three bottles of Seven-Up. Jimmy had filled his and Mickey's glasses a third of the way up, mine much less. Mickey dropped a few ice cubes into each glass. Jimmy followed with the bottle of pop, filling them to just below the rims.

"Now. Gimme' a cig, Mick, if ya' don't mind."

"The pleasure's all mine," Mickey replied, handing the open pack to Jimmy. "Sure you don't want one, Skip? They go good with the whiskey."

"No, thanks. I gave them up."

We toasted one another and then began to drink. I was surprised at the sweet, pungent taste, and the mildness of the concoction, and I downed my glass almost as quickly as Jimmy and Mickey did theirs, fearing nothing more than a loud belch.

"Man, that's good!" I said setting my glass down onto the tabletop.

"Told you so. Now, let's get to work. Mick, fill em' up again. Okay, Skip, grab them scissors an start cuttin' out some letters— about this high,"Jimmy directed me with his thumb and index finger. The space between them was close to an inch, so I found some nice ones about half that size and laid into the project, knowing I would want to edit Jimmy's composition to more than four or five words. In no time at all I had a nice pile of varying style letters, and had started on highball number three, which, I found out later, Mickey had mixed with twice as much whiskey as the first and second ones. Jimmy had wasted no time in convincing me that merely holding a Chesterfield was not a sin, and would, in fact, enhance my coolness. His reasoning made perfect sense by then. Soon enough we were all laughing, spilling our drinks, and burning holes in Mrs. McGuire's carpet with our cigarettes.

I was feeling woozy and slightly uncoordinated by the time Jimmy submitted his first draft of seven badly misspelled words.

Cliford.

Hears yor wagin bakc

The Skuls

"There. That oughta' do it." He smiled and shoved the paper across the table to me. I took one look at it and started to laugh uncontrollably.

"God, iz perfec, esept you don' know how to spell worse a shit! But, thas good cuz they prolly don't either. How zhew ever get outta firsh grade?"

We rolled on the floor over that one for quite a while. I think.

I woke up sometime later, lying on top of my sleeping bag with an unstoppable urge to turn my entire stomach inside out. Empty it. Scour it with gallons of pure Rocky Mountain spring water. Die. I did empty it, over and over again for what seemed an eternity. The taste of rotten whiskey mixed, not with Seven-Up, but with bile, made me puke some more until there was nothing left to throw up except air. I cursed myself for my inability to say no to my friends, and cursed my friends for their seemingly boundless proclivity to introduce me to vices. Vices which didn't appear to affect their ability to function. They were gone.

I crawled across the yard to the hose bib at the corner of the house and turned the faucet on full blast. I prayed that this natural instinct to drown myself with the beverage so graciously given to mankind by God would ease the pain in my skull. It helped in a way, to the extent that the cold water hitting my empty stomach made me wretch one more time. That time the vomit erupting out of my mouth tasted sweet at least. The worst was over I thought. I crawled back across the lawn, into the bag, and mercifully passed out again.

The sun bouncing off the greenhouse glass across the street awakened me with spears of pure agony. The worst was not over. The Indian neighbors' cat sat directly in my line of vision beyond the pool of vomit, and meowed when I opened my eyes. How I wished I could have traded lives with one of his in that moment.

Water, I discovered, was not a cure for a raging drunk. A hangover. I'd heard the word many times in our household, and now I knew its meaning precisely. Remembrance of the gentle tapping on my shoulder last evening, quickly followed by the image of Adam and Eve standing naked in the Garden, pointing their fingers at one another, flooded my brain. There stood the Creator in front of them shaking His finger. "See, I told you not to eat that apple, didn't I?" I somehow knew that Moses had screwed up in his translation of the text. They hadn't eaten an apple at all. Fruit is good. On that tree grew bottles of Old Crow. Of that I was positive.

"Woke up, huh?"

I turned to see who was doing the shouting. It was Jimmy, on his hands and knees peering down at me. The first thing I noticed was that his hair stood out like Frankenstein's bride's, but that wasn't the worst of him. His eyes were bloodshot and half-closed, and from two feet away I could smell his sweet, rancid, whiskey-tainted breath. Beyond him, Mickey was still dead to the world inside his flannel bag, no doubt as bad off as me.

"Oh God, don't shout," I muttered.

"I ain't. I'm whisperin'! How ya' feelin'?"

"Like a truck just ran over my head. What happened last night? How'd I get out here?"

He related how after my speech on how I thought I might try counting every star in the Milky Way later on that evening, I fell backward without a sound onto the carpet and had to be dragged out to my place of rest. He and Mickey had done their best to clean up the mess we'd made in his mother's living room, he said, and then after checking to see that I was still breathing, they took the wagon and the letter down to Clifford's house.

"Mickey kept stumblin' into trash cans, and fallin' down. I thought sure we was gonna' get busted with all the racket he made. But I got 'im back home. He had one more drink than you, too. I'm surprised he made it as long as he did."

"Did you tape the letter on the wagon?"

"Oh yeah! After you passed out we changed it a little though."

"What do you mean?"

"Well, Mickey thought it'd be a good idea to add Inky and Butch's name—under the Skulls—so we did. How do ya' spell Minkle?"

"Oh God. Tell me you didn't."

"Yeah, sure did! We figured Clifford's folks wouldn't know The Skulls from who laid the chunk, so addin' their names just made sense. An' better yet, we lugged the wagon through the yard an put it right outside their back door! Whoever goes out first this morning is gonna' trip right over it!"

Had I not gotten drunk, that terrible, tragic, idiotic, deadly mistake would never have happened. My bumbling, drunken friends had just put up a neon sign in Jimmy's front yard for Inky and Butch to see. "HERE THEY ARE!"

"Oh God. Just shoot me here and now," I whimpered.

"Huh?"

"You stupid jerks! Clifford's mom and dad are going to march right up to the Minkles' house, whether you butchered the spelling of their name or not! With that tricycle wheel—you stole!—Oh God. Did you think that maybe someone might wonder why there's only three good wheels...why would Inky want to steal a goddam' wagon wheel? And why would he sign his name to a letter. Goddamit' you're stupid sometimes, Jimmy. They're going to come flying down here again!"

"Nah..."

"Yeah! Uh-huh! Who else would they think would do something like that except us? And what if the Childers believe them when they swear it was us, not them, who swiped that stupid Clifford's wagon? Crap almighty. I can't believe you did that!"

At that moment we heard a terrible crash three doors down. To me it sounded exactly like a body smashing into a wagon with three and a half wheels. Then I heard a man's voice cursing in a way that my mom could never imagine possible.

Not very long after that, after I'd prayed fervently to another dozen powerful saints, said three more acts of contrition, and promised Jesus I'd for sure turn over a new leaf if He'd get me out of this one (again), I caught sight of an enraged Mrs. Childers, Clifford and Annie, and a limping Mr. Childers, parading single file up the street in the direction of the Minkles'. When they'd gotten out of sight I turned to Jimmy with a scowl.

"I'm going home. Don't ever talk to me again!"

Mom and Pop had missed all the fun, at least the fun I'd had. If you could call throwing up fun. They must have slept through all the cursing down at the Childers', too, though I couldn't see how. I think Mr. Childers must have been an actor, used to projecting his voice, and doing it with great conviction.

I stumbled down the steps to the cool, dark basement, and crawled into bed, praying that I'd go stone deaf for at least the next month. Every single noise was ten thousand fingernails screeching across a blackboard all at once. I could hear the spiders in my room tramping across their webs, like soldiers with hobnail boots on concrete. I cursed myself again, and pulled the sheet over my face in order to make the darkened room darker. Darker. Oh Jesus, Mary, and Joseph, how my head hurt. Light hurt. Sound hurt. My thoughts even hurt.

I fell asleep and dreamed of an invasion by Martians. Strange, gangly-limbed creatures with huge bug-eyes, antennae, and ray guns. They'd padded down the ramp of their flying saucer, one after another, scanning the area around the craft menacingly. I found myself sitting a short distance away, on a hillock watching, somehow unable to move. The sheer terror of their presence had paralyzed me. A group of the slick-bodied creatures gathered at the base of the ramp, and then looked back at the gaping hole of the entry. Jimmy sauntered out, holding a wagon wheel in his hand, then stopped and pointed up the hill directly at me.

"He's the one! He drank the whole bottle. Get 'im!"

Before I could even scream, twenty pairs of wiggling legs and green, flapping feet, brought them rushing on top of me. I closed my eyes and prayed, but I knew that nobody in heaven was listening. The creatures beat me silly with their guns and fists, while from the distance I could hear Jimmy laughing and egging them on.

"He's a fuckin' sissy. Get 'im! He's..."

I woke up with a start, sweating. The words Jimmy had been cackling in the nightmare were coming through the window of my room, but it wasn't him doing the speaking. The voice sounded all too familiar. It was Inky's. A conversation ensued that was staccato-like, confusing.

"It wasn't us..."

"Shuddup..."

"Hit 'im..."

Fists pummeling bodies, scuffling, more laughter and pleas for mercy from the mouths of Jimmy and Mick.

My head cleared immediately as the shock of realizing what was going on next door hit me like a board in the face. I jumped to the window and looked out through pain-filled eyes onto a sight that filled me with despair. My apocalyptic prediction had come true. Inky had Jimmy in a headlock with one arm, pounding his face with his free fist. Close by, Butch had Mickey trapped under his knee, working him over with both fists.

Upstairs, the muted sounds from Mom's and Pop's voices filtering through the floor joined the barrage of noises from outside. I heard the bedsprings creak, followed by the thunk of the first pair of feet landing on the carpet.

Frozen at the window, I weighed the gravity of the situation my friends had found themselves sucked into. Jimmy and Mickey might be scoundrels, I might not ever talk to them again, but I couldn't stand by and watch them taking the beating of their lives. As I hit the steps leading up to the back porch, the shrill voice of my mom surely woke the dead. "Oh Christ, LaVerne! Somebody's wailin' the daylights out of Jimmy and Skippy!"

Before either of my folks could possibly have gathered up a robe and house shoes I was over the fence and headed straight for Inky. Jimmy's neck was still firmly in Inky's powerful vice, and blood was streaming out of what I thought was still his nose. His arms dangled like wet rags, and his knees had buckled. Jimmy was taking the ten count, but Inky continued in his effort to punch a whole clear through his head. And then he spotted me and let Jimmy fall to the grass. Both his fists went up as I approached at a dead run. I should have stopped, help wasn' t far behind me, but I lowered my head and barreled on.

That's a common mistake in fighting, I thought. *A huge blunder...* The first blow I received was a right cross—or maybe it was a left, I couldn't be certain. It all happened so fast. It caught me squarely in one eye a mere heartbeat before the next one landed on the other eye. That halted my forward progress and dispelled any further notion of my being able to rescue my KO-ed friend. I fell backward onto my butt and witnessed a shower of stars in front of my face unlike anything I'd seen in the sky during the previous weeks. Butch muttered something in his trollish accent, perhaps just a congratulatory laugh. It was all mixed up with the bells clanging in my head, and another sound behind me. The chainlink fence rattling, followed by the clomp of feet landing on the grass. Pop had arrived.

The rules of civility and fairness clearly stated that an adult must never physically attack a minor. It was a common sense rule of civilized society and my family had always adhered to it, until Pop threw propriety out the window that morning and cold-cocked Inky. Lying flat on my back looking up at a dizzying array of flashing lights that had replaced the stars, I heard the solid connection of knuckles on bone, and then the voice of my usually always-quiet dad.

"You stupid son-of-a-bitch! What the hell do you think you're doin'?" Of course Inky was incapable of responding.

The fireworks display in my brain began to clear about that time, and out of the corner of my eye I caught a glimpse of Butch sneaking up behind Pop with a sawed-off baseball bat in one hand, and a look of pure hate on his face. Mickey was down for the count, he was no help, and I wasn't much better off. Butch raised the bat when he'd gotten within striking distance of Pop, but that was as far as he got. Mom appeared out of nowhere on his blind side with her frying pan, and I swear I'll never forget the terrific gong it made when it met that monster's skull. Butch collapsed beside Jimmy and Inky. Jimmy's backyard suddenly looked like the ring of Friday Night Wresting after Bobo Brazil had taken on all comers. All I could do was smile.

The cops came, the neighbors came, even Mrs. McGuire, who'd arrived home half an hour ago, stumbled out of the house with her bottle in her right hand. The Childers, of course, waltzed up the driveway, and soon enough even Inky's folks joined the free-for-all. Mickey, Jimmy, Butch, and Inky had all awakened, and everyone was yelling at once, fists raised, fire shooting from everyone's eyes, and out of their ears. Two cops with batons drawn finally separated the combatants and then took statements, none of which seemed to make any sense to them. This went on for thirty minutes or more at full volume, until the Minkles, the Childers, the Jungs, the Indian family, the confused Lindens, and even Mrs. McGuire were ushered off the property with a stern warning not to return.

I was heralded a hero. Jimmy and Mickey played dumb about the entire incident, and fortunately for the three of us the black eyes we received miraculously, and completely, masked the whiskey induced condition of our eyeballs. We were off the hook, as even the great Joe Friday would never have been able to crack the case of the mysterious letter left on the wagon with three and a half wheels.

TWENTY-ONE

To Hell With The Cyclops

I healed rapidly, that is my insides, at least, rebounded back to a state of something near to normal in no time at all. Within a day the craving for water diminished, and I was able to see clearly again, although it was through eyes belonging more to the face of Petey, the dog in The Little Rascals. My consumption of food at the dinner table began to rival that of Pop's, too. Defying all logic, he became a regular Cicero for some strange reason after the melee next door, expounding on a variety of subjects as varied as the stars in our galaxy. I had no idea he was such a Renaissance man.

"You know, Skippy," he ventured one evening during a commercial as we sat in the living room watching TV. "There's something I've been meaning to talk to you about for some time, now." He had thirty seconds before Lawrence Welk came back on.

"What is it, Pop?"

"Well, it's this business of where baby's come from. You might have heard by now that storks don't really drop them down chimneys."

"I figured as much. Seeing as how we don't have a fireplace, that is. I mean, I'd never have gotten here..."

"Yes, true." He stood up and began to pace back and forth across the floor like Sister Mary Constance—"the runner" we called her in Math class at school. Unlike that kindly nun, who'd probably never even heard the word sex, Pop looked peculiarly nervous, anticipating how to call forth the precise words to describe my conception. It wasn't a simple matter like multiplying or dividing twenty digit numbers, or finding the square root of a gazillion and three, and somehow I knew he was going to botch the effort. But once he'd opened the door and stepped into the room, not even the king of polka music could pull him back out. Or rescue him.

"Ahem," he said taking a deep breath and not daring to look at me, "you see, it begins like this..."

Lawrence bid the TV audience goodnight half an hour later, and poor old Pop was still stammering, doing his best to paint an oral picture of how I'd gotten made. His version was considerably different than Jimmy's, but in essence their renditions matched up fairly well. I sat through the entire uncomfortable episode without uttering a word, but when it was over, I spoke.

"Yeah, Pop, I know all that. Jimmy already told me, and besides, my bedroom is right below yours and Mom's."

Which was greater, his embarrassment at having done what no father probably relishes doing, or his shock at my having actually heard their bedsprings singing away, I couldn't be sure of, but he turned redder than Mom had when I busted in on them in the kitchen a few weeks back. He sat down again, and we watched Gunsmoke together in complete silence.

Pop schooled me in other areas, too, none as difficult for him as sex education, however. Basketball was one of them.

Somehow he'd squeezed enough money out of the pot to buy a backboard and rim a day or two after the sex thing, and although we had no concrete in the backyard, save the crumbling sidewalks, he mounted it onto the gable end of the garage anyway. We were going to play "lawn basketball".

"They play tennis in England on grass, you know," he informed me as he tried to bounce the ball on the moon-like surface below his feet. "Tennis is a much faster game, too. Go fetch that ball, would ya' Skippy?"

I ran after the ball wondering how the Brits could possibly manage playing any real games over there. It was no wonder they'd had to call us up to bail them out of the last war.

"Thanks, son. Now, the idea is to fake the person guarding you—here, you stand over there between me and the basket—the idea is to do this." He dribbled the ball with both hands, as it was impossible for him to control it with one, or make it to go straight up and down like it did for the Harlem Globetrotters. Between bounces, he'd glance up at me. I crouched forward a little, the way I'd seen Bob Cousy do it many times, and I sneered at him just a bit for effect. Suddenly he stopped dribbling, shifted left, then right, and then lit out around me as though I'd been completely fooled by his brilliant deception. I let him go by. One more pitiful dribble and then he was airborne. The artist of the court on wings. While in the air, both hands lifting the ball upward with unparalleled grace, his eyes became fixed on the hoop like a hawk's on a chicken, and the reality of the building standing less than a foot away disappeared entirely to his painful detriment. He hit the tin wall of the garage with a mighty crash.

I rushed to his prostrate figure, wishing I'd blocked him, or at least screamed, "Look out!" He lay there dazed for a moment, then rolled over and looked up at me with a smile.

"Guess we'll have to buy a big pole to mount that thing on instead, eh, Skippy?"

"I dunno', Pop. Think of the damage you could do to yourself running into solid steel."

"Yes, you're probably right." He asked me to help him to his feet, and then had me fetch the ball once again. "You stay out here and practice dribbling and faking. I think I'll go lie down for a bit, okay, Skippy?"

"Sure, Pop."

He limped into the house. I looked at the rutted ground again, and then I tossed the ball into the bushes next to the fence and went next door to see what Jimmy was up to.

Jimmy was still a mess. Inky had nearly succeeded in making his face a candidate for the plastic surgeon's knife. The bandages and stitches had all been removed, but he was still black and blue from ear to ear, and his nose, I swear, had been repositioned about an inch to the left. It had been flattened, too, so that he looked like a third-rate boxer, long overdue for retirement.

I found him in his bedroom. It was a Tuesday, mid-morning, and the only thing worth a darn to watch on TV was...there was nothing worth a darn on TV at that time of day. So, he was amusing himself by throwing darts at a rough sketch of Inky pinned on the wall between his bed and dresser, in the field of pits we'd left. He turned to greet me when I walked through the open door, and smiled, showing off a missing incisor, one of Inky's last gifts to him before my dad arrived. He pointed at it with his free hand.

"The dentist Mother took me to said it wouldn't grow back. After I get older he can put a fake one in though. Till then, every time I look in the mirror I'll be reminded of how that bastard an' his brother snuck up on me and Mick. Good thing you went home when ya' did."

I laughed. "I got my fair share of the beating too, you know."

Jimmy turned without bothering to answer and threw the dart. He'd been practicing I could see. It stuck in the picture of Inky, right in the mouth alongside a hundred or so other holes.

"What do you think we ought to do?" I asked as he walked across the room to retrieve the dart.

"'Bout what?"

"About getting our butts kicked every time we leave the yard."

"I dunno' about you, but I'm gonna' start carryin' a knife." He pointed to the end of his bed. I have no idea where he found it, but there on the top of the covers lay a two foot-long sword...a machete. I wondered how he thought he'd be able to conceal something that big, or worse, how he thought he could possibly use it in a fight with Inky or Butch. It hit me that the missing tooth and scarred face, the perforated picture of Inky on the wall—all of it pointed to a real hatred for the older kid up the street. He meant to kill him next time they met.

"I don't think it'd be a good idea to carry that thing around," I said.

"I don't think it'd be a good idea to let him kick my ass ever again," he replied, pitching the dart at Inky once again. "Hey, you hear from Mick lately?"

"Not since he phoned last week."

"Oh. Me neither. Wonder how he's doin'? Butch wailed on him pretty good, but somehow he musta' blocked most of the punches and kicks. I din't see much blood on his face after we got up."

"Me neither, but everything was such a mess. All I really remember seeing was you all beat...you know, with all the blood on your face." I wished I hadn't said that. I knew that even though Jimmy was not in Inky's class in a street battle, he wasn't a coward when he was cornered in a fair fight. I'm certain the words I'd chosen had only added another wound.

"Skip! Skippy!" The shrill voice of my mom coming through the open window broke the uncomfortable silence after my remark. I took the opportunity to exit the conversation with Jimmy, and ran to the window.

"Yeah, Mom, what is it?"

"Could ya' come home? I need to send ya' down to the drugstore."

"Sure, Mom. Be right there." I turned and saw Jimmy looking down at the machete lying on the end of the bed, tapping the darts in his hand on the other opened palm. "Gotta' go. I'll check back later, okay?"

He seemed lost in his thoughts and didn't answer until I'd gotten to his bedroom door. "Yeah, sure. See ya' later."

I left, very worried that something terrible lay on the horizon for my best friend. Mom met me at the front steps with her hand outstretched.

"Here's a dollar-fifty. Go on down to the drugstore on First Avenue an'get a bottle of aspirin. Get some Bactine or somethin', too. Your father has a headache and some scratches I gotta' clean up. Hurry up, now."

"Is he okay?" I asked, taking the bill and change from her hand.

"Yes, he'll be fine. I don't want you draggin' him out there to play basketball anymore, though. He's too old for that stuff. Now, get goin' with you."

"Okay, Mom. I'll for sure hurry."

I wanted to tell her that it was Pop's idea to teach me the finer points of lawn basketball, not mine, but decided to skip it. He was probably lying in bed moaning, and needed the medicine worse than I needed to try to correct Mom. She wouldn't hear my side of the story anyway.

I thought about going in the opposite direction, up to the corner to Mrs. Rashure's tiny store where I could probably find some aspirin and antiseptic just as easily, but that was in the direction of the Minkle's house, which wasn't a good idea at all. After checking to see that the coast was clear, I ran the distance to the end of the block, away from Inky and Mrs. Rashure and Butch...and away from the mortal danger to my stomach because of that switchblade. When I passed the Childers' house, I casually looked the other way, hoping Clifford's parents weren't sitting on their front porch just waiting for me to amble by. There was another meeting I had no desire to face.

First Avenue, the street under which the gulch flowed a couple of blocks to the west, was a main artery of sorts, taking traffic from Federal Boulevard, a mile to the east, all the way to the foothills, dozens of miles to the west. The stretch from Meade street to Knox Court, the corner on which the Comet Theater sat, provided a place for Larry's Barber Shop, the drugstore, a small hardware store, a gas station, and several other commercial establishments.

I arrived at the drugstore, the best maintained shop of the ragged lot, and did my business, thanking Mr. Samuelson for his speedy service before I left. Across the street at the Comet I noticed a brand new movie advertised on their marquee, "The Cyclops". Lon Chaney, Jr.'s name sat just below the title, and on the color poster pasted in the large window on the left next to the ticket booth, the image of a horrible, one-eyed creature glared out of a jungle setting. In the foreground, two figures, a man, and a terrified woman with her hands covering her screaming mouth, looked out at me, warning me that the thing behind them intended, I assumed, to catch and eat us all. I checked my pocket for the change Mr. Samuelson had given me. Twenty-five cents. Enough for the ten-cent admission, a coke, and a small bag of popcorn. Maybe Jimmy would want to come back later with me for the afternoon matinee, if I could talk Mom into letting me keep the change. With Lon Chaney Jr. starring in it, it had to be a terrific movie.

Five minutes later I turned the corner onto Meade Street and headed home. I'd been humming a song from Elvis' latest movie, "Jailhouse Rock", for the last couple of blocks, stepping lively, at ease once again, looking forward to grabbing Jimmy and heading back to the Comet later on.

Halfway up the street I glanced to my right, and every thought in my head vanished all at once, as if a lightbulb had suddenly burned out up there. Standing near the garden below the wooden porch of the small house with a hose in her hand, and looking out at me, was the dancer. I don't know if she'd disapproved of my loud humming, was put off by my two black eyes, or simply didn't like me for some other reason. Yet, there she was, staring at me. I was embarrassed and felt the blood in my ankles rush up to my face, but I stopped dead and looked back at her anyway, frozen by her beauty, forgetting all about Miss Marilou Jenkins.

Her hair—the light red-auburn masterpiece—was fixed up in ringlets, and her rouge cheeks were perfectly set above the loveliest, tiniest mouth—even more stunning—and she also wore those glasses. Not the ugly Allen-glasses that made a person look stupid, but nice looking ones. Ones that didn't want to make me yank them off and step on them. I imagined removing them, though, and touching her dark brown lashes with my fingertips. Finally, after several moments, or days, maybe, of staring like a moron at her, I gathered up my courage and spoke.

"Could you take your glasses off?"

"WHAT?"

Those weren't the best first words to say, but I was stuck with them. "Well, I just want to see your face without glasses. Could you take them off?"

"You're an idiot. Go away, whoever you are."

"My name's Skip. What's yours?"

"None of your business. Skip. What happened to your face?"

My face. I'd forgotten about my two black eyes. I must look like something out of a horror movie to her. I had to think quickly, lost in love as I was at that moment.

"I got in a fight. The other guy is in the hospital."

"Really?"

"Yes. He was bigger than me, too."

"One of the guys who was chasing you a month or two ago?"

"No. Someone else. Bigger, too."

"My goodness! So you're a tough guy, huh?"

"Only when I have to be I guess. Would you take off your glasses?" She did, and then dropped the hose and walked out toward me. It was true. The closer she got, the more beautiful she became, like Elizabeth Taylor, only a thousand times better.

"Can you see me ok?" I asked.

"Of course I can! I'm not blind, you know, just a little nearsighted. My eye doctor says he wants me to wear these glasses until I'm fourteen, then my eyes will be better."

Fourteen! That was promising. "How old are you?"

"Twelve and a half. I was born on September 10th. I'll be thirteen pretty soon. How old are you?"

"I'm thirteen, too, almost. My birthday is in August, though. I'm older than you—but not much!"

She smiled. I nearly fainted, and wanted to ask her then and there if she'd mind if I kissed her, but I thought that might be pushing it too far, too soon. I'd dreamt about it, fantasized and wondered how far I could go before it all became a mortal sin, but I'd never kissed a real live girl. Except my mom, and that was only on the cheek, thank goodness. My head was reeling. I felt a dizziness far different than the one that hit me when I'd smoked that first cigarette. An altogether pleasant lightheadedness.

"My name is Carol," she said reaching her hand out to me. I took hold of it, and that is when I completely lost control. I felt a dribble in my jeans. I was beginning to pee my pants. Her hand was silk, and satin, and soft, and should I stand there with my jeans soaked, I could have cared less. I didn't want to let loose of her. Ever. So this is what love did to you, I thought. Made you fall head over heels and pee your pants.

I was brought crashing back down to earth when Carol abruptly pulled her hand out of mine.

"Well, Skip, I have to go. I have to finish watering. It was nice meeting you. Maybe I'll see you again one of these days?"

I blinked. *You can bet on that!* "Yeah, sure thing. I gotta' go, too," I said lifting the little bag in my hand upward. "My dad's sick. Needs this medicine and...when do you think I'll see you again, Carol?"

She had turned and was walking back across the saturated lawn to the hose. She answered without looking back. "Oh, I don't know. Whenever. I have to go to dance class at two-thirty. If you wanted, maybe you could walk with me. Bye."

Walk with her? That sounded a lot like an invitation to me. I turned and headed up the street toward my house, looking back at her every other step. Two-thirty couldn't come soon enough. To hell with "The Cyclops".

Well anyway, Pop was probably in a state of near total collapse by then, and Mom was probably cussing a blue streak. As much as I didn't want to lose sight of magnificent Carol, I took off running—jumping, singing, laughing out loud, and confident that my world had just been thrust through the gates of Heaven into the lap of God. I was absolutely certain love had descended on me for the very first time in my life, and it was more than I could ever have dreamed of.

TWENTY-TWO

No Joy In Mudville

The rest of the day dragged by, towed by snails. Endless, endless seconds, and micro-seconds. I counted every one of them sitting in my room, the radio blaring, the lights ablaze, my stomach doing flip-flops every time I mouthed her name. "C-A-R-O-L". It fit perfectly, rolled off my tongue so easily, so naturally. Maybe she spelled it Karel, or Carrol, I began to think...or maybe I'd heard it wrong standing there in that swoon? It could have been Karen, for crying out loud! No, no. I'd heard it plainly enough. It was Carol all right. Anyway, the exact spelling wouldn't matter until I sent her the first gift. Flowers or something. Candy, perhaps. Maybe just a love letter. What, I wondered, *did* guys send to their girlfriends? Poetry from the heart was all I could afford, but I stunk at writing poems.

The little clock on my nightstand said two-twelve. Half an hour later it said two-thirteen. Great, I thought, in twenty more years it'd be two-thirty, and then I could go see her again. Just great. By that time I'd probably be dead. I tried shaking the clock for a while, hoping it would magically jump forward. No luck.

"Skip. Oh, Skippy! Come up here right now. Hurry it up."

That sounded an awful lot like Mom in one of her "maybe I'll murder him, maybe I won't moods". Which was it, I asked myself? I quickly went down the list of possible new offenses that needed to be answered for. I felt clean, except for those thoughts of naked earth girls. I hoped she couldn't get in my head. Nah.

Two twenty-two.

I skulked up the stairs, wondering what it was that Mom wanted to say to me. Hopefully it would take only five minutes. Not a second more. It had to, because I had a date, and the rocket trip north to Carol's house would take about three whole minutes. I opened the old door with a hefty shove and immediately wished I hadn't. I could see Mom through the doorway opening leading to the dining alcove, next to the ice box, and I could hear the nasaly voice of someone whose presence I abhorred. Allen was in there with her somewhere. Allen The Snake Charmer, The Talker, The Guy Who Had The Power To Wreck My Afternoon—my entire life. Allen Jung. Mom didn't turn her head or even bother to glance in my direction when I closed the door behind me.

Allen's voice came bouncing off the linoleum floor, the ice box, the walls, the ceiling, and even the gingham curtains covering the windows from somewhere near the doorway leading out to the patio. He was blabbering away, and when I poked my head around the corner of the archway I spotted him...and his mother, either politely holding her tongue, or else bewitched by his words. The little gathering bordered on the ridiculous. Mom stood quietly, hands clutching her tea towel as though it were a gigantic set of rosary beads, as though she were in the presence of some emissary from Rome. But of course nothing could be farther from the truth. At best, Allen could only be an emissary from Wittenberg, and that spelled serious trouble in the eating area of the Morley sanctuary. Pop sat at the table in his designated spot, with his left hand wrapped around a bottle of beer, and his right hand holding a pencil that he tapped gently on his bruised and bandaged forehead as he swam in his own insulated world of words. In front of him on the table lay the folded page of the Denver Post, opened to the day's crossword puzzle. Whatever was going on around him, he had not even the remotest interest in it.

I walked in, shooting Mom a quick quizzical look, and before I'd gotten two steps, Allen faltered in his speech, then started up again, directing his comments at me.

"Skip! Oh, I'm *so* glad to see you! Mother and I decided that you should attend my 12th birthday extravaganza. You are the first on my list of friends! We've come just to invite you." He turned to his mom who stood behind him pensively, one hand on the edge of the rear door leading out to the patio, the other on his shoulder. A wise thing to do on her part, I thought, because should Mom get tired of listening to his nutty ramblings and decide to do something severe, Mrs. Jung could have that door back open and her son yanked out before you could blink.

I glanced over Mom's shoulder at the clock on the wall next to the icebox. Two twenty-four. There was no time for politeness or congenial formalities. "Sure, I'll be there. Thanks."

As I tried to skirt around Allen and his steel-faced mother I noticed that even through the thick lenses of his glasses his eyes had grown to the size of quarters. Trouble. He wasn't going to be content simply to acknowledge my curt acceptance; it looked like he wanted to visit for a while with me and my family, tell us how the moon was formed out of yellow cheese, not green. Visit with me, the guy who liked him so much that he let him skid down the bank and take a dive in the drink back in April. This kid was a glutton for punishment. What *was* he thinking!

Mrs. Jung remained welded to the spot she'd chosen and I had to hesitate in my move for the door, which gave Mom the opportunity to push the conversation into the area I didn't want, nor had the time for. "Just where do you think you're goin' all in such a hurry," she asked. The question I didn't want to answer.

Allen's mom crooked her mouth slightly at one corner, either her version of a smile, or, more likely, a sneer. She'd probably never gotten the stains out of Allen's creek clothes— but that simply wasn't my fault. I didn't think she wanted to be in our house, but now that she was, she was bound and determined to make my life uncomfortable I think.

I looked back at the clock, cursing Allen and his mom's lousy timing. Two twenty-five. A kind of panic began to set in, and I prayed that I could come up with a quick, reasonable, acceptable answer, then get the hell out of there. "Uh...to the library. Gotta' run before it closes. Excuse me, Mrs. Jung."

Mom might have bought that except for Allen's next statement. And who but the boy genius would have known such a fact?

"Oh my! You have plenty of time, Skip. It doesn't close until five today, and even at five Mrs. Krumbody is often times..." He rambled on. His mom refused to budge. I was forced to shake my head yes several times in the next 2-1/2 minutes, smiling, glancing stupidly at the clock every other second, cursing Allen's inability to say in a hundred sentences what any normal person could say in one. If I missed Carol on account of him, I swore to myself that I'd find a pot big enough to hold him, then boil him in oil.

At two twenty-nine Allen finally shut up.

"Thanks. I'll be there. Bye." I flew out the back door and jetted toward the street. I'd never make it. I knew that. As I hit the front gate I could still hear Mom yelling for me to get back in there and...whatever.

Please Saint...Somebody. Make her late! Make her wait just another couple of minutes!

The Lindens', the Frankel's, the Childers', the Jung's. The houses rushed by me in a blur. I was Mercury, but I feared that wouldn't be enough. I crossed Ellsworth Avenue in two gigantic steps. Five more houses—or was it six—I could see a tiny piece of Carol's house, the home of a real live princess! And then I found myself directly in front of it. I was there.

She wasn't.

Maybe she'd walk out of that beautiful door any second. I'd wait. *Oh God, You're the guy I need to talk to. Your saints aren't listening! You gotta' help me out here. Please don't let her be gone. Please! That's the last favor I'll ever ask from You, I promise!*

Maybe I just oughta' march up there and knock on...no. Can't do that. What would they think? I never knocked on any girl's door in my whole life. Still...what harm in it? I mean, what's the worst they could do to me?

Shoot you, Skip.

I heard that answer, and it wasn't me offering it. That had to be Him. I was screwed.

In his great wisdom and imponderable ways, God must definitely have decided that it would be better if I didn't walk Carol to dance class that afternoon. I was devastated, naturally. I stood there in front of her house like a love-struck Romeo, shoulders slumped, words of deep affection on the tip of my tongue, but my Juliet had gone away without me. And all because of that damned four-eyed, loudmouthed Allen Jung and his doting, unmovable mother. My mom hadn't helped, either. She could have thrown them out long before I ever got upstairs. She could have.

I decided then and there to run away. I realized immediately though, that if I did, the only reasonable new address would be Carol's. I'd have to sneak into her backyard and take up residence in her dog's house. If she owned a dog. That was a bad idea, so I finally turned after ten minutes of sniveling and headed back home. I swore I wouldn't talk to my mom ever again even if she chained me up and beat me, and I swore I'd get even with Allen somehow.

***

· The sky had begun to darken outside Jimmy's bedroom. A thin coverlet of gray pushed a vanguard of puffy white, peaceful-looking little clouds eastward in the direction the late afternoon winds traveled. A black tidal wave followed, exploding veins of lightning and tremendous cannons of thunder roiling through its interior. We could easily have been standing in Dr. Frankenstein's rock-walled laboratory, looking up at God's wrath, watching the monster rise to life, shaking in our boots. But as it happened we were rolling on the floor in laughter at the foot of Jimmy's bed.

"I-I-I-I-I...like 'em!"

Jimmy agreed with Allen, or his mom, or whoever had decided that what we'd both received was simply marvelous. Yes, yes—the invitation *was* Allen, no doubt about it. Well, it was somehow appropriate. Definitely hilarious. The sky outside answered tit for tat our thunder bursts of laughter after we'd opened the invitations. In a few days Allen's party was slated to kick off. It was now official, on stationery, bold, RSVP. My best friend and I were really going to go to the Allen "extravaganza." And we were going to behave ourselves. That was sort of my solemn intention. Well, no it wasn't. We'd just have to be careful

157

doing whatever we were going to plan on doing. Actually, it was the invitations that pushed me over the edge.

The Zane Grey inspired front face of the card read:

Howdy, Pardner!
Y'all just gotta' come and help
lasso some steers!

In those horribly penned words Allen had asked all his best friends, of which Jimmy and I were somehow numbered, to come to his twelfth birthday party. There was no doubt in my mind that Frederic Remington himself had painted the scene beneath it. No doubt. A clean-scrubbed young buckaroo (about twelve years-old, I reckoned) sat atop a pony in a hell-bent gallop across a tumbleweed-infested prairie. Yep, pardner, that there cowboy would be Allen Jung, without the fruity looking, black horn rimmed glasses, of course. The cowboy sported wooly chaps, a wide-brimmed, white hat, a guitar slung (incredibly) across his back, and a lasso whirling overhead like a prairie cyclone. He rode his black and white pinto freehand, intently, fearlessly, as he and the pony raced across the dusty range, right on the heels of a terrified Texas Longhorn steer that was bigger than both him and his snorting horse put together. The terrified cow could simply have stopped dead in its tracks, turned, and gored both Allen and ole' Scout to death if it had wanted. That is what I thought as I looked at it, wondering how many of Allen's doofy friends were rolling on the floor themselves right that moment in tears of laughter.

"These are t'rrific invitations, Skip!" Jimmy laughed.

"Yeah, that they are, and that's him alright. Before his eyes went south I guess, but that's definitely him. Roy Rogers as a kid. Good grief!"

"Did Mick get invited?" Jimmy asked.

"Dunno'. I haven't talked to him this week. I hope so. It probably won't take the three of us to make him whine, but it'll be more fun if we're all there, don't you think?"

"Yep. I think Mick should be there. Yes, I do. Absolutely."

"Okay, good. I mean, we don't have to make Allen bleed or anything, but...well, he's just such a dink. Crap, he practically invites people to pick on him. If he'd just keep his mouth shut, stop pulling his pants up to his chest—you know, act like a guy instead of a sissy. And not invite us to any more of his ride 'em and rope 'em birthday parties..."

As I spoke I could see Jimmy's tongue moving inside his mouth, as though he were rubbing the tip of it over the spot the incisor once occupied. For a moment he said nothing, stared past my shoulder, a tiny bit glassy-eyed. Finally he snapped his eyes onto mine and spoke. "Ya' 'spose Inky and Butch think we're sissies?" Jimmy's mood had suddenly changed.

The storm kicked up a notch, sending gale winds and rain and hail smashing into the neighborhood in its path. Late afternoon had very quickly turned into the look of nighttime as the storm bore down on us. Though I couldn't see very far through the blackness, I could hear the sound of the trees in my yard getting thrashed, begging for mercy as their leaves were stripped and flung eastward. Jimmy cocked his head up, then went to the west-facing window that had been open during the opening salvo of water spraying against the screen. He closed it and then sat quietly on the end of his bed, looking at his reflection in the dresser mirror near the closet door, cracking the right side of his mouth open to expose the empty space.

"I'm gonna' pay that sonofabitch back for this, ya' know."

I looked over at him. He meant it I knew. I couldn't guess what depth of trouble that spelled, but suddenly Allen's un-hipness paled. I thought in that moment that I would rather live with a hundred Allens, go to a thousand neighborhood disasters with him, rather than spend one second with Inky or Butch.

TWENTY-THREE

Yippie-I-O...Shit

Allen's folks hired a clown. The Saturday of the big party the guy came dressed to the hilt in, of all things, a cowboy outfit. I thought that it was in bad taste and cast a very ugly light on cowboys everywhere, at least the kind who rode into town for the National Western Stock Show each January. Had any of those guys seen Allen's clown, I've no doubt they would have stripped him naked, snapped his bare ass with their whips, and then sent him packing back across town to wherever his clown house was located. It sure as hell couldn't be in Barnum. We would never allow clowns to live there, especially the kind who made a mockery of such a great American institution as Cowboydom.

When I saw the guy with his red ocean liner shoes, his tennis ball nose, and frizzy hair stuffed under the ten gallon hat he wore I cringed, and would have turned on my heel right then and there except that Mom had advised me not five minutes earlier in no uncertain terms to go, and, "Goddamit, Skippy, behave yourself!" No matter how silly Allen or anyone else there acted, and I guessed that included the clown. Naturally he had a horn with a big, black, round rubber bellows stuck on one end of it, and it...Oh, Lord, I remember it well...touched me as I skirted and scowled by him. He tried to goose me with that horn—while he honked it, no less. Maybe I was wrong, but had he not been about six foot-ten I know I would have called him on it. But as they say, discretion is the better part of valor. I swallowed my anger and what was left of my pride and walked on into the yard.

Jimmy and Mickey had come along with me.

"We could do somethin' to the clown, maybe. I dunno'. Start his hair on fire? I brought a matchgun," Jimmy said, pulling a brand new one out of his back pocket when we'd gotten a little past Tex the Clown on our shuffle up the driveway. "Brought some Ladyfingers, too." A group of kids about six years-old ran screaming in front of us. "It'd be cool to burn his hair up when he's playin' Hopalong Cassidy or doin' rope tricks...maybe blow off his nose, or..."

"Nope...no good. Maybe we just better leave Tex alone and go straight for Allen. He's the one who hired that fruitcake. 'Sides, that clown's bigger than all three of us put together."

As I spoke, as I began to lay out a better plan of attack on poor Allen and his even less fortunate lackey-clown, I caught sight of her. Carol. My heart murmured, clicked its heels, prodded my brain to really, really come to the party. To my dismay though, I noted that she was walking up the street toward the driveway more or less on Allen's arm. Well, more. She was with...him! In my head that was both good news and a tragedy. She was on her way, yes—though in my wildest dreams I hadn't considered that she would be invited, much less come waltzing up the walkway arm in arm with Lawrence Welk Jr. *God Almighty*, I wondered, *why would someone like her come to Dragsville with the likes of him?* Even Tex the clown stood a better chance with her than Allen. The Snake. I'd stood her up that day a few weeks ago because of stupid Allen. *That* must be why she was with him.

Carol carried a gaily-wrapped present about the size of an engagement ring box...or a wedding ring box. Maybe a "Let's go steady ring" box. Who knew? I suddenly became disoriented, lost consciousness of the clown and his annoying horn. I fixed my attention on Allen and her. Him. My girl. Him again. I—suddenly I loathed every snake in creation, horn-rimmed glasses, birthday parties—especially ones with clowns. I hated that clown. I hated that party, and my driving thought was to ruin it, bring the clown to his knees. Drive the younger kids home. Spill punch all over the spic and span patio. Hurt Allen.

I'd begun to tap the toes of one foot rapidly on the concrete surface of Allen's driveway—an old habit I'd picked up without ever knowing exactly why, whenever Mom was grilling me for having done something which I might not really even have done. My fingers had found their way onto Mick's bicep. Maybe I was trying to poke through the skin. I don't know. I don't know. A myopic vision of the world directly in front of me was all I was aware of; a world in a single, depressing shade of red.

"Hail Mary, full of grace, the Lord is with thee..." I closed my eyes and began. A flash afterimage of two figures walking happily together, hand in hand. He halted abruptly and then tugged her back to him. Took her into his red arms under the red sky in front of my blazing eyes. Then Allen kissed her. My girl. My...

"What the...? What's got into you?" Mickey stammered. "Get your fingers off...Goddamit, you're pokin' a hole in my arm!" He yanked at the claw imbedded in his muscle until I awakened with a start and released my fingers. I looked over at him as the vision dissipated in a wash of crimson down onto the concrete. Mick's eyes popped back and forth from saucer-like surprise and shock to a narrow defense—attack-if-necessary—mode. "What the hell's the matter with you?"

Jimmy had been busy in his world of plotting while all this played out, unaware that I'd melted down and tried to take Mickey's right arm with me. "I got it! You two...God, look at that twerp and his girlfriend," Jimmy said.

My knees weakened when I heard the word 'girlfriend'. The red began to re-emerge. I shot a glance back at Allen and Carol, now waltzing up the incline of the driveway together. In love, I thought. Already having planned a wedding date. The rage crept back in, and Tex bounded down to meet them. Sweet Jesus, Mary, and Joseph, it was horrible.

Goddammit', Skippy, behave yourself! But Mom had not ended her admonition with those four simple words. She'd warned me, *You start any trouble—or you let Jimmy or that Fumo kid drag you along...*I think Blessed Mary had flown like the wind from her seat at Jesus' side in the throne room high above us when she heard the plaintive beginning of my little prayer. I think she slapped my soul gently, knowing that would be so much better than having to watch Mom violently beat my ears after the cops had come dragging me up the street in the aftermath of destruction at the Jung's house. I really believed that. I don't know, though. I wasn't sure. Maybe Mary or Jesus actually liked clowns, and didn't want to see one—even one like this dressed up as a cowboy—with his wig knocked off and his tennis ball nose smashed. Or maybe she just liked Allen. I doubted that. Why would she? Protestants didn't even bother to pray to her or Joseph, her holy husband. I didn't know. But for whatever reason lost in the imponderable mind of God, the fire in my head suddenly extinguished. Another miracle.

"Hiya' fellas!" Allen spotted us.

Jimmy and Mickey instinctively understood what I was going through. Not that they were so brilliant all of a sudden, but any fool could have figured it out. The smoke pouring out of my ears, the sabers flying out of my eyes. They both grabbed an arm. My two friends—instruments of the Holy Ghost, who Mary had ordered to help me out.

"Steady there, Trigger. Easy," Jimmy whispered. He was smiling, not looking at me, but rather straight at my nemesis and my girl who were dancing over to where we stood. Tex was hot on their heels. "We'll take care of him."

"No, leave 'em be. I'm alright." Even having said that, a left-handed admission of my boundless love for Carol, it embarrassed me to no end. The cat was out of the bag entirely. My face flushed again.

I took the bull by the horns and stepped forward, handing that worthless kid the present Mom and I had picked out two days ago. The B-52 model airplane kit was in a box ten times the size of the one Carol had given to him. In that moment I wished that my present, wrapped in boring birthday print paper with a red ribbon and crushed bow, contained a couple of sticks of dynamite and a ticking clock instead of a cruddy plane. Mary slapped me again. "Happy birthday, Allen. Hi, Carol."

"Oh, thank you very much, Skip. Just place it over on the picnic table on the patio with all the others! You too, Jimmy and Mickey. I'm going to place Miss Hudson's..." and on he went in that obscene sing-song voice. Carol allowed him to tug her along. She said nothing to me or Jimmy or Mickey, didn't even look back at us. I followed them to the rear of the house, that goddam' clown clucking along beside the five of us like he didn't have a lick of sense.

"I think we oughta' just go home," I said in the most disconsolate, defeated tone of voice I could muster.

Jimmy, Mickey, and I sat on the top of the low retaining wall separating the Jung's property from the Childers'. Clifford was there in Allan's yard, too, clapping his hands each time Tex noisily twisted a long balloon and made a new animal. Jimmy was fingering his matchgun. Mick sat silently, shooting me a glance every now and then, waiting for the order to attack and kill, I thought.

Mrs. Jung exited the kitchen directly across from us with a platter of Twinkies and shot the three of us a frown. My stomach begged me to swallow my pride...but, no. She took the tray and skirted around the corner of the house where a dozen or so of Allen's other friends jumped around like little paper dolls, their trousers cinched up to their chests. Carol sat demurely off to the side, dressed like Alice straight out of Wonderland, on one of the festooned folding chairs, close to the far end of the patio. Next to her sat Allen, hands folded in his lap. The only part of him moving, of course, was his mouth.

"Well, just go over and plonk your butt down beside her, ninny!" Mickey finally said. "Do you seriously think she wouldn't pick you over...him?"

"Yeah, and while you muscle in on his girl, I'll torch the clown's hair," Jimmy added. He rose after saying that and grabbed my elbow. "Shake it off. Go get her."

"She ain't his girl!"

"Okay, okay," Mick assured me. "Go kick his butt and show him who she belongs to then." He grabbed my other arm, and between the two of them, they launched me halfway across the driveway.

Allen was busy rambling fifty miles an hour to her about something or other and didn't notice me. Carol, on the other hand, did. I know I saw her eyes brighten—her beautiful eyes resting like two pearls behind the lovely lenses of her stylish glasses. They begged for me to fly to her and rescue her from his unwanted assault. That was it! I understood everything perfectly. The little present she'd given to him was probably a Cracker Jacks trinket! Of course! He'd walked on down to her house earlier, and being the polite goddess that she was, Carol allowed him to escort her back up to his party. God, was I dumb! *Thank you, Blessed Mary!* I vowed to offer a Novena to my wonderful mother in heaven as soon as I could get myself up to church. Of course, after I'd stolen Tex's white horse, wherever he'd hidden it in the yard, and ridden off...God, Almighty! Where was I to take my beautiful prize once I'd whisked her into my arms and tossed her onto Old Paint? Oh, who cared?

I stood for a brief instant, legs spread, fingers lifting my jeans back up over my hip bones. I felt my brow drop slightly as I smiled at Carol. She smiled back. I took the first step, and I could hear Mickey mumbling his words of encouragement behind me. Jimmy's voice. Mickey again. It was all a blur-ish mix as I rose to mountaintops of confidence and determination.

Then I saw them out of the corner of my eye. Like a pair of gunslingers marching down the center of the dusty street. Both of them were sneering, and suddenly my confidence went straight out the window and into the outhouse. Whatever it was they were up to, this could not end pretty.

"Shit..." I heard Jimmy say low.

I glanced across the patio at Carol as I fumbled in my head whether to dash down the driveway and confront them—a surefire way to win her deep admiration for my courage, but a good way to receive two new black eyes—or sit tight and see what they were up to. Carol's eyes widened. She'd seen them too. Allen was still blabbering away, off in his Neverland of meaningless ruminations. The look on Carol's face suggested to me that instead of running down and trying to beat the daylights out of the Skull's officers singlehandedly, I should saunter over and yank her out of the steel-like grip of Allen and his insufferable, endlessly moving mouth. I decided to leave my two best friends alone to deal with Inky and Butch while I went and dealt with the snake charmer personally.

Tex was busy with a group of kids, and his phony hair kept getting tangled up in the branches of the apple tree he was standing under. Clifford's little sister, three other giggling, clapping little brats sat beneath him, and of course chubby little Clifford, who was more enthralled with Tex's antics than the younger kids. The clown raised his eyes as I crossed the covered patio, and then aimed and let an untied balloon loose. God Himself couldn't have gotten that thing to hit me, but Tex made the girls sitting in front of him under the tree laugh themselves silly. He made a big deal of it, though he didn't utter a word. Just made a big wide circle of his mouth, clasped his hands over his eyes and then his hidden ears. About the time the balloon did its fifth circle-eight in the air and then petered out with a last gasp, a fiery dart swished across the clown's head. I turned and mouthed, "Dammit, Jimmy! No!" That's when I saw Butch's profile entering, stage left.

I'd lost track of Allen and Carol momentarily while all this high drama was unfolding, until, out of the blue, he bounded past me in the direction of the Minkles. *Holy shit! He's gonna' lay into Butch!*

I was dead wrong. Jimmy and Mickey readied themselves for the fight of their lives, coming together like a pair of cats being attacked by a bulldog, backs against a fifty foot-tall wall. Butch seemed to sense that the fight was already won. He let that insipid grin infect his face, a toothpick dangling out of the right side of his mouth. Allen looked exactly like a novice ballet dancer stumbling across the patio stage. Before I could close my eyes and prepare for the sharp crack of knuckles on chin bone, he'd made it over to Butch. To my undying shock he welcomed him with open arms to the wild-west extravaganza. There was no figuring the wondrous and mysterious ways of God, but I kind of figured we still had a long way to go before Butch grabbed hold of the olive branch.

"Hello, Butch! I'm very glad to see you!"

"Yeah? Well we din't come ta' be a part of this...whad'ya call that thing?" He pointed at Tex the clown and broke out in a belly laugh.

"Oh...that's just a...well, you see, Mother..." For the first time since I'd known him, Allen seemed to be taking offense at someone's insult. He narrowed his eyes, I think—it was hard to see clearly through the lenses of his glasses—and dropped his welcoming arms. Jimmy and Mickey remained at the ready, but they were none too anxious to light into Butch with Inky standing with a smirk on his face down on the sidewalk.

"I think I must ask you very politely to leave, Butch Minkle. I didn't send you an invitation, and though you would be welcome under the right circumstances..."

"Shaddup, birthday boy. Nobody cares what you think. Right Ink?" Butch turned his head back to his brother. Inky neither agreed nor disagreed with the comment. He stood cracking a wad of gum on one side of his mouth, grinning, maybe waiting for Butch to clean house all by himself.

"We saw your chickenshit friends standin' here. Decided ta' come pay 'em a curtsy call."

On hearing that, Jimmy and Mickey separated and began to circle Butch slowly. Inky stepped up the driveway. Allen did something else that mystified me, totally out of character for the kid who, it was rumored, was frightened of Caspar the Friendly Ghost. He took a step backward, raised his hands and chin in a spitting image of the famous photograph of John L. Sullivan hanging proudly on the wall at Larry's Barber Shop down on First Avenue, and promptly took a right cross from Butch. Allen did not sink to his knees with the force of the punch, rather flew onto his butt, as though some gigantic, invisible hand had jerked him by the scruff of the neck. A choral response flew up from every set of lips, from every age group represented. "Ooh!"

Honestly, the razor-sharp crack it made when it lifted Allen off his feet brought an embarrassing smile to my face. I thought, *Lord Almighty that was pretty!* But, that was not the end of the fight—barely the beginning.

As delicate Carol might require protecting in the place she sat (more truthfully, I had no inclination to become victim number two), I positioned myself between her and the coming war parties twenty feet away. Inky arrived, Mrs. Jung arrived screaming. Mickey and Jimmy angled in like two P-51 Mustangs diving down on a Messerschmitt. Maybe between Allen's mother and Jimmy and Mickey, the brothers from up the street could have been bested—but I doubt it. About all Mrs. Jung was good for was clucking and cackling like a hen in a chicken coop attacked by a fox. She waved her arms, but I guess had no idea that if she swung them a little, her fists just might damage the body of the guy who'd cold-cocked her beloved son. Lying flat on his back, glasses bent and twisted, Allen didn't care. He actually looked very peaceful, even as the air above him heated explosively.

Tex arrived, finally, and he was not happy.

I've never seen a clown, dressed like a cowboy, or otherwise, with such a look of savagery on his brightly colored face. It was as though someone had committed a mortal sin—Tex, I guess. Yeah, he'd gone crazy and ripped all the statues and crucifixes down at church. Rabid, or infected with the brain palsy. Nuts. Condemned to hell, suddenly aware of it, and looking very hard for someone to take it all out on. That's how his face looked to me. And that was the best part of him. Instead of honking the horn, he grabbed it by the black ball and was fixing to jam it open-end first down over Butch's head clear to his feet. He looked like a cross between John Wayne and Boris Karloff striding across the grass onto the patio. He was pissed. I found it disconcerting that a man with shoes as long as his body was tall could move with such speed, and really, with such grace and purpose. Butch was about to discover that as well.

The scourge of Meade Street had made a foolish mistake by turning to taunt steel-faced Mrs. Jung, raising his hands high above his head, one leg raised—The Incredible Atomic Praying Mantis. Mickey and Jimmy saw Tex's rapid approach and backed off with looks of *Oh, shit!* splattered all over their faces. Then Inky bounded forward to rescue his brother from the colorful wave descending on him, but was met by Mickey, and then Jimmy, who each grabbed a handful of his pompadour. It was so weird seeing him go flat-out dead in the water. Butch saw the whole thing, Inky's look of shock and horror—more so for the violation of his brother's perfect hairdo than for what was about to happen to himself—Inky's inability to bring himself to rid the hair of Jimmy and Mickey's fingers, all of it. Mickey told me later that Butch's own face mirrored the horror of his older brother's when Butch saw just how badly the Brylcreemed masterpiece had been wrecked. And then Jimmy started wailing away on Inky's face.

About that time, Tex hit shore. Butch had wound himself up like Babe Ruth and was ready to roundhouse Jimmy, who stood pounding on Inky with one hand, half of the guy's locks in the other. He was smiling. Jimmy, that is. Butch let loose with maybe his most powerful swing ever. Tex caught it right at the check-swing point when Butch's muscles had focused every bit of their potential in forward momentum. Had I done the same thing as Tex, I would have been propelled all the way across Meade Street into the greenhouse. Tex's grasp was sure, clean, remarkable in its stability though. Jimmy sort of eloquently put it into scientific terms later. "Newton's laws of motion...all four of 'em! I saw the universe explode when the irresistible force met the impenepta...impentata...the barrier that couldn't, you know, be moved. Shit-howdy! That was two of the laws. Two others was involved..." He went on for some time as he explained those other two forces and the way...well, Butch's arm didn't want to stop, that's all. But it did. He ripped just about every muscle and tendon something horrible I'm sure, and Inky was forced to stand there and watch it all, then help his brother up the street once Tex had finally finished mopping up the driveway with him.

The really disgusting part of the whole incident unfolded almost simultaneously, although as I stood helplessly and watched it, it seemed to be happening in ultra-slow motion. When Allen hit the deck with a thud Carol had cried out, "Ooooooooohhhhhh, noooooooooo!" I turned my head toward her slowly, slowly. Too slowly. She was already on her feet rushing at one hundredth the normal speed to Allen's smiling-faced side. I couldn't catch her, stop her from endangering her body in the mess that was developing over there because I found myself moving even more slowly for that brief second when time ground down to give me a good look at her display of over-the-top concern for that little snot. Carol fell to her knees as time ripped back to 4/4 bars. Jesus. She placed her hands—I thought *way* too lovingly—on his cheeks, and kept mumbling something over and over to him. Mrs. Jung was a wreck, running in little circles, trying to cover her eyes with her own hands. Inky was getting his greasy hair yanked out and his faced punched...Butch was being swung in a circle like a dirty, wet rag. Everybody seemed to be yelling all at once, and I knew the cops would be pulling up again any second.

Watching Carol fawn over Allen, I began to grow faint. I realized then and there that girls seemed to love guys more for getting themselves beat to smithereens rather than for being tough, like me.

The party ended with Mrs. Jung cackling every detail to the two cops who finally did get there, and Carol ignoring me as she helped Allen continually adjust his mangled glasses, massage his sore chin, and, finally, open all his presents. Tex sat between Mickey and Jimmy on the retaining wall, towering over them like a battleship over a couple of tugboats. He'd given up on entertaining the kiddies and Allen, pulled his wig off, and the three of them laughed and carried on till I despaired of ever making sense out of life. I wandered home alone, totally dispirited, bested by a silly clown, the Skulls, and a four-eyed snake.

So the three of us survived again—without a scratch this time—and better yet, none of us got grounded. Allen's mom enrolled him in boxing classes at a gym downtown somewhere a few days later, and I was pretty sure he somehow talked Carol into going along to watch him perfect his Marciano abilities, because each afternoon I wandered down to her house, hoping to see her dancing, or watering the lawn. Or anything.

She never appeared.

Inky and Butch's "enemy list" continued to expand, and since Allen was now listed, I thought seriously at night (when I did my best and deepest thinking) to join forces with them—at least until he was put permanently out of commission.

But I didn't. I might have been love-struck, but I was no fool or traitor. Jimmy and I and Mickey simply laid low and stayed out of trouble.

TWENTY-FOUR

Laughing Waters, Roaring Thunder

As part of our summer routine, Pop would empty the piggy-bank, pack Mom, me, and sometimes Jimmy, into the car, and off we'd go into the high country for a week's vacation. Our destination? A small cluster of utterly charming cabins built in the 1920's and 30's in a remote, idyllic place called Cabin Creek, nestled high up in the mountains west of the city.

That year, near Labor Day, Mom invited Jimmy. After several minutes of mighty celebration following this windfall news, he and I went back to her and pleaded and cajoled her into allowing Mickey to come along too. We labored to convince her it'd be a great idea, and after a warlike assault on her from two fronts, she finally relented and gave us permission to invite him as well. Of course we already had, so all that needed to be done was to have her give Mrs. Fumo a courtesy call.

"You boys promise to stay out of trouble if I let him come?" Mom stated more than inquired as we stood there in front of her like miniature saints that evening before we left for the mountains.

"Well, yeah, Mom. Of course. We're just going to fish...and stuff," I assured her.

She gave it a little more thought, closing her eyes, scrunching up her mouth as though she'd just drunk a glass of vinegar. "Well, ok, then. I'll call his mother and ask her. Goddam' woman. Probably won't do much good though. She's so uppity...and I still think she goes to that Calvinist church, or whatever it is, up on 2nd Avenue. I don't care what anybody says." She mumbled more ugly remarks about the woman as she walked away to look up the Fumo's telephone number.

"Hot-damn!" Jimmy said, punching me in the shoulder.

I wanted to somehow include Carol (who was once again back in the forefront of my thoughts, even though she was nowhere to be found, unless I looked for Allen), but for the life of me I couldn't think up a convincing enough reason to get her invited as well. It had been troublesome enough for Jimmy and me to talk Mom into letting Mickey join us; bringing Carol into the conversation, I knew, would be pushing my dear mother to the limits.

I was certain the three of us couldn't possibly find anything up there in the wilderness to destroy. There was nothing but forests of pines, the tiny meandering creek a middling walk from the cabins, and a few cows in the mountain meadow pasture a short hike away from the buildings. Okay, the little General Store and office owned by Mr. and Mrs. Trumbull, who rented Pop whichever cabin he wanted for ten dollars a night. That, too. But surely, in even one of our most awful moments we wouldn't bring it tumbling down. No, never. It'd be safe.

After the conversation between Mrs. Fumo and my Mom ended, she came back out onto the front porch where Jimmy and I had been waiting with our fingers crossed, and announced the good news.

"That old bat said yes. He can go. Now, let me tell you in no uncertain terms before we even get started here! If the three of you even think about getting into any trouble, I'll skin ya' alive. I promise. You understand me?"

"Yes, ma'am!"

"We do, Mom. We'll be like angels, I swear it!"

"Alrighty then. He's on his way down right now. The three of ya' sleep downstairs. We're leavin' at five o'clock sharp. Mind what I told ya'! No pranks or trouble."

I couldn't let a good idea die. "Can I invite Carol?"

"WHAT?" Mom's eyes nearly popped out of their sockets.

"Just kidding," I tried to redeem the question spoken without any thought. Jimmy scowled, and Mom loaded up her rifle.

"You'd best get that girl outta' your head right this minute, Skippy. Your way too young to be thinkin' about girls like you've been doin' with that one all summer. Of course you can't invite her! Whatd'ya think I am..."

And so I received a long lecture, despite my continued explanation that I'd only been kidding about having my heart's deepest desire come along with us. The goddess who was missing. The creature I loved, who would no doubt spoil any ill-conceived notions us boys might have to burn down Rocky Mountain National Park, or shoot the cows between the eyes with our Whamos, or execute whatever scheme Jimmy might dream up and talk Mickey and me into. Honestly, I knew in the deepest part of me that tromping over the brush-infested banks of Cabin Creek, untangling a fouled fishing line every fifteen steps, falling into the water, getting eaten alive by mosquitoes, all of that would only appeal to Jimmy for about ten minutes—if that long. Besides, standing there in front of Mom, I noticed he still had his fingers crossed behind his back. He was plotting something already. A girl among us might make all the difference in the world. Silly me.

The next morning at precisely 4:33 a.m. as promised, Mom woke us up, fed us each a bowl of Wheaties, and then packed us, bleary-eyed into the backseat of the station wagon. Mickey, Jimmy, and I slept for most of the interminably long trip, but awakened just east of Estes Park, a world renowned resort Pop told us, that had been built by Buffalo Bill many years earlier. I didn't think that was true, but we raced through the charming town anyway on the way to our bucolic destination. Cabin Creek lay a few miles farther west up the canyon which had been carved a trillion years or so ago by the St. Vrain River. That, I believed, was true. Though it wasn't the Mississippi by any stretch of the imagination, the St. Vrain was an impressive body of water nonetheless, rifling down the steep, narrow, granite-walled canyon on its way to the plains below.

"They pulled two fisherman out of the drink a couple of months back," Pop said, turning his attention to the backseat briefly as we passed alongside a particularly nasty looking area of rapids. "The papers said the men must have slipped on a rock casting their lines out. River was higher then. Run-off was still heavy in June. I can't figure out for the life of me though, how two grown men could both fall in at the same time," he finished up.

Jimmy had his nose stuck out the window by then, staring down at the broiling foam below us. "Maybe somebody murdered 'em an tossed 'em into the river."

I thought that was a possibility.

"I doubt it," Pop answered him after a short pause and a laugh. "People don't murder fisherman. Least ways not up here. Never heard of any murder in these parts that I can remember."

"Well, maybe you have now!" Jimmy quipped. His statement gave rise to a series of unbelievably ridiculous questions and answers. Us four men—mom could have cared less, and was still dozing—discussed criminal activities possible in "these parts" for the remainder of the drive, none of which bore any resemblance to reality, probability, or even rationality.

A couple of miles up the highway Pop stuck his arm out the window, signaling our turn, and we rolled across the river over a narrow, ancient bridge built out of timbers and a lot of prayers. Ten minutes later we crossed another tiny bridge spanning Cabin Creek, and Pop pulled to a stop in front of Mr. and Mrs. Trumbull's General Store. He left the car, and five minutes later, exited the store, motioning that our cabin was "Laughing Waters", fifty yards up the dirt road. Good fortune. Of the half dozen cabins, Laughing Waters was the nicest—two stories tall, with a rock fireplace in the living room, and a real toilet—inside.

Jimmy, Mickey, and I whooped it up and left the car at a dead run, thankful to be free of the rear-end paralyzing confinement of the backseat. I whisked the keys to the cabin out of Pop's hand as I passed by him, tripped Mickey as I passed by him, and arrived in a dead heat with Jimmy at the base of the flight of rough pine stairs leading up to the entry door. We looked quickly at one another, then galloped up to the top.

Laughing Waters sat nobly among the stand of trees, tucked into a natural hollow in a steep, rocky hill leading off into the forest. The old cabin smelled even more delicious inside than the

175

fragrant pine-scented outdoors. I stepped across the doorway threshold into a large open room. On the left lay the living room with the massive stone fireplace. A pair of antlers sacrificed God knows how long ago by an elk, hung over the firebox and its highly polished, hewn mantle. On the floor in front of it, a ten foot-wide, oval rag rug had been placed for the comfort of guests to lie on and gaze into the roaring fire on chilly autumn, and freezing winter evenings. To the right stood the dining room with its rows of sparkling clean windows overlooking the breathtaking vista outdoors, and beyond the dining room, a small but functional kitchen with its wood-burning stove, a geriatric ice box, and another smaller table for quaint, informal breakfasts. A backdoor with gingham curtains partially covering the glass led out to a leveled-out spot for chopping wood, and beyond...the infiniteness of the forest.

The wide staircase leading up to the three bedrooms separated the living room from the dining room like a priest standing between a blushing bride and her groom. This was indeed God's country, and Laughing Waters had a peacefulness about it that humbled and performed magic on me whenever I entered it.

Mickey bounded up, shoving me into the interior of the first bedroom where I landed flat on my stomach. "You cheater, Skip!"

"All's fair in love and war." I laughed and picked myself up, raising my fists. "I'll fight you for the top bunk!"

"You're on..."

"You boys get back down here right this minute," Mom's voice came echoing through the door. "You think your father and me are gonna' lug all this stuff up them stairs, you've got another think a comin'. Hurry up, now."

We abandoned the battle for the bed and raced back down to do the grunt work. The sound of our shoes clattering back down the wooden steps made a mesmerizingly muted echo against the ceiling and walls in the quiet of the place.

Pop had already opened the rear door of the car, and he passed the lighter containers of supplies to each of us as we arrived, and then took a box under each arm himself. Several more trips and the job was completed. We all gathered in the living room to catch our breaths, and that's where Mom made an announcement in the midst of all our huffing and puffing.

"You boys take the end bedroom. Your father and I'll have the other one on the south end. Your Aunt Corey and Sylvie are coming up later this afternoon. They'll get the middle room."

"Aunt Corey?" Jimmy and I groaned in unison. We meant Aunt Corey *and* Sylvie, but the single name summed up our surprise perfectly.

So, my two aunts were coming up, and we'd have to give up a bed.

Like I said before, Aunt Sylvie's husband, some guy I'd never seen, and barely ever heard of, had run off with another woman many years ago. She and Mrs. McGuire had become sympathetic friends over that disclosure a long, long time ago, but whereas Mrs. McGuire tried to drown the memory of Fred by having an affair with Old Crow, Sylvie denounced any worldly attempt for relief whatsoever. Save fishing. She was in love with the sport, though she would never stoop to sitting on the bank of a lake to perform her magic with the rod and reel. Stream fishing was her passion, and she was good at it.

Despite the furious shaking of her fingers and the horrible twitch of her facial muscles, the woman was capable of baiting a sharp hook with the precision of a watchmaker. She knew trout more intimately, I think, than she could possibly ever have known her husband. Knew where they loved to rest, close to the shadowy banks of the creek, what bait they were most apt to go for at any given hour. I think she even knew the names of each and every one of them. She loved fish, or at least catching them, and it was she who taught me how to mercifully beat their heads against a rock after I'd snagged one and reeled it home.

"They suffer, Skip, when you pull them out of the water. They can't breathe," I remember her saying in her trembling voice on our very first outing. It occurred to me at the time that it might be more merciful not to bother catching them in the first place. But then again, it was no fun at all to sit on the bank of the creek and just watch them swim by.

I inured myself to the barbarity of the sport for hers and Pop's sake, I suppose, and in time became one of the world's finest trout murderers. A compassionate killer, once a year, along the banks of Cabin Creek.

Aunt Corey and Sylvie arrived as promised later in the afternoon while Jimmy, Mick, and me were off chasing chipmunks and running down the list of possible activities for the upcoming week. Fortunately we'd all had the foresight to bring our Whamos and plenty of quarter-inch BBs—just in case we ran across a bear or a mountain lion. But whereas Jimmy and Mickey wanted to decapitate Chip and Dale whenever they poked their heads out of their dens, I amused myself by zeroing in on less sentient things, like boulders, tree branches, and sometimes bald eagles soaring thousands of feet higher than my pellets could possibly reach.

"Those little sons-a-bitches are hard to hit," Jimmy cursed after having no luck blasting even one of the chipmunks into kingdom come several hours into the hunt.

"Yeah, well if you'd be a little quieter when you snuck up on them instead of acting like a white man, making all that noise, you might have better luck," Mickey advised him.

"Yeah," I added, "the Indians use to walk over this ground without making a sound. They never spooked even the smartest animal. Sister Mary Dolorine is an Indian, you know."

Jimmy looked at me, lowering his slingshot to his side. "You mean she comes up here an' hunts squirrels?" he laughed.

"No, stupid. I just was thinking of her when I said that. I'm sure she'd never shoot an animal, even if it was a damned old grizzly about to tear her head off."

"I sure would!" Mickey roared. "I'd do it in a minute!"

"Me too," Jimmy said with an agreeing laugh.

"Sure you would. You'd die, too. They say it takes an elephant gun to kill a Grizzly," I said to him.

"Oh, bullshit!" Jimmy began.

"Shhh! Listen! Something's up there," Mickey whispered, pointing to a boulder plugged into a rise fifty yards up the hill. "I caught a glimpse of it. It was big!"

Mickey's call for silence was an old ploy, I sensed. The bogeyman thing, meant to scare the wits out of Jimmy and me. Tired of the chipmunk hunt, I played along.

"I think I saw something, too. Let's just ease ourselves back down the mountain for a ways, and then run like hell for the cabin." As we feigned great fear and began to back down the way we'd come, the thing Mickey had spoken of poked its massive head out from behind the gray boulder, exactly where he'd pointed a second earlier. I'm not sure if it was hungry, angry that we'd been taking pot-shots at its little friends, or simply curious concerning our presence, but whatever its interest in us was, we screamed bloody murder and lit out like three Bambis for the safety of the cabin.

Not caring whether it was chasing us or not, we arrived at the back door within seconds of one another and burst into the kitchen, frightened out of our skins. Our four adult chaperones dropped their conversations and cans of beer all at once upon our arrival and peered across the room when we slammed into the kitchen wall.

"What the hell?" Pop was the first to speak. Mom sat across from him with a frown on her face, and in between them, dressed in their woodsmen best, sat my aunts.

"A Grizzly!" I shouted. "Close the damn door, Mick!"

Mickey darted back, and after a quick glance outside slammed the door shut. The three of us entered the dining room, dispensing with any greetings, and related how after innocently target practicing at knotholes in trees, this eight foot-tall, ferocious bear had snuck up on us out of the blue.

The evening passed. After a fine dinner and tons more bottles of Coors for my parents, aunt/cousin Sylvie related several suspiciously colored accounts of how she'd stumbled across a Cardinal's list of man-eating creatures in this very wilderness. Pop tried to best her stories with even more colorful ones of his own, while Jimmy, Mickey, and me sat listening in awe.

Mom and Aunt Corey cleaned up the dinner dishes and then bravely took an evening stroll together into the darkness of the woods behind the cabin.

For the next few days my friends and I were intensely schooled in angling, and true to my predictions, Jimmy quickly tired of falling into the creek and piercing his fingers with the hook on the end of his fishing line, which snagged as though every tree he walked under had branches with evil eyes and malicious fingers of its own, waiting for him. Something had to give. As the higher regions of the forest were dangerously alive with any number of beasts intent on chewing us to pieces, we decided on the third or fourth day to visit the cows in the pasture. If any creatures were to be bullied, it would have to be the cows, not us.

We received permission to abandon the fishing expedition, explaining to Pop that morning about our repulsion of having to beat the brains out of our catches. Sensing a new generation of thinking foreign to his own, but possessing a very broad tolerance for kooky outlooks just the same, he let us off the hook, so to speak.

Delighted by the reprieve, and Whamos dangling out of our back pockets, we scuffled down the dirt road past Trumble's General Store, over a weather-beaten fence, and into the north forty of the pasture. A wood-paneled station wagon roared past us just before we'd gotten ten feet into Farmer John's field, and we all turned to watch it speed up the road.

"Damn! Did you see that?" Jimmy asked.

"What? What was it?" Mickey asked him.

"Whoever's drivin' that thing is either a midget or else he's six years-old. I barely saw his hair above the window! Let's go see who he is."

We darted back across the fence, up the road past our cabin, and found the car parked fifty yards farther up the bowl in front of the last cabin, "Roaring Thunder". Sure enough, the driver had just stepped out. Either Rumpelstiltskin or some kid who couldn't have been over ten years old.

"Hey, you!" Jimmy shouted. "How do ya' drive that thing? You ain't near old enough, I'm guessin'. How old are ya'?"

The boy, as it turned out, was a girl—a tomboy if I'd ever seen one—and she shot us a mind-your-own-business glance, then hustled into her cabin without bothering to answer.

"Well I'll be go to hell. If that don't beat all. Must not be any cops in this place for miles an' miles! How old you figure she was?"

"I don't know. Who cares?" I answered. "Let's get going. The cows are waiting."

"Nah, wait a sec. She was drivin' around here, an' I know she don't have a license. I'm thinkin'..."

"Oh no you don't! Don't be thinking about anything, Jimmy. Let's just get back to the pasture. We don't need any trouble. Remember what we promised Mom."

Jimmy was off again on one of his mental adventures, not hearing a word I said, planning something I wasn't about to cave into. Not this time.

"You go on without me, Skip. I'll be there in a flash. I just wanna' check out this buggy here. Maybe that girl'll come back out...I wanna' ask her a coupla' things, too."

"No. I'm not going back without you. Whatever it is your planning, you're not gonna' do it. I'm not gonna' let you." I walked up to where he stood, put my hand on his arm, and began to pull him down the hill. His eyes narrowed, with the look I'd seen only once before. In his bedroom as he'd glared at the crudely drawn, perforated picture of Inky hanging on the wall. Before I could blink he hit me so hard that I fell backward onto my rear. I believed in that moment we'd lost a world, that Jimmy had gone mad.

I looked to Mickey to help me out. "Mick! Tell him to back off. Let's get out of here!"

Mickey stared down at me, shook his head, and then chose his master. "Goddam', Skip. You always crap out whenever you think you smell smoke. What's the big deal? We haven't done anything yet. Not a thing! What are you so afraid of?" He stepped closer to Jimmy. I gathered myself up off the ground, dusted off, and then walked back to Laughing Waters alone.

Mom, Pop, Aunt Corey and Sylvie had disappeared into the tangle of brush along the banks of Cabin Creek and its laughing waters. The fishing poles stacked neatly inside the door, the creels filled with bait and extra hooks—the hats with more hooks imbedded in their brims, the rubber boots, and cans of mosquito repellant—all of it was gone. I stepped in, glanced right, left, and then walked through the dining room into the kitchen where a tiny mirror hung alone and strangely out of place on the wall behind the door. In the worn, cloudy reflection I recognized my face with another reddened bruise beginning to swell up beneath my eye. Funny, I thought, the last time I'd gotten a shiner it was from the fist of Inky the Terrible. Private enemy number one. Really, I didn't know who hit the hardest, him or Jimmy. It might have been a tie.

Despairing at what I was going to tell Mom and Pop about this new black eye, I left the kitchen and walked into the dining room where I took a seat beneath the windows. I knew what Jimmy was up to—he intended to steal that family's car. I didn't know if he knew how to drive—I don't think he did—but Jimmy's M.O. was very predictable. He and Mickey would come flying down the hill any minute. I was certain of that.

I waited ten minutes, and then thirty. No sound outside at all. Tired of standing vigil, and hungry, I returned to the kitchen and threw together a sandwich. As I searched for the bag of chips, the shuffle of shoes atop the steps out front caught me. I was surprised when the door creaked open and in came Jimmy, followed by his little puppy, Mickey. Both Jimmy and I stared across the long space of the rooms at one another, me expressionless, he with his eyes downcast slightly.

"Where's the car?" I asked him. He answered immediately.

"Still up there. She wouldn't give us a ride. Hey, Skip...umm, I dunno' what came over me. God, I'm sure sorry. If ya' want to, you can take a good poke at me. I sure as hell deserve it, and I won't even try to block it. I'm real sorry."

I was stunned. "You weren't going to steal it?"

"Steal it? Heck no! How would I steal it? I dunno' how to drive. Cripes! Why'd ya' think I was gonna' steal it?"

"Because I know you," I said.

"Maybe not as good as ya' think ya' do. I wanted to talk to that girl, that's all—an' I did! Well, I liked the car, too. I wanted a ride in it."

"You're kidding!"

"No. I swear it. Jesus, are you dumb!"

"Yeah. You took a shiner for that?" Mickey finally spoke.

Jimmy told me how after seeing that the guy was actually a girl, he'd taken a fancy to her because of her short, black hair and funny clothes. After beating up on me, he and Mickey had stood around waiting for her to come out and tell them to leave. She did, of course, but Jimmy listens to no one when he wants something. He wanted to talk to "Ginsberg"—that's what she called herself. The weird name for a girl had something to do with Beatniks and a book called "Howl", he told me. She was thirteen, Jimmy's age now, and she'd come to Colorado at the insistence of her parents, who refused to leave her with either friends or relatives back in Manhattan for fear she'd run off with these bongo-playing, poetry-reading nuts, to a city, he said, called Greenwich Village. When her parents left the cabin to go hiking in the hills, it was her "duty", she also told him, to drive their car all over the place. A protest or something. How or where she'd learned to drive he didn't say, or didn't know. He said he was very impressed with her though. I think he found his Carol.

We had three more days until the end of our stay at Cabin Creek, and for two and nine-tenths of them, I swear Jimmy courted and wooed her until I feared he'd jump ship and find a way to stow away in Ginsberg's baggage, and then sneak back to Manhattan with her. Taking a teasing from Mickey—once again a comrade of mine—and me, he swore his feelings for her were "strictly platonic", another couple of words whose meaning eluded me at the time. "We read poetry," he explained. I know I saw him kiss her. By my understanding of the words, reading poetry had very little to do with kissing. And speaking of explaining.

My fishermen family trudged into the cabin later that same afternoon when Jimmy blackened my eye. They asked me—asked all of us—how it had come to happen.

"We were horsing around," I said, "and I tripped..."

"No he didn't. I hit 'im. He wouldn't stay with me an' Mickey. He thought we was gonna' steal Ginsberg's folks' car, an' he tried to pull me away. We wasn't gonna steal it, an' I didn't know why he was so upset. I just wanted to talk to Ginsberg—the girl in the cabin next door. I should'na done it, an I'm real sorry I did. Honest, Mr. an' Mrs. Morley. I should'na done it an' I'm sorry."

That said a lot to me about my best friend, and brought another of those rare, but glorious smiles to Mom's lips.

TWENTY-FIVE

And So I Kissed A Car

Saturday morning Mom and Aunt Corey fixed the most delicious breakfast we'd ever eaten. Better than could have been prepared by a French chef with a million dollar budget and an order from the king and queen of France to send their taste buds and stomachs into outer space. Great slabs of bacon, flap-jacks and maple syrup, blueberries, bananas, powdered sugar, eggs—sunnyside up, *and* scrambled—diced potatoes with tons of salt and pepper, freshly squeezed orange juice, and milk. And coffee! Coffee that smelled as though the patron saint of culinary arts had just ground it in the kitchens of Heaven, and percolated it with water that could only be found in the wells below our cabin. The purest, sweetest water in the universe. The amount of food my aunt and mother prepared could have fed a regiment. We were expected to devour all of it, and we tried.

"We'll be leaving at four this afternoon," Aunt Corey's gentle voice followed the aroma of the platters being whisked into the dining room. "You boys fill up. Roseanna and I will fix a light lunch later on. That will have to hold you until you get home. Eat up, now."

"Are you coming fishing this morning?" Sylvie asked me and my buddies in her trembling, cracking voice as we approached the table. She was in the process of trying to pick up her fork as she spoke, and looking at her I thought the poor woman would wind up rattling it clear off the edge of the table before she got hold of it.

"Good time to go," Pop chirped. "It's cool outside, trout'll be going for the bait like sharks."

"Maybe later on," Jimmy replied. "I got somethin' I gotta' do right after breakfast."

185

"Oh, yeah!" I laughed, followed by everyone else, except Mickey.

"Well, you just make sure ya' don't go sailing over the falls doin' whatever it is you'll be doin'," Mom chuckled.

"Falls? There ain't no falls around here," Jimmy said to her.

My parents and aunt, and poor old high-strung Sylvie roared at his reply.

"Yeah, I think there are," Mom said with a giggle. She winked in Pop's direction, but he was busy burying his plate under a mountain of food, altogether uninterested for the moment about anything else. We bowed our heads, said Grace (still chuckling), and then ate like kings.

It was a wonderful, light morning. After gorging ourselves, Jimmy ran up to Roaring Thunder, and then disappeared into the forest hand in hand with Ginsberg and her book of poetry. Mickey and I were forced to either go fishing with Pop and Sylvie, or else amuse ourselves in some other way. We found the cows and peppered them good with rocks.

At three o'clock the iron triangle hanging from the eve of the front porch sounded. The fishermen returned soon afterward with enough dead creatures to fill a cemetery; Mickey and I wished the cows goodbye with a final volley of stones. Jimmy didn't answer the call. My first thought was that he might have been trying to hike all the way back to Greenwich Village with Ginsberg.

I was sent out to find him. Mickey elected to stay and help load everything back into the cars. After nearly going hoarse shouting his name, I stumbled onto the lovebirds sitting back to back far up the hill on a flat spot near to where the bear had appeared, Ginsberg reciting a poem—that part which I overheard making no sense at all to me. Though I didn't want to separate them because I knew what land Jimmy had found himself in, I knew I must. I announced that the bus would be leaving in half an hour, then turned and went back down to Laughing Waters.

"Where is he?" Pop asked when I returned.

"He's right behind me."

Jimmy and I left the mountains in great sadness. He because he'd had to leave his kooky Beatnik Ginsberg behind; me because I'd read his thoughts as clearly as if he'd recited them on stage. School would be starting on the following Monday, too, and I would lose Carol forever to the no-man's land of Kepner Junior High if I couldn't rescue her from the arms of Allen very soon. Losing track of her there could be no worse than losing track of her at her own house, I supposed, but the number of hours I could spend standing like a homeless cat in front of it was destined to be slashed. All things being equal though, Jimmy's predicament wasn't all that bad. He'd gotten an address for Ginsberg, and a phone number. At least he could talk to her whenever he wanted, and he vowed to do just that, every single day. I absolutely knew his mother was going to skin him alive come October when the new phone bill arrived.

Mickey seemed lost in the face of mine and Jimmy's strange new addictions, not able to comprehend the power of the hormones unleashed in our lives. Of course we had no real conception of their strength either, but because of the similarity of the Siren's calls and my amazing misjudgment of Jimmy's intentions three days ago, he and I were suddenly more tuned in to one another than ever before. Poor Mickey, I feared, must have felt like a Pygmy snatched out of his African home and thrown onto the streets of New York. He said very little on the trip back to Denver.

We arrived in the city at around six that afternoon, exhausted by all the fun we'd had, desiring only to be finally home. We dropped Mickey and his things off in front of his house. Standing on the curb with his sleeping bag and pillow underarm he looked like he'd just lost his best friends. That wasn't true, and yet again, it was. We waved goodbye, and then Pop pulled slowly away, down Meade Street. We crossed 1st Avenue and instinctively I knew I must stand up. Carol's house was visible midway on the block. A car that had turned in front of us moments ago at the stop sign at the intersection eased up to the curb in front of her house. A second or two later the passengers left it—a youngish-looking woman and a girl. They began to walk up the steps toward the entry, followed by the driver, a short, balding man in a white summer suit. The girl was Carol. Come home at last, and dazzling in her Bermuda shorts. I pressed my face against the window when we neared her home and said my finest prayer of thanks, and asked, too, for a golden tongue. I was going to need it in the next half hour. As we passed she turned for some reason and glanced out, maybe only because she'd heard the sound of an engine. Our eyes met—hers dark and inviting in the fading sunlight, mine opened wide, only one blackened this time. She smiled and raised a hand, slightly, as though she wanted to wave to me, and then slowly dropped it to her side. Then she turned again and walked through the door in front of her father.

I peered back at the house until it faded into a white blur among the rest of the homes on her block. I turned quickly to Jimmy, to tell him my days of mourning had come to an end, but he was falling asleep. On our street I spotted Clifford walking toward his house. I spun the window crank around as though it were an airplane propeller and threw my head outside.

"Hey Clifford, she's back! She's home!"

He turned and looked out at me in bewilderment, stopping dead in his tracks. Mom, who had been fiddling with her rosary beads, reciting the prayers and probably cursing Mrs. Fumo in the same breath, dropped what she'd been doing in shock. Pop hit the brakes sending Jimmy slamming into the back of his seat.

"What in God's name?" Mom shouted.

"Oh, sorry, Mom. Didn't mean to scare you. Just wanted to tell Clifford that Carol's back home..."

"Goddamit', Skip. We could've had a wreck! What the hell's the matter with you anyway? Get your head back in here," Pop snarled. "Carol. I've had about enough of you guys and these girls already."

"Okay, Pop. Sorry."

Thank goodness the trip ended ten seconds later. I was torn between racing back down to Carol's house or offering to carry all the junk from the vacation into ours. Something told me that unloading the car would be the wiser thing to do.

"You guys go on. I'll bring all the stuff in for you. You're tired, I know."

"That's more like it," Pop said. Nevertheless, he grabbed the cooler with his fish, trusting no one to see to their final resting place in the freezer. With Mom leading the way, they walked slowly through the gate and into the house.

"C'mon, Jimmy. Help me get this stuff out of here. I've got a date."

"Can't," he answered. "I wanna' get home an' call Gins."

"Call her? For crying out loud, it'll take her days to get back to New York! You'll be wasting your nickel. Just give me a quick hand."

"Yeah, yer probably right. Okay, but then I'm gonna' go home an read this book she gave me. You really think it'll take days for her to get home?"

"At least." I glanced at the book he held in his hand. *Howl.* Probably love poems. Vampire love poems. I couldn't for the life of me see how he could possibly untangle romantic rhymes and verses, especially those written by a bongo-playing Beatnik, but I admired his newfound interest in literature anyway.

"Now, give me a hand, okay?"

"Yeah, yeah, yeah."

Fifteen minutes later the car was empty. I thanked Jimmy, and then raced into the living room where Mom and Pop had deposited themselves on the couch in front of the TV.

"I'll be back by dark, guys. I'm gonna' run down to Carol's and say hi to her. Bye"

"Now you wait just a minute..." Mom began, but by the end of her sentence I was long gone. Twenty-three and a half seconds later I arrived at the gates of Heaven, dashed directly up the front steps, and then drew up all my courage and knocked on her door. I prayed she'd answer, and not Saint Peter with a scowl on his face and wagging a "you're-banging-on-the-wrong-door" finger at me. Her father opened the door and I wanted to cry.

"Yes?"

"Um, hello Mr., um…sir. Is Carol here?" Those were tough words to utter. Her father didn't look offended though. He wasn't much taller than me, and his piercing eyes displayed more surprise than anything else.

"Yes, she is. And who are you?" he asked me in a level tone of voice.

"Oh, sorry. I'm Skip Morley, sir. I live up the street and just got home. I wanted to come and say hi to your daughter…my friend." Somehow my words sounded, to me at least, like an obvious lie. What I really wanted was to whisk her away and find a priest to marry us, and I wondered if he suspected as much.

"Just a moment," he replied without batting an eye. "Carol, there's a young man here to see you."

That was it. I was home free!

Seconds later she appeared in the doorway, and but for the grace of God I would have fainted on the spot. She wore the same Bermudas I'd seen her in not fifteen minutes ago, but a light pink sweater, now, that rolled over on itself at the neck. I shuddered. The image of her I'd cultivated, nourished with all my might in her absence, came back to life ten times more powerful as I stood there with a silly grin on my face.

"Hi! Where've you been? I missed you…I mean I came by a couple of times on my way to the store, and…why'd you go to the party with *him*?"

She smiled at me, and I knew whatever else I might say would sound exactly like it had come from the mouth of a first grader. So I ended the gibberish and waited for her musical voice to rescue me. She quietly pulled the door closed behind her and motioned for me to take a seat on the porch swing. We sat down, and then she finally spoke.

"We've been out of town. I waited for you that afternoon as long as I could. Remember that day? Well, when you didn't come back I went to my dance class all by myself. A few days later your friend sent me an invitation to his party…"

"He's not my friend!"

"Oh. I thought he was. He said he was."

"He lied. He's a nitwit. A moron."

"Oh, I don't think he's so bad. He certainly likes you. That's what he kept saying at the party over and over anyway."

"He did?"

"Oh yes. He thinks you and your two friends rescued him. He admires the three of you very much, even though I believe it was the clown who..."

"I would have done the rescuing, but I was worried you'd get hurt, and...you know."

Carol looked suspiciously at me and smiled. "Uh-huh..."

"But that was over a month ago. You just disappeared! I kept coming by to explain what I did...I mean, didn't do at Allen's party, and why I'd missed coming back down that first time I met you and...you were just gone! Even at night your place was dark as could be."

Carol said nothing for a long, long moment, and continued to smile at me, cocking her head slightly so that her beautiful hair hung ever so slightly over the edge of her mouth. "You came back down every day and every night?"

"Well, yeah! I couldn't let that drip Allen...you know...win."

"I see." She spoke almost matter-of-factly, and I wondered just how sour that stupid admission I'd blurted out had tasted to her. I prayed that God would reverse time, just this once, so that I could rephrase what I'd said somehow. Carol looked at me, in control of the situation. She pursed her lips. "The week following the party my family and I went to New York City. We just got back last week."

Rescued!

I thought of New York and wondered if by some chance she knew Ginsberg. "Is that anywhere near a place called Manhattan?" I asked her.

"Manhattan is New York City, silly. Along with Queens and Brooklyn and a bunch of other boroughs."

"Boroughs? What are those?"

She laughed. "Suburbs, communities—like Lakewood and Englewood and Aurora. They're all connected by trains and bridges, though, because Manhattan is an island." As she explained to me the marvelous-sounding geography of

191

Patrick Sean Lee

Ginsberg's home, the sound of music inside broke through the partially open window to her right. I took my eyes off her briefly and glanced over her shoulder into the house. Her father sat in the room, which was dominated by a huge piano like the one Liberache played, but shiny ebony, not white. No candelabras graced it, no George stood beside him, but he played every bit as well as my Mom's favorite, always-grinning, celebrity. He played every bit as well as Pop, too, I thought.

"Wow! He's pretty good," I said looking back at her.

"Yes he is. I think, anyway. That's what we were doing in New York. My dad plays for the symphony here, but it isn't nearly as good as the one they have back there; The New York Philharmonic. He went to audition, to see if he could get a job with them, but for some reason he didn't get it. Anyway, Grandma and Grandpa still live there and we stayed with them for a whole month! He kept going back to see if he could get a job almost every day. Like I said, he didn't get it."

"I'm glad," I said.

"You are? Why would you be glad? He wanted it more than anything in the world."

"Because if he had, you would have had to move back there...and I never would have seen you again. You're not crazy about Allen, are you?" I kept stumbling over my own feet.

"Allen?" She laughed. "Of course not! You think I..."

I quickly moved on, hoping Carol hadn't been offended by what I'd just said without thinking. I was overjoyed though. "What's that he's playing? It's symphony, isn't it?"

She listened for a moment to the melody that was soft and hauntingly beautiful, much different than anything Jerry Lee Lewis or Fats Domino played. More like Liberache's stuff, but more intoxicating coming from her father's fingers.

"It's a song by this guy named Rachmaninov, I think. He doesn't live here in our country. I think he's dead, too. My dad loves him." She began to hum along with the music, and I supposed she'd heard it a hundred times before. I liked the song very much; it was all terribly romantic, me sitting there, easing closer to her side. I think I would have liked it a lot better if her father had speeded up the tempo and gotten a drummer and maybe a saxophonist to sit in with him. I told her that.

"You are so silly, Skip!" She laughed. "You listen to way too much rock and roll. I'm going to tell Daddy you want him to start a band. He'll die of laughter!"

"No! Don't do that. I was just kidding. Tell him I think he's really good, and that he's playing that song just perfect."

Carol abruptly changed the direction of the conversation and looked at me very seriously. "You'd like me to take off my glasses, wouldn't you? You've never liked them," she said, removing them.

She could have worn ten pairs of glasses, it wouldn't have mattered a bit to me. Her fingers had opened me up and stolen my young soul, as deftly and gently as her father's were sliding across the keyboard inside. The glasses did nothing to alter the image, in no way diminished the haunting beauty of the pure white flesh and almond eyes behind them. Carol, for the first time nervous, I thought, played with a tiny ring of sapphire, or some precious stone, on her finger. She didn't loose her eyes from mine though. I failed to answer her question, losing all remembrance of its even being spoken as I sat there wondering if my heart was going to stay inside me, or come flying out into her waiting hands, joining my missing soul.

"What did you say?"

"Do you think I'm pretty? Now you can see me close up."

"Oh Lord. Yes! I think you're the prettiest girl I've ever seen."

"Would you like to kiss me?" she whispered.

I gazed into the eyes that were smiling at me, and then down to her soft, thin lips. If I cowered and said no, I'd shoot myself as soon as I got home, or hang myself from the hoop still on the garage, or even jump head first from the treehouse. Every daydream I'd cultivated over the last months galvanized in that instant and hit me like a shot of adrenalin. My heart in her hands didn't beat, it vibrated.

"Yes."

She turned quickly. Her father continued playing, unaware that his daughter was making my head turn to gelatin, and my knees knock like a thousand drums. Assured he was still swimming frantically in his music, she returned to me, closed her eyes, and then pursed her lips. I stared dumbly at them for the briefest of moments, and then I closed my eyes and let my heart, which had leapt suddenly back into my chest, guide me to them.

"Carol," her father's deep voice shattered me. "I think it's time you came in now. Your mother could use some help in the kitchen."

Carol pulled away from me, a heated iron jabbed between our mouths. The look of surprise on her face was surpassed only by the flush in my cheeks, my temples, and the tips of my ears.

"I've got to go. Come back tomorrow. Thank you!" She slid her glasses back on, rose immediately, and walked to the door. Opening it, she turned her head and mouthed, "I like your new black eye. You'll have to tell me how you got that one."

After she'd pulled the door shut behind her, I wasted no time fleeing the scene of the crime, shaking badly, my ears aflame and head spinning wildly. On the way home I stumbled into half the cars parked on the street. The other half received monstrous kisses.

TWENTY-SIX

They Were Laughing

It rained the last two days of September. Another mysterious dumping like the terrible snowstorm last spring, but this deluge was simply wet. Gutters overflowed and swept debris along helplessly. A few brave kids in slickers and red galoshes splashed merrily against the flow, sending plumes of gray, freezing water rooster-tailing upward. The trees seemed to be shivering in the wind, unprotected this early in the season without the gloves of snow that would arrive within a month and stick to their barky fingers and gnarled arms. Saturated leaves of red and gold and brown clung desperately to the branches, waving madly at the kids, warning them to get out, get home before the flood.

I waited in the living room in my house, staring out the front window as the sky grew darker, wringing its endless self out, refusing to budge eastward toward the plains in the inadequate, tugging grip of the wind. But then as suddenly as it had begun, the lashing ended. A warm sun falling ever farther down the horizon line peeked out and sent splintered rays streaking across the dark green grass, covered, now, with a mantle of newly fallen leaves.

It was late afternoon, October 1st, when the sound of Jimmy calling urged me out the door. For once it wasn't trouble he wanted to introduce me to exactly, just gathering all the leaves into a combustible heap.

I was thankful that he rescued me from the boredom of watching the sun; watching weak trails of steam drift upward from the street pavement. I left the house, grabbed a rake, and we began the seasonal task.

We raked the leaves into piles—giant piles in which an army of Lilliputians could easily hide. We pushed and pulled them toward the front fence in my yard and the low hedge in his.

After a while I began to feel like a salmon trying to swim up a waterfall. The leaves just kept coming down.

We talked of many things as we worked, and sometimes Jimmy even made sense. I would have listened to his wild statements and his nonsensical responses to my questions even had he not though. Jimmy was more my brother lately than ever before, and it occurred to me that Fall was not the sad ending of a weird and wondrous Summer, but rather the grand beginning of another, different, exciting chapter in both our lives. We were growing in a hundred new, impossible directions suddenly. It was confusing, but we were in it together like never before. Like only brothers could be. I smelled something absolutely kind and all-encompassing floating in the air. Some benevolent spirit coursing over the two of us.

Jimmy and I would, over the next few days, get all the leaves together, and then we'd set them ablaze—if they ever stopped falling long enough for us to herd them up. And *if* the sun had done its duty during the previous week. But if the blaze weakened because of rain that refused to be burned out of them, then we'd just smoke them into eternity. That would be okay too. There were fewer smells as pungent and aromatic as basted elm leaves.

Early fall, chilly nights, fires in the front yards; these were maybe the finest of days. Magical days that stretched across the city and the universe into an almost-eternity of falling asleep in God's lap—until the gray at last descended in what at first would seem a permanent, frozen end to an enchanted autumn life. My rake's tines scraped the surface of the mottled grass adding a bewitching sound to the smell of decaying foliage. As he labored twenty-five feet away in the cool air, Jimmy reached into his beret and pulled out his own peculiar enchantment, one that he loved.

"...who coughed on the sixth floor of Harlem crowned
   with flame under the tubercular sky surrounded
   by orange crates of theology,
   who scribbled..."

He recited the lines from *Howl* in a reverential voice, in cadence with the movement of his rake.

I loved him. I mean, since stumbling over Ginsberg's eyes and crazy notions, he'd suddenly gone from spikey-haired Puck of Meade Street to inspired sprite of the urban canticle. I don't know if he had any idea what the poetry he spewed out meant, but he spewed it out with the zeal of a tent preacher.

"Crap, Jimmy, that doesn't make a bit of sense. None at all," I called over at him.

"'Course it makes sense! You just need to listen more careful. Quit reading that 'Mary had a little lamb' shit..."

Jimmy continued to recite Howl, which got worse and worse as the stanzas dragged by. He picked up the tempo of the words. His rake reciprocated by skipping over the grass more quickly in order to keep up.

"I don't think they'll ignite," I said, trying to get him to shut up and carry on something like a normal conversation with me for a change. Instead he answered with "...who were burned alive in their innocent flannel suits on Madison Avenue amid blasts of leaden verse..."

He was hopeless today. Wound up. Synthesizing his distressing Beat world to the upbeat reality of an existence that I think rasped at something deep in his soul. *I am in this world but not of it. Me and Gins.*

Where on earth was Madison Avenue, anyway? Baltimore?

"They'll ignite. I'll get the gas can if the fuckin' things get stubborn."

I understood those two sentences very clearly. Okay, so he might burn down the Morley residence or our beloved elm tree, but at least Jimmy was making sense again. And yet, I was enthralled in a queer way with his idiotic recitations.

"Hiya, fellas!"

Well, who could that be? Whose nasaly voice was distinguishable from that of anyone else's on the planet? I turned my head but continued pulling the leaves toward the front with the rake for a moment, toward the damaged fence and a smaller, neighboring pile. It was Allen of course, who had stopped on the street sidewalk. He looked like a tourist who'd just stepped off the bus from North Dakota—a camera dangling on a braided cord from his neck, black slacks, white socks and shirt, and Union Jack-colored sport coat yanked straight off the racks at Sears Roebuck. Beside him stood Carol, ablaze in a calf-length Irish tartan kilt and a black sweater. Yin and Yang. Ugly and Beautiful.

"Geez, Allen! Where'd you steal that coat from?"

"I LIKE it!" Jimmy popped.

"Huh?" I answered.

"Moloch! Beast of San Francisco! Cowboy of the moon! Whore of Denver!" Jimmy went on. Probably the best choice of words possible—they mirrored my thoughts about Allen exactly.

Okay, maybe I was mistaken. Maybe standing out there was the very hip 1957 Denver version of Beat fashion. Sort of like Leo Peepers as the Denver version of Dick Clark, or a rowboat being just a midget version of the Queen Mary. Yeah, that was it. That would explain his high-water pants and white socks. But, nothing, nothing could explain the jacket. It just wouldn't work anywhere, in any era—but it was truly Allen, and it was truly something I could imagine on the body of a hideous beast with a hundred eyeballs crawling out of the San Francisco Bay.

To my surprise Carol left his side immediately and walked up the small incline of grass and leaves to the fence. If she was put off by his get-up, her smile masked it. As a matter of fact, she seemed totally oblivious of his presence, which kind of shocked me. I laid my rake aside and leaned my arms onto the bent top rail of the fence.

"Hi!"

"Hi."

"What's up?"

"Nothing. Just walking home."

"Oh. I'm raking leaves."

"Yes, I can see that."

"Wanna' come in?"

She beamed. Adjusted her glasses a little higher on the delicate bridge of her nose. "I suppose so. Yes, that would be nice."

I rushed over to the front walk and unlatched the gate. Allen stood silently watching this exercise in proper romantic etiquette, as if taking mental note so that someday when he met the right girl he could...and then he followed us into the yard. Jimmy? I don't know. He stood otherworldly, like a statue downtown under the courthouse portico, most likely searching through his memory banks for another goofy verse.

Carol brushed past me and walked across the dark green carpet of grass toward the neatly raked pile of leaves. She glanced back at me with a smile as a gust of wind ruffled the ends of her hair.

"Come said the wind to the leaves one day,
Come o'er the meadows and we will play.
Put on your dresses, scarlet and gold,
For summer is gone and the days grow cold,"
she said out of the blue.

When she arrived she bent over and scooped a handful up, then let them move and roll back and forth in her hands as though she were contemplating fashioning something elaborate out of them, some amazing thing out of hundreds of leaves made of pure gold. And then she tilted her head a little and threw them back up in the direction they'd just come from.

"Go back! Don't leave us for the winter! Go back!" She laughed, and I half expected the little umbrella of gold and brown and dark, dark green to obey her. To streak upward into the maze of branches and reattach themselves to the tree. They responded as instructed for an instant, then turned and fluttered downward in greater obedience to God's physics.

"Moloch! Moloch! Robot apartments! Invisible suburbs! Skeleton treasuries! Blind capitals..." Jimmy found his voice. He had laid his rake down onto the grass and hopped to the side-yard fence. What possible connection his last statement had to Carol's beautiful ode to the fallen leaves totally escaped me. Carol laughed at him, and then threw herself back into the pile of waiting leaves. I felt in that moment as though I'd raked them all up for this very instant in time. A golden bed for a diamond goddess. Jimmy bounded over the fence and joined her on his hands and knees.

"You understand?" His eyes were like those of a fish.

She turned her head quickly to look up at him, and answered, "Not at all...the words make no sense, but I think they're funny the way you've strung them all together. Are they from a poem you've written?" She sat up; I joined them on my knees. Allen stood ten feet away and began fiddling with the camera, mumbling. Carol added almost as an afterthought, "Really, though, what are skeleton treasuries! Robot...apartments? Robot! It's all too funny, Jimmy. Honestly, you are too, too weird, but I like you anyway."

A few stubborn leaves clung to her hair. I envied their fingers. She shook them free and then grabbed another handful and tossed them over Jimmy's head. He sat back a few feet from her in the crushed pile and rolled his grayed eyes, as though her questions to him were stranger than the robot apartments in Ginsberg's poem.

Click! Clicketty, clicketty, clicketty. Click! Allen moved in a semi-circle around the three of us, then back to his starting point, bent slightly to lower the angle of his shots, snapping, then winding.

"Skeleton treasuries? Society, Gins says. I mean most of it has to do with our corrupt, stulti—sulti—umm...spirit-crushin', post-war way of life," Jimmy explained.

"I don't think I understand at all," she said.

"That's what Howl is all about! How society has given up on bein' individual, sort of. I think that's what it is."

I watched Carol. She fixed her eyes on my best friend, waiting anxiously, I think, for a sermon or a loftier explanation from him. Her focus was as intent as his ramblings. Still, he was utterly absorbed in the earnestness of it all.

"Doggone! I seem to have run out of film! You guys stay here...I'll return shortly with a fresh roll. Don't go away, okay?"

Allen hesitated—waited for someone to assure him we wouldn't ditch him.

"Yeah, sure. Go get your film. Take your time," I said without taking my eyes off Carol. She tipped her head slightly, trying to read Jimmy's unspoken mind I thought. I heard Allen stumble out the gate.

What do you mean, exactly? Tell us. Individuality? Is that what you mean? Carol asked Jimmy with her stare, her delicate smile. I saw the words, the thoughts, I swear it.

Something possessed me, like the strange words possessed Jimmy. I moved my hand carefully, unobtrusively, until my fingers found hers beneath the leaves. She lifted them just a little, and I let mine stop them, settle them. I closed my thumb and index and forefinger over her fingers. Her eyes shot a glance at me without her head moving at all, and then she returned her attention to her new, crazy friend. My heart raced.

Jimmy heard her thoughts, too, I think. I'm certain. We all stopped. Everything stopped as though God had rung a bell ending the first day in the creation of the world. We knew one another intimately for a thousandth of a second. A shorter span of time than imaginable; but there it was. I tightened my fingers around Carol's. She was smiling.

"I think Ginsberg's upset that our parents want us to become like robots. No brains. Automatons or automations, or whatever. You know? Watch TV till our brains turn to black jelly so that we can just...I don't know for sure the rest of it. Gins does. She could tell you."

"She wrote *that*?" Carol asked in surprise.

"Nah. This cat named Allen Ginsberg did. Last year. It's like this eight page poem that's filled with i-er-nee an' sadness cuz all his friends are these brilliant drug addicts an' they're dyin' an' society don't care. None of us cares. Gins loves it so much that she adopted his name. She ain't Sarah Bernstein no more. Just Gins."

"She loves that they're all dying?" I asked.

"No, dummy. The poem. Howl. It's her bible," Jimmy said.

"Is she a Catholic?" I asked, getting just a little confused by the deep theological direction the conversation was heading into.

Carol laughed in a hearty, undignified way. I wondered, as she fell back into the leaves, if I'd said something altogether stupid again.

"What difference does it make what religion she is or ain't?" Jimmy asked.

"Well...uh, I guess that us Catholics don't believe in the Bible. That's all. Maybe Howl ought to be her Baltimore Catechism. If she's a Catholic."

"Whaddya mean we don't believe in the Bible? I heard Sister Dolorine say that Jesus' crucifixion is told about in the Bible. So, if we believe in God and Jesus and Mary and Joseph, an' all that stuff, then we must believe in the Bible, right?" he said with a certain air of incredulity.

I thought about it. I supposed so, even though I'd never dared crack the cover of the book because I'd heard something, somewhere, that it was like trying to understand Shakespeare, with all those thee's and thou's and begets and such. I guessed that it was okay to read it, but what for when the Baltimore Catechism had all the important stuff laid out in plain and simple English? Carol tightened her fingers on mine just a bit. I can't imagine she agreed with my thinking, but I definitely liked her fingers.

"Skip Morley, you should really consider reading the Holy Book. It answers all mankind's questions. Every other religious book is just a commentary on what God wrote inside the Bible. We don't need anyone else's opinion on what He wants for us. It's all there. The fact that Gins ranks that poem, or that guy Ginsberg, up there with the Holy Bible just means it's very, very important to her," Carol said.

"Oh." I squeezed her fingers gently, hoping that I hadn't displayed the true depth of my ignorance to her. Moreover, I didn't want to push the conversation too far and risk going to hell by thinking or doing something that the nuns and Father Blinker and the Pope might disapprove of. Like reading the Bible.

I wondered if they really didn't want us to because it was so hard to understand? Or was it...what was it? Why were we so different than Protestants? Which group of us was going to be sent to hell? God, I hoped it wasn't Carol's. Well yes I did, but I honestly prayed that she could sneak by Saint Peter somehow. I really did.

"Yeah, dork," Jimmy added.

I guessed that I was a dork.

"Is she your girlfriend, Jimmy?" Carol asked, changing the subject.

"Sure is. I'm gonna' run away here pretty soon. Maybe by Thanksgiving. I'm gonna' hitchhike back to Manhattan and then me an' her are gonna' get a pad."

"A what?" I asked.

"An apartment or a house," Carol said. I was beginning to get the feeling that maybe she knew everything. Everything. I liked that. I loved it.

"Oh. How do you think you're going to do that?" I asked Jimmy, all of the sudden realizing that his plan, if that's what it really was, was insane. "You'll flunk out of school, and your mom'll send the cops after you. You can't run away...dummy!"

"Watch me. Wanna' go with me, Carol?"

She sat up. By so doing she was forced to pull herself free from my hold. Carol looked first at me, and then brought her eyes to bear like two searchlights on Jimmy. For a moment she said nothing. I tried to find her fingers beneath the leaves again.

"I don't think so, but thank you for the invitation."

The sound of Allen's clomping footsteps returning him to our comfortable home in the pile of leaves broke the silence that followed. He rattled the gate open. "Hey! You're all still here! I got the new roll of film! It's in. Gosh, you're all still here!"

"Where else would we be?" I snickered. I stared at Carol's hair, dangling, disrupted by the leaves. She continued to look at Jimmy intensely. He smiled, suddenly, broadly. He laughed. Then he grabbed a handful of leaves and tossed them at Carol. The three of us stirred up the damp, golden feathers of leaves and began flinging them at one another.

I heard Allen's version of a curse. "Darn it! This thing is stuck! It won't move! Skip, help me get to the next frame, would you, please? It's stuck!" He sounded as though our lives depended on my answer. I glanced back at him. He was in an unknown world for a change, unable to reason the mechanical box into working correctly.

"Shit, Allen. Does your mother wipe your butt?" I rose and walked over to him.

"Skip Morley!" Carol said giggling.

I grabbed the camera from him and turned it over in my hands, tried to turn the small knob on top of it that wound the film. It refused to budge. I shot him an annoying glance. He simply looked hopefully back at me. After I tried one more time to turn the stubborn knob, ending up with the same disappointing result, I stepped beside him, and to his horror banged the piece of junk against the trunk of my elm tree. Then once again for good measure.

"Oh no! Skip!" he cried out.

I tried the knob again. It turned as easily as if an angel had slipped inside the camera and waved a finger or two at its guts. And I hadn't even asked anyone up there for help. I made a mental note to remember that trick.

"There. Try it now," I said handing the camera back to him.

Allen looked at it, then at me, and then back at the camera. He turned toward Jimmy and Carol who were sitting side by side, laughing and tossing handfuls of leaves up into the sky above them. Allen brought the camera to his eye, looked quickly over its top, back again into the viewfinder, and then clicked the shutter button. After that he bit his lip and tried to turn the knob. It made a click, click, click sound.

"Wow! Skip, you are a mechanical genius, I must admit that!"

"Oh shut up and take some more pictures. Wait'll I get back there. Get one of me and..." I stopped. And then I jumped into the leaves with my best friend and...my girl. We laughed together and threw handfuls of leaves everywhere, Allen clicking and running around us in his private, Protestant hog-heaven, until the pile was returned to its natural state of disorder in my front yard.

Ever the inquisitive type, the tinkerer of the clockworks of the universe, Jimmy jumped up covered in an armor of dead leaves and ran to Allen. "Lemme see that thing, Allen. Is it a Polaroid?"

"Oh, my goodness no! It's the latest. A Brownie Starlet 127. Very cool, don't you think?" Allen said.

"Yeah, very cool...Starlet, huh?" I heard Jimmy answer. "What hath Moloch wrought here?"

I caught Carol's eyes as Jimmy was certainly toying with the idea of changing the camera into some sort of explosive device, and in the split second that was eternity, I lifted her glasses, folded them carefully, and then leaned forward and kissed her. She'd closed her eyes when my face neared hers, and when I slowly backed away, I saw her lips slightly parted, pouting, blind and waiting for my mouth to touch hers again. So the feeling, finally, of a kiss—the feeling of Carol's wondrous lips. Stars, galaxies, lightning storms across the endless expanse of the universe. So it was that day.

Soon enough the clicking began again, and I anticipated many more explosions in the minutes, months, and years to come.

TWENTY-SEVEN

The Stars Approach

The coming days were fine, and long, and filled with the pleasantest thoughts of Carol. I drifted more and more into long daydreams of her; of meeting her constantly, constructing simple plots—each ending in a passionate kiss.

In the morning version, every day now, I'd board a bus—the same bus on which Allen bent her ear that day I was hightailing it to safety, Butch and Inky hot on my heels. The bus was always at a standstill when I expectantly jumped aboard, and conveniently she'd be the only passenger, sitting alone and beautiful far off in the rear. I'd walk back to where she sat. Sometimes Carol would be engrossed in a book, sometimes occupied gazing absently out the window, unaware of my presence. A few times sitting with her eyes closed.

I'd interrupt her; awaken her gently. She would always smile up at me, and then I'd sit down confidently, very close to her, our bodies touching, separated by only impossible denim barriers. Our conversations were simple enough.

"Where should we go today?"

"Around and around the city. All day long," Carol would answer. And so off we'd go.

In that morning bus ride I always carried a guitar unobtrusively slung over my shoulder by a strap, and it would mysteriously appear in my grasp seconds after I took my seat beside her. I'd sing to her. One day my voice would be Jackie Wilson's or Elvis Presley's, the background accompaniment vinyl or AM radio-perfect. I'd sing until the tear-jerking ending, or the bus driver would stomp on the floorboards and shout, "Goddamit', Skip, turn that music down!"

These daydreams consumed the early morning or late evening hours while lying in bed, replayed in a loop over and over with only minor variations for deeper admissions of never ending love.

Afternoons, if Jimmy or Mickey weren't with me with their distractions, I'd sit alone against a pole in the vacant lot across the street, or climb up into our half-finished treehouse, and construct a slightly more elaborate dream.

Our bus would now be a carriage pulled by a white horse, and once we'd seated ourselves, covered over with a thick Ermin blanket, away we'd go. Down Meade Street at a trot, and then a gallop, until the horse shot upward into the night sky. Carol and I would sail at ten times the speed of light through a cloud of mist into marvelous worlds far beyond the eastern seaboard, sitting under the Ermin blanket while the horse raced outward through the star-filled sky. These times neither of us ever spoke as the white horse soared by Mars and its gangly-limbed nymphs, out past Saturn and Pluto, and then off toward the center of the galaxy. I showed her Pleides and Capricorn; scooped stardust from the edge of a nearby Nova when we passed by it. She held my arm tightly as I poured the sparkling stardust, alive in a rainbow of colors, onto the fur that covered us. We watched its energetic dance, delighted. Then piece by piece, bit by bit, it would leave and whoosh by us like red and yellow and green musical notes, shooting back into the fabric of God's universe.

Somewhere in that magical journey Carol would always cuddle closer, as close as my skin—because I suspected that the vast universe was very cold—and lay her head into my warm chest.

One of my favorites though, was no more attainable than the others, but somewhat more realistic I thought. Walking up Meade Street I'd near her house and collapse for some unknown reason right on the sidewalk, stricken by some fever or accident. Carol would appear as if my presence and condition were a beacon. Out the door and down the steps she'd run, followed naturally, by her mother in great distress. Instead of calling for an ambulance, or contacting my mother who was only a block away, they'd lovingly carry me into their house and place me in a bed in the spare bedroom (which I had no idea might even exist). Weeks would pass, Carol lovingly nursing me back to health.

"He's much too sick to move, Mrs. Morley. I think it would be best if he stayed here..."

This particular dream somehow always morphed into one a little more realistic, however. I'd simply leave home and move into her doghouse in the backyard.

And so my affections for my best friend diminished in the face of my first attack of love at Carol's hands. Jimmy suffered a similar attack, but his connection to Gins was stymied following Mrs. McGuire's discovery of the first long distance phone bill. Unable to stop his calls to New York, she merely unplugged the phone and took it with her whenever she left the house, at which Jimmy resorted to writing two or three letters a day. He never showed them to me, but I could only imagine the difficulty Gins suffered deciphering them when she received them.

Even so, despite our new romantic interests, Jimmy and I bounced back into one another's orbits on a regular basis, due to the fact that school finally started up again. It had done no good for me to plead with Mom and Pop to let me leave Presentation Catholic School and enroll in Kepner Junior High where Carol was enrolled, nor could Jimmy (for the moment) leave the same and fly off to Manhattan where Gins undoubtedly attended Beatnik Junior High. We were stuck with one another.

And with Allen when the spirit moved me to bully someone.

And then Jimmy for some strange reason took Allen under his black wing.

TWENTY-EIGHT

Down The White Rabbit's Hole

Jimmy and I found Allen in his basement bedroom, a room the size of a rabbit hole. Since the entire Jung house was about 500 square feet or so, and the basement covered only a fraction of that area, it had at first seemed impossible for three or four of us to squeeze down there all at the same time. We did it though. Some men from the government space program had even visited it a few times in the recent past, Allen swore, and took a thousand photographs of it so they could use the Brownie Starlet prints to help them draw up plans for spaceships they were going to make in the near future that would take us to Mars. It hit Jimmy that it'd be cool if a person could dig underneath the Jung's basement and stick a Redstone rocket down there, then he could shoot the whole house into space in search of the sexy Martian girls with squiggly arms and legs. Allen and us along with it.

I imagined there was one of those ladies from the red planet with Allen's name tattooed on her butt, just waiting for us to splash down into one of the canals so she could get her hands on him. If I remembered correctly from Jimmy's lectures last summer in his backyard, the Martian girls were a lot wilder than earthling girls, due in no small part to their two huge, traveling green eyeballs, and three spaghetti arms and hands that could wiggle all over a person's naked body. Jimmy said they particularly liked American boys because we had big muscles and handsome faces, and other physical "features" that the Martian guys totally lacked. Like doinks.

Allen's mother let us in after some somber eye-wiggling of her own. She met us at the back door, tea-towel slung over her left shoulder. Standing there looking up at her, I reasoned that the Jung family hadn't gotten one of the new dishwashing

209

machines yet, and further that Allen must have been exempted from the loathsome task of doing the dishes by hand. Another reason to turn up my nose at him.

"Well, hello...boys. What can I do for you?" she asked with one eyebrow raised. Behind her on the end of the cabinet next to the window, overlooking the sink, hung a cat-clock. The cat was black, and it was snarling. Its pendulum tail wagged methodically back and forth, and its gargantuan black eyes followed suit in the opposite direction. It growled 4:32 P.M.

I looked nervously over at Jimmy—the quicker-witted of the two of us. He wasted no time getting straight to the point; the reason us nitwits were standing out in the growing North Pole wind on their back stoop without jackets, shivering.

"It's colder'n the hubs of hell out here, Mrs. Jung. We came to see Allen an' get outta' this gale. Is he home?"

Her mouth dropped a little at Jimmy's comment, but she stepped away from the door and pointed to the stairway railing tucked against the far wall at the end of their kitchen.

"He's in his room. No trouble, mind you. I won't be far away. I don't know why he associates..." she trailed off.

We grinned at her, politely excused ourselves, and then shuffled past her to the stairs. The sound of music very much unlike what Pop or Carol's father played, or anything I would bother listening to, greeted us. Some Jazz stuff. Saxophone and piano fighting, I'd call it. Despite the battle, a soft glow from fluorescent lights bathed the pit and gave it a paradoxical, inviting glow. Allen was so lucky, I thought. The jerk. I saw ceiling joists whenever I looked up while lying in my bed. He saw cottage cheese, and lights hidden in the plaster above his head, sort of like what Jimmy would see in his bed, only there wouldn't be any darts dangling up there like bats.

"I'm with you in Rockland!" Jimmy yelled into the void. A second later Allen's body bounced into view. A lot about him had changed, and it made Jimmy smile. He knew, of course, precisely what was going on with that kid down there because he was the author of it all. Jimmy bounded down the steps, but I remained where I stood, unsure whether any of the upcoming conversation could possibly make a bit of sense.

Allen answered. "Who threw their watches off the roof to cast their ballot..."

And Jimmy responded without breaking stride. "...for Eternity outside of Time...YES! Moloch hath wrought this. THIS! Thou art Moloch! Greetin's, distressed brother!"

It seemed obvious looking at him that Allen had set a course for absolute Beatnik craziness, and in the process had burned a whole slew of bridges behind himself. Gone was the Union Jack sport coat that made cats run for cover when he walked by, and in its place was a jet-black turtleneck sweater that had to have made witches sing, even at high noon. Light, almost tee-shirt weight. Very cool. He didn't wear a beret like Jimmy, but his horn rimmed glasses lent a certain sophistication to his face when you considered the turtleneck and the new hairstyle. Short, combed straight down all the way around his head, nearly to his eyebrows, jet-black, too. His trousers—jet-black. Socks—jet-black. Of course the shoes—jet-black penny loafers with Abraham Lincoln's image in copper relief, painted—jet-black. Very, very cool. At midnight, walking along in a dark, frightening alley, he'd appear to be a disembodied face. A disembodied face reciting disembodied poetry.

"Daddy-O. Welcome to my pad," he said to Jimmy.

In that moment, standing at the top of the stairs, I felt as though I didn't exist in the existential world he and Jimmy had marched off to, and I felt a little jealous of Allen once again. A couple of months ago it was Carol I vied with him over. Now it was my best friend. The truth of the matter was there was something about the guy with the horn-rimmed glasses that in the end sucked people into his weird orbit. Something that maybe I, Skip Morley, lacked. Realizing this potential truth, I devised a scheme in the blink of an eye to force my way down that slippery slope of coolness, directly back into their arms.

"Hey, Daddy-O's-ville! Cool clothes you're wearing. Cool pad, too. I, umm..."

211

I choked. I stopped right there because it hit me that I had become a slightly younger version, a caricature, of Mr. Peepers. Whatever spirit had touched Jimmy and Allen, made them so easily find the door into another intellectual realm, I couldn't touch. Like Mr. Peepers, I found myself wanting to be cool, but I just didn't have it. I eventually adapted a little of the slang, but my head wasn't cut out for it. Like Peepers in a way, I was bald and old and irrelevant. The best I could hope for was to look only slightly foolish.

"Hi Skipster! Come on down."

Looking down the narrow stairs into his room was exhilarating, in a way. I'm sure space had to have been a major consideration when Allen's quiet dad (who I was sure never uttered a word to anyone about anything in his entire life) was deciding where to locate the access point to the basement room. And it was a point. A tiny, square hole in the floor, with a ladder like you'd see on a battleship, only Mr. Jung painted all of it eggshell white instead of Enterprise gray. Allen's own private, personal bedroom was a safe place for him to hang out in because his mother couldn't possibly get safely down there. I was sure of that.

Standing there at the landing I wondered at first how they'd ever gotten any furniture through the galley kitchen and then through that dinky hole in the floor, but Allen had explained in a couple million words just exactly how his brilliant father had done it. He'd taken a saw and a hammer and a pile of wood, he told Jimmy and Mickey and me one day, and, "...fellas, it was something to behold. Exceptional, conceptually outside the limitations of normal building techniques. Who would ever think that someone could actually construct a bed and a matching dresser and a built-in desk right there inside a finished room? Well, my father could, and he did!"

I'd frowned, remembering farther back at that point in his speech about Pop's carpenterial efforts. The bent nails, the smashed thumbs and the cursing, the mostly ratty, kooky results—when there were even results to be seen. Jimmy took it all in stride this day, though, lifting the end of the frilly bedspread, looking at the smooth, sanded and painted legs of the bed as Allen traveled energetically down that long expository road. The drawers, too. Somehow attached beneath the whole thing, out of sight, spacially meaningful, ingenious, filled with neatly folded clothing. Mr. Jung never drank anything stronger than tea, and he built really nice stuff—maybe as a result.

Allen might pretend to be a Beat, might threaten to incinerate the White House or Wall Street or the Cathedral of the Immaculate Conception a few miles east of our houses, but inwardly he was still pure and sweet and incapable of incinerating even a match.

I followed Jimmy down into the tiny room. Stepping off the bottom tread of the stairs running against the north wall, seeing the life size traffic cop poster pasted on the far wall beyond the bed, suggested to me that I make a quick right turn, or else take the two steps forward and plop onto the twin-sized bed. On either side of the bed, twin nightstands held twin lamps with twin shades, and a variety of books and miscellany, all neatly arranged. This place was definitely not Jimmy.

"Please don't mind those model airplanes hanging over there, fella's, or the pictures of the Presidents—I just haven't had time to remove them. He gestured at three light-gray plastic models dangling from the ceiling above the miniscule walkway between the desk his father had built sitting against the other exterior wall, and the end of the perfectly made bed. The models swung lazily as though a light breeze had somehow entered the room—which none could because, unlike in my spacious bedroom, his dad had neglected to insert a single window for ventilation. Zombie spirits zooming overhead maybe, trapped, frustrated, with very little room to operate. Keeping an eye on all of us, or just searching for a way out? Allen was the worst rebel I could imagine. Guardian angels were the last thing he needed. Angry demons would ignore him entirely.

Jimmy sat down on the end of the bed. "Hey man, you need some German Zero's attackin' them B-29's. I saw a picture in Life or Look or one of them magazines where this guy melts em' together—like cars and tanks and stuff—so they look like they've just crashed into one another. It's really cool."

"You're probably referring to the Stuka, or JU-87, although any number of other Luftwaffe aircraft might be appropriate, and worthy to be hung in battle from my ceiling...well, such as the ME-109, which was a very popular fighter among the Nazi pilots. And actually, Zeros were Japanese..."

I looked around as Allen took off on a transcontinental flight. Nothing about him had really changed, not really. It hit me that first time I went down there and saw the wardrobe standing in the corner of the room across from Jimmy's long legs that Allen's world was light years from mine. Order personified his upbringing. Order and the smell and feel of new things. Furniture without rips in the fabric, or ugly dings in the woodwork. Very clean, freshly painted-looking walls. Linoleum floor instead of raw concrete with a raggedy rug thrown over part of it. Neatness. I didn't exactly know what that tall wooden case was at first though. After all, I was a child of the Twentieth Century, not the Nineteenth. I mean, why would someone need to enclose their clothing unless it was inside a separate room called a closet? A unique idea, I had to admit; the wardrobe—better than the exposed pole hanging from two heavy wires in my room on which Mom hung my shirts and pants and single belt. Still, all things considered, his room was functional, if not roomy. Not a good place to invite a gang of friends down to for a wrestling party, but more than adequate for doing homework, and then heading off to dreamland.

"...no, it's true. I saw it for real on TV last year! The Piper Cub smashed right into the Ferris Wheel back in New Jersey. It did! I saw it, Jimmy. There it hung, all smashed up with dead people falling out of the cockpit door..."

"Hey! You gonna' go to the Bazaar this year, Moloch? There's a Ferris Wheel there, ain't there Skip? Big sucker, too. Not as big as the one at Lakeside, but it's cool. We can ride it and watch for low flyin' Stukas or whatever the Commies fly nowadys. Shoot em' down!" Jimmy said.

"Well, we'd need a particular weapon of immense caliber—which none of us has..."

"Oh shut up, Allen." I couldn't help myself with this wide-eyed, gullible nut. This guy who all of the sudden was going to revolt against society. He was impossibly naive. Like when we would hopscotch down the city sidewalk on our way to the Comet and play 'Step On a Crack...Break Your Mother's Back'. Allen would disintegrate whenever he stumbled onto a chink in the concrete. On a certain level he believed, I think, that his mother actually suffered because of his clumsiness. She probably did. That's why she had Mr. Jung dig this pit to stick him in.

Jimmy laughed. "I'll bring my zip gun."

"Yeah, right," I said.

"Okay, the one I'll make, then. The plane'll have to get pretty close, but if it does, I'll shoot the Nazi bastard right between the eyes!"

"How does one construct a...what did you call it? A zip gun? And please watch your tongue..." he lowered his voice to a barely audible whisper, "...Mother might be eavesdropping, even as we speak."

"'Sjust a twenty-two caliber. I dunno'. A handle, a tube for a barrel. A bullet chamber. Inky's got one ya' know. Maybe I'll steal it from him. If I can see one, I can make it out in the garage, right Skip?" Jimmy said smiling.

"What makes you think you could ever steal Inky's zip gun—even if he has one? Maybe he'd shoot you with it, but he'd never let you get close enough to put your hands on it."

"I concur," Allen concurred.

"I dunno'. Sneak up on 'im I guess."

"You aren't serious, are you?" I said. I looked over at Allen, who was standing near the wardrobe, staring from his vantage point in another time and place at the aircraft hanging a few feet above us. He lifted his hand, fingers spread like the wings of one of the attackers, and coursed through the skies above southern England.

"Hell no. But we are gonna' go to the Bazaar. Maybe shoot matches out of the Ferris Wheel. Right Allen?"

"Whatever you say, Jimbo." He shot his cannon at a Liberator. "I'll buy some airplane glue and we'll get some matches to melt the plastic. I believe that with a little effort and...what were you saying about Inky Minkle?"

Jimmy blinked. "Nuthin'. I got some glue up at my house. Let's go get it and some matches. A lighter'd work better though. I'll steal one of Mother's. Yank them planes down and let's get outta' here. Ya' know, I saw a wreck once that this guy made...smashed a '55 Ford Crown Victoria into a telephone pole made out of a broom stick. Dead bodies all melted up, layin' everywhere. It was pretty cool."

"Help me remove the airplanes, fella's. Wait up!"

"Hang on, Allen." Jimmy returned the few feet to the end of the bed. Allen was beside himself, looking up, wondering how he would possibly be able to reach the thumb tacks holding the fishing line and the soon-to-be-melted planes. To Allen's horror, Jimmy hopped onto the end of the bed and snatched the lot of them with one sweep of his hand.

"There. Let's get outta' here now, Moloch."

"My goodness, Jimbo..."

***

"Where's Mick?"

"I don't know. Not going, I guess."

"Why not?"

"I'm not sure...but I'm not going either."

"What?"

"Well, not with you and Allen, anyway. I'm going with Carol. And my folks." I uttered the last sentence as though it was a confession of some horrible sin. It was. They'd agreed to let me take Carol to the annual Bazaar at Presentation Catholic Church. Tonight would be our first official date, and I'd be free to hold her hand. It would only be right and proper there.

I was jazzed.

TWENTY-NINE

And Across The Styx

I loved the Bazaar almost as much as I loved Christmas Eve Midnight Mass. The city of colored lights strung out on frosty poles set at intervals all along the church property announced our intentions to the world. Enter in, bring your wallet, but leave your cares (and a few of your morals) behind.

Booths hawking games of skill lined the edges of the school parking lot. Jars of jams and pickled pig's feet, freshly baked breads that had filled the air with fragrance and dominated the earlier years' merchandise were still around, though packaged now, like goods straight out of the warehouses of General Mills. Gaming tables lay tucked beneath the tall eves of the brick building housing the classrooms of our latest expansion project two years ago in 1955. To one side of it, as far away from the church's sanctuary as possible, stood a brightly decorated, flashy, but makeshift bar, stocked with enough liquor to bring every drunk in every Salvation Army across the city to his knees.

I'd put the specter of Inky and Butch far in the back of my mind; replaced the nightmare of running across them with the excitement of wandering with my friends through the noisy half square block parking lot transformed by the colorful booths and rides into a sort of Garden of Earthly Delights. Though I hadn't given a single thought to it, the gates that year were slated to be opened on a momentous evening. All Hallows Eve.

A marvelous idea burst into my love struck head as I watched the workmen from the windows of my classroom bring the truckloads of rides and booths onto the church grounds, and then erect them all week long outside.

I'd determined to invite Carol.

And so, I paid her folks a visit one early afternoon, the day the gates of Hell were beginning to swing open, letting all the restless devils out for a night of merriment at our expense upstairs. Little did I know what they had in mind for me. I ran to her house filled with expectations of an evening of magic. I wasn't to be disappointed.

Mr. Hudson answered the door and invited me in with a pleasant smile. I explained my reason for the visit, and my intentions for his daughter, who appeared suddenly from the rear of the house with her mother at the sound of my voice.

"Mr. Hudson, please let her go! She'll love it! There are rides and games of chance and, and...refreshments—it's great fun. Of course my folks will be there along with hundreds of other adults. I'll take good care of Carol. You can trust me," I told him.

"I don't know..."

"Ah, please, Mr. Hudson," I said again.

Carol rushed across the room to my side and sealed the deal. "Oh Daddy, may I, *please*?"

Her father glanced at his wife, who stood smiling, and then he shook his head.

"Well...alright. I suppose. Let me have your phone number and I'll call your father. I want Carol to be home no later than ten o'clock though."

"Understood, sir!" My heart shot to new heights at those words.

I quickly jotted down our number on the back of one his music scores, handed it to him, and then turned to Carol. I was ecstatic and wanted badly to say something romantic, like, "Our first date!" But I didn't. Instead I simply said, "Wear something warm. It's chilly at the top of the Ferris Wheel! We'll be down to pick you up at seven. Bye!"

A few hours later Pop pulled up to the curb in front of the Hudsons' house, still not quite over the shock of hearing Mr. Hudson's voice on the phone informing him that it would be fine to have Carol accompany the three of us to the Bazaar. In my state of profound joy I'd completely forgotten to tell either him or Mom about my first date, that is until the phone rang.

I checked for the number seventy-five bus that might be rumbling down the street behind us, ready to take our door along with it, and when I was certain it was nowhere to be seen, thrust the door open and took off at bullet speed across the street to her door. Mom and Pop followed at their usual crawl.

We stepped across the threshold when Mr. Hudson answered the bell. I greeted him and Mrs. Hudson quickly, "That's my dad and mom, Mr. and Mrs. Hudson," then raced to Carol's side.

Mom shook hands with Carol's parents, and the two of them eased away from the door and began chatting. Pop gasped, and nearly stumbled back out the way he'd come when he laid eyes on Mr. Hudson's baby grand that stood out in such grandeur inside the room to the left.

"My God," Pop said low as he took hold of Mr. Hudson's hand, peering over the man's shoulder at the piano. "What a beauty. Do you play...or your daughter...or...?"

"Oh, I do," said Mr. Hudson, who could not possibly have known anything about my father's melting soul at the sight of the classic Baldwin instrument. "For the symphony here in Denver, actually."

"Really!"

"Yes. For about eight years, now. I auditioned last summer for The New York Philharmonic, you know. No go, though. Pretty stiff competition back there."

Pop nodded. I had no idea whether sympathetically or in acknowledgement of the difficulty involved in getting a seat with the best orchestra in the country. He walked over to the piano shining in black, and gently rubbed his fingers along the music sheet stand. I know he would have died in ecstasy to have taken a seat, but he didn't. I know he only dreamt of it.

"Do you play?" asked Mr. Hudson.

"Oh, a little. Not on a beauty like this, certainly, but I dabble some on the parlor piano we have." He forced a little laugh.

That statement set the hook. The two of them took position on either side of the piano and spoke of composers and music and playing until I felt the evening would melt into daylight. Not once in the conversation did Pop mention the true extent of his own abilities. To this day I'm unsure just where his compositions might have ranked alongside the finest talents in history, or of Mr. Hudson's proficiency interpreting them. All my father's music has flown away, like clouds, or words, or notes—but as I remember their beauty and complexity I...well, no, I'm unsure. What can we really recall about the magnificence of yesterday's, or last year's clouds and words and notes?

I eased my anxiety about being stuck with all the adults in Carol's house until I grew a beard and sprouted wrinkles in my face by gazing into her flawless face and cautiously touching her fingertips with mine. The moments whisked by, however, and finally my parents' duties at the Bazaar overcame Pop's love affair with Mr. Hudson's piano, and Mom's propensity to query Mrs. Hudson about theology, the Irish versus the English, and the one thing that soundly bonded them—making a proper stew. We left at last for the church a mile away on Seventh Avenue and Julian Streets beneath a sky filled with twinkling stars.

Inside the car, Pop adjusted his rear-view mirror—very low, I thought—and glanced into it often, studying the angelic lines of Carol's face I was sure. Mom rarely looked forward, jabbering about everything under the sun to my guest, especially how delightful she'd found her mother—studying the angelic lines of Carol's face I was equally sure.

We arrived at the church and pulled into the reserved rectory parking lot. Before exiting the car Pop turned to Carol and me and said, "I'll be at the table right next to the refreshment stand; your mother will be manning the...what is it again, Rosie...?

"The handmade aprons and handkerchief booth at the far end of the lot. Now you two go on an' have a good time. Stay out of the church and the classrooms, mind you. An' don't go wanderin' around in the alley. Stay where everyone can see you. Understand?"

Carol blushed and said, "Yes, ma'am." I didn't reply. I was already skirting the car to help her out of the door like a young Sir Galahad.

This year Pop had chosen to man the Chuck-A-Luck table, a game in which the players almost always lost, betting on some sort of combination of dots appearing on three dice spun around in an hourglass-looking birdcage, next door, very close to the bar. The notion of paying someone—my father in this case—to watch three huge dice roll around in that wire contraption, then drop to the bottom, seemed about as interesting as watching bugs banging into a lightbulb on the patio at night. It was okay for maybe a minute or two, but beyond that time I tended to grow very, very sleepy.

Hand in hand we ran across the blocked-off street, under the strands of twinkling lights, and into the maze of bodies.

Carol was a knock-out, dressed in white peddle-pushers, Bobby-sox and loafers, and a maroon cashmere sweater. She'd pulled her glistening hair into a ponytail that bounced with every step, revealing her petite ears and a hint of the flawless white skin on the sides of her neck. She'd also removed her glasses and placed them inside her small, jeweled purse.

We slowed to a walk. I grasped her hand, and together we took in the sights and sounds. The mixture of calliope music and the horn and string sections of a local band hired to play swing hits for the dancers in the sea of revelers was a strange and disquieting combination. Like listening to opera in a honkey-tonk. Hank Williams shouting over Maria Callas. Still, here it all made a certain dazzling kind of sense, and made my blood pump the faster.

A forty-foot Ferris Wheel dominated the block, spinning slowly, carrying its cargo of terrified, elated, squealing passengers around and around. Beyond it to the north was the main boothed-off entrance, filled with people holding drinks and cotton candy, and the stuffed animals they'd won. I'd come with five dollars and fifty cents in coins saved up from raking neighbors' leaves the entire month on Saturdays. It was my intention that evening to throw a softball at the bottles in one of the booths and win the biggest teddy bear of them all. I'd give it to Carol and ask her to go steady. I'd kiss her again, too, in the shadows of the alley behind one of the classroom buildings

221

where I'd been instructed not to go. If it took my entire savings to win that bear, so be it. But, first things first. We *had* to ride the Ferris Wheel. Only fifteen cents apiece.

"Have you ever been on one of these things?" I asked her.

She laughed at me, as was her way following most of my dumb questions. But she squeezed my hand a little tighter as she answered. "Of course. We're not in Alaska. I've been to Elitch's and Lakeside, silly. Haven't you?"

"Oh, yeah. Yeah, a lot of times. I like the roller coasters they have the most. Scary. I mean, for most people...they don't frighten..."

"Good, then take me on this Ferris Wheel. They frighten me to death. It's like looking down out of an airplane without a floor beneath me. You won't let me fall, will you?"

"Heck no!"

Actually, the ride frightened me very much, almost as much as the roller coasters at the large amusement parks. I always imagined being at the top and feeling the rocking seat break loose from its anchors, or worse, the whole wheel ripping away from the central axle and taking me for my death ride across the parking lot and then down the street. Carol peered into my eyes for some hint of doubt. I hid my fear well enough though, I think. I urged her forward with a tug on her hand.

We took our seat. Mr. Chavez, the ride operator, snapped the bar securely across our laps, walked back to his control panel, and then we began the ascent. The evening air was crisp and cold as it coursed across our faces, moving us upward, upward, upward toward the apex. I glanced across the lot and the neighborhood lying beyond it, and then at Carol. Her eyes were shut tight, and she clung to me like a child to her father aboard a ship in a stormy sea. Suddenly my fear left me. I held her tighter.

"You're frightened to death. Do you want me to call for him to get us down right now?"

She didn't open her eyes when she answered. "No. I'm fine. Just don't let go of me."

"Oh my gosh! Open your eyes, Carol." I tried to be brave. "Oh, look around. We're just below Heaven. Look! You can see angels! And down there! It's Jimmy and Mick and Allen. Way down below us! Man alive, get a load of Allen's outfit!"

Carol drew even closer and put her face hard into my shoulder. "I couldn't see the angels or your friends even if I dared to open my eyes. Don't let go of me, Skip. Please, don't let go."

The wheel stopped just beyond the top of its loop with a lurch, making our seat rock. Carol dug her fingers deeper into my body, and I knew she'd had enough. When we finally swung back to our starting point at the bottom I motioned for Mr. Chavez to please let us off. Carol was nearly in tears, shaking. So far my efforts to impress her seemed to be failing.

"Let's go over to the bottle toss. Maybe I can win you something," I said as we left the ride.

"Yes, okay. Thank you for getting me off that thing. I was scared to..."

"I know. It's okay, too. I was even a little frightened. And nothing usually scares me. Do you want a Coke first?"

"No, not right now. Just go win me a prize. Something grand. I know you can!"

I led her to the booth with a brightly painted sign fixed to its lintel; "Bottle Bomber". Inside stood Mr. Moye, the school's coach, smiling, dignified as ever, and dressed in a red and white striped shirt and straw hat.

"Well, Skip! Good to see ya', son. And who's this little beauty beside ya'?" he asked.

"Hiya' Mr. Moye. This is Carol Hudson. Carol, this is our school's coach. The best darned coach in the whole city, too. I think I'm going to win her one of your best prizes, sir! She's my girl, you know!"

Carol blushed and tightened her grip on my hand.

"You don't say! Well step right up, Skippy. Twenty-five cents for three balls. I'll bet you'll knock them bottles down on your first throw. Yessiree, Bob. Have at it, son," he said, plopping three softballs down onto the booth counter.

I handed him a shiny quarter, smiled at Carol, then took aim at the bottles ten feet back in the booth. Five minutes later, and down to my last two quarters, I was still trying to figure out why the stubborn things seemed to be glued to the stand on which they sat. I'd been able to knock the top bottle off three times, and shanked the lower two once or twice, but getting all of them to topple seemed all but impossible.

"Coach, " I finally asked in frustration. "Is this game rigged? I know I hit those darned bottles hard enough to knock them down at least twice!"

Mr. Moye chuckled and then walked in two gigantic steps over to the stand. With a flick of his fingers he toppled all of them. As easy as that. He turned back to me with an amused look.

"Try again. You'll get 'em. Aim high and throw hard. It's all in the wrist. Give it another go."

Carol tugged at my sleeve as I handed the precious next-to-last coin to Mr. Moye. "Skip, I have to go to the restroom. I'll only be a minute. Can you tell me where it is?"

Embarrassed by my utter failure to topple the bottles, but bent on defeating them, I turned to her and replied, "There's one in the classroom building on the other side of the Ferris Wheel. The building next to the alley. Do you want me to go with you?"

"No, it's fine. You just win me something. Knock down those bottles. I'll be right back." She touched my hands for luck, or maybe just a silent gesture of her feelings, and then turned and walked through the growing throng in the direction of the classroom fifty feet away.

"It's cold out here tonight, isn't it Coach? It feels like snow," I said closing one eye, cocking my arm.

"Yes indeed. Way too cold for...that's right, turn those hips just a little. Yeah, you got it. Let 'er fly! Win that little gal o' yours a bear."

I ripped off the best fastball I'd ever thrown and watched it soar six inches high and to the right of the entire stack. Just like that. My aim wasn't getting better, it was headed south along with all my money. Mr. Moye walked out of the booth, bending low to clear the narrow opening, and came to the spot where I stood. I looked up at him with a look of dejection and held my last quarter out for him to take.

"No, no, you keep that, Skip. You'll need to buy your girl a Coke later on—when you give her the bear you won her. Here, lemme' see if I can help ya' get your aim down just a little better. See," he said taking hold of my shoulders and turning me slightly more sideways. "You got to get these shoulders in a straight line with your target—them bottles. Yeah, that's right. Now, put your left hand out there...no, no. Raise it up a little more. Yeah, that's right. Now, look down your arm at them bottles, like they was a bully you was gonna' throw your last rock at. Concentrate."

I did exactly as he instructed, seeing Butch's weasely eyes in the face of the bottles. Taking a deep breath and saying a little prayer to whomever might be inclined to be listening upstairs on a night like tonight, I let the ball fly. It crossed the field as though my hand and arm were still attached to it, pushing it straight and true, and crashed into the lower stack with a solid crack! The bottles flew apart. Satchell Page himself couldn't have done it any better.

"Whoo-hoo! I did it, Mr. Moye! I did it!"

"Well, 'course ya' did! Didn't I tell ya' you could do it? Now, which o' them stuffed animals you want?" he said walking back to the booth.

I knew exactly. I'd spotted it right off when Carol and I approached the booth a bit ago.

"That one," I said pointing at a fat, fluffy white one stuffed between a light brown one and a pink one. It would look perfect in her arms when she returned. And when she took it from my hands with an overwhelming display of astonishment at my accomplishment, my unbounded affection for her, I'd lead her west, toward the rear of the church property. To the tall fence, with a gate, and the stillness and quiet of the concrete alley beyond. To...I'd memorized the lines, choreographed the kisses.

"There ya' are, Skip," Mr. Moye said handing the bear to me ceremoniously. "If that don't earn ya' a little peck...well. There ya' go, son."

"Thanks, Mr. Moye! See you later." I turned, tucked the prize under my arm, and lit out to find Carol.

Another couple walked up to the booth as I turned. Mr. Moye returned to his spot inside, wishing me loads of good luck as he walked away. I pushed my way through the bodies, none of whose faces I had ever seen before, and made my way into the classroom building where I stationed myself a few feet from the Ladies Room to wait for Carol. It was odd, I thought standing there. There was no line, only a single woman dressed like a Polar bear, waiting patiently for whomever was inside to unlock the door and leave. A moment or two later the door opened, and to my dismay a girl about eight years-old emerged, smiling at the impatient lady in the fur coat as she chewed ferociously on a stick of gum. The woman skirted around her to do her business, and as the little girl walked past me I stopped her.

"Was there anyone else in there with you? A girl about my age?" I asked.

"Nope. Just me." And then she left in a hurry to melt into the thousand people outside.

I wondered if Carol had gotten lost, or gone into the wrong building. Maybe she'd thought I meant the classrooms behind the gaming tables? I left immediately and pushed my way through the bodies as quickly as I could, scanning left and right to see if we'd somehow missed one another in the mob. Seconds later I arrived at the Chuck-A-Luck table near the front entrance of the building. Pop was holding a bottle of beer in one hand, spinning the wire cage with the other, laughing with a small group gathered on the pavement in front of him. That's when I noticed someone I had seen months ago, standing beside another girl near the street side of the Bazaar. They must have just arrived. The girl saw me, too, as though some providential hand had turned our heads at precisely the same instant. She recognized me and waved.

Miss Marilou Jenkins.

I glanced at the bear under my arm, then over my shoulder to see if Carol might have reappeared somewhere close by. She was nowhere to be seen.

I raised my hand to wave back, clutching the ear of the bear as I did, intending to quickly say hello, then be off again to find Carol. Miss Marilou Jenkins' hair had grown since summer. It flowed down onto her brilliant-white mohair sweater. She and the other girl—her cousin, I imagined—moved a step or two in my direction. I saw no harm in displaying politeness, or so I thought. I could not see Carol. And so I took the bear and crossed the river Styx.

"Hello, Marilou!" I said as I stepped out of the boat onto the slippery shore two feet away from her. She wore a calf-length skirt, pink, with a little poodle appliquéd on the bottom. In the glare and spin of the red and blue and green lights it looked like a cuddly bear to me. I don't remember what the other girl wore. I don't even recall what she looked like. I do recall that Miss Marilou Jenkins looked in that moment like the statue in her foyer; the one whose robe had been made to fall to her feet— with my x-ray vision rising into perfect focus.

"Hello, Skip Morley. I thought that was you. How have you been? This is my cousin..." and she told me the girl's name and every other detail of her reason for being there on the poor side of town again. This time daddy was in San Francisco doing something medical—transplanting anuses, or...I don't remember.

"Your hair has grown. I think it looks great." I stammered.

"And you have grown more handsome. Taller! And your hair is longer, too. I like it." She eyed the bear while I went skidding down the bank, oblivious to her charming wiles and the murky water, brushing back the little wave of my hair with nervous, perspiring fingers.

"For me?" she asked in a tone of voice that I'd never heard, not even in the movies or on TV. Never. Imploring, rather. Soft enough to lie in and let the calm, steady current take me away. I raised the bear, proud of having won it, to show it to her, I guess. I didn't expect what happened next. She slipped it from my hands, with a smile, with a gentle thanks, and held it close to her breast. Mine heaved at the thought of that bear so close. So close. What was I to do?

227

Slide completely into the water and watch the world above disappear, with a stupid grin on my face, no less. That's what I was to do, and I did.

"Ah...ummm." I calculated the odds of winning another bear—the pink one, maybe. How much time it would take. How many quarters that I didn't have.

"Thank you so much, darling Skip Morley. Really. He's beautiful." Miss Marilou Jenkins stepped forward to within a foot of me, and began to place her open palm against the raging hot skin of my cheek, smiling with lips the color of fresh lava.

I suddenly woke up to a demon jabbing me in the rear with a pitchfork. Another hand came down on my shoulder from behind.

THIRTY

Miss Marilou Redux

"Hey man, what's going on?" Mickey said. I wheeled in shock. In that split second of being roused from pleasant delirium to frightful reality, I knew, knew without a doubt that the fingers on my shoulder belonged to Carol, and that I'd been caught in a swoon. Relief poured over me when I saw that it was only Mickey. He gazed at me fleetingly before turning his head toward Miss Marilou Jenkins, and then he eased a shoulder between us, paying no further attention to me. I stepped back, catching sight of one eye of Carol's prize staring out at me from under Miss Marilou Jenkins' arm, and both eyes of Miss Marilou Jenkins gazing into Mick's face. It seemed I'd been rescued. Now, if I could somehow get that bear back everything would be fine. I'd leave Miss Marilou Jenkins in Mick's hands, take the bear to Carol...all would be right in my world.

"S'cuse me," I took a step sideways and addressed Miss Marilou Jenkins. "Umm..." She didn't seem to be paying attention to me as Mick spoke symphonically to her about what a wonderful evening it was, and what was her name, and her outfit couldn't have looked any better on a queen. And so on.

"Uh, the teddy-bear," I stammered. I could have yelled it and the answer would have been the same. She hadn't heard a word I'd been saying. Her pretty eyes were locked on Mickey's. That quickly! How fickle love is, I thought.

"The bear?" I followed.

This time it registered with her. She left my friend's charms for a moment and came to me.

"You are absolutely so thoughtful, Skip Morley! I don't have one quite as wonderful as this one. This is a treasure." Miss Marilou Jenkins then sealed my fate by throwing an arm around my shoulder, raising herself onto tiptoes, and kissing me. If that weren't enough, she removed her face from mine, stared at me with a look of deep admiration and longing, feigned though it might have been. In the reflection of her emerald eyes I could see the lights of the Ferris Wheel dancing. And then she kissed me one more time for good measure. I froze solid as an iceberg of course, shocked—in fact, delighted. My second and third kisses in life, and these were every bit as nice as that other girl's. What was her name? Then to my surprise she took my friend by the arm and ambled off toward the Ferris Wheel. With the bear.

Meanwhile, a little way to the rear, just beyond the Chuck A Luck booth and the bar, Carol had seen it all, except for Miss Marilou Jenkins walking away with Mickey. Between us a crowd of revelers had gathered; eight soldiers in flashy uniforms, and their girlfriends. Drinks and popcorn in hand, dancing to the band playing *A String of Pearls.* And then another group joined them as Mickey and Miss Marilou Jenkins disappeared to the north, her cousin from lowly Barnum tagging along behind them, glancing every other step back at me.

Carol and Allen had bumped into one another after she'd left the restroom. She was on her way over to the Bottle Bomber to find me; beheld me deteriorating into a puddle of steaming water in the presence of the beauty from the eastside. Carol saw me give her the bear (or so it appeared to her), and then receive the two long kisses. I'm told Allen's eyeballs could be heard clacking into the lenses of his Buddy Holly lenses.

I finally found the two of them.

Carol stood motionless with her arms folded, looking at the side of the classroom building, legs spread two feet apart. Odd, I thought. Staring at a blank wall. Allen was timid, standing beside her with his arms folded behind his back. It looked like he might be trying to decide whether or not to ask her what her Supergirl vision had caught hold of in the bowels of the pea-green colored building. The merrymakers created a sea of noise all around. The lights and bursts of shouting splashed against the walls, the booths, and bounced off the pavement. The band played and couples danced, and all of them, all of this, unaware of the three kids near that soupy green brick wall.

"Hello?"

Allen turned to me. Carol did not.

"I do believe there might be a problem which should be left for the two of you to sort out..."

Carol unfolded her arms, but remained standing as she had been when I walked over to them. She placed a restraining hand on his wrist. "No, please stay."

"I was looking all through the crowd for you," I said.

"Leave me alone. Go away."

"But you don't understand..." I began.

Allen placed a hand atop Carol's. He concentrated on her face through those thick glasses.

"I am quite certain your, er...actions...that is..."

"Shut up, Allen. Get out of here.

"Carol, I'm sorry. You don't understand."

"Perfectly."

"No. That's the girl Jimmy lit...whose hair. I mean, I ran into her..."

"And gave her a teddy bear. And kissed her. That girl?" she cut me off.

Allen couldn't help himself. He turned his head to me, his black Jimmy-beret pulled straight down onto his forehead nearly to the tops of his glasses. "Skip, with all due respect I think the scene speaks quite clearly for itself. I would be angry..."

"Shut up."

"Really, I can understand your embarrassment at being..."

"Hit the road before I smack you and knock that stupid cap off your head. Get your hands off her and beat it."

"No, Allen. Stay."

"Carol!"

"Just go, Skip Morley." Carol left the wall abruptly, dragging the snake along behind her. Allen peered back at me for a moment as he hop-scotched away with my girl. I heard Carol. "I'm going to call my parents to come get me, Allen. Do you know where a phone is?"

"I'd be happy to give you a ride, Carol..." his voice broke off as the two of them walked away hand in hand into the chill of the night. The strangest feeling overwhelmed me. I thought that perhaps those might have been the last words I'd ever hear from Carol's lovely mouth, and an anger I'd never known welled up inside me. I ran after them and caught Allen by the shoulder and wheeled him around.

"You stupid jerk!" And then I hit him on the chin so hard that the concussion knocked his glasses and kooky beret off.

"Skip! You monster, get out of here! Never talk to me again. I hate you!"

For the second time in as many months Carol fell to her knees, and after picking up Allen's glasses and gently placing them back on his closed eyes, she stroked his forehead and hair and cheeks, crying, literally, for him to wake up.

I *was* a monster. A demon. I turned and ran away in total defeat.

THIRTY-ONE

Good King David

Amonth to the day after I said goodbye to Allen with a right cross, and Carol said goodbye to me, the first snowstorm of the season descended. Two days before Thanksgiving; full, light and merry, and terrifically cold. Despite the festive atmosphere around the house, the lightening of Mom's spirit in the face of another season of decorating, signing and mailing Christmas cards, and nonstop baking—which only reminded me in brutal technicolor of Mrs. Hudson's wonderful Saturday evening ritual—I remained inconsolably morose. Carol was long gone—off to an island all by herself. No. With Allen. Every attempt to contact her ended in utter failure. Our carriage to the stars had crashed. I kept the remembrances of it, but its dazzling colors, obedient to reality, began to fade and grow muddy.

After the Bazaar incident I'd tried in vain to lure her out of her house. I even appealed to Allen, told him how sorry I was— kissed his feet. He gladly forgave me, as befit someone of his better character, but his efforts in my behalf with Carol, the only reason I approached him, really, went the way of smoke in the wind. So, I shut myself up in my bedroom like a hermit.

And then I decided to kill myself.

I plunged into a fast to end all fasts—to starve myself to death, and watch as everyone stood by helplessly, begging me to eat a piece of bread, or even a carrot.

After a couple of days of watching my body waste away, and seeing my spirits sink ever farther down the drain, Mom threatened to drag me off to a psychiatrist, or at least to sit before Father Blinker to relate my woes to (and be preached at). I responded by asking her if she thought either of them could undo what had occurred at the Bazaar. Could they bring Carol back into my life? "Stuff the feathers back into the pillow?"

"What'd you do now, Skip? Tear up your pillow? Lord have mercy."

She didn't understand, and I wasn't about to explain it. Still, in her heart, if not her head, I'm sure she realized that I'd manage to live through that first crisis in my young life, even if she had to tie me down and force-feed me with a spoon. I knew without a doubt I would not survive.

Of course I did.

I finally relented and joined Mom and Pop at the Thanksgiving Table. What pushed me over the edge was the smell of a feast unlike any that could have been prepared in the finest kitchen in all of Christendom. I was very hungry to say the least. Two or three days of self-inflicted starvation for even the *best* of reasons was sufficiently long enough to make me question very seriously the positive outcome of such a stupid plan. If I succeeded in killing myself, where would that leave me? Where would that leave Carol? True, she would no doubt weep buckets of tears, and possibly even join me on the other side in a Shakesperean gesture of undying love if she could, but...what if she were unable to carry out her plan? I mean, what if her parents found her lying in a field of flowers atop her bed, wrists opened wide by her own hand, and then they rushed her to the hospital? Got her there in the nick of time? What if they succeeded in talking some sense into her despite her broken heart while she lay strapped to her bed in that sterile place? I would be forced to sit on a cloud with a harp and peer down on her for another sixty or seventy years, helpless. Watch her grow more lovely by the day—and possibly overcome her grief and—the worst thought of all—find Allen!

Now I was thinking straight.

I might have been delirious, or I might have been inspired—I don't really know for sure—but whichever the case, I knew from the bottom of my soul—or maybe I should say stomach—that I was ready to eat even the disgusting tail flap of the Turkey. As it turned out, my hunger strike had actually been timely.

"Well, Skippy, it looks like your nose has survived the ordeal at least," Mom noted Thanksgiving afternoon as I crept through the door into the kitchen, a kitchen alive with as many enticing smells as notes in one of Mr. Hudson's symphonies, and Pop's concertos.

"Please, Mom. I just came up to go to the bathroom. I'm not hungry," I answered her in a pathetic tone of voice. She must be feeling so sorry for me, I thought. She'd beg me, plead with me to eat something—anything—so that she wouldn't have to stand beside my lovely Carol at the funeral and weep. I was so hungry...but I'd let her beg for a little while.

"Well then, go to the bathroom. When you're finished get on over to your chair in the dining room," she sang, and then she added. "I have a surprise for you."

Honestly I could have cared less. Mincemeat pie or, or...The only surprise that would relieve my spirit would be to see Carol sitting at the table when I returned.

Mom resumed her kitchen duties without further remarks—or begging. As I rounded the corner into hers and Pop's bedroom on my way to the john I heard the handle on the front door rattling and a muffled, trembling voice. Aunt Sylvie—or cousin Sylvie—and Aunt Corey had arrived to join us. Fine and well. They were probably the surprise. I loved them, and reasoned that after the tale of woe at the Bazaar was revealed to them, and they took a long, dreadful and shocked look at me, I'd be showered with affection and concern unparalleled in the history of loves-gone-wrong.

I finished with my task and flushed the toilet. The water swirled around the snow-white bowl; down, down, down. My life in metaphor, I thought looking at it, and then the ironic, melodramatic, exquisitely pitiful words flew into my brain. "Oh...woe is me."

My self-crucifixion was nearly complete, and would no doubt be chronicled in some future age by an extraordinary poet for all young lovers to read while they sat as close as...

"Skip! Hurry it up, dear. Your aunts are here and we're just about ready to eat," Mom called out, destroying the wonderful image played by Gypsy violinists in my brain. I zipped up my jeans and resigned myself to listening to a hundred excruciatingly painful tales of twenty-four inch trout being hooked in gurgling streams and beaver ponds just below timberline much later in the evening. After much ado was made about everything in my life, of course.

Back in the dining room Aunt Corey had one arm out of her Polar bear coat, a steaming platter of potatoes in the other, helping Mom. Sylvie already had a can of beer in her trembling hand and was sitting in the living room with Pop watching the Lions finish off the Packers on TV. I eased myself into the chair in the center of the table, alone in the room, back to the wall of photographs of our family in various poses, moods, and seasons. The bookends were badly framed prints of Jesus on the left side, and the Virgin Mary on the right. Crowning the entire montage was a ceramic crucifix, painted a uniformly dull brown and glazed to a high gloss finish of absolute faux depression. Situated where I was, the burnt sienna droplets of Our Lord's blood promised to fall upon my head and form little rivulets down my face. So far everything seemed to be just right.

As I sat hollow-eyed, disconsolate, perfectly framed in suffering, the front door burst open, and in waltzed my Uncle John from far off San Francisco, showering season's greetings on one and all at the top of his lungs. He was followed by a gentleman I'd never seen before, nor had ever heard a thing about. A great din of clipped conversation, hugs, and other nonsense followed.

Lost in anonymity, and I think some embarrassment, Uncle John's companion stood quietly a foot inside the open door while all of the shrieking went on. He glanced over at me, a cigar jutting out of the corner of his mouth, and then back to his boyfriend. I assumed that's what Uncle John was to him. You see, Uncle John preferred men to women. But his companion didn't fit the mental image I had drawn of, well...the other half. He was very tall and muscular, not the body-builder kind of muscular, but trim-waisted and heavy shouldered. He was also quite handsome with his silver-black, full head of hair brushed upward and back, and his eyes were set deep in jovial drifts above thick, blush-red cheekbones. I think he was the Mister side of the relationship, and I kind of liked him right off in a tentative way for some reason even before he spoke. He had the bearing of dignity. Gentility.

"Oh my GOD! Laverne, this is David, KING David," Uncle John shouted, turning and grabbing his friend by the arm. "David, my brother-in-law, LaVerne, and his niece, Sylvia. Good lord, Syl, who did your hair? It's a-tro-cious! You did it yourself, didn't you!"

"Oh plug it, Jack. I'm n-not out to win any beauty contests today. And how d-do you do, David," she stammered.

David stepped forward and extended his hand to Sylvie first, and then to Pop.

"Well you're going to let me do it up tonight after dinner. It's simply the worst job I've seen in years," Uncle John went on.

"Glad to meet you," David said. "Who won the game? I don't think anyone is going to get by the Lions this year."

"I don't know about that," Pop replied with the crooked little grin on his lips that had long ago become a facial trademark of his. "Cleveland's got that new kid. Jim Brown. He's gonna' be hell to stop in the big game. Come on over, sit down. Skip! Get David a beer, would you, son? Get me one, too."

Of course, Pop, I thought. *I'll just drag my skin and bones out of this chair and crawl out to the refrigerator.* Which is what I obediently did. Mom eyed me from the oven a few feet away, breaking away from the conversation she'd been having with Aunt Corey.

"Your surprise is here, Mom," I grumbled, passing by her. "They're in the living room."

"Yes, I heard them. We're goin' right in. Stay outta' the ice box, now. We're just about ready to eat," she said.

"They need more beer."

"He looks just terrible, Rosie," I heard aunt Corey whisper to Mom. As I walked past her on the return fly with the beer for my unfeeling dad and those other three people in the living room, dragging one foot behind me like Igor, she gently touched my bony shoulder. "Skip you look like something the cat dragged in. Your eyes are as hollow as caves. Have you been sick, dear?"

Finally. It wouldn't be long now, I thought. My great moment of compassion was visible on the horizon. I didn't answer her, feigning deafness as well as acute emaciation, figuring a loss of hearing could only benefit my sad, sad state. As I repositioned the armload of beer I'd pulled out of the fridge, I thought of Carol going through the same hell at her house with her doting relatives—none of whom, I imagined, were anything like my twittering aunt Sylvie, or my flaming uncle.

On the verge of emotional collapse once again, I wandered back out of the kitchen under the silent stares of my Mom and my aunt, through the dining room, and into the din of the living room. Uncle John had Sylvie in stitches, dancing around in the middle of the room with her directly in front of the television set. Pop sat next to David, unconcerned with Uncle John's antics, and probably not too concerned about David's sexual preferences, for that matter. They seemed like General Patton and General Eisenhower sitting there together. Two good old boys talking about football and killing Nazis.

"Here you go," I said handing Pop the six pack of Coors. I turned abruptly with the intention of reattaching myself to the cross in the dining room. David stopped me.

"Hey buddy. Sit down here. We haven't been introduced." I turned. "I'm David, your uncle's boyfriend," he said as naturally as if his name was Martha or Sue or Rosalyn. He extended a strong-looking hand out to me.

"Name's not Buddy. It's Skip. Glad to meet you." I quickly and feebly accepted his handshake and then turned again without further niceties to resume my retreat to Golgotha. His hand stayed on mine, though, and he firmly drew me down beside him. That uneasy feeling of...but, no. Pop was right beside him.

"You look like you just crawled out of a dark hole. What happened to you? Tell me all about it. Christ, LaVerne," he said turning to Pop, "this kid looks like he needs a doctor!"

"He'll be alright. Woman problems, that's all," Pop replied. There was very little emotion in his voice, as though my physical well-being was of absolutely no importance whatsoever. That was fine with me. His lack of sensitivity was just another nail through my hands. He had his beer. He had Mom, and his football games. Me? I had nothing beyond a black, empty...

"Ah. That makes sense. Girls can be a real heartbreak," David said, smiling rather ruefully at me.

"How would you know?" I returned his kindness.

He threw himself back and laughed, then put his arm around me, pulling me into his side. "Oh, I know, I know. I was a kid like you once. Believe me, I know."

"Yeah? That's what Pop told me, only he probably really was a kid like me once."

"Alright, let's eat! Get yourselves out here before the spuds get cold," Mom called out from the dining room. "Hi, Jack! C'mon now. Turn off that TV and get in here."

How thankful I was to hear that. My comment to David had been beyond insulting, and I knew it and was glad to be able to leave him. If he'd been put off, that was okay too. I was, after all, a sick child and not at all responsible for any statements made in fits of delirium. I left him and Pop and staggered to the same chair I'd occupied before the beer run. Uncle John and Sylvie traded good-natured barbs with one another as they ambled into the dining room; more hugs and kisses by him for Mom and Aunt Corey. I watched in horror as David walked to the table and took the seat next to me, holding his smoldering cigar between his index and middle finger. If he planned on smoking throughout dinner, I planned on throwing up and then leaving. In that order.

"What's your girl's name?" he asked me in the rising swell of voices around the table. He placed his elbow on the edge of it as he spoke, and then placed his chin in the palm of his hand waiting for me to answer. I glanced over at him, a little nervous, though the question played into my idea of what the topic on everyone's lips should be.

"Carol," I answered looking down at my place setting.

"She's pretty, I take it?" he went on.

"Yes. Very. But it doesn't matter anymore."

"Oh, I see. Left you for someone else, huh?"

I looked up at him again. "No. Nothing like that at all. She was...that is..."

Yeah, she had in fact.

"David! Leave Skippy alone, you old lecher," Uncle John cackled in his nasally, shrieking voice. Everyone laughed as though it was Bob Hope sitting directly across from us. I saw little humor in it, depressed as I was, and the comment made me more than a little wary of the wolf in male clothing beside me. David, once again, didn't seem to be offended or embarrassed. He shoved his cigar back into his mouth, smiled, and told Uncle John to clamp it. Then he spoke to me again as the first platter of food turned the corner of the table.

"We can talk about it after dinner if you like. I'd like to hear about your girl. She must be something. I mean for you to go off the deep end like you have. If you like."

Well, if no one else was going to rub salve into my wounds, I guessed David would have to do. It would have to be in the company of Pop, or at least Aunt Corey though. Who could say, maybe he *was* an old lecher. I sure didn't want to become his lecheree.

Mom had brought a bottle of Mogen David wine to the table, and all the adults toasted our many blessings over and over again. Between the wine and the unending bottles of beer I was surprised they found any room for the turkey and ham and all the trimmings, but they did. David drank like a seasoned pro, but he ate as though he were two men—or one man and two women. I managed to end my fast with half a plate of the delicious food, and half a glass of the wine, which hit my stomach with a delightfully warm sensation. Throughout the feasting David continued to query me in spurts and snippets about school, sports, my friends—like any normal man, any good friend of my dad's would do. Much to my dismay he made no more mention of the topic which would send swords into my heart. Nor did anyone else.

The feast ended with Pop groaning a little, holding his stomach, moaning for just one more Coors to settle the rumbling down there. Mom and Aunt Corey sat for a bit talking about doilies and salt and pepper shakers. Sylvie and Uncle John took their drinks and their reminiscing out to the kitchen table, leaving David, his cigar, and me to hash over politics, romance, and the weather.

"Come on, Skip. Let's go for a walk. It's colder than a well digger's ass outside, but it's quiet. You can tell me more about your Carol, little buddy. Walking and talking go hand in hand. Whatd'ya say?"

"I don't know, David. It's too depressing," I answered. That wasn't precisely true. It was depressing, but I wanted terribly to spill my guts to someone. His cigar somehow made me feel a little less apprehensive, and the instant visual of a man with his bare butt hanging outside a bucket, thirty feet down inside a well, made me smile and drop my defenses just a little. "You aren't, you know, like interested in my body, are you? Like Uncle John? He whistles and hoots at everyone." I figured I might as well set the ground rules.

"Not me," he chuckled. "Your uncle is more than I can handle. No, if you were...well, say you were this Carol, and I was a straight guy, it'd be the same. I might whistle at men, but kids are off limits. Do you think we're all perverts?"

"I don't know. You hear stuff...you know."

"Don't believe everything you hear, and a lot of what you think you see. Most of us are pretty good people, just like your folks. Come on, let's get some air."

I liked him a lot, really, despite his infirmity. And I trusted he meant me no harm. We got up, put on our heavy winter coats, and left.

Another front had moved in while we were eating; frigid, filled with snowflakes that drifted lazily down in the darkness and dusted the brown lawns and the sidewalks and streets with a thin blanket of white. David and I turned left outside the gate and headed north in the direction of Carol's house—which I'd

241

been forbidden to walk in front of under penalty of death by her father. It was David who surreptitiously chose our path. Even so I offered no objections.

"Well, tell me all about Carol and yourself," David said as we took our first few steps along the sidewalk. I began at the beginning, describing the several flitting visions of her last spring—the divine vision of her standing in front of her house with the garden hose last summer. By the time we neared her house I hadn't spelled out half the events prior to that night of the horrible Bazaar, nor a quarter of my feelings concerning her timeless beauty. I stopped when we reached her front walk, went quiet, and pointed across the street to the door.

"That's it?" he asked, placing a hand on my shoulder.

"Yes."

"I see. Well, what do you want to do?"

"I don't know. Maybe wait and see if she comes out. I don't know."

"And what would you do if she did?"

"Don't know that either. Run up to her, I guess."

"And what if she didn't want you to?"

"She would. I know she would. She's just being stubborn. I think."

"Well then, go up and knock on her door. Why wait for her?"

" I can't!"

"Why not?"

"Her father. He said he'd shoot me if he ever saw me around here again."

"Ahh! I see. What did you do to her to make him so angry?"

And so I had to tell David the entire story of the incident at the Bazaar, every detail of it standing there in the snow in front of her house, and how I'd come down week after week, desperate, and how I'd kept throwing pebbles at her bedroom window. Mr. Hudson had come out and kindly asked me to leave—which I did—and then I returned a few minutes later when he'd gone away, and started up again. The next time and the time after that and the time after that when he came out to chase me off, his temper seemed to grow, until he finally threatened to shoot me if I didn't leave and not return.

"My daughter doesn't want to talk to you, Skip, and after what you did to that other boy, I don't blame her. Go away and don't come back."

"But I just want to say I'm sorry and that I don't really mind that chickenshit Allen." This was the year for sticking my foot in my mouth. I bit my tongue and cursed the feathers that kept flying out.

"Just go away. Both of you are way too young for this kind of nonsense anyway. Go."

When I finished relating my Greek tragedy, David tugged me gently on. We retraced our steps back toward my house, though I would gladly have stayed where we were and freeze like an ice statue, just to be near her.

"How old are you, Skip?"

"Thirteen...and a half."

"Thirteen already! My, my. And you're going to marry this Carol?"

"Someday."

"Yes, someday. Someday when?"

"I don't know. When we get older. Why? What difference does it make? Just someday. Well, I was going to anyway."

"Think of it like this. You have a lot of things to see before that day. A lot of things. So does Carol. Both of you have to complete school, you know, maybe even date some other people while you're growing up...getting all set to marry one another."

"I don't want her dating other guys. I couldn't stand that."

"Why? Do you think she'd love one of them more than you and you'd lose her?"

"Maybe. I couldn't take that chance."

"But you have to. The awful truth is this: Neither of you is anywhere near being old enough or mature enough to seriously think about tying yourself down in marriage. Her father was right. I'm not saying you're not madly and truly in love—you might be for all I know—I doubt it, but it boils down to one further, painful fact—at least painful in the short run. You have to let her go for a while. If she loves you she'll be back someday. Let her go. Put some weight back on, for crying out loud. Read some more books, the real classics. See some movies. Force her out of your mind. That will be the hardest thing you've ever done so far in your life, but it's your only course."

"I don't think I can, David."

"It isn't a question of thinking whether or not you can. It's a simple question of what must be done. You really have no choice."

As we turned and walked up to my gate I considered what he'd said. It was bad news, and up to that point the thought of pushing Carol out of my mind hadn't even arisen. With my stomach full once again, my reasoning was forced to revisit. He was correct I guessed. Much as I loathed the idea nearly as much as I loathed my days without Carol, I knew pushing her out of my head was the only course. Well no. I could drive myself crazy.

I died one more time. This growing up thing was proving to be a bitch all of a sudden.

THIRTY-TWO

Merry Christmas Inky

I spent the remaining six days of David and Uncle John's visit gorging myself on left-over turkey, plowing through the pile of books on the floor in my room in a vain search for the perfect novel of adventure, talking to David, dreaming about Christmas. I crowded into David's counsel like a starving child in a soup line. They slept in a spare bedroom in the basement at the front of the house. It embarrassed me to think of my uncle and another man crawling into the double bed in that room. I kept my radio turned on every night now—low enough so that any sound that might come from the other bedroom would be drowned out, but I never heard a thing.

During the day while Pop was busy working, Uncle John and Mom busied themselves shopping, lugging out the Christmas ornaments, reliving old times, doing those kinds of brother/sister things. David and I sometimes sat in my bedroom on the floor, or took more long walks in the snow. He told me all about the wonderful city he lived in and its glorious bridge that shot through the fog with timeless beauty and grace. As though its architect had been handed the set of plans by God himself and instructed to thrust the catenary across the impossible distance of the bay. There was a street there that climbed a hill so steep, and swept back on itself so often, a person needed track shoes and the lungs of an athlete to make it to the top. Cable cars with musical, clanging bells. Foghorns in the night calling out to the ships entering the bay. I was entranced by his words, and I grew to like him more than I thought possible because of the portraits he painted of his beloved home, and of course his quiet, gentle manner. He lifted my sagging spirits, continuously asking me how I was doing that day, that hour, that particular moment.

"Does it ever snow in San Francisco, David?" I asked a few days before he and Uncle John were slated to leave. We were sitting alone in my bedroom as usual—he on the end of the bed with his back against the wall beside the photograph of Jimmy and Carol taken in the snowstorm of leaves, me with my back against the headboard underneath the crucifix. A new guy named Sam Cooke sang *You Send Me* on the tinny little radio on my nightstand, and the unshaded light bulb hanging from the ceiling joists above us flickered sometimes, a tribute to Pop's wiring prowess. Outside, the dreary sky looked mournfully in on us. Lots more snow, no more sun, and many more months of steady, unrelenting gray.

"Never...at least that I've ever heard of." He chuckled and then went on. "It's wintertime out there for a good part of the year though. Not quite as cold as here, and no snow, but freezing in a different way because of the fog. Mark Twain said it best, I think. 'The coldest winter I ever spent was a summer in San Francisco.'"

I ran those words through my head for an instant and then laughed out loud. David smiled at me in that infectious way of his, ingenuous, wedded with his sparkling eyes.

"Let's get out of here, Skip. For some reason today this room could make a clown sit down and cry. I'll walk with you up to the little store on the corner and buy you a bottle of pop or a hot chocolate. Want to go?"

"Sure. Okay."

And so another day passed. And then another, and I began to smart a little less.

When Uncle John and his lover left on Sunday afternoon, two weeks before Christmas, David hugged me, holding his cigar between his fingers, and I know I saw a small tear forming in the corner of his eye. I told him how much I would miss him, and that when I was old enough I'd fly out to San Francisco and visit him.

Sometime in July, midwinter in the city of his birth.

***

With David gone and Christmas fast approaching, with all my books thrown into the corner of the bedroom, with the frigid air and drifts of snow calling me out of hermit existence, I hopped the fence and went to find my missing friend. It was early afternoon, and I didn't bother to knock for fear of waking up Mrs. McGuire. I let myself in the always-unlocked door and crossed the living room. Then I turned the corner into the small vestibule separating his room from the bathroom and Mrs. McGuire's bedroom, and pushed Jimmy's door open. He sat cross-legged at the head of his bed. Mickey was at the foot, waving a hand in the air. He was saying something to Jimmy about how the two of them should give Inky and Butch a Christmas present.

"Hiya guys."

"Hi-ho, Daddy-O. So ya' decided to crawl outta' yer' hole, huh?" Jimmy called back. He seemed happy enough to see me, and he smiled at me, sporting the hole in his teeth.

"What's up, stranger?" Mickey said turning to me.

"Nothing much—just came to see what's going on. My uncle and David are gone, now, and I can...umm...come out."

"Those guys...they're queer, aren't they?" Mickey said, and then started up his tale of the possible Inky adventure again without waiting for a reply. The way he said it—I didn't dignify the remark about my uncle and David with an answer. Instead I sat down on the floor at the end of the bed and absently shuffled through Jimmy's pile of Mad Magazines and just listened to them.

"We could TP their house. Whattya' think, Jimmy?" Mickey said smiling. Jimmy just stared at him without answering.

I immediately knew that that was a very bad idea. They hadn't been around for ages. Doing something stupid like that would only open up old wounds, and God knows our signature would be on every leaf of toilet paper dangling from the trees in front of the Minkle's house.

"Why would you want another war?" I asked Mickey. "We haven't had any trouble with them..."

"In a pig's eye. While you were in your house kissin' that uncle of yours ass, I was getting mine kicked by fuckin' Inky. Minkle's got a long memory. He cornered me two weeks ago when I went down to get a haircut..."

Mickey related how after he'd left Larry's Barbershop Inky appeared out of nowhere alone a few doors down at the drugstore. The fight didn't last long because Mickey was faster than Inky, and my friend had gotten away, but not before Inky knocked him down with a solid punch, and then kicked him in the ribs a few times.

"How's Gins?" I tried to change the subject.

"I dunno'. TPn' ain't no good. That's kid's stuff, but I think I've got a better idea," Jimmy answered, getting back to the subject under discussion. My memory was long too, and I remembered vividly enough how if Pop and Mom hadn't shown up last summer when the brothers were wailing on us in Jimmy's backyard, all three of us might be long gone from this world.

"I think we ought to just forget it. Maybe if we leave them alone..." I began.

"You could make a bomb 'an set it on their doorstep," Mickey cut me off.

"Nah, I don't wanna' go to jail for murderin' 'em, but what I'm thinkin' will sure piss 'em off. They *won't* have no idea who done it, neither."

Whatever it was he was cooking up I didn't want any part of. Just like after the Clifford wagon incident, Inky would put two and two together, and this time cook up a plan of his own. This time Mickey's ribs would become part of his backbone or worse, and Jimmy would crawl away without any teeth. If he was lucky.

"You guys are gluttons for punishment. Just forget it, whatever it is you're planning, Jimmy. Someone's gonna' get hurt bad if you don't."

"It ain't gonna' be me, even if they do figure out who done it. I got my machete, an' 'sides, they won't know who did it. I'll be across the street watchin' though. I wanna' see the look on his face after he answers the door." Jimmy laughed. Mickey was all ears, smiling.

"It's real simple. We can do it tonight."

I got to my feet before he laid out his newest plan to get us all killed. "*You* can do it tonight. I don't want any part of it. You never learn, Jimmy. Why don't you just go call Gins or something? Forget Inky and Butch. See you later. I hope not in the hospital." I turned and started out of the war room.

"Yeah, go find your fag uncle and his boyfriend," Mickey called after me.

I left without looking back or saying a word. As I walked back to my house I thought of what a terrific friend David had become, and what an asshole for a friend Mickey had disintegrated into. Knowing Jimmy's hatred for Inky and Butch, and his ability to dream up capers that seemed always to come back and bite him on the ass...but I wondered just what this one would be?

I'd find out exactly within a few days.

THIRTY-THREE

Hi Chickenshits, We're Back

There was no sign of Mickey and Jimmy, save the light bleeding out of Jimmy's bedroom window on the first two nights after they did whatever it was they did to Inky. I quit glancing over the fence after that, and steered clear of him. I had no idea where Mickey was either, or what he was doing, and besides, Christmas was only a week away.

Lawrence Welk came onstage dressed as Santa Claus on one of those nights when I *should* have been raising hell with Jimmy and Mickey. Myron Florin was dressed as an elf, along with Bobby the dancer, and...it was the same old polka crap, just disguised as Caroling, and with thousands of bubbles floating around instead of snowflakes. I left Mom and Pop sitting in front of the twinkling lights on the tree, Lawrence smiling and waving his baton on the TV next to it at them, and wandered down to my room to read, or listen to the radio. Or both. The clock on my nightstand said 7:45. I grabbed a book, turned the radio on, and then lay down absently to read.

Within ten minutes I was fast asleep, discouraged with life in general.

The next morning I awoke at just past the crack of dawn, knowing I would have to get out of the house or else lose my mind. I was beginning to think about Carol once again, and I had to fight myself on that account, or else risk plummeting into a new and maybe worse depression. Jimmy's and Mickey's company was a no-go. Love them as I did (although I didn't admit that to myself), I didn't want to be anywhere near them because of Inky. I knew he'd take revenge. I hated the guy, but not enough, I thought, to kill him—and that's probably what it would take to keep him away for good.

I thought about taking a walk, but both directions, north and south, held peril for me. Carol north, Inky and company south. That's when the treehouse standing unfinished and freezing cold entered my head. Maybe this morning would be a good time to finish making the five gallon-can stove.

I rose from bed, dressed, and wandered up the stairs to the rear door. There it stood, a Little Huey plopped atop the stump of a tree. The sight of it nearly made me laugh. A crooked roof sat, un-shingled, but still there. The window facing the back of the house had stiff plastic tacked onto three corners. The fourth moved back and forth unencumbered, dancing every now and then in the capricious breezes that came and went.

I trudged through the snow out to it, climbed up the wooden rungs nailed onto the trunk of the tree, brushing small patches of snow from the tops of them as I ascended, and then I pulled myself into the living room with its raggedy piece of carpet Jimmy and I had found a couple of blocks away in someone's trash and dragged home. Beneath the windows, mounds of snow had accumulated, ending in dissipating white foothills as they stretched toward the dry center of the room. On a small platform in one corner sat an empty five-gallon drum, sealed on both ends. Beside it sat two pieces of tin pipe about four inches in diameter. Beside those on the floor in front of them lay a hatchet, a hammer and a dull chisel, plus a roll of Jimmy's miracle welding material—duct tape.

Months ago Jimmy and I had hacked a not-quite-round hole approximating the pipe's diameter in the shallow pitched roof, but had given up on hooking up the heater soon afterward.

There it all sat, waiting for the incision in the front of the can that would become the firebox opening, and some sort of hole in its top for the exhaust pipe connection. I stared at the thing for a while, thought about how miserable I was again, and the unfairness of Jimmy and Mick's happiness, but that was a useless endeavor. I picked up the hammer and chisel and began the evisceration of the front of the small drum. With any luck I'd have the project finished before darkness fell; have the windows

251

tacked closed again, and a friendly fire warming up the interior. With any luck I'd wake up years later, like Rumplestiltskin, and there would stand Carol, returned to my lonely life, smiling down on me...

***

I'd been working on the stubborn can for half an hour or thereabouts when I heard them clomping across the yard, their voices growing louder with each step. They punctuated their conversation with laughter, and said stuff I couldn't hear over the noise of my surgical tools. Up the ladder they came, thanking me for letting them know exactly where I was with all the noise I'd been making. Then they joined me in the project that we'd postponed far too long.

"I'm going to invite Rosie to go with us up to the lake..."

Somewhere over the weeks that had passed between the Church Bazaar fiasco and my desertion of him, Mickey had joined the ranks of the smitten at the hands of Rosie Gonzalez, a pretty girl in his class.

"No you ain't," Jimmy snapped. "No girls. If Gins ever comes out from Manhattan, okay, Rosie can come with us, but I don't want no chicks otherwise."

"That's no fair," Mick said, "Gins won't ever be out."

"And Carol will be an old lady before I get to see her again...probably won't want to skate anymore by then, either," I said to them.

"Oh, dry up," Mickey told me. "Hold the end of that pipe for Jimmy while I get a piece of tape ready." Already he was beginning to get weary over my ongoing state of melancholia, but I did as he said and grabbed the lower section of the pipe that was seated reasonably flat on the top of the stove while Jimmy crimped the end of the next section to be joined to it.

"Well, what did you guys do to Inky?" I asked as I worked away with the hatchet.

Jimmy laughed. "Oh, we got 'im good didn't we Mickey?"

"Yeah, he won't forget his stinky shoe for a while."

"Stinky shoe?" I asked.

Jimmy laughed again. "Yeah, real bad stinky. We loaded up a paper sack with fresh dog shit and then lugged it up to his front doorstep. I knew he was right inside somewhere 'cuz I could hear 'im talking to shithead Butch about somethin'. I counted to three, and then took out one of Mother's lighters, opened the top of the sack a little, an' then lit it on fire. After it caught good, I rang the doorbell twice, and then ran as fast as I could across the street to where Mickey was waitin'. We ducked behind that big tree and waited until the door opened, and Inky stepped out and screamed, "Shit!""

"Yeah, it was shit alright," Mickey laughed loud.

"Inky did what anyone, 'cept maybe dumb-ass Butch, would do. He started stomping on the bag for all he was worth. It didn't take 'im long to find out his shoes and socks was covered with fresh, gooey dog shit. The fire was out, though."

I had to laugh with them. Mickey had rolled over onto his side, holding onto them as he thought back. "So...you think they figured out who did it?" I asked.

"I don't care," Jimmy said. "I got my machete," he patted his leg on which the fearsome looking blade was strapped in a makeshift scabbard. "If he gets anywhere near me, I swear I'll cut his fuckin' arms off."

"You're nuts," I said back. "You'd better hope he didn't figure out who it was. I hope for your sake, too, he has loads of other enemies."

Everything was going along smooth as silk—the conversation had drifted back into the mechanics and physics of stoves—until we were interrupted by the bang of a rock on the alley wall of the treehouse. That sound was awfully familiar I remember thinking, and it could mean only one thing. Our old friends had eliminated the possibility of every other one of their enemies except us. Inky had returned.

"Jesus! Can it be?" Jimmy whispered. "I don't believe it."

"Yeah, I think it can be," I said. "If it's who I think it is, we're goners."

Jimmy stood up, or stood up as far as he could before his head met the roof rafters, and poked his head out of the window facing the alley. I joined him, followed by Mickey. Standing below us in the alley were Inky and his little puke of a brother.

"Hiya' punks," he called up. "Haul your asses on down here. We need to talk. I got some shit I wanna' give back to ya'." He and Butch stood there, unarmed and alone, Inky holding up a paper shopping bag. But it didn't matter. Had he brought Norbert and Bobo and Chinky and a hundred other thugs, I would have risked certain death just to see Jimmy scare the hell out of him with the machete. Besides, I had a hatchet. I turned, opened the floor hatch, threw the hatchet out, and then climbed back down the ladder.

Jimmy was right behind me as I bent over and picked up the hatchet. Mickey lingered in the safety of the treehouse until we'd gotten to the gate, but then he climbed down and joined us out in the alley. We stood five feet from Inky—who looked so confident and threatening this close up, and who glared at us with real malevolence in his eyes. He tossed the sopping bag at Jimmy's feet in the snow. Butch didn't exist in my head during those first few seconds, but I should have known. More so than Inky, he would have something up his sleeve beyond a switchblade. Slouched near his older brother's side, he had one hand in his dirty jean back pocket.

Inky addressed Mickey first: "Well, well, well. If it isn't chickenshit number one. Or maybe it's number two...or three. These other two dicks are way ahead of you, I guess. Real pussies."

"Ink, we don't want any trouble...I ain't gonna' say..." Mickey began.

"Shut up. Why's dickhead Morley carrying a hatchet then? You think we came to hurt you?" He shifted his eyes to me. "Did you, Morley?"

My courage rose, solidified in that instant. Why had I been so stupid to bring the hatchet if I really hadn't intended on using it? I thought, *Maybe I will. Maybe I just will.* I began to shake a little thinking about that—the whole scene that would be played out in the coming moments.

Defense. Don't swing it, just scare him and Butch with it. Don't hit him. Don't even try. Don't kill him, or cut him even, but do chase him away. Make him and Butch run.

"Here's the present you left me when you snuck up on us last summer." Jimmy bared his teeth, showing Inky the hole in his smile.

"Yer gonna' be missin' all of 'em in a second or two," Butch chimed in. He pulled his hand out of his pocket, holding the shiny switchblade I'd heard so many rumors about. There were no trashcan lids today, no wooden swords or sling shots. This was something out of the Bowery, and I had the ugliest feeling someone was going to die before it ended.

It began.

Mickey was the first to move, skirting around Jimmy and me to take a flanking position to the right of Inky. Inky backed up two steps, crouched low and forward, and then reached into his back pocket, retrieving a longer switchblade than his brother's. I had the hatchet, but I'd never been in a fight like the one facing me. I wondered just how to use it to my best advantage. I wondered again if I could. I could run. I wanted to, but no. We'd end it here.

Jimmy moved to my right and grabbed a short, broken tree branch lying beside the fifty-gallon trash barrel in the alley behind our fence. At the same time Mick removed his jacket and wrapped it around his left arm. For a long moment there was complete stillness as each side sized up the other. Inky made the first move, a frightening feint to his left, and then he lunged at me with the knife extended and drawn like a boxer's glove, shooting for the opening in my defenses. I had the hatchet. I'd have to be the first to go. Butch moved on Mickey with a growl, figuring, I'm sure, Mick's would be the easiest side to jam his knife into. Once Mick was down, he could concentrate on Jimmy.

I took a step backward in the snow. More quickly than I could see or anticipate, Inky veered to his right after the short jab and swung his arm in a wide, high arc. The blade whistled through the air and slashed across Mickey's tee-shirt. Mick screamed and stumbled backward into the face of the Andrews' incinerator on the far side of the narrow alley. A long, ugly red line spread outward as he stared down at his chest and stomach in horror. Inky immediately turned back to me. Butch turned to face Jimmy. It was as if he and Inky had choreographed their movements a hundred times in other battles.

I turned first to Mickey, whose eyes were stretched wide open, and then to Jimmy. A half second, no more. Jimmy cocked his arm, took one fierce step forward, and caught Butch attempting to duck the coming blow. His calculated move was a mistake. Jimmy's club, the last remnant of the Spring storm that lay in the garden all summer and was finally tossed out a day or two ago, ripped downward with every bit of force Jimmy could bring to bear. The meat of the branch caught Butch in the side of the head with a sickening crunch. He fell, and I thought for certain he was dead. Inky rushed to his side and knelt over him for a moment, as though a momentary truce had been called. He gazed down at his brother for several seconds, and then leaned across his body and plucked the knife Butch had dropped in the snow. He stood, a weapon in each of his hands now, waving them in tight circles at Jimmy and me. His eyes narrowed and I saw no fear or emotion in them at all.

Jimmy eased right, I instinctively moved left, wondering if I had the courage to swing the hatchet into his body. Strangely, I thought of Carol walking away from me with Allen in tow. I thought of Carol. Without blinking I brought my arm up and back and made my move. The blow would have killed him. He'd shot a glance at Jimmy, I think more afraid of his club than he was of me. For reasons I'll never be certain of, Jimmy swung again—but not at Inky. The branch met my wrist at the height of its descent, deflecting the hatchet just enough so that the full force of my swing, the death blow to the monster who'd made our lives hell all year long, was halved, or quartered. The dull cutting edge missed his head and landed instead on his collar bone. The knives fell from both of his hands and he dropped to his knees, but he didn't utter a sound. I glanced sharply at Jimmy, then lifted the hatchet for the final blow.

The wail of sirens was the nest thing I noticed. And then Jimmy's hands grabbing my arm. I shot a glance at Mickey lying in a growing pool of blood...over to Butch, to Inky, to the gray blanket of clouds above me. I wanted to kill him; I would have I think. Adrenalin and a moment of real hatred. Insanity.

I began to shake uncontrollably as the squad car screamed down the alley and skidded to a stop fifteen feet away. And then I began to cry and I let the hatchet fall to my feet.

***

Three ambulances arrived very shortly after, and the two brothers and Mickey were hurriedly loaded inside and rushed away in a discordant howl. Mr. Linden was deaf, I'd always thought, but he swore to the line of officers in his breaking old-man voice that he'd witnessed the entire incident.

"Those two boys are no good. No good at all. They've been terrorizing this end of the street for as long as they've been able to hold those knives they carried. They're no good. Skippy, McGuire, and the other boy are good kids. I watched them build this fort; watched them other two come down months back and pick a fight with them, too. They ought to go to jail. They're no good. How's the little guy that got cut? It looked bad from what I could see. Is he going to make it? God Almighty, I saw kindlier battles in Europe forty years back..."

The cop listened to Mr. Linden for as long as he could bear the war remembrances that followed his account of our fight in the alley, and then he pulled Jimmy and me aside after thanking Mister Linden.

"That true what the old man said?"

"Yes sir, every word of it. I swear we was mindin' our own business. That sonofabitch...sorry, sir...that's the same guy that's been makin' everyone's life miserable down here on this block. We was only defendin' ourselves," Jimmy said to him.

"Where did that hatchet come from?" the cop asked.

257

"We were cutting a hole in our stove—in the treehouse," I told him, pointing up at the ramshackle house in the tree. "Then I tossed it out before I came down because I saw Butch, the one who's unconscious. He had a knife."

"Why didn't you kids run for the house or call out for help?"

"Cuz they'da just come back tomorrow after they got their hands slapped," Jimmy answered. That was the truth.

The last I heard, Inky was brought up on more assault charges—attempted murder is what the police told my mom and dad, I think. We were promised he'd be gone to juvenile hall for quite a spell this time. Butch was placed into a sanitarium, or nuthouse, after he gained consciousness two weeks following their attack. From what I heard, he made slobbering noises instead of his normal slurred, guttural speech, and he ranted like a chimpanzee whenever someone entered his room. That's what I was told, anyway. I felt sorry for him, but I couldn't help but think the world was a better place with Butch the Chimp inhabiting it instead of Butch the Terrible.

I confessed my sin of vengeance at church soon after hearing all of that and taking the time to consider just what I'd done. I don't know if Jimmy bothered to. His hatred for the brothers coursed deeper into his soul than mine. I couldn't live with the weight of it. I think he could. But say what you will, or think as I might, Jimmy stopped me from killing Inky that day. I suppose his hatred for Inky had a bottom after all.

THIRTY-FOUR

Barnum Lake

C hristmas came, and Christmas went, with no real excitement, unless a new sweater I really didn't need or want could be called exciting.

There were no further incidents due to Inky being locked up, and Butch being institutionalized and as coherent as a rock. Carol was a bitter memory, but her image was beginning to fade a little in my mind. Jimmy was even having second thoughts about running off to Manhattan to find Gins. Mickey was the only one of us who was caught up firmly in love, and that was with Rosie of course, who he hung onto like the snow on the trees everyday at school. I guess I was happy for him. So, life marched on for all of us, until the strange night and the dream came, and rocked my world.

I awoke before dawn that Saturday morning, February 1st, to a litany of wind outside my window. The shadows of the naked elm tree branches coursed back and forth across the dead grass in the fractured haze of the moon like ghosts, unsure of what direction to take to leave this life. Although my bedroom was comfortably warm, I lay beneath the covers sweating as though I'd been asleep in an attic in mid-summer. As I blinked my eyes I tried to recall what manner of nightmare had visited me to turn my bedclothes into sopping washrags, but nothing came. I had awakened as though what I was looking out at was my first-ever vision. I suspected the sweating had something to do with Carol—haunting my sleeping subconscious—and so I prayed.

"God, if you refuse to answer me, at least don't torture me in my dreams." I couldn't bring myself to thank Him for another

259

day of life or even ask His blessing on this new one. I lay there for a long while staring out at the silver-gray sky devoid of texture, wondering if I should get up and change into something dry. A sudden shriek of wind hit my window and more eerie shadows whisked past. I threw the covers aside, jumped onto the rug, and stripped the sheets. The wind continued to howl. I undressed, throwing my clothes into a pile at the foot of the bed, crawled on top of the first blanket and then pulled the others over me thinking I'd fall back asleep until dawn arrived to chase the gale away. It was 3:00 A.M.

I awakened again later to the sound of voices outside my room—the stairwell off the back door to the kitchen. I blinked and glanced over at the clock on my nightstand. Nine o'clock. The voices became clearer as the shades of my deep sleep began to evaporate. They belonged to Jimmy and Mickey, laughing, calling back to someone on the main floor. My Mom. Yes. I could hear her muffled voice, something she'd been saying to them when I opened my eyes. "...drag him out of bed! Goddam' kid. Nobody should sleep this late."

"You betcha', Mrs. Morley! We'll each grab a leg," I heard Jimmy say as the door to the basement opened with a hurried creak.

"Hey, wake up in there, you lazy good-for-nothin'," Mick yelled. They entered my bedroom that was awash with bright sunlight. I glanced out the window and noticed a sky light blue and cheerful. Both of them stopped at the end of my bed. They were dressed in blue jeans and sweaters, more appropriate for an early Spring day than the dead of Winter.

"C'mon, get up," Jimmy said, "we're headed up to Barnum Lake. We're gonna' do a little skatin'. Mick's gonna' show us how to do a figure eight, kinda' like what Inky did on his belly!"

Mickey thought that was a great joke, and pulled his sweater and shirt up to his chest. I looked over at his stomach and cringed.

"Pretty cool, huh?" he said.

It wasn't. A long purplish line with dots on either side where the stitches had been threaded wound from just below his breast down to the top of his jeans.

"Whoa! That's ugly. How's it feel?" I asked him sitting up. "Turn on the light so I can see it better." Jimmy darted around Mick to hit the switch on the wall, raking his index finger across Mick's back as he did.

"SWISH! The steel cuts quick and deep!" he joked.

I pushed the covers aside and crawled to the end of the bed to have a close look at the scar. "That is...wow! Did Rosie, you know, put Baby Oil or something on it? I'll bet she did. You two have been like Mutt and Jeff this whole semester. How'd it feel to have her fingers massaging your stomach?" I laughed.

"Eat your heart out! She has hands that move like clouds. She's a Mexican princess!" Mickey said rolling his eyes and stroking his belly. "Hey, let's move it. Get some clothes on! You always sleep naked?"

I looked down at myself. Well no, not all that often. Only after...I felt my forehead, my arms, my own stomach. Dry as a bone, and thankfully normal again. I peered over the end of the bed where I'd thrown the wet nightclothes several hours ago. Mickey had one boot on the pajama top.

"That was one weird night," I said woodenly.

"Huh? What was weird?" Jimmy asked.

"Uh...nothing I guess. Thought it was all a dream...nothing. Okay, let's go! Throw me those pants over on the chair. I want to see Mick light up the lake! What's the temperature outside, anyway? You guys are dressed like it's summer."

"I dunno'. In the high twenties, I guess. Sun's real warm, though. It's perfect," Jimmy replied throwing my jeans at me. "Where's your skates?"

"I'm not sure...out in the garage somewhere I think." I pulled on my engineer's boots and tied the laces in record time. "Okay, let's get out of here."

The night had been spooky; a strange, otherworldly fever maybe, that had hit me suddenly, then vanished just as quickly. Hopping up the steps I still felt the clamminess of my pajamas, and shuddered at the figures that had whizzed by my window in the wind. Jimmy, Mickey and I ran to the garage and conducted another of our frustrating searches through the mountain of junk. We found the skates and then lit out of the yard, down the street. The sun was warm, and by the time we arrived at the lake in half an hour I figured we'd be skating through slush. That was okay, though. At least we wouldn't have to shovel snow or put up with TweedleChilders and TweedleJung.

As if by fate...

"Hiya, Daddy-Os. Long time no see. Where are you going?" Allen sang out from the rear of his driveway as we passed by.

"We're goin' to the creek to look for hibernatin' bears, Moloch!" Jimmy answered with a smile.

"Ve-ry funny. No, really, where are you going?"

We stopped. Mickey and I looked at one another. Should I invite him and find a thin spot in the ice? Nah, he'd probably break through it and sink to the bottom, this time in water over his head, and never come up again. Then his mom would really be mad at me. My lost Carol more so.

"We're taking our skates...see 'em?...down to the pawn shop," Mickey chirped. "After we collect our money, we're gonna' buy a crossbow and go looking for those bears. Want to come along?"

Allen thought about the statement for a minute. "Ah, you guys. Where are you really going? Skating? Can I come along? Let me go get my wallet. I'll chip in—maybe for those arrows. Hang on!" He dropped whatever he'd been doing and headed for the back door to his house.

"Crap, Mick! Let's get out of here. I don't want that nitwit tagging along," I said laughing.

"Wait a sec," Jimmy said. "What's the big deal? He's ok. Why're ya' always so down on him, Skip? For cryin' out loud, he's bringin' his wallet. We'll get him to buy donuts and hot chocolate!"

"No way. Let's go," I answered. And so we yanked on Jimmy's arms and took off at a run down the street, skipping across patches of thin, black ice like three clumsy characters in a

Laurel and Hardy movie, not quite sure if we were supposed to fall or not. I closed my eyes when we passed in front of Carol's house, holding onto the back of Mickey's sweater, imagining she was glued to her front window, waiting in tears for me to flash by. I saw her face—absolutely distraught, beckoning to me with eyes that had burned clear through my soul and now refused to let me go. How I wanted to stop and run to her and touch her lips again. And then I thought of David and what he'd said. How foolish I was to risk coming down this street. Even if I'd ripped my eyes out of their sockets, the deeper eyes of me would have remained as sharp and penetrating as a hawk's.

I pushed Carol's face out of my mind and concentrated on visions of flying across the ice; playing crack the whip with Jimmy in the lead, Mick in the middle tethering me. As we passed by the block of stores on First Avenue, and then turned north on Knox Court, I squinted up at a sky without even a wisp of a cloud anywhere. The sun heated the asphalt street and sent ghostly tufts of steam rising. Someone's dog shot out of their front yard, a portion of its frayed rope dangling from its neck. The animal chased us out of its territory with a ferocious amount of barking; a warning not to return. We slowed to a walk two blocks farther up the long incline of the avenue, out of breath, and safely beyond the point where I thought Allen could catch sight of us— or the dog would have any remaining interest in our presence. Across the street on the west side sat a tiny brick church with a small spire reaching heavenward, and a black-framed billboard identifying the name of the congregation. "Christ The Savior Lutheran Church". Below that the sermons for tomorrow's services were announced.

"9:00 A.M. Jesus Walks On Water"
"5:30 P.M. Searching For Jesus"

Mickey looked around us on the ground for a rock, but luckily for the sign there wasn't even a pebble large enough to bother slinging at it. Anyway, two men were standing on the sidewalk a few feet away from it. We couldn't hear what they were saying, but the taller of the two, dressed in a black suit and clerical collar, pointed at it, scratching his head. Had Mickey found a decent rock I know he would have thrown it, and we would have been off and running again. We shuffled on.

We arrived ten minutes later at the lake. It lay at the bottom of a steep, two hundred yard-long hill dotted with dead-looking elms, and conifers that refused to give up their color to the bleakness of the winter months. Tucked into a depression on the southwest end of the lake near the boundary of the park, Weir Gulch meandered in, two or three feet deep. Just below a thin layer of crystal clear ice we could see the current dropping down the slope to disappear into the lake's shimmering, frozen covering. Across the surface of the lake small mounds of snow lay piled here and there marking the efforts of earlier skaters who had cleared it in days past. A few hundred yards away Federal Boulevard rose above the steep bank, alive with traffic at this late hour of the morning. We sat down near the edge beneath a tree and changed into our skates.

"Wonder if Allen put the puzzle together?" I laughed at the thought of him staring down Meade Street, wondering why we'd gone away without him.

Jimmy clinched the last knot of his laces, picked up a dirty scoop of snow from the base of the tree we sat under and threw it at me. "Jesus yer mean sometimes, Morley. He ain't ever done anythin' but be nice to ya'. Ya oughta' be ashamed of yerself. '...streets of shuddering cloud and lightning in the mind leaping toward the poles of Canada...'"

"Ah, shut up!"

Mickey followed suit with more snow, and then they bounded down the hill together and jumped out onto the ice. They whisked along in clumsy circles as they gained their bearings, rusty since the last time we'd flown like the wind across a frozen surface. I watched in silence for a minute or two, then followed them out onto the brilliant surface of the ice. I met them seventy-five feet away from the bank. Both of them stopped as I leaned and dug the sharp edges of my runners into the ice beside the first low mound of snow.

"Who said it got too hot this week? This stuff's hard as a block of granite," Jimmy assured us, jumping up and down.

"Wasn't me. Let's crack the whip!" Mickey said, tossing his gloves onto the pile of snow.

"Okay. I'll lead the pack. Grab onto my hand. Skip, grab his!"

When we'd locked ourselves together in a chain, Jimmy dug the tips of his skates into the ice and we all took off, gaining speed as we shot across the ice toward the east shore. The shiish of our blades on the frozen surface was musical, the only sound except for the occasional clatter of studded tires on the pavement of Federal Boulevard a hundred yards away. Near the shoreline, Jimmy pumped his strong legs like the wheel connecting rods on a locomotive, and then leaned hard left in a sudden U-turn. Mickey flew behind him, tightening his grip on Jimmy's hand, loosening it on mine. I knew what was next as I quickly entered the turn with rising momentum. Mickey yanked his hand free, and I shot like a cannonball out of the barrel into the wall of dead foliage hanging down onto the ice. The crunch knocked me backward onto my rear.

"Oh, that was no fun!" I grabbed my belly with a forced laugh.

"Good show! Very graceful!" Mickey shouted from where he and Jimmy had stopped thirty feet away.

I rolled over onto my stomach, glanced at the ice beneath me, then pulled myself up onto my haunches. My reflection was dark and contorted in the rippled surface near the shore. Mickey skated over to me and stuck his hand out. "You ok? I didn't mean to let go of you."

"Liar. You wanted me to split my gut wide open so I could get stitched up like you!"

Mickey giggled. "Oops! You got me. Let's race to the far end!"

"You're on!" I said, and took hold of his hand. He pulled me up, and then we joined Jimmy who was crouched low already, arms bent and ready for the push off.

"On my mark," Mickey said. "Last one to the north end has to kiss Sandra Beaudine! Ready. Set. GO!"

Mickey and Jimmy lit out like a pair of Cheetahs. My rear skate raked the ice when I dug in and pushed forward, and I fell to my knee. By the time I'd regained my footing both of them were twenty feet ahead of me and accelerating. I thought of Sandra; a nice girl in Jimmy's class, but loaded with acne, and with hair that must have been dunked in an oil vat. I'd have to close my eyes and pinch my nose if they called my losing hand in the race. Before I'd gotten five feet in my desperate but useless attempt to make up the gap, a shout pierced the air from my left. Mickey heard it too and hesitated, allowing Jimmy to rocket on ahead.

"Hey fellas! I found you! Wait for me!"

Allen. Wearing his best black, too. I stopped completely, knowing it was now impossible to salvage even a second place. Our pestering friend stood on the bank in his gleaming skates by the inlet, one toe daintily poking at the ice.

"Wait up! I'm coming."

Not that there was any hope of getting back into the race, but I wanted to thrash him good. Just for his persistence. Just for his stupidity in finding us. Just because he was Allen and wore horn-rimmed glasses. Mickey glanced in front of him at the back of Jimmy, then threw up his hands, turned, and motioned for me to come with him to welcome Allen. We met a short distance away from the kid who was going to be led to the inlet somehow, and we stopped. Mickey furrowed his brow when he turned his head to me.

"Do you want the honor, or should I nudge him?"

"I think you'd better do it. Your mom probably won't beat you half as bad as mine will if I do it."

Allen tried to join us as we spoke, skating as though he had fifteen legs all working against one another. Why would God create such a drip, I thought? Other than the glasses, his total lack of coordination, and his absurd devotion to being punished by me—what was it that made me want to pick on him? Especially in the light of what the Minkles had done to us over the months? It hit me that we were very much like them. They must have seen us as Allens.

"Wait, Mickey. Leave him be. Let's go get Jimmy—let that twirp hobble along after us if he wants."

"Huh?" Mickey curled up his nose.

"Yeah. C'mon. Let's go.

"Hey Allen! Welcome aboard. We'll see you over at the north end!" I gave Mickey's arm a tug, and then we turned and sped off to catch up with the winner of the race. Allen clomped along, his ankles twisting with every step as if he were learning to walk in high heels.

Mickey and I flew like the wind, expecting to see Jimmy lounging at the shoreline, laughing and ready to demand that we both kiss Sandra. As we approached the gentle dogleg turn fifty yards from the shore, a momentary shot of confusion fell on me. He wasn't there. I scanned the steeper shoreline to my left where a tangle of brown vegetation hung onto the earth, plummeting down into the ice. Mickey stopped dead, digging his skates into the frozen surface beneath us, grabbing hold of me. The force of it and my momentum made me fall to my rear with a thump. Mickey's outstretched hand pointed across the field of ice straight ahead. Halfway between us and the bank near a lone mound of snow I saw Jimmy's head and arms break the surface of water, waving wildly as he tried to get a grip on the jagged rim of the broken ice above him. His face was the color of a clean sheet of paper. The beret he wore constantly lay bobbing like a cork in the churning water. He saw us and screamed in a high-pitched, exhausted tone, "Help me." Then he lost his hold on the slick, water-drenched ice and disappeared.

"Jesus! He's gonna' drown! Quick, we gotta' pull him out! What the hell happened? Jimmy, hang on!" Mickey screamed.

Jimmy reappeared once again, dripping and half frozen, his hands batting aimlessly at the churning water. Somehow he found the edge of the ice, cracking jagged pieces away each time he put any weight on it.

Mickey yanked the neck of my sweater. "Quick! Go find a stick or a branch—anything! Hurry." He left me and shot forward, pulling his own sweater off as he did. I jumped to my feet and turned in a rush of panic toward the steep embankment behind us

"Oh sweet Jesus, get me a branch!" A long root, I thought...a hunk of abandoned rope. A limb! There, at the top of the bank. Its thick end sticking out, tangled among overgrown, dead grass and weeds. I raised myself up onto the serrated tips of my skates and exploded toward the wall of dead grass. When I reached it, two, three breaths later, I scaled it as if I had claws instead of fingers. I grabbed hold of the inch-thick woody end and yanked it, the steel tips of my skates buried in the side of the low cliff. The branch gave immediately and followed me downward again, onto my back atop the ice. I raised myself up and returned close to the spot where Mickey lay on his stomach, throwing his sweater out like an anemic lifesaver, over and over and over. Jimmy clung precariously to a semi-solid shelf, shivering. "Not enough. Closer. I can't get my skates off..." He disappeared again when his grip failed, but somehow returned a short second later, gasping for air, exhausted from the struggle and the freezing water. Mickey scooted closer, roundhousing the sweater. It fell short again.

"Mick! I got it!" I screamed. Mickey turned his head as I tossed the branch. He released his hold on the sweater and snatched the long branch, then quickly shoved the end of it to Jimmy. Jimmy's head was barely visible, now, but one set of fingers still clutched the ice. I prayed more fervently than I had ever prayed before. Mickey raked the end of the branch across Jimmy's knuckles.

"Grab it! God, please..." And then I saw Jimmy's hand loosen slightly. He took hold of the slender end of the wood; a tenuous, feeble grip, as though whatever remaining strength and will to be saved was wrapped up in his frozen fingertips. The top of his hair barely poked through the water's surface. His head popped up, and then the other arm. He took hold of the branch, but the look in his eyes seemed vacant.

"Skip, get over here, quick!" Mickey shouted.

I eased forward to within a foot of Mickey, listening for any sound of cracking, any feeling of movement of the ice under my feet.

"I've gotta' go help him. Take the end of this thing," he said.

"No, Mick! Don't do..."

"Just do it!" He sat up, ripped off his skates, and then began crawling toward Jimmy. "If the ice starts breaking under me just don't let go. I'll get him!"

I heard the sound of skates clomping on the ice behind me as Mickey closed the distance between himself and Jimmy. It had to be Allen. I turned my head and yelled at him, "Go for help, Allen. Run! Take your damned skates off and go find somebody. Now!"

"Oh gosh! Oh..."

"Go!"

Allen stared at the scene for a split second, and then as if he had been born to it, undid his skates and flew off like the wind. I turned back to Jimmy and Mickey. Mickey was at the edge of the hole, one hand on Jimmy's fingers and the end of the stick. Jimmy's head had gone beneath the water again. And then I heard our best friend's death knell; a low, terrible crack, followed by several more in quick succession. The ice beneath Mickey gave way. He rolled on his side as it split and followed Jimmy under the water. A fraction of a second later Mickey re-emerged, gasping from the shock of the freezing water, still hanging on to the end of the branch. Jimmy didn't come up with him.

"Hold on," he said to me with a gasp. "I'm going back for him!" He shot head first under the water. I waited, eyes glued to the spot where they'd been. The black, broiling water calmed. It felt like minutes—too many minutes. Mickey was in trouble, too. And then he burst out, arms flailing, eyes wide open. He grabbed hold of the branch, and as he took in a huge breath of air, shook his head. "Going back. Lost him..."

"No, Mick! You're turning blue already! I'm pulling you out. Oh God, Jimmy!"

Mickey let go of the branch and dove under. Seconds later he resurfaced, gasping again. "I can't see, I can't find him. Goddamit!"

"Grab on, Mick. Hurry. You're gonna' freeze and die, too. Jesus, hurry up before you don't have any strength left. Do it!"

Mickey grabbed onto the branch. I dug the spikes of my heels in and pulled with all my strength. Holding onto the branch with his left hand, he found the solid edge and struggled out. He was half-frozen, soaked and shivering uncontrollably, but he was alive. I fell to my rear and cursed God through my tears. In front of us the waters breathed up and down, up and down, and then grew calm and serene, reflecting the mid-morning sun off the infinitely small ripples coursing across its surface.

THIRTY-FIVE

Aftermath

"**W**y did you boys go near that end of the lake? Didn't you see the Danger sign? Oh, Lord Jesus!" Mom wailed. She paced the floor, shaking, wringing her hands one moment, then covering her face with them the next. Pop sat in silence across the table from me, staring down, and deep in shock.

"There wasn't a sign. We didn't see one. Jimmy went over by himself. Me and Mickey were talking to Allen. I don't know...I don't know."

"Well there was! The police said they saw it," Mom replied on the verge of tears. She looked at me, then at Pop, and then she turned and walked hurriedly to the kitchen door. "I'm going over to Ruth's. God help us. She's probably layin' all in a pile. LaVerne, take care of Skippy. Talk to him. Oh my God, my God..." She walked out, leaving the door wide open.

I didn't envy her trying to console Mrs. McGuire. I imagined the woman was wailing like a banshee and yanking all her hair out. I lowered my head onto the top of the table and cried some more. The only person I knew who had died was Grandma Cowden—and she as was old as the hills when she simply failed to awaken that morning so long ago. The old are supposed to die, but not the young...not Jimmy.

Mom wound up calling our family doctor, Michael Ryan, after she'd sat with Mrs. McGuire for a while. Ruth had been drinking when the police knocked on her front door, but I knew the shock wave of news sobered her up in short order. It had to have. Mrs. McGuire was wandering through the rooms with an open bottle dangling from her hand when Mom got there—sobbing, shaking, but she was cold sober. It would do no good for the woman to continue drinking, Mom said afterward, and so she

271

gently removed the bottle from Mrs. McGuire's hand and helped her to the sofa in the living room. Mom sat with her there, holding her, crying with her, wishing the hours could be undone. Doc soon enough arrived with his satchel and a hypodermic needle. A short time later Mom returned home and poured herself a stiff shot of whiskey.

"I'm goin' back over in a bit. When she wakes up I don't want her there by herself. I'll stay with her. God Almighty," she said downing half the glass, "there ain't nobody but us to help her through the funeral arrangements. I better call her boss, too. Jesus."

During those bleak hours Pop consoled me as best he knew how, assuring me it wasn't mine or Mickey's fault, but really, what could he say?

"You two did the best you could, Skip. I'm proud of you. Don't take this on your shoulders. There was nothing else you could have done. I guess God just decided it was time Jimmy came home."

And now this cop out. How did God think? Why? Why would He do this to Jimmy, who hadn't even had time to straighten out—to me and Mickey, and especially to Mrs. McGuire? What kind of God was he? Within the span of four short months everything in this world that harbored any importance to me, contained any joy at all, had been ripped away. For what reason?

"He's cruel. I hate him!" I replied to Pop's nearsighted statement; his feeble, silly superstitious explanation of divine reasoning. I wanted no more of this. Any of it. God or Pop or my lost-in-the-Church Mother. I left Pop sitting by himself and went to my room where I turned the radio on as loud as I could tolerate. I lay in bed unable to sleep for hours, listening to the hits of the day, hoping they would drown out the bitterness and sorrow. I never wanted to hear the word God again.

The next morning I missed my assignment to serve Mass. I refused to go when Pop woke me up at five A.M. After a minute or two of shaking me without a response he left by himself. Whether Mom left Mrs. McGuire and went with him I had no idea. I couldn't imagine her not going—I'm sure she had a lot to talk over with God.

The weather had taken a turn for the worse at dawn, with a frigid Arctic front barreling over the northern Rockies, bringing at first a sputtering flurry of snow, and then an onslaught of white savagery. How appropriate that it should beat on us and try to lock us up in isolation. An hour after Pop left I heard the front door open and then close, and then a single set of footsteps meandering around upstairs for a while. Then silence.

"I'm not going to school today. I'm staying here. I don't want to see anyone."

"You are goin' to school," Mom informed me, though her manner was almost conciliatory. "You aren't gonna' lock yourself up down here like you did after the doin's at the Bazaar, Skip. You can't. It ain't healthy. The other kids'll help you get through this. Maybe Sister Dolorine, or Father."

"I'm not talking to either of them. I know what they'd say. I just don't want to go back until...until after the funeral. Please, Mom."

"No, honey, you got to. Now's the time you have to be around other people who'll be mournin' just like you. Come on now, get dressed and let your dad see if he can't get through all this snow and drive you to school. Come on." She looked down at me with agonizing sorrow plowed deep into her face. She loved Jimmy too, I knew. Her heart was as broken as mine in a way. I got up and put on my clothes.

We ate breakfast quickly, somberly, with nearly every word pulled from our mouths like aching teeth. Mom was uncharacteristically silent for long stretches, and the short questions by Pop had to be asked twice, sometimes three times before she would reply in equally short sentences. Pop's answers to her queries, "Do you think you can drive in this mess?" "You gonna' drive Ruth and me to the mortuary?" were, "Yes. Yes." Devoid of emotion, even for him.

Through the window I watched the snow continue to fall, lazily now. It was cold. I heard the air coming through the furnace duct over the doorway, constant in its effort to keep the rooms alive. Beyond the glass everything was freezing solid again in the face of the storm. I thought about the hole in the ice at the lake—probably sewn up overnight by the hands of the freezing wind.

Pop and I left thirty minutes earlier than usual, anticipating a grueling, fishtailing climb up the long hill of Knox Court. It would be hours before the city trucks manned by workers with huge shovels arrived on our side of town to throw salt mixed with pea-gravel across the roadways. I sat beside him in the front seat, thankful, at least, that he hadn't turned on the radio. He didn't say a word, I supposed because his thoughts were focused on keeping the car from spinning sideways into the gutter or another car. When we arrived twenty minutes later, he stopped in the middle of the road on the pavement crown, slipped the gear shift lever on the steering column into neutral, and then turned to me.

"You take care of yourself today, son. Try not to think about Jimmy...I mean...you have your lunch? Will you be all right?"

I opened the door without looking back at him. "Yes, Pop. I've got my lunch, I'll be okay."

"Good then. I'll be back at three-thirty. Try not to think..."

I closed the door and made my way through the knee-deep snow toward the classroom building, thinking a lot. Sister Mary Dolorine had just gotten there. She stood on the low step, keys in her hand, dressed in a Saharan mantle of black. She noticed me trudging across the roadway immediately. She unlocked the door, turned, and waited for me with a sad look on what was visible of her face.

It was going to be a long, miserable day.

THIRTY-SIX

A Rosary And Carol

I placed my lunch and books in the cubbyhole inside the door after Sister greeted me solemnly.

"I didn't see you at early Mass yesterday, Skip. Were you hurt when you and Mickey tried to, to...". She hesitated.

I looked away momentarily, uncertain of what answer would be appropriate, given that the most important thing in her life was an unflagging internal insistence to serve her God no matter what distraction or tragedy befell her. Though I blamed none of this on Sister, I no longer found it in me to share her point of view.

"Yes, Sister, I guess I was. I'm sorry. I'll probably be better by this coming Sunday. I hope he's not too angry."

"Father?"

"Yes, him too."

I glanced up into her face and could see by the sad, startled look that she understood what I'd meant very clearly.

"Father has requested that the student body take part in a Mass for Jimmy before class begins. Go along, now, over to the church. I think the two of you have a lot to talk about."

I understood just as clearly who she meant. We had nothing to say to one another though. I turned and left her standing there to greet the rest of the students with the good news that all of us were to be blessed before our day began with the opportunity to throw prayers up into the celestial realm. I doubted whether anyone would be home there, or if they were, even remotely interested in receiving them. No, maybe Jimmy would be. I decided to at least say hi to him and tell him how broken I was that he'd had to leave us; how badly I missed him. That I loved him.

A moment later I entered the church, and would have taken a seat in the last row, as far away from the altar as possible, but I

275

knew the Sisters always gathered there in order to have an eagle's-eye view of the rest of us. I chose a point inconspicuously near the center of the church, did not bother to genuflect, and moved halfway into the long, glistening pew. I sat in the quiet atmosphere and gathered my thoughts together. How strange it felt that I'd have to carry on a conversation with Jimmy in which I'd receive no reply, no poetry verses or bursts of laughter. I wondered if he was watching me—or was he more likely looking down on his mother? It made no difference, really. I needed to talk to him. Talk at him. Ask him if he, at least, knew why this had all happened. Had God explained the reason for this latest injustice? I closed my eyes and thought of Jimmy's smiling face, and then I began.

Hi, Jimmy. Can you hear me? Do you see me? Gosh, I just want to let you know how much I miss you already. How much...You must have seen that me and Mick tried as hard as we could to help you. Didn't you? We really tried, honest, but that water was so cold, and the ice kept breaking, and...and I knew Mick was next. I'm so sorry. I'd give anything to have you back here. Anything. None of this makes any sense.

Did he tell you why? You know, why you had to go so soon? What was the big rush? Maybe tell him for me that I'd like to know the answer to that. I used to think he listened to my prayers. I don't think he ever really did. Maybe he'll listen to you.

I was thinking back on summer last night. How you fell head over heels for Gins. How you two sat up there on that mountain that morning like a couple of stars that crossed paths and got hooked by each other's brightness. It made me smile, Jimmy. Something happened to you when you met her, you know. I mean, I didn't feel like I'd lost my best friend or anything, but you grew up a little after you crossed her path. I liked that. Oh, God, Jimmy, I miss you so much! Why'd you have to leave? Why'd he do it? I don't think I can ever forgive him for what he did. You can tell him that too. I don't give a hoot if he strikes me dead. Who cares?

Do you get loads of ice cream and stuff? Or do they let you smoke all the cigarettes you want, and drink whiskey if it makes you happy? Do you run into any Martian girls? Don't tell me the answer to that 'cuz I'd probably slip someday and spill the beans to Gins! Especially if they're cute like you said they were that night when we slept out in your backyard. She'd be pissed at you. Rosie's going to write and let her know what happened. We'll look after her 'til she gets over it. You don't have to worry.

I didn't want to come back to school this morning. You probably saw that, huh? Jeez, it's bad enough you drowned, but having to come back and listen to everyone asking a million questions about it...especially Sister Dolorine. I mean, I still really like her and all, but right now I just can't bear going over it again. And I know she'll corner me sometime and tell me how much Jesus loves me...and you...and how it's not our place down here to question...What did he say to you, Jimmy? Can you somehow let me know? Can you come back for just a second or two and let me know it's okay? That you really are happier there, and that there was a good reason? Even if he won't let you tell me what it is? You don't have to show up like a ghost or anything, or even talk if you don't want to. Just come back and let me know? Ask him, too, about Carol. I still miss her. What was the deal there? Would you do that, Jimmy? It all just seems so cruel. All of it.

Well, I'd better go. Father's saying this Mass for you. I don't want to be here, but since it's for you—I guess I don't mind so much. I miss you, Jimmy. I...I love you.

When I opened my eyes I saw Mickey. He was sitting quietly beside me, but I hadn't heard him come in—hadn't heard anyone. My eyes were filled with tears. That embarrassed me, and so I quickly wiped them away with the cuff of my coat. The church was half-full. Rosie sat next to Mickey, defying the statute that Student Body Masses be segregated by sex. Another foolish rule, but that's how it was. I supposed no one had the courage to come forward and move her, seeing as how Mickey must certainly be in deep mourning; an exemption today. I was thankful to see them.

Rosie had her right arm around Mick's waist, low enough so that it was invisible to the prying eyes of the Sisters behind us. The bottom of her uniform skirt lay well above her shapely knees, and on any other day she would have been dragged out by one of the nuns, had the hem lowered by rough hands, and told in no uncertain terms what she was. Or what they thought she was. Not today. She reached across Mickey's chest and touched my arm with her free hand, and she smiled sadly at me. I crinkled the corners of my mouth in return, then looked at Mickey. He mirrored my greeting and his hand followed Rosie's to my arm. I felt for the first time since Jimmy went away that I wasn't suffering alone after all.

The three tiny bells in the sacristy rang softly announcing the start of Mass.

***

I made it through classes Monday and Tuesday with only a brief encounter with both Sister Mary Stanislaus and Sister Mary Dolorine. They'd cornered me Monday afternoon while I waited on the sidewalk for Pop to pick me up. After a brief time of questioning and serving up platitudes, they must have despaired of my sullen mood and clipped answers, though. Seeing in my silence that I refused to be comforted or struck by the Almighty finger of acceptance, Sister Dolorine finally hugged me and whispered that she'd pray for me, and then both nuns left for the piet solitude of the convent.

Jimmy's Rosary service was held the following evening at McConaty's Mortuary on the far east side of town. Mom had thought it wise to bring Mrs. McGuire along with us, knowing her worst hours had not yet arrived, and that she'd need all the help she could get. When we entered the chapel under the cloud of organ music played low and depressingly slow, and on seeing Jimmy's casket draped on its lower half in white at the front of the main aisle, Mrs. McGuire broke down and began to weep. Mom responded as though it had all been scripted by putting her arms around Mrs. McGuire, and gently urging her on to the front pew where the four of us must sit. The closer we got to the casket, the louder her sobbing and bursts of crying became. The Rosary was a callous service, I thought. To whose advantage and

278

comfort was it directed? Certainly not to Mrs. McGuire's. And she would have to go through it all again tomorrow morning at the cemetery—a hundred times more painful than tonight. I began to hate God even more for what he'd done. I wanted to turn and run, hide myself until everything was only a black, foggy memory. But that would be useless, and so I followed my Mom and Mrs. McGuire, at my father's side, allowing more of my own tears to begin their escape. When she reached Jimmy's casket sitting amongst a garden of flowers beneath the pulpit, Mrs. McGuire halted and placed a hand on it, heaving with emotion. Pop held me well away from Jimmy's satin-lined bed while Mrs. McGuire bent over it, whispering and shedding tears onto her son. Some moments later she sorrowfully turned away. On the arm of Mom, head hung low, handkerchief covering half her face, she allowed herself to be escorted into the front pew. After seeing Jimmy's lifeless face, what little life she'd hung onto up to that point must have perished.

Pop allowed me a few moments by myself with my friend after Mrs. McGuire was seated. I stepped up to the casket, looked down at him, and then closed my eyes immediately. Try as they may have, the morticians had been unable to capture anything of what he'd been. His unruly blonde hair was washed and combed and neatly parted. What could they have known about the way he failed miserably, constantly, with a comb? His beret was nowhere to be found. They'd put him in a brown suit, too. Even in death I knew he must be horrified and uncomfortable. His face though. It was a poor mask—powdered and colorless, and his lips were drawn too tight, with a frightening tinge of purple in them. I stood quietly for a moment surveying the near-specter beneath me that once harbored laughter, sadness, joy and fear, and I began to cry convulsively. They would shut the lid after we'd all gone, and then it would be just a highly polished box, lowered into the earth tomorrow amidst a final round of weeping and goodbyes. That moment standing there was the most difficult of my entire life, worse by degrees than seeing Carol walk away hand in hand with a beaten Allen last Fall. I bid

Jimmy farewell, and then turned away to join my parents and Mrs. McGuire.

We waited as the chapel filled with other mourners, many of them making their way to where we sat, offering condolences and more tears. Finally Father Blinker strode in with his missal and rosary beads. He stopped when he'd gotten to the front, leaned over the rail of the pew directly in front of Mrs. McGuire, and whispered something in her ear. A hand touched hers, she nodded, and then he walked up to the Prie Dieu and began the memorial service.

"In the name of the Father, and of the Son, and of the Holy Spirit..."

The litany of Our Fathers and Hail Marys rolled dolefully onward, one following another until the last of the beads on a hundred rosaries slipped though the thumbs and index fingers of everyone present who held them. Father remained kneeling for a short time after the completion of prayers, his eyes closed and his head bowed reverently, and then he rose and stepped across the immaculate white carpet to the pulpit. He placed his rosary beads into his jacket pocket, opened the missal and placed it onto the top of the stand, and then he looked across the room to Mrs. McGuire. As though he were her closest, most loving friend—and at that moment he was—he said to her in his strong, kind voice.

"Ruth, join me in remembering our beloved James." He paused, focusing his eyes on her—capturing what was left of her and lifting her briefly from her grief. Then he gazed out at the crowd.

"I see that many of you here tonight are young men and women—friends of James. Your faces are downcast and your hearts are broken. I can well understand your grief. I grieve too. I knew him well myself. Imagine though, for a moment, if you can, something remarkably different, from James' perspective. It is true the circumstances of his death were tragic, but I know that in the short moment of his passing his spirit left in great joy to join that of Our Lord and Savior, Jesus Christ. We mourn him, we who have known and loved his carefree ways, his courage and selflessness. But James is far happier now, I can assure you, than he ever could have been in this life. Do not mourn him, rejoice with him."

Father smiled and left the pontifical dryness of the podium. He walked to the edge of the carpeted platform, surveyed every eye with a sweeping glance, and then continued as though he were sitting at a festive table amongst his closest friends.

"Jimmy shot a BB some months back from the choir loft. I don't think his aim was true...was it Skippy? You remember the evening quite well, I'd guess," he said with a guarded laugh, turning to me. I dropped my gaze, recalling the shot that traveled in a long arc and hit the half dollar-sized glass of the Monstrance containing the body of Jesus.

"Who do you suppose he was aiming at, Skippy?"

I was forced by the question to look up. He waited patiently for my answer.

"X, Father. He meant to hit X."

"Yes, so I heard afterward. Do you suppose, my friends, that Jesus was outraged?" He paused again, capturing every tear-filled eye. When he was certain the question had sunk in, he answered it with great authority. "I can tell you that He was not. He surely chuckled at James' terrible aim. Though it was my duty to scold him, I chuckled too. Later in the rectory of course.

"You see, our Savior doesn't live in Monstrances or Tabernacles...or even in churches. Those things and places are merely reminders for us that He *does* live. He lives within us. Of course all of you know that, don't you. How silly of us to think that James could possibly have incurred His wrath for a childish prank gone terribly wrong. And you may trust that He has already walked in the most beautiful gardens with James at His side, laughing with him, holding him close to His heart. You must not be sad, when James is rejoicing. It is time, now, for all of us to let him go, hard as we may find that.

"But why, you ask, did He call James home?" Father looked down at me, and I knew that the question really was meant for me. Somehow he had peered into my heart and soul.

"I don't know. I wish that I did. I would tell all of you, make your sadness fly away on the wind. I can only remind you that His knowledge is infinite, His love for us fathomless. For whatever reason He chose this time to call James home to His heart, trust that it was driven by motives of the greatest love imaginable. James is exactly where he should be, where he was destined to be from the moment of his conception." He finished. Once again Father walked to Ruth, sitting beside my mother, leaned close to her, touched her cheek with the palm of his hand, and whispered something to her.

I covered my face with my hands and wept. Not in sadness, or out of the bitterness that had overwhelmed me in these days past, but because I sensed Father's words might be true. I desperately wanted them to be. I wanted to believe again that everything God did was for our best, that he heard our every prayer and loved us...and loved us. But, what was the use of taking Jimmy? Where was the good there?

I thought I felt a tug on my shoulder, a soft set of fingers. When I turned I saw only Mr. and Mrs. Fumo and Mickey sitting with their hands laid in their laps. I expected to see Jimmy standing between Mickey and me, but I was mistaken.

Beyond them, near the rear of the chapel, I saw the reason for whose ever delicate fingers had stroked my shoulder. Carol and her parents had just risen and were readying to leave. I thought for a moment that I should remain seated in deference to the occasion, but that thought disappeared as quickly as it had arisen. I gathered up my courage, or my foolishness, and stood up.

"Excuse me," I blurted out to my folks, Mrs. McGuire, and Father, and then I left the pew in a rush. A few of the mourners had begun to stand and make their way out of the chapel. I walked as quickly and respectfully as I could through their ranks, and out the doors into the cold of the night.

Carol and her parents were nearly to their car when I caught up to them. I had no idea what I would say, or if Mr. and Mrs. Hudson would even allow me a moment in their presence.

"Carol! Mr. and Mrs. Hudson..."

They turned and looked at me as though I had just climbed out of the casket inside. No one spoke for a long, tense minute. When I was certain they would shun me and turn away again, Mr. Hudson did the unexpected. He glanced at his wife, then pursed his lips and touched Carol with his hand. He and his wife left her there facing me, without a word, and entered the car.

"Hi."

"Hello, Skip. I...we heard, you know. Daddy thought it would be good to pay our last respects to Jimmy. They didn't actually know him, but...I'm so sorry it happened. I really liked him. Really. I'm sorry."

My mind shot a thousand questions to my tongue, but I was paralyzed with confusion over which of them to start with. All I found myself able to do was look across the inches dividing our faces, wishing I could turn back the clock to the night I'd ruined us at the Bazaar.

"I miss you. I..."

She placed a finger on my lips.

"I have to go. Tomorrow, maybe. At the cemetery. We can talk then. I'll ask them if they'll take me. I have to go."

She left me standing in a cloud of hope and despair. Seeing her, hearing her voice, Jimmy gone.

Mr. Hudson started the engine after she'd gotten into the back seat, and then they drove away. I remained rooted to the frozen pavement and watched until the taillights faded into the blackness.

THIRTY-SEVEN

Mount Olivet

I awoke Thursday morning from a dream of Jimmy. He'd been laughing at something, and I couldn't help but notice that in the dream his missing tooth had been replaced, and that it fit perfectly in his mouth. We were sitting with Mickey and Rosie, Gins and Carol, on a hill somewhere—a vision mixed up with vague remembrances of that familiar spot, and others overlaying it I'd never seen before. It was sunny and warm, and below us lay a city, much like some futuristic image from a science fiction movie, where gleaming towers sent showers of golden-colored shadows over the streets below. I think we'd been talking about the giant chicken from outer space. Maybe that was it.

Some dreams are so very difficult to leave, but my sleeping hours had done their duty, and so I was ushered back to consciousness; much, much too soon. The covers of my bed lay over me as though throughout the night I hadn't twitched a single muscle, as though for some reason every unconscious thought had been like the dream—filled with strange peacefulness and overwhelming joy.

The clock on the nightstand said 6:35. Three hours until the final chapter of the dreadful week was written at the cemetery. Three hours until my eyes would come to rest on Carol again. Outside, the twinkling stars were beginning to give way to the patient advance of the pre-dawn light. At least there would be no snowstorm to add further gloom to the misery of the interment. I said thank you to God. And then I bit my tongue. The floorboards above me creaked against the joists, and I heard the muffled voice of Mom.

I lay in the quiet of my room for another moment or two trying to pull the images of the dream back up into my consciousness. Only Jimmy's smile...and Gins. Carol sitting so close to me. Rosie below us with Mickey's head in her lap. The city had vanished.

The sound of the toilet being flushed, and then water hammering through the exposed pipes running under the joists when the tub faucets were turned on. I eased out from underneath the covers, found my clothes and dressed, and then left the dark shadows of the basement to join Mom and Pop when they found their way to the kitchen.

It was Pop's undeclared job to brew a pot of coffee each morning. He stood at the counter by the sink in his house shoes and robe, ready to drop the basket into the metal pot, when I pushed the door open. He glanced at me with eyes still half-closed, and managed a smile straight from a cheerless awakening.

"Good morning, Skippy. Did you get any sleep last night?"

"Yes Pop, I think I did, and I had the most wonderful, strange dream. Very peaceful."

He noted my answer with a nod of his head, only vaguely aware in his fumbling with the coffee pot, I think, of what I'd just said. He placed the glass-domed lid on it, stepped drowsily across the floor to the stove, and then set it on the rear burner.

"Dreams are funny things, you know. Don't mean a thing usually." The burner refused to light. He cocked his head a little to look under the pot, then grabbed a wooden match from the cardboard container on the top of the grease splash and struck it near to the grate where the gas hissed out.

WHOOMP! The burner lit. So did his eyebrows and the tips of the hair on his scalp.

"Damnation!"

"You okay, Pop?"

"Yeah...I guess so. *What* was I thinking, anyway?" He turned to me rubbing his face. "Where were we? Oh yes, dreams. You say you had one last night?"

"No, just before I woke. A really neat one I think. Jimmy was in it. And Carol. Mickey and Rosie, too."

"Your Mom?"

"No. Rosie Gonzales. We were all there on a hill together. It was so peaceful. It made me feel...I don't know...relieved, or comfortable. Like everything was okay."

"Umm. Don't think I know this Rosie."

"What I'm trying to say, Pop, is that I don't feel so much like my soul's been yanked out this morning. I'm still so sad Jimmy's gone, I really am, but I think that was actually him in the dream. Somehow. I think he was trying to tell me he was okay. Oh gosh, Pop, I miss him so much, but I think he's...well, at peace. He's resting on a hill, waiting for his friends to join him someday. Does that sound nutty to you?"

Pop forgot about the pot of coffee, the burner now sputtering out a constant circle of flame, and turned his seared face to me. "No, Skippy. That isn't nutty at all. If there's a God in Heaven, I think maybe he sent Jimmy down to hold your hand one last time. He probably saw as well as any of us that you especially, needed it. You're a lucky boy."

Lucky might not have been the right word, but I got to thinking that perhaps Jimmy being gone, and my getting him back, was something like emptying the feathers of a pillow from the top of a church spire in a wind storm. Try to collect them all and stuff them back in. Not so easy. There wasn't a blessed thing I could do about it except begin to move on. Even so, his being here, needling me, laughing with me, leading me madly astray, just *beside* me—it was too soon. Save his body, he was still right here. But the dream was like one of Mr. Hudson's or Pop's piano concertos. It left me in a different frame of mind because of its loveliness. The blackness wasn't quite so overwhelming suddenly.

"LaVerne? Come in here and zip me up, would ya'?" Mom called from the bedroom. Another of Pop's undeclared jobs was to work the zipper on the backs of Mom's dresses. He left the pot on the stove, me in my contemplative state, and shuffled off to get Mom's hatches battened down. I gathered up a bowl, the box of Wheaties, and the half carton of milk from the refrigerator. I sat down at the table and began breakfast.

"For God's sake, La Verne! What happened to your face?"

We arrived at church at 8:15, just as the man from McConaty's was preparing to take the sprays and vases of flowers inside. The back door of the hearse was still standing open. Thank goodness Jimmy wasn't in it. Mrs. McGuire sat for a moment beside me in the back seat of our car, silent, her face powdered nearly as heavily as Jimmy's was last night. I looked over at her briefly as Pop walked around to open the door for her. There was nothing there. She wasn't sobbing or taking in deep gulps of air at intervals like someone just finishing up a good cry would do. Her eyes stared straight ahead, devoid of any sign of life.

Pop pulled the door outward and Mom leaned in, gently grabbing hold of Mrs. McGuire's hands.

"C'mon, hon. Let's get it over with. Take hold, now. Let's go."

Mrs. McGuire let herself be led like a lobotomized patient out of the backseat, into the church behind the mortician and his assistant with their bouquets, and once again up to the front beside Jimmy's coffin.

Father Blinker said a low Mass, dispensed with a further eulogy, but he did not fail to walk up to Mrs. McGuire when Mom helped her to her feet after the service. This morning he hugged her, then walked with her behind the casket to the rear of the church, holding her hand. From my limited vantage point behind them I'm quite sure I saw color returning to her face when she turned her head to respond to something Father had said to her halfway down the aisle. Perhaps, I thought, she also might survive.

Despite the solemnity of the march outside, I glanced left and right to see if Carol and her parents were sitting in the midst of the people in attendance. Either they had left early or hadn't even come. What had she said to me last night? Tomorrow, at the church...or was it the cemetery? She must come. I couldn't stoop to asking God to help me out. If I had, I knew with certainty she'd never be there. I asked Jimmy instead.

I rode with Mom and Mrs. McGuire in the mourners' limousine while Pop drove the station wagon in the long, gloomy procession through the city to Mount Olivet Cemetery northwest of the church. I watched through the side window as two mortorcycle cops hop-scotched from traffic light to traffic light, assuring us an unimpeded crawl clear to the gates of Jimmy's final resting place. His time among us was limited, now, to another short hour. Another sixty minutes, maybe less. Suddenly just the presence of his lifeless corpse gained in importance. I wondered as we passed under the black, wrought-iron arch and up the paved roadway, what Mrs. McGuire was thinking. Only a few more moments, now? Could she please, God, just have him back for one more day? One more hour?

We wound among hundreds of gravesites, many with urns, or small bundles of flowers set on the dry, dormant grass beneath their granite markers. Row after row, section after section, until we pulled to a slow, respectful stop behind the black hearse a short walk from the excavated site carpeted in green felt where Jimmy's casket would be set onto the lowering device. His final moments in the bright sun. More tears would follow; many more tears.

I was fine for the most part throughout the service, scanning the faces of the crowd assembled around the grave every other second. Standing between Mom and Pop and Mrs. McGuire on the little knoll, I was half-distraught, but still half-filled with the anticipation of merely seeing Carol. I apologized to Jimmy for that bit of nagging joy in my heart during this somber occasion dedicated to him, hoping he'd understand. In my heart I was certain he would.

After Father had read the short prayers and blessings written in the small black book he held, he stepped back and lowered his head while a man from the mortuary turned the lever on the web-strapped stand holding Jimmy. As the casket slowly lowered, a ray of sunlight caught the silver finish of the crucifix on its top. I shut my eyes when it hit me, and said goodbye to my dearest friend.

Mrs. McGuire walked forward with a white rose in hand, stood strangely emotionless for a moment, then dropped it into the mouth the hole. I joined her, removing the boutonniere from the lapel of my jacket, and let it fall down beside her rose. After a moment of silence I turned and hugged her, then walked away. Moving toward the crowd the first person I met was Mickey, on his way to toss his boutonniere alongside mine. Our eyes met for an instant and he touched my arm with his hand as he passed by me.

Farther down the slope I stopped and surveyed the long line of cars parked at the edge of the road. One after another I checked them off in my mind as my eyes searched for Carol's. I didn't see it, and so I scanned them all again. The Hudsons hadn't come. I dropped my gaze to the ground ahead of me and walked on to the mourners' limousine where I waited in utter despair for the final service to come to its end.

THIRTY-EIGHT

The City On A Hill

Two weeks slipped by on the back of a cruel and loathsome horse after Jimmy was laid to rest on that sunny, cold morning. Mom continued to look in on Mrs. McGuire each day. Pop settled back into making a living, composing marvelous works on the piano, and eating like two men once again. Life and the Colorado weather resumed something of a less frantic pace for the briefest of moments.

But the last week of February arrived, and with it another storm that raced out of the north, dumping a foot of snow on the city. The temperature hovered just above the zero mark on the thermometer hanging outside the kitchen window. The next series of storms was even worse, and they followed so closely in succession during the last two days of the month that all the city schools were shut down on Friday the 27th due to their ferocity. Mickey called a few times but he hadn't shown up at my door since the morning of Jimmy's drowning. I ran into him every day at school of course—him and Rosie that is—and maybe that would have to do. He talked to me, sometimes even at length, but the glue binding our affections had somehow weakened to the point of breaking. Our conversations were never quite the same—our plans for the days no longer included one another. When I saw Rosie and Mick together on the school grounds where they were careful not to openly display their affections, or in the deli a block away where they were free to hold hands at one of the tables, I began to look away. It brought to mind the dream in which the six of us had sat in great contentment on that high, magnificent hill. But, like Carol, the dream had vanished, shattered into pieces and scattered everywhere. I climbed back into my closet of despair. I might have stayed there wallowing in self-pity had it not been for Allen. The kid I had no use for. The creature lowest on my list of conceivable instruments of God.

He came knocking on my door. It was a Saturday morning, about nine o'clock. Mom invited him in. Had he come along with his mother I'm sure they would have been made to stand outside and state their business in the frozen air on the front porch. But he was alone, no threat to Mom, and so he was welcomed.

I sat downstairs in my room entertaining thoughts of having a stunning picture of my latest ravaged countenance painted on every other billboard throughout the city. Receiving notes of sympathy and understanding from thousands of touched souls. Having God appear in the flesh to comfort me. Being compared sometime in the future to Job.

Allen waited on the couch in the living room like a suitor in a parlor might have in the last century while Mom walked to the end of the kitchen, opened the door, and called down to me.

"Skip, you have a visitor. Come on up here."

A visitor? I immediately eliminated God, unless by chance he'd arrived in disguise, but the next person in line was Carol. Something told me, though, that *that* hope was destined to be dashed. As I left my room and made the trip up the blisteringly cold stairwell, I checked off the faces and names of potential visitors. The matter-of-fact tone of Mom's voice told me it couldn't be Father Blinker or any of the Sisters, worried sick at this latest terminal attack on my spirit. Coach Moye? No. Maybe Mickey. Yes. But no, he'd be here with Rosie, for sure, and even Mom knew the subtle grammatical difference between visitor and visitors. I opened the door to the warmth of the kitchen. Mom stood indifferently at the counter, humming the melody of *That Old Rugged Cross.* Strange. A Protestant hymn if ever there was one. Whoever it was, he or she didn't warrant great excitement, but on the other hand the song she'd picked strongly suggested it was someone of at least some spiritual standing. I tapped her shoulder and mouthed, "Who is it?"

She ended the tune abruptly and answered with a cryptic flick of her tongue on her teeth, "Allen."

Allen? Allen Jung? I shook my head in surprise and dismay while she motioned with hers for me to go into the living room. I left her to pick up on the hymn at the bar she'd ended at.

"Allen," I greeted him coldly, "what's up?"

He reacted as I might have expected, jumping to his feet, expounding on the amount of snow that had fallen, the reason for the freezing temperature, in Beat verse. Would I like to go with him to Ellsworth Avenue—the short, Alpine-like street dividing Carol's block from ours? A few younger kids had already gathered there; the fresh snow was packed, slick, and hard as a rock. The whole scene would be too cool...

With him? I couldn't see it, but I answered politely. "I don't know. No, I don't think so. Not right now."

"But it's perfect outside. I haven't seen you in weeks, and I thought since Jimmy is gone and all, you might accompany me..."

That sounded all too much like an invitation for a date to me, and worse, it rankled me that he'd dare use Jimmy's name in the same sentence. Still, I masked my abhorrence at such an idea. "Thanks. Maybe later. I've got some things I've got to do."

"Oh. All right. I just thought I'd ask," he said dropping his eyes a little. Looking at his dark pupils through his thick lenses made them seem twice as big as they actually were, and I had to look away for fear I'd lose my balance. He walked to the door and left rather sadly with his shoulders slumped. Standing at the front window, I watched him leave the yard with his shiny new sled, tugging it behind him, dressed in his heavy, black sweater, immaculately pressed black trousers, his beret, tip-toeing over the deeper drifts of snow on the sidewalk. I turned when he'd gotten nearly out of sight and walked back to the door leading out to the back porch. Mom was still at the counter where she'd been a moment earlier, quiet though when I re-entered the kitchen.

"Why don't you go on down and do some sleddin', Skip? You and Jimmy always used to like it so much. It was nice of Allen to come up and invite you," she said without turning.

I wasn't going to answer at first. I reached the door and pulled it open, but then I reconsidered.

"He isn't Jimmy, that's why."

"You wouldn't be goin' for Jimmy. Or for Allen. You'd be goin' for yourself, 'cause you need it." She turned just as I was about to step out onto the concrete landing of the back porch. "Wait a minute. Come back here...please," she said in a tone of voice that up until that moment I hadn't often heard.

Even so, I readied myself for another lecture, leaving the door ajar just in case it became unbearably melodramatic. Mom walked over to me, paused while she put her fingers under my chin, and then she wrapped her arms around me and drew me close to her.

"Oh Skippy. I love you so much. I miss you—kinda' like you miss Jimmy. You're gone, too, sweetie. Don't you realize that? You've left with him and it's breaking my heart." She removed her arms from around me and placed both hands on the sides of my face. She stood there silently for a long while staring deep into my eyes, and I saw in hers the pain she was enduring. I wanted to help her, but there was nothing I could do. She couldn't help me because she didn't have the power to bring anything that was important back into my life. Right or wrong, childish or otherwise, that's just how it was.

"Go on and go, sweetie. Get your mind off all your troubles. The fresh air and snow and other kids'll do you a world of good. The world ain't gonna' stand still now that Jimmy's gone. You just have to get back on it somehow."

"It isn't only Jimmy, Mom, it's..."

"I know, sweetheart. I know. None of it seems right or fair, but that's the hand you been dealt right now. You can't fold and walk away, you gotta' pull up your sleeves and wait for a better one. You gotta' stay in the game. I love you sweetie, and I know you can do it if you want to. I got faith in you. I hate seeing you like this."

Mom was right. I was getting sick of listening to the radio and staring at the pictures on my bleak walls. If I didn't get out of the house I was certain I'd go stark raving nuts before too much longer. Better to endure Allen. Who knows, maybe there'd be a brand new face in the crowd that I'd never seen before.

I left the Flexible Flyer tucked away inside the shed in the backyard and walked to the corner just in time to see six screaming kids come flying down the hill on their sleds, straight across the intersection without a care in the world, as though someone had banned the traffic on Meade Street. There was a wonderful anarchy ruling the street; shouts in decibels at the top of the scale, a couple of dogs barking, chasing and nipping at the runners of their masters' sleds. A kid I'd never seen, chasing a girl I'd never seen, with a gloved mitten full of white, freezing snow. He caught her and baptized her golden hair. The boy might have been a year or two younger than me—the girl a year or two younger than...

Mr. Kimple stood in front of his flower shop at the corner, hands on his hips, watching all of this with a smile. His six month-old crop of carnations thrived in the new section of greenhouse stretching up the street. Tufts of steam escaped a missing pane of glass high up near the ridge. Inside, the greenhouse was only warm mist and thick gray fog.

I glanced upward toward Newton Street, toward Mickey's house on the corner. There at the top I saw Mickey's back, and Rosie's. In front of them stood Allen, facing me fifty yards away. He had hold of his sled, which he'd painted glossy ebony to match his clothes, his hair, his glasses, and probably his new outlook on life. I chuckled inwardly, not being able to imagine a kid with his temperament looking out at the world with anything less than Norman Vincent Peale's positive attitude. The sled stood on its end runners next to him and he patted it intermittently as he spoke, like he would a close friend, or a puppy. He had hold of Mickey's and Rosie's ears, too, with his gesticulating, and non-stop string of forty-dollar words I imagined. Mickey stood motionless, one arm draped over the shoulder of Rosie's heavy-knit, maroon sweater, but every now and again I could see him turn away from Allen, Rosie too, and look straight ahead, as though listening to someone else's replies; someone standing invisible to me in front of them.

I began to ascend the hill through footsteps beaten into the crust of white lying atop the sidewalk. Near the alley, which split the steep hill exactly in two, down which the Skulls had wandered in their Hun fury what seemed so long ago, I stopped. Between Allen, whose cracking voice was beginning to overcome

294

the screams of the kids and the barking, and Mickey's left shoulder, the top outline of auburn hair bobbed. Suddenly Allen laughed, then stepped sideways abruptly for some reason and glanced down the hill. Three more kids streaked by, screaming. As they shot by me, little bundled up electrons blasted clean out of their orbits, Allen's eyes caught mine. His arms went straight up, the sled went down like a tree. It hesitated for an instant after meeting that last crack of the axe blade. Mickey first, then Rosie with her long black hair swirling as it followed the quick rotation of her head, wheeled to follow Allen's gaze. And then Carol's face peeked out from behind Mickey's body.

Allen rattled off a greeting loud and clear, "Don't let that horse eat the violin!"

I looked around. So odd. I thought I'd just heard *Jimmy* shouting those words. The timbre of them, the ridiculousness. I half-expected to see a horse readying to open its mouth and take a bite out of a Stradivarius held in...in whose hands? Visions in my head, that was all. No horse, no violin, no Jimmy or anybody else holding it. Just crappy reality. Allen reciting a line from one of the atrocious Beat poems. He'd taken up where Jimmy had left off, and that was the way it should be, I supposed. Jimmy had befriended him—taken him under his nihilistic wing, only Allen was too perfect a spirit of optimism to fit the clothes precisely. Too innocent. He just looked the part of one of the anarchists marching over American mores and values. I caught his eye and couldn't help but laugh.

"Clouded with snow the cold winds blow,
and shrill on leafless bough,
the Robin with its burning breast alone sings now!"

I rejoined the game, of course drawing a pair of deuces— but, I was in again.

To my surprise—my delighted and everlasting surprise— Carol stepped forward and clapped. A bright Springtime smile leapt onto her face, eclipsing in me all of the dark hours I'd endured in her absence. She wore polished black slacks tucked into white winter boots with fur-lined tops, and a white-hooded parka, the bottom which was lined with the same texture of fur as the boots, and which ended in a kind of Coco Chanel perfection at her waist. I stood with melting emotions, recalling her face—on the porch swing, on the corner below us when I'd walked her home through the blowing Fall leaves. Her smile was stolen from the museum masterpieces; Mona Lisa's, Venus', Saint Catherine of Alexandria's, so stunning, and oh, so lovely. Mickey and Rosie simply continued to look down at me, though Rosie's eyebrows raised, I think a little amazed that the rat had at last emerged from his dark, depressing intestine of the Leviathan. All four of them skirted around a group of kids and another yapping dog getting ready to fly down the hill. They made their way on uncertain, skating feet to where I had stopped at the alley. Delighted by my appearance or simply curious, my friends gathered round me.

"Welcome back to the land of the living," Mickey said smiling.

I was thankful.

Rosie touched my shoulder and added, "We were worried about you. Why didn't you come to the phone when we called?"

"I don't know. Just didn't want to talk to anyone about anything."

"Yeah, well we did. "D'ja ever think of that? You okay now?" Mickey asked.

I dropped my gaze for a split second; thought of Jimmy and the ten thousand footsteps of our lives, the last of them on shoes with soles of sharpened steel, and suddenly their cutting pain seemed to diminish. I felt an ungloved hand on my shoulder. I was thankful.

Mickey's mouth was moving; Allen's mouth was moving faster. Rosie held onto Mickey and shook her head at some remark he'd made. Carol took hold of Allen's hand, smiled her goddess smile, and then reached out to touch mine. The hand on my shoulder urged me to accept it. And the world stayed mute. I took hold of Carol's hand and immediately wondered what had become of our carriage to the stars? What had become of everything? I'd died, but never my hope.

We began the descent toward Meade Street—the five of us, at someone's command. Allen's I think. He seemed to have taken on the mantle Jimmy might have wanted me to don, but that I'd turned my nose up at. The great floppy-eared black dog woofed and rumbled like a massive flour-covered rug down the street. It stopped unexpectedly when it got beside us to look us over, its tongue wagging red and steamy, and its tail sweeping the air behind it. It turned its head a few degrees to the left, and then to the right, then content that everything was right, the dog continued on its way, with paws the size of snowshoes, kicking white cyclones up effortlessly.

"I miss him."
"So do I."
"Me too."
"Yeah, we all do."
"Yeah."
"Where you wanna' go?"
"Rashure's, I guess."
"Do you have any money, Carol?"
 Laughter. "Allen, guys buy, not girls!"
"I've got a dollar..."
"Mrs. Rashure makes really good hot chocolate. Has fresh cookies sometimes, too."
"I have some change."

We ambled past my house, and then by Jimmy's. Through his front window, Mrs. McGuire's ghostly image suddenly appeared and peered out at us. Her head swayed a little as she watched us walk by, and so did her emaciated frame. She hadn't brushed her hair in ages, Carol remarked in a whisper. I could see the top of her bottle of Old Crow clutched by its throat in her right hand, not a lover any longer, but her demon companion. Her lord. Her dead Jimmy. Then, as quickly as she'd appeared, she turned with a ratcheted effort and let the drapes fall closed, like a coffin lid. They rustled momentarily until their weight, and one of Jimmy's strange Physics laws, brought them to a halt. We walked on. Not far, now.

"What was the deal with the horse and the violin?"

"Just a line from a neat poem...Jimmy lent me one of his books..."

"Ah."

"Somehow I can't see a horse chomping on a violin!"

***

Winter slowly passed, as it always had, as it always would, and with it, a dreary granite-grayness, a forever-twilight season. I stayed among my friends as though my life depended on it and witnessed a new, rising sun that climbed every day higher toward the solstice. Every so often I lifted the "September" ring from my pocket—the one I'd once intended to give Carol—and looked at the scratches on the blue stone; tailings in the glass facets from coins that had sat alongside it in my pocket. Even marred, the sunlight reflected off it and through it, as if a magic, spell-casting one foot-tall miner had pulled a real, precious sapphire from deep inside the earth and given it to me just for her. Then I'd place it back into my pocket.

Carol smiled at me whenever we inadvertently crossed paths, but she sat on her front porch beside Allen more often as the days lengthened, listening to poetry he probably wrote, being read to her from a piece of wrinkled notebook paper—or just conversing. I never saw her dancing anymore. I began to notice Rosie though, now that she and Mickey had lost interest in one another. She was very pretty, and she kissed well. Sometimes we sat down beside Allen and Carol in front of my house, or walked together up the warming street to Mrs. Rashure's little store to buy a bottle of pop or two. Now and then the four of us encountered Inky and his younger brother sitting on the steps, but they had become harmless in the wake of everything that happened in that fateful year, now long gone. Inky had, in fact, relieved his head of twenty pounds or so of hair, and looked surprisingly like a monk without robes. His voice of greeting was kinder, softer, too. And Butch? His eyes were vacant. His mouth drooped open slightly, and drool leaked out of the corner of it constantly. That's all.

I often heard Jimmy's voice, which had not even had time to rebel against its own childhood squeakings. Funny, I could see him sitting cross-legged in the company of his old friends, high on that hill above a magnificent and golden futuristic city, regaling the cruel age of machines and thieves and liars, but dreaming, now, in verse about a brighter tomorrow.

"'I saw the best minds of my generation destroyed by madness, starving hysterical naked, dragging themselves through the Negro streets at dawn looking for an angry fix.'

What are we gonna' do about it?"

His tone was somber, as always, but his eyes twinkled as he and Gins, Mickey and Rosie...Carol and I...sat, like figures in a painting. And who would lead the charge but the kid who showed up late on the artist's canvas inside those dreams. The kid who bumped into light poles, fell into swollen creeks, and who cringed at actually touching the slithering body of a garter snake.

The End

Made in the USA
Las Vegas, NV
03 October 2022

56509765R00167